Until the Next Time

Until the Next Time

a novel by

Kevin Fox

Algonquin Books of Chapel Hill   2012

Published by
Algonquin Books of Chapel Hill
Post Office Box 2225
Chapel Hill, North Carolina 27515-2225

a division of
Workman Publishing
225 Varick Street
New York, New York 10014

This is a work of fiction. While, as in all fiction, the literary perceptions
and insights are based on experience, all names, characters, places, and incidents either
are products of the author's imagination or are used fictitiously.

LIBRARY OF CONGRESS CATALOGING-IN-PUBLICATION DATA
Fox, Kevin, [date]
Until the next time : a novel / by Kevin Fox. — 1st ed.
p. cm.
ISBN 978-1-56512-993-1
1. Irish Americans — New York (State) — New York — Fiction.
2. Irish Americans— Ireland — Fiction.   3. Ireland — Fiction.
4. Murder — Investigation — Fiction.   I. Title.
PS3606.O954U67 2012
813'.6 — dc22   2011022798

10 9 8 7 6 5 4 3 2 1
First Edition

To Kate, whoever you are . . .

This book is for all those with eyes that see and ears that hear. You know who you are, and although you might not find the answers you look for in these pages, perhaps they will help you to remember.

For I tell you, that many prophets and kings have desired to see those things which ye see, and have not seen them; and to hear those things which ye hear, and have not heard them.

—Luke 10:24

All these things are done in parables: That seeing they may see, and not perceive; and hearing they may hear, and not under-stand; lest at any time they should be converted, and their sins should be forgiven them.

—Mark 4:11–12

"Open your eyes, ya bleedin' eejit. I told ya everythin' ya need to know. Jus' look. The whole bleedin' truth is right here if you'd just see it, ya amadan."

—Declan Murphy, September 1998

PROLOGUE

I was standing on the O'Connell Bridge in Dublin when I saw her for the last time. There was a light rain, and the thin traffic splashing through the puddles made a soothing sound that reminded me of home. I had tickets to New York in my pocket and was resigned to go back to finish school when I caught sight of the woman I've loved forever. She was obscured by dark, rain-splattered glass, staring at me from the back of a taxi, her green eyes holding mine for just a moment as the traffic snarled on the bridge. She smiled as if she recognized me, and then in a blare of horns, the traffic started moving again and she was gone.

That was almost four years ago, and I'm still looking. I'm still obsessed with finding what I lost—what I never even knew I *had* lost until my twenty-first birthday, thirteen years ago. That was the day that my father handed me my uncle's journal and told me about a man I had never known. The journal changed my life, but she changed me in an even more important way. I hope what you read here will explain what I mean by that.

In publishing this book, which includes not only parts of my uncle's journal but my own experiences as well, I'm hoping to recover what I've lost. Some of you who read what follows, those of you with "eyes that see and ears that hear," will understand why I had to publish this.

Sean Corrigan
Inchmore
May 23, 2009

Sean

"Read this," my father said as he tossed a leather-bound journal at my chest, trying to catch me by surprise. He did. Not because he woke me up at 6 a.m. but because he was actually giving me something. Aidan Corrigan wasn't exactly a hands-on, doting father. He believed children learned survival skills by surviving. Surviving *him*, mostly. I looked at the book with its yellow dog-eared pages. It smelled musty.

"What is this?" I was still half asleep, and I was asking the question in a general sense, meaning: "What the hell are you doing in my bedroom before the sun is up with a musty-smelling piece-of-shit book?" He took it literally, as always.

"Wha's it look like? You never seen a book before? It's a feckin' birthday present. What'd you expect, hookers and tequila?" He snarled, always the sentimental old man. I hated the way he slipped into a bogus brogue when he cursed. The only brogue he'd ever heard was secondhand, from his father, Jim Corrigan. And even my grandfather did his best to lose his accent as soon as he got to America. They all did. Back then, speaking with a brogue wasn't sexy or cute, and it didn't win you the hearts of women. If you spoke with a brogue, people assumed you lacked an education, money, and common sense. Most of the time they were right on all three counts.

Unfortunately, my grandfather's brother Sean (whom I was named after and who my grandfather came over to join as a partner in the creatively named Corrigan's Tavern) never lost his brogue. It may have cost him his life. Great-uncle Sean arrived here in 1921 when he was just sixteen, running from the original Troubles, I suppose. He never quite outran them, because on March 18, 1946, the morning after St. Patrick's Day, my father found him in the alley next to Corrigan's Tavern, the victim of an apparent mugging that turned violent. He was barely alive when they found him and only said one thing in Irish before he died. *"Ni dhiolann dearmad fiacha,"* which translates as "A debt is still unpaid, even if forgotten." No one knew what it meant, but the police thought he probably owed the bookies some money. It was definitely possible.

The assumption was that after he locked up the bar, either the bookies showed up for something he owed them or someone pegged him as the owner by his brogue and tried to take the night's receipts. The strange part is that he had the cash in his pocket when they found him, a flask of whiskey by his hand, and his head propped on his coat. You would have thought he was peacefully sleeping off a "bout with the stout" if not for the hole in the back of his head. Maybe whoever tried to mug him was remorseful afterward, but it never made any sense to me.

Right now, neither did my father. He was still staring at me, waiting for me to say something about his sudden awareness of my birthday—a birthday I had forgotten myself. Well, maybe I hadn't quite forgotten it, but I certainly hadn't remembered it yet. Like I said, it was early, and last night's birthday celebration had only ended a couple of hours ago. My body's alcohol content was probably still over the legal limit, since I had been drinking to celebrate both being legal and to forget that my girlfriend, Sarah, had dumped me two weeks before. She was already dating some guy from Princeton, and I had seen her sticking her tongue in his ear at Conti's Pizza the night before. That's when the drinking started. Not that I ever liked her tongue in my ear—I just liked the idea of it in someone else's ear even less.

The way my father was staring at me was giving me a headache. To avoid the look, I opened the book, glancing through it as he lit his cigarette and flicked ashes on the floor, just like he always did right before he made an excuse to leave in order to avoid talking about anything real.

The pages of the book were worn and water-stained. The first page was headed "Notes for Dr. Sorenson," but Dr. Sorenson's name was crossed out, and next to it, someone had written "the Next Time" so that it now read "Notes for the Next Time." Every few pages was a dated entry. Inside the front cover was a name: Mike Corrigan.

"It's a journal," I muttered.

"Really? And your mother thinks you're stupid . . ."

"Who's Mike Corrigan?"

He shrugged before I even finished asking, taking a long drag on his cigarette, as if he couldn't speak without smoke coating his vocal cords.

"You were named after him and your great-uncle. He was Michael Sean, and your great-uncle was Sean *Michael*. Names don't come from nowhere, boyo. He was my brother." As he said this, he stood up and was out the door before I could ask the question that kept repeating itself in my head: "What the fuck are you talking about?" I had no Uncle Mike. My father had no brother.

Shows you how much I knew. Shows you how easy it is to hide the past and change history when people refuse to remember. As I opened the journal once more, a newspaper clipping fluttered out. Dated December 10, 1973, it was a terse report concerning an American fugitive, Michael Corrigan, who was killed by MI5, the British Security Service. They thought he was working with the Provos, the Provisional IRA.

I felt like I was reading fiction as I went on, trying to focus on the faded type: "a former New York City police detective assigned to a joint federal task force investigating subversive groups up until the time he was arrested, accused of murdering a Negro civil rights worker in rural Pennsylvania. He fled from prosecution to Ireland earlier this year."

So. I had an uncle. I had an uncle who was an NYPD detective and killed by the British while working with the IRA, *after* he killed a black civil rights worker and fled the United States to hide in Ireland. And I had his journal in my hands. Fuck.

I started to read.

Michael

JANUARY 17, 1972

Notes for ~~Dr. Sorenson~~ the Next Time

Okay, Doc, you told me to write it as it comes to mind, so here goes.

I'm not really sure why I'm writing this. I know you think it could help at a trial, if there is one, but no matter what you think is going on in my head, I didn't shoot that morning because of combat fatigue or post-whatever stress disorder like those guys coming back from Vietnam. I can't get off on an insanity plea. I knew exactly what I was doing. I shot Jimmy Butler because he was shooting at me.

At least I thought he was.

You said not to analyze what happened and just to write it down exactly as I remember it, but how can I? I remember him shooting at me. I remember getting hit in the face with pieces of rock as bullets ricocheted off the shale around me—but when I got to Jimmy Butler's body, there was no gun. When the investigators tore through the site, there were no bullets. I have shards of rock in my face, yet they all swear no one but me fired a shot. They all asked if I saw a gun. I didn't. You know that. It's not like I ever lied about it. Why do I need to see the gun if I can see where the bullets hit?

I know. I'm getting ahead of myself. Being defensive. Just write what I remember, right? Well, it was cold. I remember that much. My hands felt like they were cracking, since I wasn't wearing gloves. I never wear gloves when I'm on a stakeout, especially if they have me set up as a sniper. You need to be able to feel the trigger pressure. You need to have a sure grip. Gloves don't cut it.

We had arrived the night before in Wellsboro, a little town in north-central Pennsylvania that looks like the town that time forgot. An NYPD informant had tipped off the task force, so they'd called us in to assist, but since we were out of our jurisdiction, the FBI had taken charge and was calling all the shots. It was a good thing, I guess, because I was out of my element. The calendar said it was 1972, but from the look of Wellsboro and the surrounding area, it might as well have been 1941. On the way into town, we got stuck behind a 1939 Ford 9N tractor like my uncle Jackie used to have on his farm—driving right down Main Street with a load of manure on the back. It was hardly the place you'd expect to find a couple of cop killers holed up, especially guys associated with the Black Panthers. Wellsboro is full of Polacks and Germans, so around there those guys'd stand out.

At about 4 a.m., we left the Penn Wells Hotel and drove out Route 660, then headed off some dirt roads past a place called Cherry Flats. We had county maps and a local state trooper to guide us, or we never would have found the place, especially in the dark. And it was *dark*. Not like it gets here in the city, where there's always some sort of light coming from somewhere. Looking around that little county at four in the morning, you'd swear the lightbulb had never been invented.

About two miles from the place they were supposedly hiding, we pulled off the road—which was more like a logging trail, just dirt and ruts, with grass growing up the middle of it where the tires didn't keep it down and dead. The snow that was on the ground had melted a bit the day before and made the ruts muddy. We couldn't have driven farther if we wanted to.

That's when the four of us decided to split up. The federal guys on the task force, Agents DeMarco and Davidson (the latter the token African American the feds liked to assign to anything that dealt with civil rights) were going to take up positions on the road in case anyone came in from the outside; Detective Green, one of our NYPD guys, was going to take the downhill side of the cabin to cover the back and the logging trail that went off into the woods; and I was going to take up position above the place, watching the front door. Our orders were to watch and observe until the guys from St. Paul arrived to make the arrests and ID the suspects. We were to stop them only if they tried to leave.

I remember taking up position on a large flat rock overlooking the cabin and the field in front of it. I chose the rock because it was one of the few places to lie down that was not completely wet. The sun had melted the snow off it, dripping down into the seams of the rock. I had a view of the cabin that was slightly obstructed by a couple of scrub pines, and at about 6 a.m. a light inside came on. That was it for another hour, and it seemed like every minute of that hour it got colder and the wind bit a little more.

I heard the door first, before I saw him. Then I looked up through the leafless trees to see him down the hill in an army surplus coat, closing the door behind him and lighting a cigarette outside the cabin.

I didn't know his name was James Butler—that only came after he was dead. At this point all I knew was that he was a Vietnam vet with a big afro and dirty clothes, suspected of being a Black Panther and one of the guys involved in a cop killing in St. Paul, Minnesota, on New Year's Eve. Whoever killed the police officer in St. Paul had shot him in the back when he answered a bogus call about a woman in labor who needed help. He'd been shot with a military issue Colt .45, a Colt like this guy Butler must have carried in Vietnam.

Butler looked up the hill in my direction as I looked down at him, although I'm not sure he saw me. He started to move, but not toward me. He walked toward the woods, out of my line of sight. I couldn't see him, but I could hear him, and he was moving around me. I thought he might be trying to outflank me. I couldn't use my radio to call for help, because he might hear me. There was no way I was going to compromise my position or the stakeout if he hadn't already seen me. My job was to sit tight. That's what I did.

Periodically I thought I could hear him moving off to my right and behind me. It bothered me, because I was facing west, toward the cabin. That meant that if he decided to come up on me, he'd be coming from my east, and if I had to look up at him, I'd be staring right into the rising sun. He was a former marine, so he'd know this.

About fifteen minutes later I heard something directly behind me. It could have been a rock shifting under his weight, or a dried-up leaf crackling under his foot. Whatever it was, it made me turn.

I slowly rolled over, trying to find him through the brush, but he'd gone silent, and the sun was in my eyes. I was squinting into it for what must've been ten minutes when I noticed a shadow moving across the snow. I couldn't see him through the brush, but I knew where he was by his shadow.

To be safe, I lined up his hypothetical position in my sights, pretty sure that my rifle was pointed right at his head, although I couldn't see it through the branches of a Norwegian spruce. My hands were cramping from the cold and my ears were burning from it. I was wondering how long I could stay still.

That's when it happened. To my right, an inch from my ear, the rock I was lying on exploded. I jerked to my left but still got hit by a shard of rock, right in the temple, less than an inch from my eye. The next one threw up splinters of rock right in front of me, cutting open a gash just above my left eye. Blood dripped into my eye as more shots hit all around me . . .

I fired. I fired again. And again. I fired until the rock around me stopped exploding. I fired until the shadow on the snow stopped moving. My ears were ringing as I lay there, watching the snow around Jimmy Butler turn red. I stared for a long minute, unable to move. I listened to see if I could hear his partners coming to help, or him moving, or moaning, or anything. All I could hear was the ringing in my ears, and then, slowly, gradually, the wind. That was it. The next thing I heard was my own footsteps, crunching in the snow, headed toward his body, my rifle reloaded and ready for any movement. Ready to shoot again if I had to.

I didn't know who he was then. I didn't know he was a war protester, a decorated vet home just two weeks from Vietnam. I mean, I knew he was a vet, but none of that other crap. I had no idea he was a pacifist who swore he'd never fire a gun again. I knew only what I'd been told: in the cabin I was watching were three men, alleged Black Panther members, who had shot a cop in the back in St. Paul, Minnesota, and had fled cross-country to Wellsboro.

I looked down at him, his blood seeping out onto the snow, melting it and sending up little wisps of steam. I was angry, scared, shaky from the adrenaline rush, and frightened of the slowly fading ringing in my ears. Frightened because I might not hear his partners if they came running up.

There were no other footprints in the snow, no sounds louder than my own breathing. Finally, I moved toward the body, wanting to make sure he was dead, to make sure that if I walked off, he couldn't shoot me in the back.

He'd wet himself. His muscles had relaxed. He was dead all right, but the only thing I found underneath him was a urine stain in the snow. And blood. No gun. For a second I thought he must've had a partner, someone else who was shooting, but then I saw that there were no other footprints.

I sat there staring at the guy, watching his blood slowly spread in the snow. It didn't make any sense to me. I even reached up and touched my cheek, pulling out a splinter of shale to make sure it was there. My hand came away with an inch-long splinter of rock and a healthy dose of my own blood. Finally I rolled him over again, looking for his weapon. I still go over it in my head, trying to figure out how he got rid of it, but no matter how hard I looked, there was no gun.

I know they're making it out like I killed him because the government told me to. I know they're saying we're some vast conspiracy trying to silence the opposition, to exterminate the black man. But that's all bullshit. I don't care what happened to Malcolm X or Martin Luther King, or what the damn National Guard did at Kent State. I shot him in self-defense.

Christ. You know what the scary part is? If I were on a jury and heard a guy tell me they shot someone in self-defense and no one ever found a gun on the other guy, I'd send him to the chair. I'd send *me* to the chair. I thought it even then, as I knelt over this guy, patting him down, trying to find where he put the gun. The more I thought about it, the angrier I got.

I didn't realize I had my blood on my hands when I rubbed them through my hair, when I wiped the sweat off my face. Yes, I was sweating. I was sweating because I was panicked. I was ripping his clothes open to find the gun. He *had* to have a gun. I killed him because he shot at me. I *knew* he had a gun. I had pieces of shale in my face to prove it. It was not "disrespect" or "desecration" that made me rip open his jacket and shirt and pants, it was *desperation.*

When DeMarco and Davidson came up through the woods and saw me tearing at the dead guy's clothes, it wasn't because I hated him and had wanted him dead. It was because I knew that *I* was as good as dead. And I *was* angry at him. I was pissed off that he made me kill him.

Yes, there was blood on my face. Yes, there was blood on my hands. Yes, I ripped open his clothes, and yes, I even kicked the body in frustration. Because I was angry. I was angry that he was dead.

Why did he come up behind me if not to shoot me? Why was he hiding out in the woods? I know what they all said later, but that's gotta be bullshit. He wasn't, and he couldn't have been, "trying to get away from it all" after getting back from Vietnam. He *circled around me.* He wasn't out walking to clear his head. He was out walking to put a hole in mine. I can't believe anything else. Not with a face full of rock shards.

But where was his gun? I still don't know. I don't know what happened out there. I was hit in the face with rock. I heard gunfire. And I killed James Butler. And I know how it looks.

God help me if I get a jury of my peers, because I'd hear my lame-ass explanation of how I got his blood on my hands and I'd send me straight to the fucking chair.

Sean

Shit. I mean really. Shit. I was lying in bed at 6:07 a.m. on my twenty-first birthday, and I'd just realized how little I knew about my own family. If they could keep a killer uncle secret, what else was hanging in our collective closet? What else had been forgotten?

In three minutes the alarm would go off—in an hour I had to be at work—and I was only ten pages into the journal. It's not as if I liked my job, but I really needed the money to go back to college. If I didn't go to back to school up in Binghamton, I'd have to live with my father and work all year, and I was smart enough to know that my father was a pain in the ass and work was overrated. Actually, at twenty-one, I'd learned that most things in life were overrated. My life had almost no purpose except for avoiding work and trying to develop some kind of meaningful, or at least sexual, relationship. And since my last attempt at a relationship with Sarah had been a dismal failure, even that wasn't much of a reason to get out of bed in the morning.

And now I had a hell of a reason to stay in bed. There was no way I was doing anything else until I finished that book. I called in sick—claimed a family emergency. It wasn't even a lie. I was just calling in about twenty-one years too late.

I didn't get out of bed until almost four thirty. I read the entire journal, trying to decipher the notes in the margins, looking at the grainy photos stuck in between the pages, most with names written on the back.

The pictures all looked familiar to me. Their subjects' faces were eerily similar to those of my cousins, siblings, and other relatives. When I looked at a few of the photos, I felt like I'd been there when they were taken. It was almost as if I could tell you what was lying beyond the frames of the photos.

But what I couldn't tell was why there were so many blank spots in Uncle Mike's journal. Pages had been torn from the book in a half-dozen places, leaving bits and pieces of words behind. Why would someone tear entries out of a journal? What could anyone be hiding that was worse than a racist–killer–former-cop uncle?

As I flipped through the book, a few loose pages fluttered to the ground. One of them was a letter.

Dearest Sean,

I know when you read this it may not make any sense to you, but you must come and find me. You must find out how, and when, it all ended.

Don't let them make me a martyr to their bloody cause. Martyrs are dead people, and I won't be dead, no matter what you think at first. And if ever I become a martyr, I'll be a martyr to my own cause, not theirs. I'll be a martyr for us. Only us. That's all that will ever matter to me and Mickaleen, right? Trust me, my eyes are wide open, I'm wide awake, and I know what comes next. It's not so hard once you've done it before. We both know we will find each other again. Just as I know you will try to find me. I believe in soul mates, in love. It's the hopeless romantic in me, but I know it's true and can say it because I've lived it. I'm the proof that it exists, and now I refuse to settle for anything less. I'll see you on the other side, and I vow to you, I will find you. If anything goes wrong, please, please, come looking for me . . .

Love,
Kate

Stuck to the back of the letter was an old, faded photo. I knew who it was the minute I saw it. It was her. Kate. It was dated December 8, 1972, and had the caption *Kate on the Rock of Boho.* The picture was a beautiful Irish landscape taken from a hill of bare granite, with rich, rolling fields and cattle and sheep in the background. It looked like a scene out of an idyllic fantasy—but I saw none of that until later. In that moment, all I saw was Kate.

I had no idea how she changed my uncle's life, or how she was about to change mine, but my chest tightened and a nervous tingling energy made me shiver. I *knew* her. I knew, even though the photos were black and white, that her eyes were green and her hair was a rich dark auburn and that in the summer she would have freckles. I knew that her voice was much huskier than you'd expect, that her smile was more crooked when she was really happy, and that if she laughed too hard she would start to hiccup. I also knew that she would cure those hiccups with a shot of whiskey.

And yet I didn't know her at all. I remember thinking that I must have heard bits and pieces of her story as a child and buried the information somewhere in the back of my head. Perhaps Kate had come to the States at some point and visited us. But regardless of how I knew her, I knew that I needed to find her in the journal.

I skipped ahead to a page marked January 19. The handwriting was a bit sloppier here, and it seemed to start right in the middle of something. I found out later that January 19 was the day that my uncle Mike's name first appeared in New York's *Daily News,* in an article that described "the murder" of James Butler. It was the day Uncle Mike left his own apartment in Bay Ridge and went to my grandparent's house out in Prince's Bay, on Staten Island, hoping to get away from all the press and the people who wanted to lynch him. After I knew all this, the next entry made a lot more sense.

Michael

It didn't take them long. They didn't even use a brick. They used my mother's leprechaun statue, with its faded green paint and sickly smile, the one she's had in her flower garden for the last twenty-two years. She called him "Lucky." Very original, I know. "Lucky the Leprechaun." Maybe it was accurate, though, because as Lucky smashed through the bay window in my parents' living room, he got caught in the drapes and fell straight down onto the couch.

I was the unlucky one, because that's where I was sleeping. Lucky bashed me right in the forehead and left a nice welt over my left eye. But all that happened to the little green bastard was that he lost four fingers from the hand he was waving, leaving Lucky an obscene little fellow, telling the world what he thought of anyone who might consider tossing leprechauns through windows in the middle of the night. I liked him better now. As my eyes stopped tearing, I noticed that Lucky had a note taped to his ass: *Dye raceist Mick pig.* Very eloquent, and so close on the spelling. I doubt the irony of calling me a racist and a Mick in the same sentence was appreciated by these particular vigilantes.

"Oh, sweet Jesus. It's Lucky." I looked up and saw my mother, Margaret. The gash in my head, the broken window, the squealing tires outside—she noticed none of it. But Lucky? Him she noticed. She scooped him up off the floor as my father shuffled down the hall, turning on every light in the house and humming "Loch Lomond" under his breath. When he saw the broken glass, he just shook his head.

"Are ye all righ', Mickaleen?" he asked, falling into the brogue that tended to creep out when he was tired. The faux accent wasn't as bad as the fact that he'd called me Mickaleen. Mick was his dead brother Sean's nickname. He'd been killed in a robbery gone bad before I was born, and my father rarely mentioned him until he got a touch of the old-timer's disease and started to forget who we all were. When he first started losing his shit, he used to tell me that I looked just like Mick, but now he just thinks I *am* his brother.

"Who would do such a thing? Throwing Lucky through our window like that?" my mother wondered as she crawled around looking for the severed fingers. She hadn't even looked at me. "I really can't believe this. Do any of you see Lucky's thumb?"

"It's the damn Tans," my father muttered, coming to sit by me on the couch and taking one of my mother's precious doilies off the coffee table to staunch the flow of blood from my forehead.

"Those guys were more than tan," Aidan said as he wandered in, yawning widely. I noticed that he had a pistol in his hand as he peered out the curtains. Aidan was always up for a fight, but the fights he showed up for were usually over by the time he got there.

"He's talking about the Black and Tans, you amadan. The British," I muttered, suddenly wishing I had stayed at my place in Brooklyn. At least in Brooklyn it would have been a brick that came through the window, and after it did I could go back to sleep instead of listening to these three.

"I know what he's talking about. Do you think I'm a feckin' eejit?" Aidan asked, knowing the answer. "You know what I don't understand? Why didn't you guys just plant a gun on the nigger? It's not like you killed him on purpose, and what's it gonna solve blaming you? It ain't gonna bring him back now, is it?"

"It would just make things worse."

"Worse? How do you figure? Now I've got to go to bed in the middle of January with the wind blowin' in and freezin' my balls off; Ma and Da gotta fix that damn window; and you're going to the chair. How do you feckin' figu—"

He was cut off as one of Lucky's loose fingers hit him square in the mouth, bouncing off a tooth. He touched his lip and came away with a spot of blood. My mother never even looked up at him. I'd hate to see that woman with a knife. As Aidan continued to complain, I got up and went to the kitchen with my father, got a washcloth to replace the doily, and called the police.

Twenty minutes later I had a fifty-year-old sergeant named Malone sitting on the edge of the sofa taking my statement and telling me how he supported a fellow officer of the law in times like these.

"I'm tellin' ya. You did what you had to do, am I right? Too bad you were workin' with the damn feds. They gave you up in a heartbeat, didn't they?" he asked, shaking his head in disgust. I honestly wasn't following him.

"Excuse me?"

"One less of them is what I'm sayin'. Like it matters if there was a gun. If you're not behind the war and our troops, you're a traitor, am I right? And our Constitution says we have the right to execute traitors."

"He was a Vietnam vet."

"I know. And I agree with you. That makes him even worse. Turning his back on his brothers in arms. Of course, guys like that don't want to be Americans, do they? They should go back to where they came from." I didn't bother to tell him the guy was from Toledo, Ohio, and the last of his relatives to see Africa probably arrived in America two hundred years before this ignorant Mick with a badge and a gun. I just didn't think he'd see it my way.

A half hour later Sergeant Malone left, and I put Lucky back out on the lawn. I'd let his middle finger tell the people of the world what I thought of them.

Sean

I read and reread for another five hours, trying to figure out why all this made so much sense to me. Parts of it felt familiar, but sometimes the story took strange turns. I wondered whether the missing pages would've helped me put all the pieces together.

I needed some answers and my only hope was my father. I closed the journal, threw on some clothes, and walked down to the kitchen and into the haze of smoke that hovered over the Formica table. Within the haze, my father calmly sipped at his coffee, listening to Karen Carpenter sing "We've Only Just Begun" on the oldies station. He looked up at me as if he'd been waiting there the entire time I was reading. He didn't even have his *Daily Racing Form* open.

"What is this?" I asked, holding up the journal.

"I thought we already established that. You told me it was a journal, remember?" And he took another puff, blowing smoke at me, never looking away from my eyes. It was a challenge, but a challenge to *what*?

"How come I never knew about it? How come I never knew I had an uncle Mike?"

"You chose not to know."

"Bullshit."

"Tell me the truth, Sean, did it really surprise you? Or does it all feel a little familiar, like you knew about it and just forgot?" he asked, and I answered by looking away. It *was* familiar, as if I'd read the book, or seen the movie, or heard all about it in another lifetime. He smirked when I didn't answer. "I thought so."

"Was he racist? Did he really murder that guy?"

"You tell me. You spent the whole day locked up with that piece of shite."

"Well, whether the guy was armed or not, your brother pulled the trigger, didn't he?"

"So what? He killed a coon who shot at him first," my father said, and I realized he was just provoking me. My father has a foul mouth, but he's no racist. He hates everyone equally. "Why are you asking me any of this shite? You read the journal. It's all in there."

"No. It's not."

"No? What's missing? You know more about it than I do?"

"There are whole sections missing. About Declan and the Battle of the Bogside—and about this, this—cult. What's with this 'awakening' bullshit?"

"You think I know? Or give a rat's arse? Go do your own damn research. Go check your facts, then come back to me with some real questions. Not this shite. 'Is it true?' What a stupid feckin' question."

Just say the damn word, I thought, turning to leave. I was halfway out of the haze of smoke when he stopped me.

"Here. You'll need this, ya amadan."

"What's this?"

"Your real present."

Reluctantly, I waded back into the toxic fumes and he handed me an envelope. Inside was an airline ticket. JFK to Shannon, for the eighth of July. Three days away.

There was a price on the ticket—over eight hundred dollars. The last time my father had spent eight hundred dollars in one place was when he bought his house in 1974. The most expensive car he'd ever bought was a 1971 Cutlass, for six hundred dollars in 1982.

"Who are you?" I asked as I looked at him.

"Don't ask *me* who I am. I decided a long time ago that I dinn't want to know. But if you want to go find out who your dear departed uncle was, take the tickets. He paid for them."

"Bullshit."

"You callin' me a liar again? Your uncle Mike left some money behind when he got his head blown off. He wanted you to have it. Last letter he sent said all his crap was to go to the next Corrigan born. That was you. So you

get the journal and the chance to go back to Ireland. Fuck if I know why."
What happened to "feckin'," I wondered. He must have been really pissed
off to use the *u*.

"What about work? Next semester's tuition? I can't just leave."

"Are you deef? I told you, the little shite of a brother left his money to
you. There's a little over thirty grand in the bank."

"Why didn't you tell me?"

"You never asked."

"How could I know to ask if I never knew I had an uncle?"

"Didja ever ask if ya *had* an uncle? You think you're smart but you never
ask any questions. Nobody's hidin' anything from you, boyo—you're just
not lookin'."

He was full of shit. He was hiding Uncle Mike from me and he knew it.
There was no Uncle Mike in any family pictures. He was never talked about.
He'd ceased to exist sometime in the early seventies. It was all very Irish. I'm
not kidding. That's what the Irish do, you know. If we don't want something
to exist, it doesn't. My great-grandfather had thirteen brothers and sisters and
only four of them existed after 1921. We, as a race, are great at denial.

In Ireland today you'll still hear people say, "Ireland has never been conquered." This in spite of the fact that from the time of Oliver Cromwell until 1921 the British had armies on Irish soil almost continuously—and still
do if you consider Ulster to be part of Ireland. It works in small ways as well.
"My husband never drinks." "My wife is a saint." It's as if the statements
alone can make it so, and if there are no statements, it never happened.

So Uncle Mike, who didn't exist before July 5, 1996, was suddenly born
again, and I was going to find out why. I was going to find out why no one
ever told me about him, and why there were so many things my family never
talked about. I didn't know then how dangerous it could be to go after the
truth, or what lengths some people would go to in order to hide it.

If I knew then how close I would come to dying, or that there would be
bombs going off in Ireland because I asked the wrong questions, I might
have stopped right then. But I didn't know, and I'm glad I didn't, because
what I found there made it all worthwhile . . .

Michael

It's 2:37 a.m., according to my alarm clock, and I got up to write this because you told me the dreams might be important. They better be if I'm going to get up in the middle of the night and write this crap down.

I should just tell you up front that they're not like regular nightmares. I just want to be clear on that. There was the same fear, and the cold sweats, but I never woke up wondering if the dream was real. No, I woke up wondering if what I saw when I was awake was really the dream. It's hard to explain, but what I saw was actually more like a memory than a dream. It seemed as if the whole time I was dreaming I were watching something that was already done, something I knew that I'd live through and regret long after I woke up.

The first thing I remember was my hands, cold, gloveless, and cracked open from dryness, but this wasn't outside of Wellsboro, and these hands were too small to be mine. But they *were* my hands. Like I said, it was a dream, right?

Anyway, I remember all this detail. Stupid details, really. Like the boots I was wearing, with frayed laces, made of heavy, stiff leather. I remember thinking that the new soles I had put on were worth it, even though I've never had new soles put on any shoe in my life. The soles were about the only new thing I had. My pants were made of a coarse canvas material and my shirt was thick wool. It itched, but in a way that I was used to. I can't stand wool usually, but this didn't bother me. The rifle I was carrying was old and not very well maintained. The wood on the stock was gouged from careless use and the whole thing needed to be cleaned.

I was waiting for something, leaning on a tree as the sky grew lighter and the wind ripped through my jacket. I was tired and cold, and I wanted to get up and walk home to get in front of a fire I somehow knew would be there.

Then I heard it. The crunching sounds of boots on gravel, just over the rise. I lowered myself to the ground, face first, onto a broad, flat rock.

That's when I noticed the rock. It was just like the one from the day of the shooting. It hit me even in the dream as déjà vu. I'd been here before.

I could see him approaching through the trees. I caught glimpses of his faded jacket. He almost looked like one of us. I knew I needed to wait. If I fired too early, I would ruin it. But then, suddenly, he opened up on me. There were bullets hitting all around me, fast. More shots than he could possibly fire so quickly. I started firing back just as he stepped into the clearing, and it was then that I saw his face. Right after I fired my last shot. The shot that hit him in the forehead. I remember hearing his skull crack as it went in, like brittle oak branches snapping under your feet. He stood there for a moment, just looking at me. I was shocked that there was so little blood. That he just seemed surprised, not even in pain. He just looked confused, curious why I'd shoot him in the face.

My good friend. Liam.

It didn't make sense. How did he get there in front of me? And why would Liam shoot at me?

That thought made sense in the dream, Doc, but I don't know who the fuck Liam is. I mean, I see him clear as day in the dream, reddish brown hair, blue eyes, and he's small, like a kid, really. In the dream I've known him forever and his name just keeps going through my head as he falls . . . Liam Liam liamliamliamliam.

When I woke up I heard myself screaming his name. I lay there in the dark, disoriented, not knowing where I was until I heard my father's voice from the doorway, calling out in a whisper:

"Go back to sleep, Mickaleen. It's just the dream again."

Sean

I found Dr. Sorenson in the yellow pages. I was prepared as I dialed the phone to be told that it was the wrong Dr. Sorenson, that it was his son and that the old man had died, or that he wouldn't talk to me because of some kind of doctor–patient confidentiality thing. The only thing I wasn't prepared for is what actually happened. After I told his receptionist my name (three times) and told her I was calling about my uncle (whose name I had to repeat four times), she put me on hold. I was pretty sure the last time she repeated my name she asked me if it was "Culligan," like the guy in the commercials who delivers water softener. There wasn't much hope I'd get through to the good doc if I had to do it via this woman.

Ten minutes later, I was in the middle of eating a peanut butter and jelly sandwich, trying to hold it in one hand, a glass of milk in the other, and the phone in the crook of my neck, when I heard a voice on the other end of the line, practically yelling.

"Is it really you?" His voice startled me so badly that I nearly choked. I finally managed to speak.

"Uhh, umm, I'm trying to get Dr. Sorenson."

"I know. Felice tracked me down here in the Vineyard when she heard who it was." Obviously, Felice, his receptionist, had screwed up again.

"I think you misunderstood. My name is Sean Corrigan, and I'm—"

"I know who you are. Where are you now?" He was still yelling, the way people do when they think they have a bad connection.

"Prince's Bay. On Staten Island. But—"

"How soon can you come see me?" Sorenson asked intently, as if my seeing him were a matter of life or death.

"This isn't actually about me. It's about Michael Corrigan, my uncle."

"Of course it is. Tomorrow works for me. Make it tomorrow. Better sooner than later. I don't want to risk missing you. You could get hit by a car and I'll never get to talk to you."

This doctor made me nervous. Something wasn't right about the whole setup. I was beginning to think this Uncle Mike's journal thing was a practical joke planned by my feckin' father, but I had to know for sure.

"Tomorrow's fine. I can—"

"Perfect. I'll drive down tonight. Say ten o'clock, at my office on Fifty-second Street. Felice will give you the address." He was moving too fast for me. I hadn't even told him about the journal yet or what it said about him and the hypnotherapy he did with my uncle. He had to be confused about all this. I sure as hell was.

"Uhh, yeah. Okay. I got your address from the phone book, but don't you want—"

"Of course, bring whatever you have. By the way, what's your birth date?" By this point I was getting suspicious.

"July fifth, why?"

"What year?"

"Nineteen seventy-six."

"Perfect. Perfect. Ten o'clock. Don't make me wait any longer. You can tell me everything else then." And he hung up. He knew I was going to show up, and I knew there was something really odd going on. I needed to know exactly what it was.

DR. SORENSON'S OFFICE was not what I expected. He was in a brick building wedged between two modern structures, a coffee shop on one side and a sushi place on the other. There was a cracked plastic buzzer next to a gray steel door on the street, right next to the vile smelling Dumpster from the sushi restaurant. Fortunately, Felice responded to my buzz quickly, and I bolted inside.

The elevator shuddered as it moved down for me, its cable squealing as it rubbed on the pulleys. The doors cranked open and inside was a frail waif of a woman with liquid-blue eyes and jet black hair worn in a ponytail. Her fists were clenched so tightly that her knuckles were turning white. She didn't step out.

"Please. Get in. I'm not getting out."

I got in, standing as far away from her as I could in the small space. I kept my eyes off of her and faced the doors. The shuddering of the elevator distracted me until she started breathing slowly in and out, so loudly that I couldn't help but notice. I risked a glance at her.

"I'm sorry. Closed spaces freak me out. I had a bad experience a long time ago."

Dr. Sorenson's office was on the fifteenth floor. The elevator was crawling upward, having made the third floor, at best, by this point.

"Really?" I pushed the button again impatiently.

"It's exposure therapy. I lock myself up in small places. I ride the elevator for an hour before every appointment. I usually take the first one of the day so I don't make anyone uncomfortable. You're not uncomfortable, are you?" she asked, and then took a deep breath, sucking air.

"Me? No. Of course not."

"Good." She smiled tightly and closed her eyes, rocking slightly back and forth as she breathed in and out, in and out.

Once her eyes were closed, it was finally safe to look at her, and I was surprised to see that she was beautiful. I know, it was a strange thought. Crazy is not beautiful. But her skin was like porcelain, perfectly smooth, and her dark lashes fluttered sweetly as she worked at keeping her eyes closed. Obviously the black hair was a dye job, but it suited her. And her deep breathing was going through me, the way a deep bass subwoofer makes your whole body vibrate.

As I took her in, she opened her eyes and addressed me.

"Thank you. You can get off now."

I could barely hear her, she was whispering so low. She reached out and touched her palm to my face. It was soft and dry.

"Excuse me?"

"You can get off," she said with a shy smile, and nodded to the elevator doors as they opened. We'd arrived at Sorenson's floor, where directly in front of the elevator Felice sat at a battered Formica desk, staring at us.

I stepped off and held a look with the girl as the doors closed. It was the strangest two minutes I'd ever spent with a person, but it made me want to ride the elevator with her again.

"You must be Culligan. I see you met Annabelle." I looked more closely at Dr. Sorenson's assistant. She was well over fifty, with thinning hair that was probably gray when not dyed an unnatural orange.

"She's really improved a lot. You should've seen her a year ago. She didn't bother you, did she?"

"No."

"Good. She's making progress. Take a seat. The doctor will be out in a moment." I sat down on a leather couch and tried not to think about Annabelle. Dr. Sorenson had comfortable furniture at least, and the waiting room was soothing in a way that let you know someone with a degree in both art and psychology designed it. Pastel colors, fresh flowers, a feng shui flow of movement through it. Unfortunately, places that are designed to make people comfortable and relaxed always make me uneasy. I feel like I'm part of some psych experiment, being watched by invisible eyes. They make me want to scream. Ten minutes later the door to the inner office opened and a small man with a trim white beard glanced out.

"Felice, send in Mr. Corrigan," he called out to her, never looking at me. It was kind of hard to miss me in the tiny waiting room, and he could have asked me in himself, but I guess it was some type of social dominance ritual to ask the underling to send me in. I followed him into his office.

As soon as we were inside, he closed the door and smiled at me. "My, my, how about that. You look great." He was walking in circles around me, examining me like matador might a prize bull. Finally he motioned to two chairs across the room, next to the gas fireplace, offering me a seat.

"So. You've come to tell me about your uncle," he said as he sat back, watching my face.

"Umm, no. Actually I came to ask about him. He left me this journal," I said. Dr. Sorenson's smile grew brighter, and he leaned toward me, obviously eager.

"Good. Good. Where is it? Give it to me," he demanded as his eyes darted around, looking for it.

"Excuse me?"

"It's mine—the journal. Part of our therapy." He said it as if it were a challenge.

"But he's dead. There can't be any more therapy."

"I know he's dead. If he wasn't, it'd still be *his* journal. But if he is dead, the journal's mine. Or maybe *ours,* if you like, but we agreed a long time ago that I could read it and get all the information from it." Sorenson was speaking faster. There was a desperate edge to his voice. I was missing something here.

"He left it to me. No one told me anything about you, except that he started the journal as part of his therapy. I just have a few questions about what it says, so . . ."

All the excitement went out of Sorenson's voice, and he deflated. "I can't tell you anything."

"Why not? If he's dead, doctor–patient confidentiality doesn't really matter anymore."

"I can't tell you because it wouldn't be good for you." He stood, moving to the window, looking down over the city.

"I already read it. I know what he did."

Sorenson didn't react for a moment, but when he finally looked up, I could see his eyes reflected in the window. He was watching me, studying me. I got the impression that I'd disappointed him somehow, and I wanted to please him, but I didn't know what he was expecting from me.

"Why did you come to me?"

"Some of the pages have been ripped out. Whole sections are missing. "

"Who would do such a thing? That journal is the proof—" He stopped himself and pressed his lips back together.

"Proof of *what*?" I asked, genuinely confused. I felt like Alice in Wonderland. No one around me was making any sense.

"I can't tell you."

"Why not?" I asked. He just shrugged, looking away from my face and hiding his own by turning away. He didn't want to look me in the eye. I had no idea what to say next, and he wasn't turning back around, so there was a moment where we were both trying to figure out what to do. Sorenson saved me the trouble when he finally spoke.

"I learned a lot from my sessions with your uncle. About what happened out there in the woods, and about what happened . . . well, what happened before all that." Sorenson looked up at me again, but this time he had pity in his eyes, looking at me the way people look at you right after they find out you've been fired or have cancer or are incontinent. It only lasted a second before he went on. "Your uncle agreed to keep a journal so we could prove what happened to him between the time James Butler was killed until his own death, and after that . . ."

His voice trailed off, and I assumed "after that" meant that after that Sorenson lost track of the journal. He was raising more questions than he was answering. His shoulders slumped and his voice trailed off. This was the same guy who had rushed back from Martha's Vineyard just to see me. Something wasn't right. He was hiding something, keeping secrets like my father did. It never occurred to me at the time that they might both be trying to protect me, so I kept asking questions, determined to find out what he was hiding.

"What did he mean by 'Notes for the Next Time'?"

"It doesn't matter," Dr. Sorenson said, and then turned back to me, a glimmer of interest returning to his eyes. "Who did you get the journal from, anyway?"

"My father. He was holding it for my twenty-first birthday."

"And where did he get it? Did he give you anything besides the journal?" Yup. There was definitely some interest back in his voice, but what I couldn't figure out was why.

"An airline ticket to Ireland." I answered, and he nodded solemnly. I was getting tired of being the only one who had no idea what we were talking about, but he was apparently satisfied that he had figured it out.

"Smart. Very smart." Then he turned on me quickly, his voice tight. "Can I hypnotize you?" he asked out of the blue, staring me in the eye again as if looking for a specific contraction of the pupil.

"Not a chance." It came out a little too harshly, but what do you expect? I've seen people hypnotized on television, and they did some pretty funky shit. "No offense, but no. I mean, really, no. I'm not really comfortable with that." I stammered as if I were the one being unreasonable. He just nodded, disappointed.

"I had to try. Your uncle didn't like it much either." He seemed to have given up as he walked to a small safe behind his desk and knelt down, spinning the dial as he kept talking.

"I guess there's really no choice. You need to see for yourself to believe it, so he sent you a ticket. He probably thought you'd get the whole journal, but the messenger took parts of it out. He should've known that no one really wants to know the truth."

"Look, Doc. You're not making much sense. Just tell me what's going on. If I was supposed to get the whole journal anyway, what difference does it make if you tell me?"

"No. I'm sorry. Come back to me after. You wouldn't believe me if I told you now." And then he turned to look at me, even as he pulled an envelope out of the safe, with a sad look in his eyes.

"You mean you want me to find the rest of the book?"

"To begin with. I can give you one thing to help you." And he handed me the bulky manila envelope. "It's a tape of Mike's last hypnotherapy session with me. The first half of it, anyway. He stole the rest of them."

"Stole them?"

"Yes, before he knew what I was trying to prove to him. Listen to it carefully." He stared at me until I nodded, and then he opened the door and held it until I took the hint and walked out. By the time I thought of what I wanted to ask him, he'd closed the door, shutting me out.

"And the reluctant hero is sent forth to discover the mysteries of life." I turned as I heard her voice. It was Annabelle the elevator girl, sitting on the couch, calmly reading a magazine as she looked me over. "He did that to me the first time, too. It's cold, but it's effective."

"You know what he's talking about?"

"When you come back, you can buy me a drink and we'll talk about it. If you don't find what you're looking for, of course." Annabelle smiled, then pulled up the magazine, shutting me out.

I was on the street before I thought to wonder how Annabelle had known I was going on a trip. I tried to buzz back up, but Felice took forever to answer and the sushi Dumpster was warming up in the sun. I rode back to Staten Island with the old cassette tape of my uncle's last session in my pocket, wondering what he had to say.

When I finally got home I rushed to the garage. There's a portable radio there that my father keeps to play his old cassettes that are so stretched and abused they sound like they're playing at the wrong speed. I popped in the tape and heard Sorenson's voice.

"Begin by focusing on your breath. With each breath going more deeply within. Let yourself go deeper and deeper into a beautiful, relaxed, serene state . . ."

His voice was a soothing monotone. It pissed me off.

I fast-forwarded through the drone of Sorenson trying to be serene. To be honest, I didn't want to suddenly wake up and find myself back in his office, having been somehow tricked into being hypnotized by the tape. I've heard guys like Sorenson can make you do weird things when you're hypnotized. Definitely not for me.

I stopped a couple of times, waiting to hear Uncle Mike's voice. When I finally did, I thought I might have gone too far, because he already sounded wired.

"I remember seeing the white pieces of bone, and the trickles of blood, and all the way into his skull, to the gray lumpy brain matter covered in watery blood. There was something unreal about it. There was a hole, right in his forehead. I put it there. I couldn't move for a minute, and then suddenly I had to. I had to get out, to run—anywhere, as fast as I could—and then I heard him moan."

It was my uncle's voice. I knew it as soon as I heard it. It sounded like my own, just a little different from my father's. With every word he spoke, the images he described became more unsettling. Still, I couldn't stop listening.

"His eyes were fluttering. Then they opened, staring straight at me. Accusing me. But I knew I couldn't save him. The bullet was in his head. Bullets can scramble your brains, ricocheting off your skull without killing you. I'd seen people like that, mumbling and moaning, shitting themselves for their mothers to clean up, drooling oatmeal out of their half-opened mouths. They would have been better off dead.

"So I shot him again. He didn't move anymore. I know it sounds cold to you, but it was a different time. What else could I do? He had a bullet in his head. He was never goin' to be whole again."

And then the tape stopped abruptly, as if it had run out.

Something about the way all of this was playing out made me wonder if I was ever going to be whole again either. How many pieces of my life were missing? Would I ever be able to feel like I knew myself or my family if I didn't find out what happened to him? Why had he chosen to send his journal to *me*?

Sorenson knew more than he was saying. So did my father. I was the only one walking around in the dark. I had to find the missing sections of the journal. I had to find out why my uncle wanted me to have it. I started packing for Ireland.

Michael

Doc, by now you know that I've taken all your tapes and all the transcripts I could find. I'm sorry, I know all about doctor–patient confidentiality and all that, and that you couldn't turn me in even if you wanted to, but I heard that last tape. If anyone ever gets their hands on it, I'm gonna be sitting in Old Sparky. I stopped the tape after listening to myself admit that I shot him again. I don't remember it that way at all, but you have my voice on tape, admitting that I put one in his head when I knew he was still breathing—and unarmed.

I know I wasn't supposed to listen to what I said during a session, Doc, but you left it in the recorder and you should know better than to leave a cop alone in a room full of tape recordings and incriminating papers. I don't know what I'm going to do. I'm still writing in the journal, just in case. In case of *what* I'm not sure, but I want you, or whoever reads this, to understand what happened.

No matter what it says on that tape, I didn't shoot James Butler again at close range. Maybe you "suggested" it when you hypnotized me and made me think I did, but I didn't.

I read the other transcripts, too, and I can see why you think I might be losing my shit. Maybe it is that posttraumatic stress stuff, maybe it isn't, but either way I can't talk to you anymore. Let the bureau suspend me. Let the grand jury indict me. It was an accident, and nothing I said to you while you were messing with my head under hypnosis will ever change that.

LEAVING YOUR OFFICE I saw the evening edition of the *Daily News,* with my police academy photo on the cover. It made me look guilty. I remember the day that picture was taken, twenty-one years old, I couldn't help but smile I was so proud. I smiled until Sergeant Sacristano growled at me, pissed off and impatient.

"Wipe the stupid grin off your face, Corrigan. You're a cop, not a door-to-door salesman. The law is serious business." So I scowled. And now that scowl made me look mean. It made me look guilty. I turned away from the newsstand and kept walking, hoping with the few years I had on me, and longer hair, that I didn't look so mean anymore.

As I drove home, I noticed a dark-colored Ford with two men in the front seat. They were following me, staying about fifty yards back. The car was clean, recently washed, with no dents and nothing unique about it. Definitely a federal car. The New York cops were at least smart enough to blend in. I thought about losing them, but they were there, supposedly, for my protection. After the whole Lucky incident and the lynching in the press, I decided to slow down. I remember thinking at the moment, Let them watch me, I'm not going anywhere. Funny, isn't it?

When I got home tonight, I went straight to the garage for a gas can. I wanted to burn the tapes I stole from your office, but my father was in there already, sitting on a milk crate with the door open, chain-smoking. I could see a dozen black marks on his immaculate concrete floor—scars from the cigarettes he had put out. If he was scarring his floor, he had to be tense. He was obviously waiting for me, because when he saw my car pull up, he crushed out the cigarette he was smoking, even though he had just lit it. That cinched it. The cheap bastard usually finishes my mother's half-smoked cigarettes by stripping off the paper and rerolling the tobacco—and she smokes Virginia Slims. He hates Virginia Slims. It's an image thing, I think.

He recovered quickly, bending over and picking up the crushed cigarette and slipping it in his pocket to be rerolled later. Then he called out to me in what he must've thought was a whisper. It was no whisper—it sounded more like an emphysema patient screaming on a roller coaster.

"Don' go in the damn house, will ya? They're lyin' in wait," he hissed. It was clear that he was agitated. It was one of those nights. I didn't really have the energy to deal with his particular type of insanity, but at least his delusions might be entertaining. I decided to humor him.

"Who's lying in wait, Da?"

"Never you mind. You can still get away. Go back to Glasson, to the Portlick Pub, and find your cousin Declan. Give him the package for your uncle Martin. He'll help you take the right of passage." My father was getting the past and present mixed up again. He always talked about Portlick when he told stories about my great-uncle Sean, the one killed behind the bar. Tonight he was in rare form, whispering hoarsely as he went on, grabbing my arm, his eyes wide.

"I don't even know what you're talking about. I'm not going anywhere."

"The right of passage. It's the law. We have to cross the neighbor's land and get to the island or we forfeit the right to cross. That land's been in our family since we were banished to Inchmore in 1763, and if no Corrigan walks it by the first of February, we'll lose the way. I can't make it and Aidan doesn't need to go—he's an eejit anyway. It's you who needs to go. And it needs to be tonight."

His eyes were frantic, practically bugging out of his head, as if he thought they could convey some secret meaning. I couldn't help but think that he looked like Peter Lorre in *Casablanca,* with his eyes popping out of his head every time he got excited. Still, it showed he cared, I guess.

"Look, Dad, this is your thing. Aidan can go if he wants. I'm not. I don't know anything about Ireland or our cousins. You made sure of that. You cut us off. I don't even know their names—"

"You never asked."

"What was I supposed to ask? You go back every year, but hell, until I was seventeen you told us it was a business trip. You never let us come with you. You've been keeping these secrets all these years and now you suddenly want me to go back? Why? What's the catch? Is it just so you can get rid of me now that I'm a problem?" I asked, but I really didn't think it was the only reason he was sending me back. He had some ulterior motive, I could see it in his eyes. I had reasons to be suspicious. I'd only learned about the right of passage a few years before, and part of me thought it was bullshit—a convenient excuse to leave us all behind for a few weeks. My father was so cagey about the whole thing, I thought that he might have a girlfriend over there, or even a second family. I swear he looked guilty every time he came back.

"It's not like that. You don't understand. The past, it's . . ." His voice trailed off, but he tried again. "It's not like you think it was. The war and the killing and everything. It was another lifetime, but it's all still right there. You need to go so you can understand. I swear to ya, you'll understand if ya go," he pleaded.

"Why should I go? Send Aidan."

"Just do as I tell you, Mickaleen. You need to go back to Glasson. Make the right of passage before it's too late. Besides, I told your cousins I'd send gifts. You can take those, too." And with that he pulled a ticket out of his back pocket. I could see the Aer Lingus logo on it and my brother Aidan's name as he pushed it at me.

"I'm not going anywhere. If I leave now, they'll think I'm guilty." I walked past him, headed into the house, annoyed that he'd insinuate that I might need to run, although I knew deep down that he was right. Whether or not I did anything wrong, they needed to hang me.

I had the tapes that would incriminate me in my jacket, ready to burn, but even without the tapes, it made political sense to scapegoat me. Ever since the King assassination, race riots had been breaking out around the country. Now, four years later, after the shootings at Kent State and all the rest of the things that had gone on, no one seemed to trust the government. Both the feds and the NYPD were eager to have someone to hang in order to prove themselves fair and impartial. And after James Butler died, I was the obvious choice. It was only a matter of time before a grand jury indicted me and some ambitious U.S. attorney made a political career out of me. I knew which way the wind was blowing. I just didn't need the confused old man rubbing it in.

"But you *are* guilty, Mickaleen. They all know it. They saw you shoot him. They all saw him lyin' there dead in the cold." I wasn't even to the door and the bastard was still pushing it. I put my hand on the knob, but he kept going. "If you make the right of passage, maybe you can make up for it. Face things instead of runnin' for once . . ." His voice trailed off as I turned on him and he saw the anger rising in my face. I wanted to hit him, even though I knew he was out of his gourd and mixing me up with his brother. When I saw the look on his face, the sadness and confusion, I couldn't even yell at him. I just opened the door, a blast of warm air and the smell of roast beef greeting me. That's when I knew it was going to be bad.

I knew it because my stoic and coldhearted mother is insensitive to every human emotion except one—hunger. Cooking was her answer to every crisis. If you lost a puppy, it was chocolate chip cookies. If you broke a bone, it was steak. Pneumonia, the flu, or chicken pox and it was soup. It was liver and onions for a broken heart (don't ask), and apparently, for a potential murder conviction, it was roast beef. With mashed potatoes.

I should have listened to my father. I should have run at the first scent of roast meat, because they *were* lying in wait for me, sitting around the kitchen table, congealing leftovers still in front of them. "They" were my mother, the damn priest, and the lawyer she'd hired.

The lawyer worried me the most. He was the best lawyer she could afford, I know that, but he was still Thomas Cahill, the twenty-six-year-old son of our church organist. His hair flowed down to his shoulders and he was wearing an "off-the-rack at Sears" suit. I had known him since he was in elementary school with me, back when we called him "Two Thumbs Tommy" because he had two thumbs on his right hand. That's why he never learned to play the organ, I guess. I had heard that one of the Quinlan kids cut off the nub with an ax at Boy Scout camp, but I hadn't seen Tommy since to confirm that it happened the way I heard it.

Now here he was, reaching out to shake my hand. Yup, with only one thumb.

"It was Patrick," he said with a straight face. For a second I almost didn't know what he was talking about. Then he clarified everything. "And they exaggerated. It was a Swiss Army knife. You can't trust a Quinlan with an ax."

I almost turned to make a break for it, but my mother caught me too quickly, her claws digging into my arm as she pulled me toward the priest, who kept fingering his rosary.

"Thank Jesus you're here, Michael," she wheezed. "I was just telling Father Finn that I was worried something might happen to you before you received absolution. I'd never forgive myself if you were forever damned because I didn't get him here fast enough."

"What the hell are you talking about, Ma?"

"You watch your language, son. Your good mother's just concerned for your eternal soul. I'm here to save you." Father Finn stared me down. It might have made me nervous, but the gravy on his cheek from the pot roast he'd already sampled made him look ridiculous.

"You're gonna save me? All by yourself? Then what's the lawyer for? Is he the devil's advocate or yours?" I looked up at Tommy. I was smiling, but he wasn't smiling back.

"I wouldn't be joking now, Michael. Thomas has been to confession and God has forgiven whatever sins caused his deformities. But you, you've taken another man's life. You're going straight to hell if you die." Father Finn slammed his hand down on the coffee table, scaring everyone in the room. After a pause to gauge our reactions, he slammed his hand down again, making a point.

"BAM! Bam! It will be that quick. I warn you, son, one time crossing the street, you'll get hit by a Mack truck and then it'll be an eternity in flames for you."

"And if it's a Peterbilt, do I go see St. Peter?" I couldn't help myself. Father Finn's face went red and the burst blood vessels in his nose looked like they were about to start gushing. I was saved from the moment by Two Thumbs, interrupting the exchange.

"Hell is only one of your worries. The grand jury handed down an indictment. First-degree murder." I finally looked past the scar on his hand and caught Tommy's eye. He was scared. The guy who had Pat the crazy Quinlan cut off an appendage with a pocketknife was scared. "First-degree murder's a capital offense in the state of Pennsylvania. That means the chair. Frying."

"I know what it means. But Jesus Christ, it was an accident. How the hell?"

"Watch your language, boy," Father Finn said through gritted teeth.

"Please, Michael, you're in enough trouble without swearing," my mother whispered as she served cheese and crackers. If she thought that was swearing, I wonder what she'd think of what'd be coming out of my mouth when I had a thousand volts going up my ass.

"They say it was revenge because he was a cop killer. That it was all planned," Two Thumbs went on, trying to get this intervention back on track.

"Understand, Michael, we all know the negro deserved it, but it wasn't your place to judge him and take his life. Only God has that right." The priest was back on the high ground, apparently unaware that a jury had the same rights as God under the law and that they could judge me and take my life just as effectively as the big man.

"It's political, if you want the truth. Nobody wants any more riots. If they convict you, they can keep the peace. You're a sacrificial lamb."

"Now don't go using those kinds of phrases in reference to a sinner, Thomas. It's not proper." Father Finn stared at Two Thumbs and Two Thumbs looked away as the priest took another cracker, chewing it and spraying crumbs as he turned back to me. "Confess to me now, tell me what was in your heart and I can make it right with God. I'm willing to help you, I'll even testify at your trial because your mother's always been a God-fearing woman and has tithed to the best of her ability."

"You mean she's bought your testimony because she gives to the church?" I know. I shouldn't have said it, but I'd seen coerced testimony too often to ignore it.

"She demonstrates faith."

"I'll say. She certainly doesn't display good judgment."

"Michael, that's enough. Confess to the priest. Tell Father Finn your sins," she demanded, as if I were still eight years old. "Tell him all the facts so we can figure out a story to get you off the hook. When it's all over you can show your appreciation by donating to the building fund for the school at St. Thomas's." And there you have it. It didn't matter if I murdered a man. Only that my mother had tithed and that I bowed before the priest, admitting that I sinned. Even if I hadn't. Then he'd make it right with God—for a fee.

"So you all think I'm guilty?"

"None of us actually wants you to suffer, Michael. As long as you're genuinely sorry." The priest reached across and took my hand to make his point. I could feel the clammy sweat of his palms. "You killed a man, Michael.

Accident or no, it's a sin on your soul and you have to pay. Pay and confess to God, or it's the chair and straight to hell."

"And this loving God, our Father, there's no middle ground with him? There's no chance for a little bit of purgatory?" Father Finn looked at me like any good DA would have. I wasn't getting any reduced sentence without pleading guilty.

"That's it, Margaret, I tried. Your son doesn't care about his soul. If he changes his mind, I'll be in the rectory." With that, Father Finn stood, walking out, grabbing a couple of crackers on the way. As he reached the door, he turned back. "And if, when you do need me, Margaret, you happen to have some of your Irish soda bread, it wouldn't go unappreciated." Father Finn smiled and then was gone. I couldn't help but think that if I did go to hell, I might be able to buy my way out with some soda bread and a little pot roast, because someone like Father Finn was sure to be guarding the gates.

"Now look what you've gone and done. All our hopes are on poor Tommy Two Thumbs here." My mother sighed, then turned to Tommy as she poured him more coffee. "No offense, Tommy, but you never were the hope of nations."

"No offense taken, Mrs. Corrigan. I'm glad to have a case at all." He smiled at her.

The only good news so far was that the grand jury had indicted me. That meant they were moving fast. I wouldn't have to wait so long to find out what they intended to do with me. I walked out of the room, ignoring my mother as she called after me.

I SAW LIAM AGAIN. It was only for a minute and it was all mixed up, but I saw him. All I can remember now are bits and pieces of images: fire in a fieldstone fireplace that smelled thick and earthy and looked like moss burning; a woman kneeling by the fire, her hair, the color of maple leaves in the early fall, hanging loose, covering her face. I remember getting up, wanting to get to her, interrupted by a door of wooden planks slamming open and letting in a blast of cold damp air. Liam was in the doorway, a fine mist settling like dew on his shoulders and hair.

"We just got word. They're coming." He was excited, I could see that, but he was frightened, too. In the dream—and I knew I was in a dream, even as I dreamed it—I wondered who "they" were. For some reason, "they" felt, in a way that only makes sense in a dream, like the police, the priests, the people who tossed Lucky through the window, and everyone else who wanted to see me hang.

I knew Liam was right, no matter who "they" were. They *were* coming, and I was running out of places to hide. I looked over at the woman, but I couldn't see her face. Only her eyes. They were the most familiar eyes I've ever seen, more familiar than even my own. I didn't realize then that I would see them again, or what they'd mean to me, but I felt it somewhere deep inside.

I watched those eyes as she spoke one word, and her eyes said the same thing she did, only more clearly.

"Go."

I woke up on the couch with my heart racing. I was wide awake, cold, holding every muscle stiff even though I was ready to bolt. The boarded-up window with plastic over it was leaking air, which explained the cold but not the racing heart. There was no possibility of sleep now. In the logic of dreams, of the subconscious, I had just been told to get my ass out of bed and move. But who listens to dreams?

Me, apparently. I got up, convincing myself that something must have set off the dream. Maybe someone was outside again. I looked, but all I could see was the dark-colored Ford with two white guys in it, parked in the shadows.

I went out the back, through the scraggly rosebushes my father kept, scratching my forearms on all the thorns. Then I went over Mr. Liggio's fence and out his front gate. The morons in the Ford never saw me.

Ten minutes later I was walking past the Quinlans' darkened house on Amboy Road, wondering if Patrick still lived with his parents or still owned that Swiss Army knife—and what he did with the thumb once it was cut off. I wasn't really thinking about it by choice, it was just one of those thoughts that crosses your mind. I was walking to clear my head and to try and come up with some way out of a death sentence that didn't involve bribing a priest, and the old neighborhood usually helped put things in perspective. On the corner of Amboy and Seguine, I made a right, past Nick's Country Store, headed up toward the train station and the Prince's Bay Pharmacy. I was thinking that a ride on the good old Staten Island Rapid Transit might be better than walking, as my nose and ears were starting to sting from in the cold. Then I saw him.

He was in the bank parking lot across the street, in a red Chevy Nova, slumped down in the driver's seat and looking in my direction. I don't know how he got there or what he was doing, but it looked like he was waiting for me, watching me. I know I shouldn't judge anyone by skin color, but he was dark, so dark he blended into the shadows, and if he was watching me, I had to assume there was only one reason. I'd killed a man, and a lot of people thought I did it because he was black. That was enough reason to put me on trial—or take revenge.

I pretended I didn't see him, but I walked a little faster and reached under my coat to rest my hand on the grips of my off-duty gun. Halfway up the small hill to the train station, I heard the click of the Nova's door latch. I still didn't turn. At this distance, he'd need a rifle to hit me, and odds were he only had a pistol. I was taking the odds. All I wanted to do was to cross the tracks on the street overpass and get to the stairs that ran down to the train platform. If I did, he'd have to follow, silhouetting himself as he crossed after me.

It worked. I ducked into the stairwell and stopped, practically holding my breath so that it wasn't visible in the frigid night air, listening to his soft footsteps as he approached. I heard him hesitate at the other end of the overpass. He was smart enough to know the risk he was taking.

He followed me anyway, and I realized too late that I'd expose myself if I moved too soon. If I spooked him, he might pull a gun, and then I'd have to shoot him. If I did, I'd definitely be meeting up with Old Sparky. Maybe I could get back into my parents' house without anyone noticing I was gone. Then the two morons parked out front could be my alibi for another dead black man. Yeah, them and the priest. I wondered how much baking Mom would have to do for that one.

His footsteps were coming faster. The only thing I could do was to jump him and try to disarm him. I timed it well. One of his feet was just hitting the stairwell as I bum-rushed him, put him in a headlock, and slammed the barrel of my pistol to his head.

"All right, what the fuck do you want?" I said, even as I smelled his nasty cologne and it registered that his shoes looked like they came from Thom McAn. This was no vigilante. This was a fed.

"Jesus, Mike, it's me, Davidson. It's me . . ." I let him go, spinning him around, still holding the gun on him.

"Are you an idiot? Sneaking up on me? In the middle of the night?"

"Me, an idiot? Who goes out in the middle of the night when he's got a target on his back and a price on his head?" Davidson shook me off, straightening his suit and tie. A typical agent, he always wanted to look clean shaven and freshly pressed in case someone saw him out on the street in the middle of the night. He couldn't tail someone if his life depended on it, but damn, he could iron a mean crease.

"Twyman Meyers sent a note to us down at the Federal Building. It was a hit list. You're at the top. Next to your name is your address—and your parents' address." He glanced nervously up and down the street as if Twyman and his self-styled revolutionaries from the Black Liberation Army were already watching. If Davidson, a fed, was nervous, that made me nervous. Still, something wasn't making sense.

"If the BLA wants me, I'm flattered. But why are you telling me? You and your FBI cronies never did us any favors before. You didn't even want us on your task force. So why didn't the department let me know? Why you?"

Davidson looked away from me with such a guilty expression, I almost knew what was coming before he said it.

"Word is that J. Edgar doesn't mind if they get you. Better a cop than a federal agent, right? Then he can blame you for Butler's death and when the BLA's killed you, Hoover'll have a good excuse to use everything he's got to destroy them, no matter what Nixon wants."

"And what does Nixon want?" Davidson looked away again, obviously uncomfortable.

"I'm not actually in on these things, you know, but the boys are saying he wants you convicted. It'll get Nixon the blacks and radicals in time for the election in November. Going after you shows that the Justice Department is fair and balanced." He paused then, looking genuinely torn. I knew that this was hard for him. He was betraying the bureau and Hoover by telling me this. Not to mention helping a white man who'd just murdered another black man—and a lowly cop at that. The thing is, Davidson was just a good guy, who followed his gut and did the right thing. That's why I knew he was telling the truth. There was no upside for him to be doing this, no angle to play.

"Look, Mike, you've always been straight with me, so I'm here to tell you, half the people want you dead and the other half wish you already were dead. You and me, we know you're a straight guy, but that don't matter anymore." I nodded. He was right. My choices seemed to be limited: Old Sparky or a hail of bullets—a hail of bullets that might take my mother, father, and Aidan with me, not to mention Lucky. It was a tough decision, but I'd feel bad about my dad. And Lucky.

I left Davidson there at the entrance to the station, standing in the dim light of the Prince's Bay Pharmacy, two doors down. I never even thanked him. I just walked away. He understood. I was walking away from him, distancing him from all this. I was walking to clear Davidson and to clear my head. But my head wasn't clear. It was muddled with dreams of Liam and a woman with green eyes and a place more familiar to me than the neighborhood I was walking through. The whole way home, one thought kept crowding in. I was walking in the wrong place. I needed to go walk the land. I had the right of passage. I just needed to take it.

Sean

I found Special Agent Timothy Davidson easily enough by calling the local FBI office. It never occurred to me that it'd be so easy, but I guess they're supposed to be able to find people and if they couldn't find one of their own agents, it might be embarrassing. I left a message for him at his office in Manhattan, explaining who I was and asking if I could meet with him to talk about my uncle. In less than an hour, I got a return message.

"Sean. Timothy Davidson. I'm here all day. Twenty-second floor of the North Tower. I'll put your name on the list. If they say I'm not here, call me and I'll chew their asses out. After today I'm on assignment and back in three weeks, so make it today if you're in a rush." And then he hung up, no good-bye, all business.

Two hours later I was leaning into the perpetual breeze that slid between the two towers of the World Trade Center, heading for 1 WTC. The concrete barricades that had been up since February of last year had become makeshift benches for the inhabitants of the World Trade Center complex as they ate their dirty water dogs and pretzels. None of them seemed to be concerned with the reason the barricades were set up, the truck bomb that failed to take down the buildings, but instead treated them the way New Yorkers treat everything from the homeless, to tourists, to an abandoned car—like furniture, walking around them, ignoring them, or using them for whatever they could be used for.

It was the middle of the afternoon, after the lunch hour rush, so I had an easy time getting through security. Davidson must've warned them, because they called him immediately, escorted me personally to the elevator, turned a key, and sent me straight up to the twenty-second floor.

Agent Davidson was standing outside the elevator, staring me down before the doors even opened all the way. Gray-haired and potbellied, he still scared me as he started firing statements at me.

"If you came for answers, here they are. One, there was *no* gun on James Butler. Two, I testified that there was no gun on him, because there wasn't. Three, I also testified that I heard at least *two* weapons firing, from two distinct locations. There was a clear difference between the sound of Detective Corrigan's gun and the other one, wherever it came from." Talk about defensive. Davidson looked like he wanted to end the meeting before I stepped out of the elevator.

"Actually, I wanted to know about the night you came to warn him, and . . ." Before I could finish, he was on the elevator with me, stabbing the buttons to close the door, pushing me back in and using his body to hide me from anyone who might be watching.

"Wait, what are you doing?" I stammered, a little nervous about being stuck in a confined space with this guy. I wasn't having good luck with strangers in elevators the last few days.

"Shut up," was all he said. I tried to say something twice more, but each time, he just repeated himself.

"Shut up." Simple and to the point. Yeah, that sounds right. When the elevator doors opened, he started striding across the lobby without looking back at me. I followed him, not knowing what else to do. Finally, halfway across the lobby, I tried again.

"Can I talk now?"

"No. Shut up." And he kept walking. I kept following. I almost stopped as he crossed Church Street, darting between cabs, then headed down Dey, but he looked over his shoulder as he crossed and called back to me.

"Get a move on." Then he kept walking. I caught up with him on the other side of Broadway, as he headed down John Street. He was making a beeline for the tattered awning of the Roxy Coffee Shop. Davidson didn't wait for me to follow him in, and by the time I got inside all I caught was the tail end of his order to the waitress.

". . . and make them runny. I don't want rubber." He saw me then, but looked away, waiting for me to sit down.

"I'm not buying you breakfast," he said, finally looking up.

"Uh, can I buy *you* breakfast?" I asked, not sure if that was what he was hinting at.

"Are you stupid?" he asked. Somehow I knew there was no right answer to that one, so for a change, I just shut up.

"Sit down," he commanded. I did, and then he was silent again. I was beginning to think I should stand back up when he finally continued, his voice low, his tone discreet. "Do you realize that if anyone thought I warned Mike of anything, I could be charged with aiding and abetting?" Davidson asked. "I could be charged as an accessory after the fact. And who the fuck told you I warned him?" His eyes bored into me. Looking at him, I could understand why people make false confessions. It beats pissing yourself. I couldn't help but answer him.

"He did. I got his journal."

"That asshole. He put something in *writing*?"

"Yeah. I have most of it, but—"

He reached out his hand, cutting me off. "Give it to me."

"I don't have it on me." Davidson narrowed his eyes as if he didn't believe me and even gave my coat a once over for any telltale bulges. Finally he sighed heavily.

"Destroy it. No good can come of it. The past is the past. Leave it there. Nobody cares about it anymore."

"I do." He ignored the comment for a moment while the waitress delivered almost uncooked eggs, a toasted bagel, black coffee, bacon *and* sausage, home fries, and a tomato juice.

As she walked away, around a mouthful of bagel drenched in egg yolk, he managed to mutter, "You'll end up like your uncle if you're not careful. You're an idiot if you go over there. I told him the same thing, but he had that same look in his eyes as you."

"I just want to do what's right."

"Bullshit. You're looking for something you can't find. Nobody cares anymore about what your uncle did. It's ancient history. The BLA, cop killers—they don't matter anymore. Terrorists do. They're our new breed of 'idiots with ideologies.'" He glanced around as he said it, holding up his empty coffee cup that he had downed like a shot of whiskey so that the waitress could see he needed a refill. The waitress obviously knew him well. She ignored him.

"Idiots with ideologies?" I prodded him.

"Yup. The most dangerous men in the world."

"You could say the same thing about the people bombing abortion clinics. About any fanatic."

"True. They're all crazy, and it won't stop until they're un-crazy. Gotta teach them to think differently. Good fuckin' luck with that, right? You got any answers to that one, kid? Some way to stop people from trying to kill each other?" I just shrugged. Of course I had no answers. I couldn't even stop my ex-girlfriend from thinking I was a boring schmuck *and* fuck. Yes, those were her exact words. Cruel, aren't they? I thought I was just inexperienced.

"Your uncle ran away from it all and ran into something just as dangerous. He wrote me once from Ireland, you know." Davidson stopped, waiting for my reaction.

"He what?"

"Yeah, that was my reaction, too. He had some balls. He coulda jammed me up but good."

"You still have it?"

"I burned it. I don't like things in writing. But I remember a line from it. It made me want to go home to Ireland like he did, even if it wasn't home for me—and even though it killed him." He paused, trying to remember the exact words. "He wrote, 'I found it, Tim. A place where it all makes sense. A reason for fighting the good fight, even if I lose.' That's what he called law enforcement, you know. 'Fighting the good fight.' "

"But he did lose. They killed him over there."

Davidson nodded. "Yeah. But before that, he found something I never did. That place wasn't safe for him, but he loved it, I'll tell you that much." Then he looked back at me, suddenly all business again. "Look, kid, you should know—your uncle was a lost soul. Never really fit in on the task force or even in the NYPD from what I heard from the other cops. He thought for himself too much. Top-down authority didn't work for him. That's why

I liked him, I think. We were both outsiders, looking for something more, I don't know what. Just something more, I guess. Maybe he found it. If you're like him, maybe you will, too. Just don't let it kill you."

Davidson threw some money on the table and stood up, moving stiffly as he grabbed his jacket.

"And if you find what he found, let me know. I'm getting to an age where I could use a little of it." Davidson looked back at the table, as if he could find "it" somewhere there. But he hadn't left a crumb of toast, a scrap of bacon, or a drop of coffee behind. He looked disappointed.

"What did Uncle Mike find exactly? Did he say?"

"No. He was talking a little crazy in his last letter. It was that same kind of crazy thinking that got him killed, I'll bet. Don't let it happen to you." And with that, Davidson walked out. It was the last time I ever saw him.

I tried to follow him. I had more questions. I wanted to ask what Uncle Mike wrote that was so crazy and what Davidson knew about how he was killed, but the waitress caught me at the door, stopping me.

Agent Davidson had stiffed her on the bill.

I paid for breakfast. So did he, apparently. I tried looking him up when I got back from Ireland, but I learned that two weeks after we had breakfast together, his heart gave out over an egg-white omelet. Apparently he was trying to get healthy.

Michael

I came back into the house the way I left, scratching myself on the Liggios' fence and then even more on my father's damn rosebushes. The warmth of the house felt good, but the heat never sank into my bones. If it did, I might never have left. When I got back to the couch, where I had been sleeping, I found an Aer Lingus ticket sitting on my pillow, along with Aidan's passport. I could feel my dad watching me from the hallway. Had he been standing there the whole time I was out, just waiting?

"Write to your mother. She'll miss you," he said calmly, as if I were going off to Boy Scout camp. He was sucking down a cigarette, the ash glowing as brightly as his tension.

"I will." No sense making a drama out of it. I grabbed the tickets and noticed another bag at the foot of the couch. I knew what was inside: Dallas Cowboys Super Bowl jackets to give to my cousins and stuffed Mickey Mouse dolls for the kids—things from the States that no one on the other side would want. My father insisted on sending things like this over every year.

"Nobody watches American football over there, Da."

"Maybe not all the time. But Staubach won it twenty-four to three. They had to notice that now, dinn't they?" I couldn't see his face, but I knew he was smiling. For some reason, these completely inappropriate gifts were funny to him.

"I had to rush to get those jackets on time. The Cowboys are fresh off the win, you know. Just give that package to your cousin Declan. The jackets will keep them warm, and if the little ones are too big for Mickey Mouse, they can make a quick buck sellin' them to some other poor child. And make sure you tell them that the gifts are from Mickaleen himself." It wasn't worth arguing with my dad. He was an old man and taking the gifts would make him happy.

"I'll need their addresses. I don't know how to get in touch with them."

"Ahh, shite. Sure you do. Say the name Corrigan in the town of Glasson and a relative will be within earshot. If not, go to the pub in Portlick. One of them's always keeping a stool warm there. You'll know them when you see them, won't you," he said. It wasn't a question.

"I've never met them."

"So? They look just like you but different. Especially the women. They're different in a nice way."

"I'm sure I'll figure it out."

"You will, but be careful over there, Mickaleen. You know what happened the last time you let your guard down. Liam came and got you, didn't he? And she'll be there waiting again, I'm sure . . ." His voice drifted off. It was like he suddenly heard himself and how crazy he sounded. Or maybe he noticed that I was staring at him. I was staring because he was talking about Liam—and it struck me that he knew who Liam was, somewhere in that addled head of his. But how did he know? Or do crazy people living together just synchronize after a certain point?

"Who's Liam, Da?" I asked quietly, trying not to startle him into sanity by pressing him.

"Who's who?" Bullshit. His expression was blank, but he wouldn't meet my eyes.

"Liam."

"I have no idea, do I? And even if I did, he wouldn't be anyone you know now, would he?" Talk about evasive answers. I wasn't going to let him get away with it, but a light suddenly snapped on, blinding both of us.

"Where the feck's he going?" It was Aidan, squinty-eyed and shirtless, rubbing his potbelly.

"Never mind, Aidan. Shut the light and go back to bed," my father ordered as he shielded his eyes.

"Like hell I will. This ain't Christmas and he ain't Santa Claus, and unless there's going to be a present here for me in the morning, I want to know what's going on."

"I'm leaving." It just came out. There was no reason to hide it, really. He'd know as soon as he woke up in the morning. Aidan opened his eyes wider in surprise, then squinted again, still too sleepy to handle it. No one said anything for a moment, but finally Aidan just nodded as if he saw the logic.

"Good. About time. Better off. Da's gonna have a heart attack with everything going on and Ma's gonna burn down the kitchen if you stay. And I could use some sleep, myself. Two nights in a row, up all night."

"I'll miss you, too."

"Don't be snide. You're runnin'. So what? Run. Go. It won't matter to us that it makes you look guilty or that it makes us look stupid." Which of course meant it *would* matter. It was the way my family, and most other families of Irish descent that I knew, spoke. A lot of things meant the opposite of what they appeared to mean.

"I'm sorry, Aidan."

"For makin' me look stupid, for runnin', or for not tellin' me you were gonna?"

"For everything except making you look stupid."

"Yeah. That one's not his fault. I blame your mother," my father said.

"Well, I'll forgive you for that one, too, if you give me your car." Aidan smiled. I guess he wasn't so stupid after all. He was going to get my '68 Mustang out of all of this.

"It's yours." What could I do with it, anyway? But Aidan shook his head, suddenly serious.

"I don't mean that way. You can't just go fly out of here. The two square boys in the car out front will stop you. Give me your car and your jacket. I'll take off somewhere. They'll follow me." I was impressed. Aidan's a bit dense sometimes, but apparently he was sharp enough to notice the team watching me.

"You'd do that?"

"If I get to keep your car, it's worth it. Better'n havin' to buy my own now, inn't it?" And Aidan smiled again. This was the happiest I'd seen him in a long time, but it wasn't really surprising. He'd always liked doing the right thing for the wrong reasons. I tossed him my keys and jacket and he grinned widely. I didn't even see him pull out—I just heard the squeal of the tires as he made it to the corner and gunned it.

The boys out front apparently head the tires too, because I went to say good-bye to my father, not even really thinking about it, just rushing to get out, but he stopped me by doing something strange.

For the first time I can remember, he hugged me. I mean, I'm sure he must have done it occasionally when I was a kid, but this was the first time I ever remembered him doing it. As he held me close, I heard him muttering.

"Write to her. Otherwise she'll act like you were never born. She'll hide your pictures. Forget your name. Write to her so we can remember. So we don't forget each other again." He wasn't making much sense anymore, so I just hugged him back. Then I went out the front door and tried not to look back.

THREE HOURS LATER I was walking through the international terminal at Kennedy airport when I saw the early edition of the *Daily News*. On the third page there was an article about me under the headline CORRIGAN TO SURRENDER, with a statement from my "lawyer," Thomas Cahill, the two-thumbed organist's son: "Detective Corrigan maintains his innocence and is seeking solace in his family and his church . . ." Fortunately, the accompanying picture was so small and blurry that I didn't have to worry about being recognized.

What a load of shite, as my father would say. I wasn't seeking solace, I was running. Maybe I was a coward, maybe I was stupid to think that I could get away. I don't know. It seemed like I had no choice. Besides, what was there to stay for?

As I got on the plane a little while later, a little old woman looked at my pale Irish face and asked me if I was going home.

"I hope so."

Sean

That was it. He was gone. There was no manhunt. No charges were officially filed. Civil rights groups screamed about it, but what could anyone do when no one knew where he'd gone? Nothing happened, not even to my father, because the cops didn't want to admit they'd lost track of Uncle Mike while following his brother on a trip to New Jersey to buy cigarettes and a case of Pabst Blue Ribbon.

As I waited for my flight in the international terminal at Kennedy, I realized that I must be somewhere near where my uncle sat some twenty-four years ago. I sat there thinking about all the things I never dreamed were possible, like having an uncle who was a murderer, and my father doing something that wasn't completely selfish (even if he *did* get the car), and the fact that the car I rode in as a child once belonged to the uncle I never knew.

I remember that Mustang so well. My father used to let me pretend I was driving it. I remember the smell of it, the smooth feel of the wheel. I loved that car. When he wrecked it on the West Shore Expressway one night, I remember being angry at him. I wanted that car when I grew up. For some reason I had it in my head that he was going to save it for me. And now I find out that it was never even really his. It was Uncle Mike's.

It's pretty strange when you find out something that makes you look at your entire life from a different perspective. It makes you wonder how many other things are out there that you know nothing about. And if you did know about them, would they change the way you looked at the world?

I had a philosophy class once that spent a semester on the idea that the world as we know it is just a collective dream. All of us agree what things look like, what colors are in the rainbow—all of it. And then we dream the dream until one person, with strong ideas and enough charisma, decides to change the rules. When one person dreams their own dream and forces us to look at it, the whole world can change. The example the professor gave was, ironically, flying. He said that before anyone could ever fly, they had to dream that they could. Then they had to believe it. Then, by inventing a science that made other people believe, they built up enough faith in the collective unconscious to make it a collective dream. Once enough dreamers dreamed it, it happened.

The Irish in me, always worrying, wondered what would happen if it worked the opposite way. What if I were flying to Ireland, let's say, and people suddenly stopped believing planes could fly. Would they all come crashing down? When my flight was called and I walked to the jetway and looked out at my plane, the thoughts came back again. I had no faith. It was too big. Too heavy. That lumbering giant couldn't possibly fly. What if other people were thinking the same thing? What if enough people thought about the impossibility of flight all at once? Would my plane would come crashing down?

It was all just nervousness. Some part of me was jittery about going back to Ireland, to the place where my uncle had been murdered. Part of me knew that the world had changed, that the dream had shifted the minute I found out I had an uncle that I never knew that I had before. My uncle had been killed by MI5, and murder was suddenly part of my life, part of the dream that I lived. I realized that I wasn't really worried about the plane going down. I was worried about it landing. When it did, I would have to start seeing the world in a different way, a way that included an uncle who might have killed a civil rights worker—and I might run into the people who killed him in turn. I thought about turning around. If I stayed home, nothing would change and I'd be safe.

If I turned around, I could keep dreaming the safe dreams. I'd never have to worry about planes dropping out of the air or murderous uncles. I could live in healthy denial. I kept walking up the jetway. At the time I didn't know why, but even after I found out what it was that made me hesitate, and even after learning about the bombings and what happened to Kate, I know it was the right thing to do.

As I walked up the aisle of the plane, I kept trying to picture this vessel flying, hoping that everyone else would just keep believing that planes can fly. That they'd have faith and dream the collective dream. I kept thinking, Planes can fly . . . Planes can fly . . . I'm not sure I really believed it would work, but it was like an atheist praying when he's about to die. What if he gets to the other side and finds out that he was wrong?

What if I got to Ireland and found something I wasn't expecting? It had been less than a month since the Provisional IRA had blown up the city center of Manchester, and if they were willing to blow up complete strangers, why not the nosy nephew of a man they'd killed twenty-three years before?

Michael

"Raison fer ya visit?" I heard a voice mumble. It took me a minute to realize he wasn't actually offering me a *raisin,* as in "Would you like a raisin for your visit?" His accent was that thick.

I looked up to see the customs agent examining Aidan's passport. He hadn't even glanced at me. That was good. If he had, he'd have seen the fleeting moment of panic on my face when I answered in my head that the "raison" for my visit was to flee a "mairder" charge. Finally he looked up, but by then I'd settled into the lie.

"Visiting relatives and claiming my father's right of passage," I answered. I don't know why I told him about the right of passage. Maybe it was because in law enforcement you always distrust general answers as easy ways to lie. Details have the ring of truth.

"Good luck to you then. Keep the land in the family. Somebody wants to take it away, make 'em pay for it. Anything to declare?" he asked, already opening my bags. I'd like to declare my innocence and get back on the plane, I thought, but that didn't seem like the best plan, so I went with plan B.

"Just some gifts for the cousins that my father sent over."

He finally looked up at me, lifting the bag as if calculating its weight. After a moment he smiled, and I was sure he knew something. What he knew I wasn't sure, but whatever it was, he was enjoying it.

"Heavy, inn't it? Presents for the lads, eh?"

"Some for the nieces, too," I told him, and for some reason he laughed. I could smell his stale cigarette and coffee breath as he did, but he was still smiling at me as if I were *his* long lost cousin.

"Yeah. The nieces. Our lasses are as mean as they come when they get their minds set, aren' they?" And then he handed the bag to me, nodding respectfully. "Welcome back, Mr. Corrigan. It's good to have yer kind come home agin."

"Thank you, but I've never been before."

"Are ye sure now? Wit' the look a you? An' a name like Aidan Corrigan? I'da thought you'd never left until ya opened up yer gob." He narrowed his eyes at me and for the first time looked at me as if I were lying. Then he glanced at my passport, genuinely surprised. "Well, look at that. Yer passport agrees with ya, don't it? I guess ya must have a good raison fer that." He handed me back my passport and waved me on, but before I got two steps away, I heard him call after me.

"Don't let the boyos get you involved in any a their troubles, will ya? There's been a lot of it lately." I turned back to look at him, confused. He must've seen my look, because he went on. "Yer cousins. The ones the heavy stuff's for. Don' let 'em sell you on anyting. 'Snot yer place. But give 'em my regards." Then he winked. I turned and headed for the doors, just another American tourist in a place I thought I understood—but clearly did not.

I was still trying to figure out what the hell he was talking about as I reached the sidewalk and stepped out into something that was too light to be called a drizzle and too heavy to be fog. This was what my grandmother used to refer to as "misting." I knew it wasn't nearly as cold as New York had been when I left, but the rain made it seem colder. It wasn't just your skin that got cold here, it was your bones. In spite of the cold seeping into me, I had to smile. Even here, right outside Shannon, there was a smell you couldn't find in the States, something both fresh and old, warm and heavy. It reminded me of the smell of a wood fire on a cold day. Even when you were too far from it to feel any warmth, you knew it was there waiting for you.

Even the rain felt welcoming. As I walked through it to rent an old Vauxhall Viva from a woman named Patricia, I felt like I was heading home. The car wasn't very old, but it looked long abused and drove like it, too. The smell of stale cigarettes and pipe tobacco lingered in the ceiling liner, the wheel kept pulling to one side, and the shocks didn't do much except slam loudly every time you hit one of the ever-present potholes. Just driving it here was an abuse. Irish roads aren't like our roads. They never go straight, they're rutted, and they end when you least expect it. It would be hard to judge the age of a car after time spent on Irish roads since an hour on one could do years of damage.

Distances are also hard to judge in Ireland. Especially for Americans. Our roads are mostly straight and you can calculate how far you've come by the time you've spent traveling. Not here. Here you stop for sheep, cows, old women, random dogs, and hairpin turns.

It took thirty miles and almost an hour before I saw the green that Ireland was so famous for as the sun came through the clouds for an instant. It made the whole trip seem worthwhile, at least for that moment. The green did seem greener, if only because the mist and rain make everything else seem grayer.

After another hour spent traveling in more rain, I wound up back where I started. At least I think it was where I started, because the house at this particular crossroads looked familiar. It was bright yellow, and last time I came through I would have sworn it was white, but it had the same fence, the same car out front, even the same cat in the yard, hiding under a hedge. I stopped, looking at all the possible roads I could take from here, almost positive that I had already taken them all.

This is the culture that gave us the Celtic knot, and they seemed to work spirals and knots into every aspect of their society. Including the roads. After a few hours driving, you begin to realize that everything—roads, minds, and even conversations—are as twisted as their jewelry. Once you see the pattern it's beautiful and complex, but to an outsider it just looks like a jumbled mess.

I know, I've heard the theories of why the roads here are like this—that they follow the old cow paths and animal trails, or it's because the country is so old, but I think the confusion is purposeful. I think the locals use it as entertainment. I swear I saw the same two old men on the side of the road four different times, and each time I saw them, they were laughing harder at me. Maybe they used them to confuse the British. I don't know how anyone can conquer a country when you can't even find your way around it.

I was already down to a quarter of a tank of gas when I saw my turn. I was sure it was my turn. It had to be. It was the only one that didn't look familiar to me. Every other turn was starting to look like a turn I'd taken before. I really was afraid I was going in circles. The roads looked too familiar. That's when I saw what looked like a light-colored taxi with a little blue light on top coming up behind me. It was one of those boxy-looking Hillman Avenger saloon cars that they had all over the place. I was wondering what a taxi was doing all the way out here in Westmeath when I noticed that the sign on top didn't say TAXI but GARDA. The cops, the Garda Síochána na hÉireann, Irish for "Guardians of the Peace of Ireland." It took a moment before it hit me in the gut—I wasn't on their side anymore. I didn't want to talk to the cops. Looking back, I might have been better off if they arrested me right then and there.

But then I would have never met Kate, and she's what made all the rest bearable. For a second I thought about hitting the gas and running, but I knew I had nowhere to go. All the policeman would have to do is sit right there on the side of the road, and soon enough I'd probably be back asking him for directions. I pulled over.

As he got out of the car, slowly, I ran through what I needed to say and remember. Like a mantra, I kept repeating, "I have to be Aidan, I have to be Aidan, I have to be Aidan." After two or three times, I forced myself to stop. I didn't want to be my brother. Not that he was a bad guy, but to be honest, he was a bit of a self-centered asshole—a likable go-to-the-football-game-and-get-drunk kind of asshole, but an asshole nonetheless. If I tried to act like him, I'd start cursing the Irish, their roads, their road signs, and eventually their police force, blaming anyone but myself for getting lost. So I decided to be me. With Aidan's name. The garda stooped and peered in the window, smiling.

"You've been this way before, haven't ya?" Maybe it was a smirk, not a smile. He was enjoying this.

"Probably," I answered, not really knowing if I had been. He nodded as soon as he heard my accent.

"A Yank, are ya? Can I see yer passport?" Suddenly he was all business, and it crossed my mind that a warrant might have been issued after I'd fled. If the department figured out I had my brother's passport, they might have alerted the Irish Garda. I tried to distract him by playing the part of the lost tourist as I handed him my paperwork.

"I'm trying to find my way to Glasson."

"Good luck to you then. You can't get there goin' this way, can ya?" he said, without looking up from the passport.

"Obviously, I don't know. I'm lost." He looked up at that, staring at my face, looking at my eyes. I thought for sure he knew who I really was, and I started to sweat in spite of the chill.

"Are ya sick?" he asked, backing away a step.

"Me? No . . ."

"You look pale, boyo. And you lost some weight since this passport photo was taken."

"I'm fine. Better, actually." I tried to act natural but couldn't figure out what natural should be when you're lost in a strange country talking to a cop worried about your health. Then I noticed the garda nodding slightly, as if he had just figured something out.

"Ahh, got off the bottle, did ya? Ya look like a drinker in this here photo. The drink'll bloat you, and when it starts seepin' out you do look pale. Am I right?" He was nodding more rapidly, pleased with his detective work.

"Yeah. That photo's of a man who drinks too much. That's for sure," I agreed as he stared at the passport one more time.

"Corrigan, is it? From the island or the mainland?"

The question didn't register for me at first. What mainland? What island? Ireland itself was an island. Was he trying to trip me up? Did he know from the passport that my parents lived on Staten Island? Luckily he saw my confusion and clarified his question.

"Your *folks*. Were they the Corrigans from Inchmore—in Lough Ree—or the mainland?" he asked, and it suddenly fell into place. I remember my father telling me about taking a rowboat or something to church every Sunday, no matter how harsh the weather, and fishing for eels in the shallows of the lake.

"The island."

The garda smiled. "You're lucky there now; I don' like the other ones much, do I?" he said as he handed back Aidan's passport to me. "If it were the mainlanders, I'd tell you that you might want to stay lost."

His words reminded me of the little family history that my father had imparted. The Corrigans of Inchmore were the branch of the family that had fled when the British took their land for agitating rebellion in the Troubles of 1867. Living around the lake, on the "mainland," were all his cousins. The cousins kept their land by either going along with British rule, saying nothing, or not getting caught. I was lucky that I'd answered that my family were the islanders.

"Nasty backstabbin' lot, them mainland Corrigans. Their women are one of the reasons these roads are so damn twisted," the garda continued.

"Their women?"

"Fer certain. Since time began their husbands have never wanted to go straight home after a long night at the pub, because the ol' hag might be up waitin'. So they wander around drunk, making twisted paths so well worn the horses started to use 'em. Then the cars jus' followed. Yer sure you want to get to Glasson?"

"It's where my family is."

"Aye. That's as good a reason to leave as it is to go there, but if you insist, take the first right, second left, third left, first right, and you'll be there in fifteen minutes, won't ya," he answered, walking back toward his Hillman. I called after him, trying to remember what he'd just said.

"First right, second left, third left, first right," I repeated. He turned back for a second and smiled.

"Very good. I bet you couldna do that when you were still on the bottle, could ya?" And he got in his car as I repeated the directions over and over again in my head, wondering if I'd have to pretend to be a reformed alcoholic to pull off stealing my brother's ID.

An hour later I came around a bend in the road that had hedges growing into it so far they scratched the car. It was there that I found a greengrocer's set back on the other side of the road. This was the first hopeful sign I'd had for a while. I knew for a fact that I had not passed a greengrocer's before, especially not one with a gas pump out front. For the last ten minutes the gas needle had been resting on empty, so it was something I'm sure I would have noticed.

The bins for fruits and vegetables were mostly empty this time of year, but the small store inside was lit up and the primitive gas pump looked like it was working. I pulled up onto the loose gravel next to the pump and went to the door, pulling out the Irish pounds I had exchanged at the airport.

The smoky warmth of a fire hit me as soon as I entered, taking the chill out of the air. So warm it felt like my clothes might steam from the heat. I looked around for the clerk, distracted by the differences between this place and a store back home. None of the candy or chips were the same. Here, the soda was all kept warm, stacked in small bottles. Even the Coca-Cola looked different. I was picking one up to look at it when I heard a woman's voice from the back of the little store.

"*Céad mille fáilte*," she called out as I turned to find her, carrying a crate of something, and my breath caught in my throat. She had an ease about her and her green eyes had flecks of blue and gray that seemed to look into me and through me all at the same time. Her hair was the color of maple leaves in the early fall, hanging loose.

"*Dia dhuit*," I answered, without thinking, taking the crate from her and piling it on top of several others that sat by the counter. I knew I was staring at her but couldn't look away. I could tell just by looking at her that she'd have freckles across the bridge of the nose in the summer and that her dark auburn hair would grow more red in the sunlight. I had no idea how old she was—depending on the light and her mood, she could have been twenty or thirty—but I'd guess she was somewhere in between, because her voice had a husky heaviness you wouldn't expect in a young girl. I wanted to hear it again, so I kept talking.

"*Ta me i gcruachais. Ta me ar strae.*" She just smiled as if I were flirting or teasing her. I smiled back, wondering how I'd remembered these phrases.

"No . . . *Ta tu mall. An bhfuil tu ag lorg duine eigin?*" she asked.

"*Ta bron. Nil Gaeilge maith agam. An Bhfuil Bearla?*"

She laughed as I finished, and somehow I knew that if she laughed too hard she would start to hiccup and that she could cure her hiccups with a shot of whiskey. It was just one of those things you know somehow, even when first meeting a person. I know it sounds like horseshit, but I found out later I was right.

When she laughed, it hit me hard. Butterflies in the stomach and all that other crap I'd never taken seriously before. She wasn't beautiful—at least not when I first looked at her—but when I looked back, and she was laughing at me, I saw it all there. All the things that came together to make her uniquely perfect: the delicate skin that would be too pale on another woman, the eyes that reflected the light, even in darkness, the smile— everything. When she finally stopped laughing, she shook her head and just turned away, moving behind the counter.

"Thank you. I needed a laugh like that. Don't know Irish, do ya?" She smiled again, putting a warm Coke and some potato chips up on the counter, pointing out that I had remembered more than I claimed to know.

"Does it sound like I know it well?"

"Yer cute, are ya? Well, I'm Kate Ryan, and now that ya know my name, ya can be a polite gentleman and innerduce yerself."

"Excuse me?"

"Stop puttin' me on, and innerduce yerself."

"Oh, sorry, I'm . . ." I stopped. I'd completely blanked. It wasn't that I didn't remember I was Aidan. I didn't even remember I was Michael.

"At a loss fer words? Tha's odd, inn't it? Ya don't look like you've been in the sauce yet." She looked me up and down, taking me all in, making me feel like an idiot. "Ya look like a Sean if ya ask me."

"No, not Sean. Sean was my uncle." That came to me pretty easily and helped with the rest. "I'm Aidan. Aidan Corrigan." It came to me as soon as I stopped thinking about it.

"Praise Jesus, he's remembered himself. And if Sean Corrigan's yer uncle, then yer da must be Ole Jim Corrigan. No wonder you and yer Irish sound so familiar to me. The Corrigan men have wonderful voices."

"You know my family?"

"As well as ya know yer Irish."

"But I *don't* know Irish. I'm an American." I protested, aware that I'd responded to her with Irish phrases, but unsure why, or where they'd come from. Maybe I'd listened to my father more than I'd realized as he rambled on, mumbling under his breath.

"Yeah. *Irish* American, right? Now go pump the petrol and tell me what ya owe me when yer done, *Aidan* Corrigan. Ya can do that much, can't ya?" It sounded like a question, but there was no doubt she was telling me what to do. I did it, too confused about what just happened to question her.

I really was at a loss for words. As I pumped the gas, I replayed our conversation in my head. She'd welcomed me when I walked in with the traditional greeting, *céad mille fáilte*—a hundred thousand welcomes. I'd somehow answered her with the equivalent of an Irish hello, literally "God be with you," and then the conversation went on:

"I need your help. I'm lost."

"No, yer just late. Are ya looking for someone?" she had asked, smiling as if she knew I was. She was staring at me, and I wanted to answer in Irish, "I'm looking for you," but it sounded so ridiculous that I responded, "I'm sorry. I can't speak Irish very well. Do you speak English?" And that's when she laughed.

Thinking back on it, I can understand why she thought I was lying. I was speaking to her in phrases that I must've picked up from my father or my uncles. I was trying to recall when last I'd heard my father speak in Irish, when another phrase started going through my head: "*Bean mo chroí.*"

I had no idea what it meant, but it started an avalanche of others: "*Tá tú go hálainn*" and "*An bpósfaidh tú mé?*" A conversation was playing out in my head, but I couldn't understand a word of it.

I watched Kate reading a book through the steamed-up windows and thought about going in and asking her what the phrases meant but decided against it. What would she think of a man who claimed not to know a language he'd been speaking moments before? She looked up at me as I watched her and the thought "*bean mo chroí*" rattled around my head again as I looked away. I was going to have to find out what that meant.

When I went back inside to pay she was sitting on the counter reading *The Little Prince* and watching me over the top of the book. I couldn't think of anything witty or even rational to say in English, so I pretended to count my Irish pounds and grab some snacks off the shelves. Even they confused me. I wasn't used to Irish snack food, with their Tayto Crisps, Mikados, coconut creams, and their Barm Brack cakes. All I wanted was a good old American Twinkie—or at least a Ho-Ho.

I kept my eyes on the snacks but couldn't help glancing up at her, feeling her eyes on me. She caught me looking. So much for all my experience as a cop. Some detective I was.

"Still lost?" She grinned. "Nothing looking familiar to ya?"

"I've never been here before."

"That doesn't answer the question now, does it? Does anything look familiar to ya?" She repeated this as if I were a bit slow, which I guess I was at that moment.

"You think I should recognize something even though I've never been here before?" I asked, squinting, trying to see what kind of food I had picked up in the little yellow bag with a girl's name on it.

She smiled and nodded, holding up the book in her hand. " 'That which is essential is invisible to the eye.' It says so right in here. This place feels like home, even though it's not, donn't it?" She stopped speaking, but her eyes held me. She expected an answer. Her logic was as winding as the roads, but I suspected I could follow it if I listened long enough.

And maybe it did make some sort of sense. This place, the greengrocer's, the roads, all of Ireland—it did feel like home in a strange way. But like a home I'd lived in when I was a little kid, before someone else moved in and changed all the furniture and painted all the rooms. Still, I wasn't about to explain all that to a stranger, so I lied.

"No. I'm completely lost. I've been driving for hours, but every time I think I know where I'm going, the road turns the wrong way. I went by this same yellow house four times, sure that if I turned right there I could get straight on the road to Athlone, but I kept getting turned around."

She nodded solemly. "Ahh, the FitzPatrick place. Ya haven't been able to go right there for fifteen years. They turned the road around because they found some old ruins when they tried to widen it, and now ya have to go up the other way past the O'Haras'."

"You mean I could have gone right?"

"Up until fifteen years ago."

"Well, how do I get there now?"

She laughed at me again, shaking her head as if I had asked something stupid. "Ya can't get where yer goin' from here, Yank. Ya gotta get back to where ya started first. Where are ya coming from?" She looked at me like she really cared to know where I'd been, but all that really mattered was that I was here now. Where I was coming from was irrelevant. But then again, so was arguing with her.

"Shannon Airport."

"Ahh, well, ya better sit down then. You've got a few hours to waste." Kate must have seen my look and went on, "Travelin's way too quick nowadays. Ya go so fast ya leave part of yer soul behin' and now ya have to wait fer it to catch up. So sit. Have some tea. Wait for it to catch up with ya and then it'll be easier to find yer way." She grabbed a teapot and started to pour.

"You're having fun with me now, aren't you?" I asked, noticing that I was starting to sound like a real Irishman, answering a question with a question.

"Am I?"

"You are. And thanks for the offer, but I really want to get where I'm going before dark." I grabbed the crisps, Kimberleys, and Coke, pulling out my Irish pounds and almost dropping Aidan's passport as it came out with my wallet. Kate laughed, enjoying how nervous I seemed to be.

"Don't bother with that. I've got what ya need right here." I looked at the counter where she pointed to see a bag of crisps, Kimberleys, and a Coke sitting there. She already had exactly what I had picked up waiting for me. I set the passport down and picked up the Coke, taking the bag she had ready. "Ya won't need much more than that there. Just head up the road a stretch to the first left, straight on to the third left and then ya will see Lough Ree. Keep it on yer left and ya will be in Glasson in no time."

"How'd you know I was going to Glasson?"

"Where else would a Corrigan be goin'? If yer an island Corrigan, which I can see by yer eyes ya are, you'll be lookin' for the Portlick Pub. Pass Glasson and take the third left near the lady picking flowers." I had no idea what she was talking about, so I just nodded.

"Thanks. For everything." I didn't know what else to say, so I took the stuff as she bagged it and turned to go. "I really do appreciate it."

I'd already turned to leave when I heard her calling after me.

"*Ní dhíolann dearmad fiacha,*" she said, and this phrase I recognized. They were my Uncle Sean's last words. My father had translated them for me a hundred times. "A debt is still unpaid, even if forgotten." I turned slowly to look at her, suddenly cold again.

"What debt?" I asked as she put out a hand, never losing her grin.

"Fer the crisps and petrol, yeah. You forgot to pay me." She picked up Aidan's passport from where I'd left it on the counter, holding it hostage. "Yer identity is a terrible thing to lose, especially if ya came all the way back home to find it. Fer the price of a fillup and some Kimberleys I'll help you get it back." I reached for the passport, but she pulled it away, teasing now, waiting for the cash. I counted it out as she watched me, and then we traded, her eyes on mine the whole time.

"Thanks," I said as I turned away, still not sure what was going on. I knew I'd probably never see her again and probably shouldn't. I came all the way over to Ireland to keep a low profile, not flirt with the woman at the green-grocer's. I just needed to find my cousins and stay there. As I opened the door, the cold air hit me again and I hesitated, not wanting to leave.

"Are ya really gonna do it *again*?" she called, and I looked back as she said it. For the first time since I'd met her, there was no grin on her face, no light in her eyes. It made her look older.

"Do what?"

"Leave without sayin' good-bye."

I thought she might just be giving me a hard time, but I really couldn't tell. She seemed genuinely annoyed. Somehow I never really thought of Ireland as a foreign place, since my father was born there and we share a common language, but I was starting to think that I didn't understand these people at all.

"I don't know how to say good-bye."

"I never met a man who couldna say good-bye."

"I meant that I don't know how in Irish." With that, her grin was back.

"Well then, I'm not going to be the fool woman to teach you. Jus' say, '*An bpósfaidh tú mé.*' "

There was no arguing with her. When she told someone to do something, it was accepted that it'd be easier to do it than not. It would be months before I really knew what she was making me say, but somehow, even that first day, she knew I'd want to know how to say it. *"An bpósfaidh tú mé,"* I relented.

"Very good. And then I say, *'Bpósfaidh. Tá grá agam duit.'* And then it's all settled, inn't?" She laughed softly without explaining herself and turned back to her book, dismissing me with "Two lefts and you'll see Lough Ree on the left. Don't get lost again. I don' want to have to come find you, Sean."

"It's Aidan," I choked out, fighting not to say Michael. I needed to work on my fugitive skills.

"Don' look like an Aidan to me," she said without looking up. I stood there for a minute, waiting for her to say something else. I wanted to leave and I wanted to stay, but she just hid behind her book, invisible. Finally, to save myself from looking more like an idiot, I stepped out into the soft cold rain, wondering if I could find my way back here if I did get lost again.

As the cold started to seep back in, it reminded me that I already *was* lost, in the middle of a foreign country, pretending to be my brother, running from a murder charge. If she was right, and the only way to find my way was to get back where I started from, I was going to be lost for a long time. Maybe even long enough for my soul to catch up.

Sean

I felt like I was at a bus station somewhere in Ohio, surrounded by over-weight Americans and the industrial-strength smell that is common to all transit hubs, whether it's an international airport or a bus terminal in Cleveland. But I wasn't in Ohio, even if it could have passed for it. I was waiting for my luggage in Shannon Airport in the west of Ireland and was severely disappointed. As I watched the people around me, complaining about the airline food, the usual travel delays, and the rude passengers they'd traveled with, I started to wonder if there were actually any native Irish in the place.

As I grabbed my luggage, I finally noticed a few natives, easy to spot. They didn't push, just waited patiently and watched for whatever relative's luggage they needed, sliding back out with a deft "Excuse me" and "Thank you" once they'd retrieved it. I took my cue from them and waited patiently. My flight had gotten in a little early and I'd cleared customs two minutes before I was originally due to land.

I had no idea who I was meeting or what they might look like. My father's only comment was that it would be "one of yer uncle Patsy's kids. How the feck should I know what they look like? Like a cousin of yours, I'd bet." He was always so helpful. As I waited, I overheard a bit of conversation that I couldn't ignore.

"Jaysus, 'ave ya ever seen such a brilliant mass a amadans in one bloody place?" It was a woman's voice, sweet, almost lilting. If I didn't understand her words, I would've thought she were reciting poetry.

"Yeah. Yer da's place at holiday time." That voice was male and typical Irish. He mumbled. I turned to look and spotted a young woman no more than twenty years old, with a face that definitely did not match her words. She had fine, almost elfin features with a smattering of freckles and reddish blond hair. You might have called her delicate until you saw her eyes, which had the sharp look of a fifty-year-old con artist—the kind you see at the baccarat tables in Atlantic City. She was sipping a Guinness, even though it was only a little after noon local time, and as she turned I noticed a streak of blue in her hair. She seemed to be trying hard to overcome her natural beauty.

The man with her was the opposite: clean shaven, sharply dressed, and handsomely dark. He looked like he'd stepped out of a *GQ* ad. I never would have looked at either of them twice if I hadn't heard what the foul-mouthed little elf said next.

"I don't know why the feckin' eejit picked me to meet this Yank gobshite of a cousin, do you?"

GQ kept glancing at his watch as if he had somewhere he'd rather be. "He's got me here wit' ya now, don' he? A damn chaperone to keep you from runnin' any more garda off the road. I've got better things to do now, don' I?"

GQ followed the girl toward the arrivals board.

"Ahh, Jaysus. His feckin' plane got in early," she said as she read it, quickly glancing around the terminal.

"You think he'll be pissed off you weren't here to pick him up?" I asked as her sharp eyes fell on me, questioning who the "feck" I thought I was to be talking to her.

"If he's like the rest of you Yanks, he will. Yas think the damn earth revolves around the United feckin' States. You all should—" I couldn't hide my smile, and she stopped midsentence. "Ahh, shite. It's you, isn't it?"

"Me who?"

"Aidan's asshole son himself, that's you, inn't it?" She moved closer into my space, almost daring me to contradict her.

I took a step back but then stopped. If she was anything like my father, it would be better to stand up to her now rather than be her whipping boy later.

"I guess it is me, then. Who are you? Patsy's rude bitch of a daughter?"

"Sure 'nuf. It is you. Look at 'im, Kevin. You see the family resemblance?" She grabbed my jaw, hard, forcing me to face Kevin.

"Not quite, but I hear it now, don' I?" And he offered his hand, smiling. "Kevin O'Connell, and my apologies for the greeting."

"Ohh, shut the feck up, would ya, Kevin? He knows it's nothing personal, don' ya, Yank?" she asked as she punched me in the arm.

"To tell the truth, if you didn't talk to me like this, I might not believe we were related. In fact, if I go too long without someone calling me a feckin' eejit, I start to feel like an orphan."

"See? Now get his damn luggage, Kevin, and stop acting the maggot. Is this how you welcome my cousin, lettin' 'im carry his own bleedin' bags?" Kevin grabbed some of my bags while Anne started for the doors, empty-handed, talking the whole way. "I'm Anne by the way, Anne Ryan. And I'm not really yer cousin, least not by blood. By marriage somehow, through my aunt Kate—at least that's what they told me. And what should we call you, besides a feckin' eejit?"

"Sean. Corrigan."

"Well, Sean. Corrigan. First thing you should know is that you pack like a girl. An American girl. Everything's too big, overstuffed, and probably won't fit in the boot of the car, will it?"

"I packed a lot because I might be here for a while," I said.

"And don't we have ways of washin' yer clothes here in backward Ireland?" Anne asked as she walked into the street to get across to a parking lot, forcing traffic to stop without even looking up to see if it would. A Volkswagen squealed its brakes, but she didn't seem to notice. "Well? Don't we?" she demanded again.

"Sure. But I wasn't sure I'd be greeted so warmly and was afraid I might need to fend for myself."

"Are ya bein' nasty now?"

"He'll fit right in," Kevin mumbled, letting my luggage tumble to the ground behind a beat-up Ford Sierra Ghia.

"And who asked you to open yer gob?" Anne snapped at Kevin as she opened the trunk. Kevin muttered something I didn't catch, putting my stuff in the trunk as Anne responded, "No. You just put his stuff in the boot or you might have a boot in yer arse." Then she moved to get in the car. It took me a moment to realize that she was getting in on the driver's side, since it was the opposite side I was used to.

"I thought he was driving," I said before I could stop myself.

"Are ya kiddin' me? You think I'd get in a car with him? He's dangerous."

"Didn't he come to make sure you didn't run anyone off the road?"

"Sure 'nuf. And he will. Keep yer eyes open, Kev. It'll make the Yank feel better if ya warn me."

Kevin just grinned in response and climbed in the back, muttering. "You can have the front, boyo. I'll give a shout if it's goin' bad."

"Yer a coward, Kevin. Puttin' the Yank in the suicide seat, are ya?" Anne was starting the car, and I was still outside, hoping they were putting me on.

"You were drinking a Guinness in there," I told her, in case she'd forgotten.

"And? Would you feel better if it was a Harp?" She revved the engine, impatient. "Look, Yank—"

"My name's Sean."

"Right. Get in the car. I've waited too long for you to get here, I'm not waitin' anymore."

"You didn't wait, you were late."

"Are you arguin' wit' me now," she asked, although it was more of a statement, because she backed out of the parking spot, missing my foot by inches. She started to pull away, then hit the brakes, leaning out the window, doing her best to be what she apparently thought was a gracious host. "Last chance . . ."

Kevin opened his window and shrugged, a real apology in his weary look. "Don't feel too bad, boyo, she's like this with everyone."

"She doesn't have many friends, does she?" I asked as I reached for the door handle. She tapped the gas as I did, smiling, making a point.

"She has family. She doesn't need friends. It's the Irish way," Kevin muttered as I jumped in, afraid if I didn't she'd start moving again.

"You're family, too?" I asked, looking back, not seeing any resemblance.

"Me? Of a sort. My cousin's aunt by marriage has a sister-in-law that's got a brother married to her aunt," he explained. I took his word for it. "Seriously, boyo, can we go? One of us actually works for a living." I realized as he nodded to the door that I hadn't shut it. As I reached for the handle, Anne slammed her foot down on the gas and the door swung shut, slapping me in the head. When I looked at her, she was smiling.

"Sorry. Trying to help." Then she looked up in the mirror at Kevin, changing her focus. "An' you. You call that work? Answering phone calls all day?"

"I help people solve their computer problems," he protested, wincing as Anne exited the lot through the entrance rather than the exit to avoid paying for parking. An incoming car barely missed us on its way in, its horn blaring. Anne didn't even blink.

"You're full of shite is what you are," she went right back at Kevin. "You read a checklist and then tell them to reboot, and when that doesn't work you hang up and pretend they got disconnected." She continued to accelerate, looking for a lighter as she flicked a cigarette into her mouth.

"That's what we're trained to do. And if we don't get moving, I'm going to be late again." Kevin reached over the seat and took Anne's cigarette, lighting hers with his lighter, then his own.

"So what? All them poor souls will be on hold for an extra ten minutes. They expect it, don't they, Yank? After all, most of them come from your side of the pond." She looked at me as if expecting an answer, which made me nervous because she wasn't looking at the road. At all. I wasn't sure what to say, so I said the first thing that popped into my head.

"Are you like this with everyone?" As soon as the question was out, I regretted it, afraid of her response. But she just shrugged.

"No. There's some I don' like. Them I'm not so nice to. Why are you here, anyway? What kind of person goes on a holiday with no family or friends? Where's yer girlfriend?" she asked. I could tell she'd just keep digging if I didn't respond, so I answered honestly.

"I don't have one."

"Ahh, a boyfriend is it? You do dress a bit like a poof." She looked me up and down, and I couldn't help look down at myself.

"No I don't. And I came here because my uncle Mike left me a journal." Anne looked at me like I'd just admitted to something more than being a poof, then traded looks with Kevin, who just shrugged.

"You came all the way to Ireland because someone left you a journal? You changed continents fer *that*?" she asked as she cut off another car, nearly running it off the road.

"Umm, Anne. That was—" Kevin started.

"I saw 'im. He should learn how ta drive. Now let the Yank explain himself."

"My uncle paid for the airfare. He left me all his money when he died."

"A dead man paid fer this little holiday?"

"He wanted me to clear his name. He was accused of murder back home and of working with the IRA over here. He was killed outside Enniskillen by the British in 1972 and my father gave me his journal for my birthday. I think the journal was supposed to help me prove his innocence or something, but some of it is missing and a lot of it makes no sense, so I had to come over to track down what really happened." I noticed as I spoke that the car was slowing down. For the first time traffic was passing us. When I looked up, I saw that Anne and Kevin were both staring at me with blank looks.

"And how are ye intendin' on doin' that?"

"Well, he mentions a lot of people in his journal. I think if I can just talk to Declan Murphy, ask him a few questions . . ." I stopped because my chest had slammed into the seat belt, knocking the wind out of me. Horns blared all around us as Anne hit the brakes and jerked the wheel, pulling into the slower lane, cutting off cars in the process. She was looking straight at me, now completely ignoring the road in front of her.

As I caught my breath, I managed to ask the only question going through my head, "Are you nuts?"

"Me? Am I feckin' nuts? Have ya looked in a mirror, ya feckin' amadan?" Anne yelled, taking one hand off the wheel to shove her rear view mirror toward me.

Then, from right behind me, right in my ear, I heard Kevin mumble, almost growl, "Declan feckin' Murphy? You came here to ask Declan feckin' Murphy questions about what happened back then?" He was leaning over the seat, breathing heavy.

"I just have a few. My uncle's journal says that he and Declan were together a lot. They were like friends."

"Jaysus. 'Like friends,' he says. Pull over, Anne. Pull the damn car over. I need to get out and breathe before I strangle 'im."

"Leave him be. Remember what the damn priests say. We need to protect and care fer the feebleminded. Maybe we can talk some sense into 'im." Anne pulled off the shoulder of the N19, stopping near a small stand of trees. I suddenly got a flash of being kneecapped by the mumbling GQ boy in the backseat.

"Maybe we can put 'im on the first plane back. Say he never showed up," Anne suggested. "Or maybe it doesn't need to be that hard. Maybe it's all a misunnerstandin'. Let's jus' get a few things clear, Sean. Am I right in sayin' you have evidence agin' Declan Murphy and you want to confront 'im on it?"

I had never thought about it that way. It was just a story. A story about my uncle. Until now I hadn't thought about the other people in his journal as much more than characters. I tried to justify myself. "I guess you could call it evidence, but I don't care about the guys he killed or the bombs or any of that. I just want to find out what happened to my uncle." Anne just stared at me, a twitch in the corner of her eyes like she was trying not to smile.

"See, Kevin. He don' care about the killin's. He don' care that he has proof that a prominent and respected politician was once a murderer an' a terrorist. All he wants to know about is 'is uncle. So I'm sure after years of killin' informants and such, Declan will open right up to 'im and spill 'is guts. Don' you think?" Anne asked as she turned to Kevin, who was in the backseat, moaning.

"I don't need the sarcasm," I told her, even though I was starting to see her point.

"I think you need a good beatin' to knock some sense into yer head. I'd ask Kevin to do it, but he's really just a sap. Look at 'im back there. Thinkin' of Declan turns his bowels to jelly." She looked disgusted with both of us and pulled out another cigarette.

"I can't listen to this. Jus' drop me off at work, Anne. I promise, I won't tell anyone what 'e said. I don' wanna know." I was starting to appreciate why Anne found Kevin so irritating. He whined.

"What are you so scared of?" I asked. "It all happened twenty-two years ago."

"You think tha's a long time? People 'round here are still pissed off about shite that 'appened in 16-feckin'-90. An' do ya know how many men Declan

Murphy's killed?" Kevin's voice had gone up an octave as he spoke. Anne was already halfway through her cigarette, sucking it back so hard the red glow of the tip reflected in her eyes.

"The journal only mentions like five or six, not counting the bombings, but—"

"Look, Sean, a word of advice," Anne interrupted. "I know you want to find out what happened to yer uncle Mick, an' you will. But maybe I should help you. Keep ya clear of the tetchy stuff. Curiosity not only killed the cat, it killed half a County Westmeath over the centuries, ya know? It might be best ta leave Declan out of this." She stubbed out her cigarette, suddenly calm and collected.

"But he's my father's first cousin. My great-aunt's son. He's sort of related to me. Why would he do anything to hurt me?"

"There's about four million Micks on this island, boyo, and we're all sort of related. But that don' stop us from killing each other," Kevin said, his tone mournful.

"Yeah. Relations do each other in sooner than strangers. We need more strangers. I'm gettin' tired of the lot I got here. Saps. Every one." Anne glared at Kevin, who looked away. I was starting to get uncomfortable. I'd been here a half an hour and I was already breaking up friendships.

"It's really not that big of a deal. I can show you the journal," I offered, trying to pacify them.

"Don't! I don' wanna see it. I don' wanna know. You have to burn it. That's it. Let's burn it." Kevin's expression was almost hopeful. "Where is it? In here?" He grabbed my backpack and dumped it on the seat, catching the journal before it even hit the vinyl. He stopped, looking at it for a minute, then put it down, wiping his hands on his jeans and pulling out a lighter.

"Wait! What are you *doing*?"

"I'm burnin' the damn thing." He flicked the lighter and was ready to put it to paper as I stared in disbelief.

"You can't." But he was. I could see the paper getting darker, ready to burst into flame when Anne slapped the lighter out of his hand, bouncing it off a window. We both turned to look at her, shocked.

"He's right. You'll get ashes and smoke all over my car." This from a woman who'd just smoked two cigarettes in less than three minutes. "I'll do it."

She snatched the journal from Kevin before either of us could react, then kicked her door open, striding around the car toward the stand of trees.

We hadn't even made it off the N19 and here she was disappearing into the only stand of trees around, ready to burn the journal that held the only clues I had to what really happened to Uncle Mike. Kevin put a hand on my shoulder, trying to soften the blow.

"Sorry, boyo, but it's better this way." As he said it, I decided Anne was right. Kevin was a sap. I started after her and had just reached the berm when I saw the bloom of flame.

Anne tossed it into the underbrush as it lit, and the dead leaves made it burn more hotly. I was still twenty feet away when she turned back toward me.

"Look around you, Sean. See how green this land is? Ya know why that is?" She paused but didn't expect an answer and went on, "It's green 'cause blood makes brilliant fertilizer. Every place you go, if yer not stepping in sheep shite, yer steppin' on a grave. Trust me, ya may be a Yank, but yer blood'll spill jus' as fast as ours." She walked toward me as she spoke, positioning herself between me and the journal.

"I can still find Declan and ask him anything I want."

Anne winked at me and patted my face as she passed me, going back to the car. "Ya can. But now ya can't prove nothin', so he doesn't need to kill ya. I jus' saved yer life."

"Declan might kill 'im anyway. Jus' fer askin'," Kevin piped in from the back of the car.

"Yeah. But it's off my conscience, inn't it?" Anne shrugged, climbing in the car and slamming the door. I stood there, looking between the burning journal and the car, completely lost.

"What am I supposed to do now?" I asked, my tone more pathetic than intended. I wanted to be angry, but I was too shocked. Anne just rolled her eyes.

"First, get in the damn car," Anne called out. "It's wet out here. Then ya can enjoy yer holiday. Come meet yer Irish family. I'll take you to see the Giant's Causeway and the Ring of Kerry or even the Cliffs of Moher. You'll have some good craic. On my honor, you will."

"She's bein' nice, Sean. She hates them places. They're like the Disneyland of Ireland, full of fat Americans," Kevin chimed in. If he was trying to make me feel better, it wasn't working. I'd been looking forward to seeing those things until he put it that way.

I stood there for another twenty seconds, watching the fire. Then I heard the door I had left open slam and the car engine rev. Anne was making her point and I knew it wasn't a bluff. If she'd burn my journal, she'd leave me behind.

I walked to the car, taking my time. I have my pride. For the next forty minutes we rode in silence. I kept trying to figure out what to do next. I had no copies of anything in the journal and only a vague memory of what it said. How was I supposed to find the people and places without referring back to it? How could I know if the people were lying about what happened if I couldn't double-check the facts?

As we approached Athlone, Anne reached across the front seat and put her hand on my leg. I tried to ignore it, knowing that she was trying to get me to look at her, to apologize. She didn't take being ignored very well. She moved her hand up my leg, stroking it until I finally looked at her and pulled away. I could see that she was smiling through the haze of smoke from her latest cigarette. As I caught her eye, her face turned serious and she nodded to me, reassuringly.

"It'll be all right, Sean. You'll find what ya need. I'll help you if I have to," she said. But her eyes weren't on me. They were on Kevin's pile of software manuals.

"Help him? Are ya out of yer—"

"Shut yer gob, Kevin. I'll drop ya at work and then we'll talk no more about it, unnerstood?" Anne glared at him in the rear view mirror and he looked away sullenly. The silence didn't last long.

"Every time the dead come up, even in conversation, they drag one more of us down with them," he mumbled. "And they always come up again', don' they? Risin' from their graves and startin' troubles all over again. Better the dead stayed dead."

"Ahh, but that they never do, do they, Kevin?" Anne said, and we rode in silence again until we dropped Kevin off in downtown Athlone. I barely noticed him get out of the car. Anne just handed him his software manuals from under the front seat.

"Where's the rest?" I heard him call out as Anne pulled away in a rush and he fumbled with the books. It was then that I remembered Anne's glance at the pile of books and looked down to see that there was still something sticking out from under the front seat. She shoved it back under deftly as I wondered if I would have to remember everything I'd read in the journal. I hoped not. Without it I was lost.

Michael

I drove for another twenty minutes after I'd left the greengrocer's, something I knew only because I looked down at my watch. Otherwise I kept losing track, both of where I was and of the time. Neither the miles nor the minutes seemed to pass in any consistent way. Five miles went by in a minute, while the next five took an hour. My eyes kept going back to rock walls and fields and sheep, and my mind kept going back to Kate. I had no idea why. I wasn't even sure I liked her—I hadn't understood our conversation well enough to tell. I got the feeling she was making fun of me, the way an adult might tease a precocious kid. Like she knew something more than I did and was waiting for me to get the punch line.

Yes, she was attractive, but she wasn't really *beautiful*. Some people would look at her and not give her a second glance. Her smile was crooked, and her nose had a bump right on the bridge where the freckles were. One eye had flecks of gold and the other was more green. I could pick out ten things that weren't quite right about her. Yet somehow the whole was greater than the sum of its parts.

I wanted to write my attraction to her off to stress and hormones, except it wasn't the physical bits of her I kept thinking about. It was the way she smiled—like she had a secret to share. Like she was making fun of me even when she was being utterly polite, almost distant. I had to stop obsessing over her or I'd end up in Belfast. According to my father, that's where anyone who stopped thinking straight ended up.

I figured that I must be almost to Belfast when I saw an old man walking with what at first looked like a cane but when I got closer turned out to be a gnarled piece of wood that his hand had worn to a glossy smoothness. He clearly didn't need it to walk, because as I slowed down and rolled down my window, he sped up, outpacing the Vauxhall. I tapped the gas to keep up and called out to him, even as he refused to meet my gaze.

"Excuse me, sir. I'm looking for Glasson."

He turned and looked at me for a brief moment, then turned away again, calling over his shoulder, "You found it, dinn't ya?" And he kept walking, as if I were ruining his time on a four-minute mile.

I looked around, skeptical. A few sheep and an old man couldn't really be called a village. Maybe it was a rhetorical question. Maybe I'd passed the town already. I tried again. "I'm looking for the *village* of Glasson."

He kept walking, and I hit the gas to catch up to him. He wasn't really acknowledging me but seemed to be purposefully speeding up and slowing down so I couldn't quite keep pace with him.

As I got even with him, he grumbled at me. "You want to have a chat, have the courtesy to keep up, Yank. Even better, get out and walk to keep an old man company. It's rude to ride when I'm walking." And with that he turned off onto a worn path through a field, giving me no real choice. I pulled the car to the side of the road and got out, rushing to catch him before he disappeared. I twisted my ankle as I hit the field, but I kept after him, suddenly understanding the walking stick. The ground was so uneven and full of stones the stick acted like a rudder, keeping him balanced and straight. It took almost thirty yards to catch up, and I was breathing heavy as I fell in behind him.

"Could . . . you point me . . . in the right direction," I gasped, trying not to sound out of breath. He smiled at me, enjoying how hard he was making me work.

"You'll be wantin' the Portlick Pub, am I right?" he asked with a sneer, making me wonder if I'd offended him somehow.

"How'd you know?"

"Lookit ya. Ya got the eyes of that murdrin', desertin' bastard Sean Corrigan, don' ya? Where else would yer kind go? I know what yer here for, don' I?" His words held a challenge, but to what, or for what, I couldn't figure out. He obviously had known my uncle, hadn't liked him much, and had decided I was more of the same.

"I just came for the right of passage. My family has land and—" I started to explain, but he interrupted.

"Don' ya figure I already know all this, ya eejit? I wouldna talked to ya at all if I dinn't. Them bloody amadans've been waitin' on ya, so ask yer question and get it done, will ya?" I had no idea what he was talking about, but he was apparently going to answer a question, so I gave it a shot.

"How do I get to the Portlick Pub from here?"

"That's easy now." He sighed as if he'd been expecting something harder. "Keep going straight on until you come to a track—not the first one, mind you, but the second. The first will put you someplace you don't want to be now, won't it?" He grinned, breathing easily, avoiding every pitted, ankle-twisting step, leaving them for me. "Go to the second track, on your right, headed backward toward Lough Ree. That's the track by the boulder that looks like a woman's arse. That'll be the one you want now, isn't it?" He picked up the pace as he headed up a small rise in the field, toward a field-stone wall.

I was confused and increasingly anxious. I had lost sight of the rental car parked halfway off the narrow road behind me and was alone with a man who thought my uncle Sean was a deserter and a murderer. "A rock that looks like a woman's ass," I muttered, starting to catch my breath.

"That's right. And a fine one it is, too. Don' look like none of the women in my life, does she now?" He turned to face me as he asked this last question. But what did he want—me to agree with him or compliment the women in his life?

I played it safe. "What's a track?"

"A track? It's like a road only less so. Go down that one there and mind the trees and Ol' Jim Quinlan, fer sure. Can you manage that much?"

"Jim Quinlan?"

"Ahh, yeah. He's got a way of comin' down the track at you after he's tipped a few, he does. There's hours yet to go before he leaves. Yer early fer 'im to be ready to quit yet, aren't you?" The old man walked faster. I was keeping up, but barely.

"About how far is that?"

"Ahh, it's a good walk." He picked up the pace as if trying to leave me behind.

"And how long is 'a good walk'?"

"Depends. How fast do you walk?" He grinned sourly.

"Slower than I drive, and I'll be driving," I told him, getting tired of the games. All I wanted was a simple answer.

"Well, you best drive slower if you want to find it. Drive as slow as you walk and it's just a few minutes." He stopped abruptly where the path dead-ended next to a fieldstone wall that stood at the height of his chest, and if he wanted to outpace me now, he'd have to climb the wall to do it. "If you miss it, don' go farther. You don't want to be runnin' into that crowd that keeps themselves up there."

"How will I know if I missed it?"

"Oh, you'll know. You'll remember it when you see it, and once you see it you won' fergit it agin, will you?" He smiled, and I got the feeling he was setting me up for some practical joke. His whole attitude seemed to have shifted since the conversation started and I needed to keep him talking. I needed to find out more before I stepped into whatever this was. I knew that there was one thing he said that must be the key.

"You knew my uncle Sean?"

"I did. And I'd say 'God rest his soul,' but its obvious that didna happen, did it?"

"Did you know he was murdered?"

"I know he paid fer what he did and it's all settled now. Why else would I be talkin' to you?" I didn't know what to say to that and he nodded at me as if the matter were settled.

"His penance is done and he's forgiven, boyo, but it's never forgotten. Not here." And then he turned to the fieldstone wall, walking up and over it as easily as going up a flight of steps.

He was gone down the other side and lost in a field of high grass before I even saw how he managed it—a few stones jutted out from the wall, make-shift stairs that you'd never see unless you knew they were there. The wall was no obstacle if you knew about those stones. I was starting to feel like everything in this place was like that. The roads, the conversations, the relationships, even the walls—they were all barriers if you didn't understand them but easy to follow if you knew their secrets.

I heard him start whistling from beyond the wall, seemingly happy now that he'd left me behind. From somewhere beyond where I could see, I heard him call out to me, "Don't get lost again, Yank. They won' wait fer you forever."

And then he was gone. I started walking back toward the road and my car, a bit wary of following his directions. He seemed a little too self-satisfied and smug, like he was working some kind of angle. Maybe it was the cop in me that didn't trust him, but I didn't know what else to do.

Before I got back in the car I cleaned the windshield with my sleeve, making sure I could see well enough not to miss the track. I drove another mile or two as slowly as I possibly could, trying to figure out whether this track would look something like a road, or if it was something "less," what exactly "less" would look like.

I found out a few minutes later when I saw the first track—two ruts disappearing into a field of amber-colored barley. The second track was more obvious. At the edge of it was a large boulder that stood about three and a half feet tall, wider at the top than the bottom, with a crack down the middle of the gently curved halves. If you glanced at it quickly, it looked just like a woman wearing gray slacks, bending over in the field, and Kate's description of "the lady picking flowers" suddenly made perfect sense.

Even if the old man hadn't warned me, I probably would have slowed down to take a better look, it looked that real at first glance. In fact I almost missed the turn while staring at it, waiting for it to move. Then, at the last minute, I saw the muddy ruts almost hidden by the grass and I yanked the wheel around until the tires found the grooves worn in the earth.

I went forward slowly, as the track wound through grass so high that I couldn't see above it or around the slight curves in the track. Luckily, I heard the sputtering diesel engine before I saw it and I quickly pulled to the right, halfway into the field, trying to get out of the way. Then, too late, I remembered I should've pulled to the left, since I was in Ireland. The VW that came racing down the track didn't make the same mistake. It pulled to the left, headed right toward me, then overcompensated and spun into the field, disappearing into the tall grass. I heard the engine sputter and die as I got out, running to make sure the driver was okay. When I reached the car, he was already out of it. He was coughing and wheezing and didn't look good. A big man, muscular, maybe forty, his face was bright red.

"Are you all right?" I asked, hoping he was. He was too big to carry out of there, and there was no way I'd find a hospital in time to save him if he wasn't. He was wheezing badly, like an asthmatic.

"And why wouldn't I be?" he said, gasping. I realized he wasn't having an asthma attack but was laughing. Or maybe it was both. It was a terrible sound.

"You're not hurt? I ran you off the road." He laughed harder at that and grabbed his car door, pulling himself up to a standing position.

"Road? It's jus' a wee track, inn't it?"

"Still, I'm sorry."

"Sorry fer what? Serves me right fer tryin' to go home early and fer lettin' the woman tell me what to do. First time I listen to her in three years and this is wha' happens. No good deed goes unpunished, does it?" He grinned and started walking through the field, not directly back toward the track but diagonally back the way he came. I watched him for a moment until he turned back and nodded to me. "Walk with me. Let's get to business. I'm parched." And he began walking again. I was ready to give up on making any sense of things, so I followed him, leaving our cars right where they stopped.

"You're not upset?" I asked, just to make sure this "business" wasn't about paying penance like my uncle Sean did.

"'Ell no," he said with a grin. "Now I've got an excuse fer a couple more pints, and you've got an excuse to buy 'em fer me. Am I right?" He clapped me on the back and winked. As he did, I got a whiff of alcohol off of him that made my eyes water.

"You're Jim Quinlan." It dawned on me as he grinned, holding out a hand to me, still walking, emerging onto the track a bit farther up, closer to the lake.

"My reputation precedes me, donn't it?" He walked a few more feet and sighed as he emerged into someone's backyard. A white two-story house with a newer addition to one side was ahead, with several cars parked where a lawn might be, and a shed falling down beyond it. I looked farther up, where the track cut past the edge of the property. I could see the waters of Lough Ree, with a half-dozen boats lined up on its shore where the track met the water and the grasses turned to reeds. There was nowhere to go except to the lake or back the way I came. I stopped, wanting to get back on the right track.

"Look, it's really nice to meet you, Jim, but I'm looking for the Portlick Pub. You know where it is, right?" He turned to me with a wry grin and laughed again but kept walking. I waited for the owner of the house to emerge to find us, an American and a drunk, walking across his yard.

"Do I look like tha' much of an eejit? It's right through that door," he said as he pointed at a red door on the newer part of the house. I was beginning to wonder just how drunk he really was.

"That's a house."

He shook his head, exasperated, as if I were the one who was drunk. "No. *That's* a house," he told me as he pointed at the older section. "*That's* a pub. The ol' woman doesn't like the spirits in the house. That's why Christy has the pub in *there*, inn't it?" He walked up a worn stone path, headed for the red door. I still hesitated. It looked like a house to me, but he grabbed the pitted brass knob and twisted it, pushing the door open. He disappeared into the shadows inside as I stepped up behind him.

It was so dim inside that it took a minute for my eyes to adjust. The "pub," which was really just a big room with some tables, chairs, and a bar, was not very well lit, and the rich, warm character of it came as much from the layers of peeling paint that seemed to hold the place up as anything else. The first thing to come into focus was the brightest spot in the room, the large fireplace at one end. Made of fieldstone, the hearth and chimney took up an entire wall of the pub, and the heat it radiated took the edge off the dampness with that same earthy smell I remembered from my dream back home. The one where I shot Liam.

As I thought of him it somehow came to me now what the smell was— peat—the dense, dried vegetation from the bogs, cut out into bricks and burned because wood was always scarce and peat was always cheap. The smell was peat mixed with a host of other kinds of smoke, a wall of it and not the kind you find in the States. It wasn't that acrid bitter cigarette smell at all. It was warm and sweet, soothing, not dry. Pipe smoke and cigars as well as cigarettes. Prince Albert in a can type of smoke, all spicing up the comfortable, earthy smell of peat.

As my eyes adjusted I noticed the twelve men inside. They were all looking at me—at least until I looked back at them, and then they turned away. Conversation had stopped and no one spoke or moved until a man in a chair by the fire, his back to us, spoke without getting up.

"What've ya got there, Jim? Is it the package we've been expectin'?" His voice was soft but carried. He never turned, and no one looked at him, but they were all paying attention.

"It is. Just blown in 'e is. Ran me off the track and offered to buy me a drink," Jim told him, still standing by the door.

"You're himself, aren't you?" said a hulking red-haired man off to my right, seated on a stool. I turned to look at him.

"Himself?" I asked, unsure how anyone could be expecting me, worried that they thought I was someone else. They didn't look too happy to see me.

"Mickaleen," whispered the man in the chair by the peat fire, and I turned toward him to find him looking straight at me. I knew I shouldn't have responded. I knew better than answering to my own name. I knew it was a trap, but I was caught unprepared. I was prepared to ignore "Mike" or "Michael," but nobody called me Mickaleen except my father—and he only did when his old-timer's disease was kicking in and he confused me for his brother. I was Mike. Still, they were all staring at me, and I had to find some way to respond.

"I'm Aidan, not Mike. Mike's my brother."

The man in the chair stood. He was lean to the point of being sinewy, with a few cuts on his face that made him look as if he'd been in a fight recently. "Did I say Mike, now? I thought I said Mickaleen, fer sure. But yer sure as hell no bloody Aidan. Next you'll be tellin' me your not a Corrigan, won't you?" He walked toward me as he spoke and was now right in front of me, staring me down. "I bet yer lookin' fer yer cousin Declan."

"You know him?" I was suspicious. If I'd met this guy when I was on the job, I would've pegged him for some kind of criminal, a low level drug dealer maybe.

"I *am* him," he answered, then suddenly grinned, holding out his hand. "It's good to see ya, Mickaleen. Wasn't sure I ever would, was I, lads?" I took his hand, hesitant, as everyone in the room watched. Declan saw my hesitation and grinned.

"Lookit 'im, boys. Nothin' ever changes with the Corrigans. He don' trust nobody, do you, boyo?" He was looking right at me, smiling, even though his eyes were cold.

"I was expecting someone else. You don't look like your pictures . . ." It sounded like a weak excuse, even to me. The last picture I'd seen of Declan was at least fourteen years out of date, when he was about ten. But still, there was something familiar about him. Something about his eyes.

"I grew a pair since I let anyone take a picture of me, isn't that right?" He smiled and patted me on the arm. "I'll tell you what, boyo. If you have a package with you to give your uncle Martin with a note from your da, Ol' Jim Corrigan himself, that says 'Martin, use it in good health,' will that be proof enough for ya?" His eyes were on mine, and even though they were filled with humor, there was an edge there, something waiting to be set off by a wrong word. Nobody else spoke for a moment, and then I heard the door slam behind me.

"I got his bags for him." I turned to find that Jim Quinlan had slipped out at some point and was in the doorway with my bags and the presents for the cousins. "Anything else I can do fer ya, Mickaleen?"

"I'm Aidan," I protested weakly. "You want to look at my passport?"

"Sure, why not," chimed in the hulking red-haired man on the stool, putting out a hand. Declan glared at him, a warning.

"We don' need to see any such thing. We know who you are. You're himself," Declan told the man, who just grunted in return.

"As you like it. He's himself. Can't argue with that now, can I?" The red-haired man backed down, but didn't look happy about it. He seemed to be the only one there willing to defy Declan.

"Who are you?" I asked the redheaded behemoth, unable to quell my curiosity. If anyone was going to be a problem here, I was sure it would be him.

"Patsy Ryan," he grumbled.

"He's the garda 'round 'ere," Declan informed me with a smile.

"You're a cop?" I asked, a little stunned, given the company he seemed to be keeping. These seemed like a group of hard men. Or maybe I was just used to soft Americans.

"It pays for the Guinness now, doesn' it?" He grunted sarcastically, reading my disbelief accurately. "You have a problem with the Garda?"

"Me? No. It's just that one of your guys stopped me outside Athlone. Gave me some bad directions." I'd barely finished when Patsy laughed, finding something genuinely funny.

"That'd be Tom Doyle. Sent you to the greengrocer's, I bet, didn't 'e?" I nodded and he continued to find humor in it, explaining, "His family owns the place. He was jus' tryin' to steer a bit o' business their way. Nothin' personal I'm sure . . ." His voice drifted off as he said it, and his mood seemed to darken as if he'd suddenly thought of something else.

"Tommy's a good man. Just a little too intense, he is. Out there tryin' to solve the *Maidstone* escape, pullin' over every stranger aroun', I bet," Declan explained. He must've seen my blank look and took pity on me, steering me toward the bar, where Christy, a bald, red-nosed man in a suit, was tending bar. He put down a Guinness for me as Declan went on, "Everybody's a little tense. Seven Provos slipped off the *Maidstone* prison ship in Belfast Lough a few days ago, wearing nothing but their drawers, some grease, and butter. It's said they headed south and might be near here. Hard cases they are, dangerous men, aren't they?" He looked around and got varied responses, from serious agreement to laughter. "So ya see why we had to take a good lookit ya and make sure yer not one a them." Declan nodded to Jim, who put my bags down next to me and set the one full of presents up on the bar.

"Did ya talk to 'er?" Patsy growled from over the top of his Guinness, staring me down as if he'd heard none of what Declan just said.

"Talk to who?"

"Ya know damn well who. You were at the greengrocer's, weren't ya? She was workin' today, wasn't she?" He was slurring his words a bit, and now that my eyes had adjusted, I could see that his were bloodshot.

"You mean Kate?" I asked, trying to understand Patsy's sudden attitude.

"So you did talk to her. What'd she say, seein' the likes of you?" Patsy stood, standing a good four inches taller than me and twice as broad. Declan stepped between us to diffuse something. I'm not sure what it was, but Patsy wasn't happy. Declan started to say something quietly when the door slammed and I heard a voice from behind him.

"Let the fool go, Declan. He's too drunk to hurt anyone. He just thinks that since 'e's my brother he's got to defend my honor." I turned to find Kate in the doorway, hanging her coat on a coat rack, calm and cool. "Eejit that he is, he should know my honor's never been tarnished."

Declan was smiling now, along with the rest of the crowd. It was clear they all knew her, and that in her presence, they were all a lot less dangerous. "There she is herself. How are ya, Kate? I take it ya met Mickaleen?" Declan asked, gently pushing Patsy back into a sitting position.

"I'm familiar with him."

Declan handed me my glass, diverting my attention from Patsy and Kate for a minute. "She told everyone an old friend would be coming through today. She's got the twitch in her, ya know," he said as he watched her cross toward us, appreciating her as much as I did, it seemed.

"The twitch?" I asked.

Christy, the bartender and pub owner, casually interrupted. "The twitch of the witch. Second sight. She knew you'd be here. Rang us up and told us you were on the way."

I had to smile at that. "I don't know how much of a gift she's got. I saw her at the gas station less than an hour ago."

"Gas?" Christy looked confused.

"He means petrol," Declan said as he moved over to let Kate squeeze between us.

"Ahh, I thought he was havin' some intestinal troubles." Christy smiled as he handed Kate what looked like a brandy.

"She rang us up yesterday, boyo. She's got the knowing in 'er, all righ'."

Declan said quietly. "Unlike Patsy here, who just has the drink in him." Kate shook her head. Patsy's temper was a familiar problem, it seemed. I turned to her, trying to understand.

"Why didn't you tell me you were coming here? You could have just showed me the way."

"You never asked," she answered simply, sipping her brandy.

"How could I know to ask you to show me the way if I didn't know you were coming here?"

She turned it around on me again.

"Didja ever ask if I was going to be comin' this way? Did ya even care if I needed a ride? You think you're smart, but you never ask any questions."

"Okay, fine. Then I'll ask. Explain to me what's going on here. Why's Patsy got a problem with me? Why do they call me 'Mickaleen'? Why didn't you tell me you were coming right behind me and already knew I was on my way?" I challenged her, but she just looked at Declan, who answered for her.

"Calm down, boyo. Nobody's hidin' nothing from you—you're just not seein' what it is that's right in front of you."

He was full of shit. So was Kate. This was getting irritating. They were hiding something. I stood up, calling their bluff, ready to walk out. I had no idea where I'd go, but when someone lies to you straight up, you can either sit there and take it or leave, and I was done taking it. Declan stopped me with a hard, tight grip on my forearm and an almost desperate look in his eyes.

"Fine. Let me show you." He held on, waiting until I nodded, then he reached for my bags—for the one full of presents. That's when Kate spoke up, quietly but with a tone that carried weight.

"He's here for his right of passage, Dec. Don' get 'im involved in the rest of it." Her voice was barely above a whisper, but the bar seemed to grow silent as she spoke, and once again I noticed that everyone there was looking at us while trying to seem like they weren't interested.

"He chose to come. It was supposed to be Ol' Jim or even the other brother, but he chose to come. That means somethin'." Declan sounded defensive as he opened my bag right on the bar.

"Not to him, it don't."

"He brought the gifts," Declan said as he pulled out the Cowboys jackets and the stuffed Mickey Mouse dolls.

"That don' mean 'e knows what's in 'em." Kate held his gaze. This was some kind of standoff, but I couldn't figure out what they were arguing over. Finally Declan looked away from her and turned to the men in the rest of the pub.

"Look, boyos. Some American football jackets fer us Cowboys, and Mickey Mice fer the wee ones," he called out. Kate glanced at me with a pale apology in her eyes, but I had no time to wonder why. I was wondering whether Mickey "Mice" was the proper plural or whether it was only proper in Ireland. By the time I looked back at Declan he had a knife out and was slashing Mickey's throat, and bundles of cash were falling onto the bar. Two-inch-thick bricks of U.S. currency. I stared, even as he took the knife to the football jackets, dumping more dead presidents on the bar.

Declan was grinning from ear to ear, winking at me. "The little ones've outgrown Mickey, but we all can use this, can't we, boyos?"

I turned as I felt someone move closer to me, putting a hand on my shoulder and speaking in a low voice, not quite threatening but ready to threaten. "Your da's a good fellow. Always lookin' out for the poor cousins over here. He understands what you owe." Patsy's breath wafted into my ear, and as I looked up at him his eyes seemed a bit more clear, if more dangerous.

"Green is a wonderful color, isn't it, boyo? You Yanks got it right with your money, that's for sure," Declan went on as he sliced and diced the presents. "Damn. There's more here than he said. The Ancient Order of Hibernians come through again . . ."

I turned to Patsy, the corrupt garda who had allowed this to go on. "I knew nothin' about this," I told him.

"I know. That's why you're still alive. But sooner or later, you'll know all about it, and then we'll decide what to do with ya." He stared at me as he spoke. For some reason it intimidated me in a way I hadn't been intimidated since my grandfather had died. I looked away first, glancing at the red door to the pub to see how far it was and if I had a chance to reach it. When I glanced back, he turned abruptly away. Kate was moving toward us, and it was her that he was running from.

"I'm sorry," Kate said simply as she touched my forearm. An energy seemed to flow through her fingertips.

"For what?"

"All of it. What happened. What's coming. All of it." She glanced after her brother, then at the men in the pub, all picking up cash off the floor.

"Knock it off, will ya, Kate?" Declan called from across the pub. "Mickaleen's done a good deed today. See that he gets a good meal and a place to stay fer as long as he needs." He laughed, stuffing the cash back into the empty bag the presents had come in. I turned to Kate, but she wouldn't look at me.

"What am I supposed to do about this?" I asked, aware that I had just provided cash to the IRA—aware that my supposedly addled father had been funneling money back this way for years. I might not have murdered James Butler, but now I was definitely guilty of funding a terrorist organization. So much for running to Ireland to stay out of trouble.

"There's nothin' to do, except come home with me and let me take care of you. I'll get you to bed," Kate said matter-of-factly. She must've seen my face when I turned, but I hoped the pub was dark enough that she couldn't see me blush.

"After yer long trip, I mean. You'll need the rest. Ya can stay at my ma's. We're almost family and she puts people up from time to time." Kate turned away, but I thought I saw a tinge of red on her face as well.

"What do you mean we're 'almost' family?" I asked as I followed her toward the door.

"Declan's cousin to both of us. His ma's yer da's sister, and his da is my ma's brother."

"So are we . . ."

"Good question. Now yer learnin'. No. There's no blood between us. Not that way." She stepped out the door. The sun had come out for a moment, and it blinded me as I followed her. It was the one piece of good news I'd heard all day.

Sean

I'd never realized that all those Irish cottages you see in pictures, with their frail-looking thatched roofs, were all actually made of heavy fieldstone with walls that were up to three feet thick. Maybe it was the thatch and white-wash that made them look so unsubstantial. I was standing outside of one, looking in through a leaded glass window set into the wall, which was at least three feet thick at the bottom and tapered to just under a foot at the roofline of the second story.

I guess the walls of this house needed to be thick, because the roof wasn't thatch. It was heavy gray slate. Its floor plan was so classic that even without stepping inside, I knew the kitchen was in the back, the window over the sink looking out toward the barn and fields. Of course, I could probably picture the whole thing in my head because this was the house where my uncle Mike stayed when he first came over, the Ryan house where Kate's family had lived for generations. I was about to enter the house he'd stayed in with Kate, the place he'd confronted Patsy, and where he probably would have lived out his days if things had turned out differently.

I felt like I was following in the footsteps of his spirit as I moved closer to the house. I knew this place well from the journal, so well it felt like I'd been here before. I knew that the front staircase had uneven steps that would trip you up in the darkness, purposefully designed that way to screw with the Black and Tans and all the other representatives of authority who had raided it over the years. At least that's what Kate's mother, Bridey, had told my uncle. He didn't believe her, feeling that Bridey made up stories to explain things she didn't want to talk about.

But many of the stories my uncle put down about this house had the ring of truth. One that stuck in my head was that the original owners of the house were killed by Cromwell's men in 1650, and the dark red stain on the wood at the base of the front stairs is their blood. In the rebellion of 1798, the Ryans got even and a whole squad of the king's soldiers who had come to burn them out were buried in the basement. According to family legend, they were lured inside by the woman of the house, a Ciara Ryan, who claimed her husband had fled and left her alone. As soon as they entered the house, they were ambushed and hacked to death with kitchen knives.

I put my hand up to block the sun, trying to see inside the house, when I heard footsteps on the gravel driveway behind me.

"Ya dirty lil' bastard, whatta ya think yer lookin' at?" a deep male voice growled at me from behind, making the hair on my neck stand on end. I turned around to see a bald-headed man with piercing blue eyes, rubber boots that came up over his knees, dirty jeans, a red flannel shirt, and canvas work gloves. He was staring at me in a way that felt like an assault. I'm not usually easily intimidated, and I'm not one to babble, but it was as if the weight of his look forced the air out of my lungs and words came tumbling out.

"Uh, yeah, I'm ... I'm here—" I stammered, but he interrupted, stopping me before I could tell him my life story.

"Shut up," he ordered as he stepped closer, staring at me. Then he stopped, his eye twitching as he inspected me. Finally, he spoke again. "Damn, ya eejit. It's you. Inn't it?" He moved even closer. I tried to back up but only scraped my back on the rough stone of the house. "It's you, ya bleedin' persistent bastard. Ya made it."

I didn't really know what to say to that. It seemed pretty obvious that I'd made it, so I just stammered, "Uh, yeah, I flew into Shannon this morning..."

He looked at me like I was a moron and did a good job of making me feel like one. "Who do ya think sent Anne after ya? I'm jus' surprised it took so long. It's about time, inn't it," he grumbled. Then he turned away, picking up a pail of something dark brown and congealed, shaking his head in frustration. "If ya came looking for her, she inn't here."

"She just pulled the car around," I answered, not really understanding why having sent Anne to pick me up, he'd still think I was looking for her.

His expression softened a bit. "Ahh, you're talkin' 'bout Anne. I thought, since you were here and all, that ya knew, but you don't, do ya?"

"Knew what?"

"All of it. Never mind. You don't know so you can't know, can you?" Before I'd read Uncle Mike's journal, it had never occured to me that there could be a language barrier in Ireland. I thought he'd been exaggerating his confusion for effect, the way most of my family stretched facts, something we jokingly referred to as "the Corrigan Factor." But here I was, breathing the smell of cow manure and talking to a man who spoke in Zen koans.

He must have thought I was disappointed and not just confused, because he put a hand on my shoulder. "I miss her, too, you know," he said, looking genuinely empathetic. I was saved from explaining that I didn't quite follow when Anne came around the side of the house from wherever it was that she parked her car.

"Da. What do ya think you're doin'? Don' be talkin' to 'im like tha'," she ordered, thankfully getting him to take a step back.

"This is your father?" I asked, incredulous. Talk about your beauty and the beast. Not that he was really ugly, or Anne that classically beautiful, but he was a big brute, scarred and bald, and she was . . . Well, she was hot in a tough "trying not to be" sort of way.

"Can' ya see the resemblance?" she asked, putting an arm around his waist. Her shoulder barely reached his hip. He squeezed her gently and offered his hand to me.

"Patsy Ryan. And yer Sean Michael himself, ain't ya?" He smiled, and then I saw it—the man he used to be, the man I'd read about in the journals. The big red-haired man in the Portlick Pub. Kate's brother. God, life had been hard on this guy.

"You were the garda," I managed to say, shocked to shake hands with a man who until now had only been a character in a story.

"Ahh, I was. But I retired. I'm a gentleman farmer now."

Anne looked him up and down, from his manure-stained boots to the scar that ran across his cheek. "An' ya look like a real gentleman with yer muckin' boots full of shite and yer horror-show face."

"I'll have none of that from you, unnerstand," Patsy threatened mildly. "I know I'm a gentleman 'cause I've a spoiled little sketch fer a daughter to prove it." He turned to me, confiding, "I got what I deserved, in more ways than one, trust me. She reminds me of my sins every day."

Anne grinned. "It's true. Ya shoulda been nicer to yer ma. I've come to make ya pay fer that."

"Ah, she's my karma, she is," Patsy smiled and winked at me. It was strange seeing the two of them together. There was a lot of love there. But I was still trying to make sense of how this man in front of me fit in with the man in my uncle's journal. I had the sense from what I read that they weren't exactly close.

"You knew my uncle?" I had to ask. I needed to know more, what he was like, why he did the things he did.

"Dinn't we all?" Patsy dismissed the question, his smile suddenly gone.

"So you know what happened to him?" I pushed, and Anne stepped between her father and me, smiling forcibly.

"Jaysus. Lookit 'im. Jus' like all the other Yanks, come home lookin' fer dead relatives an' expectin' us to tell stories all night. Come on, Sean. Let's get yer things." Anne took my arm to pull me away, but Patsy didn't move. He was staring at me again with an intensity that held me to the spot.

"Well? Do you really need me to tell stories, Sean? Or do you already know some things?" His voice was quieter now, more subdued. Clearly, he wanted to know what I'd read about him, but Anne didn't give me a chance to answer.

"If he knew anythin' would he be askin' you for answers now," she blurted, tugging my arm forcefully toward her car. Patsy just held up a hand, stopping us both.

"Go on in. I'll get his things."

"I can get them, really," I protested.

"Don't be ridiculous. Yer our guest. I can carry a few bags. I bet the boot's full of 'em, inn't it?" Patsy touched my shoulder again, then turned away, the gravel crunching under his heels for a half-dozen steps before Anne said anything.

"Let's go in. I'll show you yer room," she said, more subdued than I'd seen her. Following her through the heavy oak door, I had to rush to keep up.

By the time I got in, she had moved through the kitchen and was at the far end of the house, in front of a large window. Below the window was a small table with a single photo and a candle.

The photo was of a petite brown-haired, blue-eyed woman who could have been Anne in another lifetime. Anne seemed to be frozen in place looking at the pictures. I stood next to her, feeling self-conscious, unsure of what to do. Finally, I broke the silence.

"Who's that?" I asked.

"My ma. God rest her soul," she muttered quietly.

"Oh. I didn't know."

Anne's eyes flashed for a second, "Did yer da tell ya nothin' about us?" Then she turned back to the window. She seemed to be distracted, not looking at the photo, not paying much attention to me, but just looking outside at something I couldn't see.

"I don't think he knows much."

"So all you know is what's in that journal?"

"What I can remember of it, now that it's gone," I retorted, with more than a little bitterness. She smiled and shook her head, then nodded out the window. I stepped around her to see what she was looking out at.

It was Patsy taking my bags out of the car. He was going through each one, expertly rifling them so that I'd never even notice anything out of place.

"Ya can thank me anytime," Anne said, staring at her father. "If he found that journal, he might not be so nice to ya anymore."

"What makes you think it said anything about him?" I got defensive, suddenly worried about being a guest in the house of a man that my uncle had accused not only of harboring Provisional IRA killers but of possibly being an enforcer for them himself.

Anne looked at me as if I were hopelessly naive. "I've known me da my whole life, ya eejit. Ya think I don' know what things he's done? Ya think I want to see him put in jail because some arsehole Yank wants to know how his precious uncle died?" She had a point. To me, the journal was history. To her, it was her father's life story.

"All I wanted to do was—"

"Shut yer bleedin' gob, will ya?" Anne said suddenly, turning away and moving quickly to the front stairs. "I'll show ya to yer room. It's the same one yer uncle stayed in. The very same mattress. Possibly even the same sheets." She had just reached the bottom stair when I heard the reason for her haste.

"I've got to go out," Patsy called out, dropping my bags by the kitchen table. "Some things I need to take care of. You'll make sure Sean gets some supper, Anne?" He sounded calm, almost amiable.

"I'll manage." Anne forced a smile until the door closed behind him, then turned to me and hissed, "The door at the top of the stairs on the right is yer room. The bathroom's across the hall."

She raced to the kitchen window to make sure he was really leaving. Once she was satisfied that Patsy was gone, she sat down by the door, pulling on her shoes.

"Where are you going?"

"I'll tell ya later. I've no time now. I gotta talk to the sap an' get back before he does."

"Get back from where? What's going on?" I asked, but Anne ignored me. I stood in the doorway, calling after her as she made for her car. "I'll come with you. I need to eat anyway."

She stopped and shook her head, annoyed. "Jaysus. Don' they have refrigerators and stoves in the States? Can ya not find yer way around a kitchen?"

"Well, yeah."

"Good. Then ya won't starve to death and leave me to bury ya in the basement. Feed yerself. Clean up. Do whatever it is ya need to do. I'll be back." And then she disappeared around the corner of the house.

Ten seconds later I heard a clutch pop and tires spinning, throwing up loose gravel as she raced out of the driveway. I was left utterly alone, somewhere in County Westmeath, wondering what was going on.

I went back inside, noticing how the late afternoon light cast long shadows, highlighting the dust mites that hung in the air. It was quieter here than anyplace I'd ever been. The floors creaked, and the wind whispered through the gaps in stones of the old house. I stood in the middle of the kitchen for a minute, and from there I could see the cranberry-colored stain at the bottom of the front stairs—it really did look like dried blood. I'm not much for ghosts or spirits, but I was overtired, and between the noises the house was making, the stories in my uncle's journal and the darkened wood at the base of the stairs, I was a little freaked out. What if Patsy got back before Anne? I wouldn't want to deal with him on my own.

In the midst of my exhaustion and confusion, I remembered something Uncle Mike had written in his journal. Something Kate had said to him. *Flyin's done too fast nowadays. You go so fast you leave part of your soul behind and now you have to wait for it to catch up.* I understood what she meant. The world had shifted around me, and everything was a bit off. I was a stranger in my own head.

I went through the refrigerator and found a slab of ham, some bland cheese, and a slice of rough, hard bread. It wasn't very good, but it was filling.

Between the rustic sandwich and the claw-footed cast-iron tub I found myself showering in fifteen minutes later, I felt like I had stepped back into Uncle Mike's life. He was here, in exactly this same place, twenty-two years earlier, probably eating almost the same food and standing in this same tub with the same slightly sulfuric water trickling over him. The water barely dribbled down my back, but at least it was hot. I stood there until it got cold, trying to figure out what to do without the journal.

I figured I could ask Patsy a few questions, although he didn't seem eager to chat. I could go talk to Declan Murphy, but according to Anne and Kevin, that was an "eejit" idea. I dried myself off, then realized that I had left all my clean clothes in the bedroom across the hall.

The clothes I had taken off had been worn for almost twenty-four hours. They felt stiff and smelled stale. I really didn't want to put those back on, so I wrapped a towel around my waist, opened the door a crack and peered out. The hall was empty. I hadn't heard anyone come back in, and I was pretty sure I was still alone. That thought didn't exactly comfort me, but I decided to take the risk that I might not be and pulled the towel tighter.

In two steps I was across the hall and into the small bedroom, closing the heavy oak door behind me. My suitcase was on top of the dresser and I opened it quickly. As I fumbled with the zipper, my towel fell off and I heard something move behind me.

"Now that's a brilliant ass, inn't it?" It was Anne's voice. Right behind me. I turned to face her, not thinking, and she flipped the light on. It blinded me and I raised my hand to shield my eyes, forgetting to cover the rest of me.

"Suddenly I unnerstand that nursery rhyme 'Wee Willie Winkie,'" she said, giggling, and I managed to cover myself with the first thing I grabbed from my suitcase, a shirt. As my eyes adjusted, I saw that Anne was sitting cross-legged on the bed wearing nothing but a T-shirt. I noticed that an open book was resting on her thighs. Actually, I noticed the birthmark high up on her right thigh before I noticed the book, and even then, Anne had to draw my attention to the book.

"What the hell are you doing?" I demanded, as if it weren't obvious that what she was doing was laughing at me.

"Enjoyin' the view. Seems like yer doin' the same." She put both hands on her breasts and pushed them up, tight against the cotton shirt. "They're not big, but they bounce." She let them drop to prove it. I looked away— because if I kept looking I might have to do something about it, and as tired and disoriented as I was, I wasn't crazy enough to think that would be a good idea.

"Know what else I'm doin'," she asked playfully, and I heard the blankets rustling.

"I'm not looking. Whatever it is, you can do it in private."

"Well, you got a dirty mind, ain' ya? I'm jus' readin'. Yer uncle's not a half-bad storyteller. Not much of a writer but fun to read. Especially since I know all the characters." She had me, I turned to look at the book that was in her lap and saw more than her lap this time. It was Uncle Mike's journal sitting there, open.

"But you . . . ," was all I got out. Not much of a statement, but I was naked and I'd have sworn I saw her burn it. I did. I knew I did.

"I burned one of Kevin's computer manuals. Trust me, it helped 'im as much as it helped you. Ya ever try to read that shite? Besides, he's safer thinkin' this little bit of incendiary material is turned to ash." She sat up, curling her legs under her and arching her back, as if getting comfortable in order to read. "Sorry I had to run out on ya, but Kevin'd notice that he was missin' a manual an' I had to convince 'im I used it as kindlin' and burned it with the journal. Otherwise the eejit woulda tipped off my da that the journal might still exist."

"So Kevin doesn't know?"

" 'Course not. The amadan don' wanna know an' he never would've agreed to ride us up ta Dublin tomorrow if he knew." She lifted the book up as if to read, exposing her legs. "This is entertainin' shite, inn't it? Did ya read this bit about Mickaleen bringin' cash over fer the lads?"

"You mean the part where your father threatens him?"

"Yeah. There. Yer eejit uncle didn't even realize that he was in the pub with three of the *Maidstone* Seven. Right there with the men who escaped a prison ship by adoptin' a seal and seein' how he got through the wire on the lough. Kinda sexy thinkin' of seven 'ard men covered in nothin' but butter, don' ya think?" she asked, staring straight at me and stretching out, lying on the bed now. "Jaysus, I could read this all night."

"I thought you believed curiosity killed the cat," I said, trying to find something I could put on without dropping my T-shirt.

"And half a County Westmeath. But satisfaction brought 'im back, dinn't it? And it was only one a nine lives he used up, so there's no harm done. I'd always rather indulge my curiosity. How 'bout you?" Anne was smiling. Thinking back on it, if I'd called her bluff she probably would've just left, but I didn't know that then. After an uneasy moment, she let me off the hook, holding up the book again.

"Whatta ya think my da would say if he knew you had this?"

"I don't know. What do you think he'd say if he knew you were in here and I was naked?"

She smiled, thinking about it. She had a twisted sense of humor. "I think he'd whack yer wee willie off fer either offence. Or maybe he'd jus' be happy if I tricked you the way Kate did yer uncle Mike and get ya to ask me '*An bpósfaidh tú mé?*' " She grinned, holding the journal open to the page that phrase was on.

"Wait, you know what that means?" I moved closer, trying to see what she was looking at.

"A course I do. I had to sit through Irish class in school now, dinn't I? Kate made him ask, 'Will you marry me?' An' then she answered that she would. The first time they met, too. I have to say, ol' Kate was brilliant, wan't she? Here, sit, read with me." She patted the bed beside her and held up the book to read. I didn't move.

"Are you going to give it to me?"

"Am I goin' to give you *what* exactly?" she said, stretching.

"The journal."

"Ah, that depends. *An bpósfaidh tú mé?*" She was joking, I know she was, but I didn't know what to do. So I did nothing. Said nothing. And I'm not sure what expression was on my face, but hers suddenly changed. She was done teasing, and I couldn't tell if she was disappointed or relieved.

"Don' bother answering," she said. "Ya already did." She was staring at me as if I knew what she was talking about. I didn't. Not then, anyway. Not until much later.

"I just want my journal."

Anne knelt on the bed, edging a bit closer to me. Close enough that I could almost feel the warmth of her body in the chilly room.

"Yer journal? Not yer uncle's?"

"He left it to me," I said, reaching out for the journal with one hand, covering myself with the other.

"I jus' have one question. What's the real reason you want to find out what happened to 'im?" Anne looked up at me quizzically, and I could see that she really wanted to know, and that I wasn't getting that journal unless I answered.

"Uncle Mike? I'm not sure."

"You know he killed that man by accident, so it's not that, is it?"

"I know he said he was innocent."

"And you know why he helped Declan. You know all them things he done. You know he betrayed them all in the end. He says it 'imself."

"I know," I admitted, trying to keep my eyes on her face. As she spoke, I could feel her breath on me and see down her T-shirt. She wasn't wearing much more than I was.

"So what's left to figure out?"

"I don't know," I said, trying not to look at her.

"I think you do." Her stare seemed to be accusing me of something. She was not teasing now. Her eyes were hard, her tone serious. It took me a minute, but I finally realized the one question the journals never answered or even hinted at.

"What do you think happened to her?" I asked, even though part of me wasn't ready to know.

"Ya mean Kate?" She sighed, sitting back a little, as if I finally asked the right question.

"Who else?"

Anne climbed down off the bed, tugging at her T-shirt as it rode up one leg. She still held the journal. "Yeah. Who else? Who else has it ever been about?" Then she looked up at me, and for the first time she didn't intimidate me. She looked very young suddenly, younger than me. She was smiling slightly, but it didn't have the knowing, bitter edge it had before. Then she walked around the bed, closer than ever. I thought she was going to do something I might regret, but she just shook her head.

"Here," she said as she slapped the journal into my bare chest.

"You're giving it back?"

"If yer lookin' fer that kind of answer, I'm not gonna stop ya. I'd like to find what yer lookin' fer too someday . . ." And she turned away, walking to the door. She stopped when she got there, her hand on the knob.

"Get some sleep. You get to drive to Dublin with me an' Kevin the chaperone in the mornin' to meet Declan. Maybe you'll even live through the experience." She snorted with amusement as she slipped out into the hallway and I was left to wonder whether she was talking about living through the drive or meeting Declan.

As I went to close the door behind her, I saw her silhouette in the hall, standing in the dark, watching me. I couldn't make out her face, but I heard her mutter, "*Sonuachar chugat.*" I didn't understand the words, but I recognized the sad tone.

"I don't know what that means."

"*Póg mo thóin,*" Anne said bitterly, and turned away. I knew that one. *Kiss my ass.* I sighed with relief. If she was being nasty, I hadn't really offended her. Having been raised in a traditional Irish family, I knew that it's when they stop telling you to kiss their asses that you're in real trouble.

I closed the door and looked down at the journal. Feeling a strange sense of déjà vu as I realized that I was standing in the same room he'd slept in twenty-two years before. This was probably where he wrote part of this journal. This was where he'd spent time with Kate. How different his life had been from mine, and yet here I was in the same place.

If there was one part of his life I envied, it was Kate. If only there were a Kate here now . . . All I had was Anne. I looked down at the journal, wistfully thinking of Kate, and sat down to read. I needed to read it through one more time to memorize whatever I could. I didn't want to risk losing it again. It felt too much like losing all the memories of my uncle's life. He'd left them for me, and it seemed like it was my job to keep them intact, to keep them alive.

Michael

I drove my rental to Kate's parents' house in the near dark, growing more furious with my feebleminded father at every knotted crossroad. How could he set me up to deliver cash to the Provos? Whether or not we were related to Declan and the rest, they were terrorists. And if I got caught, I wouldn't be the only one to suffer the consequences, because I was traveling on Aidan's passport.

Maybe I should have stayed in the States. Sure, at home I was wanted for murder, but here in Ireland, I'd become a full-blown terrorist. Perhaps I should keep running while I could and get out of this country, too, but I was afraid that if I moved on I'd only upgrade my crimes. What next, England as a serial killer? My head was still spinning when Kate spoke up from the shadows of the passenger's seat, her face lit softly by the lights on the dash.

"Wait fer yer soul to catch up before you worry too much about it. Ya make mistakes when yer soul's not in it with ya, don' ya?" she asked. I guess she could see the worry on my face.

"About how long does my soul take to cross the Atlantic?"

"Generally? A week or so. But since yer from here originally, maybe yours is more familiar with the journey. I'd say give it a week." She didn't crack a smile and I couldn't tell if she was joking or not.

"You don't really believe that, do you?"

"Why shouldn' I? You ever see the way people act when they're on vacation?" And then she smiled. I wanted nothing more than to relax into the moment with her, but I couldn't shake the image of all that money tumbling out of the beheaded Mickey Mice.

"No sense gettin' upset about the money. What's done is done, inn't it?"

She startled me by placing a gentle hand on my arm, and I nearly went off the road. I tried to cover my reaction, concentrating on keeping the car on the wrong side of the road. It took a moment, but then I was back to being angry.

"My father set me up. I could've been arrested at the airport and they would've sent me right back home to face . . ." I managed to catch myself before giving anything else away and turned to look at her. She just looked out the window. After a moment, I heard her speak, softly, her breath forming a mist on the window as she did.

"Did he ever tell ya why he left? Why he keeps sendin' things over?"

"My father?"

"An' his brother Sean. The one they called 'Mickaleen.'" She turned to look at me, waiting for some kind of reaction. My instincts told me she knew something I didn't and that this was a test to see what I did know. The part of me that thought like a cop knew that if I were working her as a suspect, I should probably bluff to try to get more out of her. I thought about it for a second but realized I didn't want to play games with her. I'd been playing enough games recently.

"I assume they left for all the usual reasons. Money, jobs, opportunity . . ." I trailed off, seeing her look. A wall had gone up behind her eyes and I knew she was trying to decide how much to tell me. She looked away again and her voice got so soft I had to strain to hear her over the noise of the car engine.

"They were runnin' away. From a lot of things." She glanced at me, to see how I was taking it. I saw her out of the corner of my eye, but I kept my focus on the road. It kept twisting, a new surprise around every curve. After a moment, she went on, just as quietly. "But mostly they were runnin' from family and friends. The law, too. An' from guilt. They thought they could break the cycle. But no one can really do that. I guess that's why yer da still sends money over."

I was trying to absorb it all, and then it clicked, and I muttered out loud. *"Ni dhiolann dearmad fiacha."* The last words my uncle Sean had said. Was his debt tied into some IRA deal? Had he paid with his life?

"Right. A debt is still unpaid, even if forgotten. Maybe they didn't run far enough," Kate said.

I was busy putting the pieces together: my uncle Sean being killed, my father paying off some debt by sending cash back every year, and my father never returning to Ireland until after Uncle Sean had been killed. He probably worked out a deal to pay off his debt after he saw what happened to his brother. But there were still pieces missing.

"What did they do? What did he feel so guilty for?"

Kate shrugged, watching my eyes. "He never told ya, an' you think I should?"

"My father did something that he's been trying to pay his way out of for over twenty-five years, and now he's put me in the middle of an IRA plot. I think I deserve to know."

My words didn't seem to impress Kate. She looked down at her hands for a moment, and I was beginning to think she had decided to stop talking altogether when she finally spoke. "Yer father did nothin' except stand by his older brother. As he should have. It was Sean. Poor Sean." She looked right at me then, with so much emotion that I had to look away.

"What'd he do?" I finally asked, not sure if I really wanted to know.

"Shot his best friend, Liam, dead," Kate said simply. "Wasn't neither of them more than nineteen at the time."

Liam. The face from my dream flashed in front of me and I swerved, almost missing a turn in the road. My body felt flush with adrenaline. I tried to tell myself I was overtired and rationalizing why I might have dreamed about shooting someone named Liam. Maybe I'd heard my father talking about him when I was a kid, and the stress of accidentally killing James Butler had brought it all back from some dark recess inside my head. Then I noticed Kate watching me, her hand once again on my arm.

"You all right?"

"Just in shock, I guess. I never knew any of this."

"Never knew, or forgot—either way, it doesn't change what happened, does it? It was an accident. They were gonna ambush the Tans out on the Mullingar Road and it all went wrong. They got turned around in the mists and it was so cold the Shale Ghosts were out. It was them that started the shootin'." Kate was nodding calmly. As if ghosts explained a half-century-old killing.

"Shale Ghosts?"

"Yeah, sure. Had to be. Why else would Mickaleen kill 'is best mate and warn the Tans by jumpin' the gun? If he hadna shot, the Tans wouldna killed them others either. They lost the element of surprise. Sean and Ol' Jim were lucky to get away at all. Either that or they betrayed the rest, sold 'em out to the Tans. I never believed that, though the Murphys did for a long time. They lost three boys that day, Liam, Killian, and Aidan."

"The Murphys? Declan's family?" My stomach was churning. The local Provo's family had a grudge against mine for murdering three sons and betraying the cause. Welcome home, Michael Corrigan.

"Who else but Declan's family? It's one a the reasons he hates the British so much. But don' worry. Declan's one of the few that don' blame Mickaleen. He's the one who told me about the Shale Ghosts." Kate was absolutely serious. I could see it in her eyes, hear it in her tone. She'd seemed so down to earth, so normal until now. I was alone in the dark, being led down the back roads of Ireland by a woman that believed in ghosts and thought I was from a family of murderers—or, worse, traitors. I slowed the car, wondering if I should find a town or well lit street, somewhere safer to be right now. Kate was oblivious to the effect she was having on me, rambling on.

"As far as I'm concerned, ya don' owe me or nobody else here anything. Not fer what Sean done so long ago." She patted my arm, but it didn't reassure me. It only made me doubt her judgment.

"Is that why Patsy doesn't like me?" I asked, thinking about his reaction to me in the pub.

"Patsy? He's not seen the light yet, tha's all. One of these days we'll wake 'im up and he'll see that he doesn't know everything." She stopped, abruptly pointing into the darkness off to the right. "Better turn here or we'll be in real trouble."

"Real trouble?"

"Late fer dinner. My ma would kill us." She smiled, not realizing that her ma was the least of my worries. I made the right, sliding a little bit on the gravel track that I turned off onto. "That's the place. Been in the family since the seventeen hundreds, though it's been added to since. We're one of the few families aroun' here to keep some of our property. It's one reason some don't trust us."

I squinted farther up the driveway, surprised to see a large two-story whitewashed house with a heavy slate roof. I guess I'd expected either a small thatched cottage or something much more modern. I had no idea that houses like this still stood or that one family might own it for centuries. According to Kate, her mother had been taking in American tourists, offering a bedroom and breakfast for about five years, ever since Kate had moved out. Now that Kate had moved back home, they'd stopped taking people in, even though they still had the extra room.

I stopped the car where the driveway came up behind the house. It was pitch black when I turned off the headlights, the only light coming through a kitchen window. As I went to open my door, Kate grabbed my arm, stopping me.

"Look, Aidan, or Mickaleen, or whatever it is ya want to be called, no matter what my ma or da says—what anyone says—if ya have questions, come ask me, okay? Promise?" I nodded, and she seemed relieved. "The only thing Sean did wrong was not facin' up to what he done. Ya can't run away from karma." Kate shook her head, her expression absolutely serious. It made me smile for the first time since I saw the cash on the pub floor.

"Karma?"

"Yeah, it's the—"

"I know what karma is. I just didn't think I'd hear about it in rural Ireland."

"An' why not? Ya think we're a bit backward?"

"No, but karma's like a hippie thing, and you're all so Catholic." I got out of the car, going to the trunk for my bags. She followed me out, smirking at my arrogance.

"The idea that yer good an' bad deeds come back to ya is a hippie thing? What happened to reaping what you sow? Inn't that a good Christian concept, even in the States? Inn't Thomas Merton an American?" Kate asked. "An American an' Trappist monk that worked wit' the Dalai Lama himself an' you don' know about him, but ya think ya know about karma?"

Kate was right. I had no idea who Thomas Merton was and what I knew about karma was interpreted through hippies I'd arrested. Suddenly this seemed like an argument I couldn't win. So I did what I usually do when confronted by a woman smarter than me: I changed the subject.

"You said you moved back in a few months ago?" She nodded, then turned away, moving toward the back door. "Why?"

"The Troubles. You know . . ." I clearly didn't know, but it was just as clear that she didn't want to talk about it. She pushed open the door and I was hit with a blast of warm, sweet-smelling air. Somebody in the house was cooking, and the warmth of it spilled right out into the night. I followed Kate into the shadows of a utility room off the kitchen. The light filtered in, along with the sound of the radio playing in the kitchen. RTÉ Radio was discussing a planned peaceful march on the Magilligan Internment camp in the north as well as reports that the *Maidstone* Seven had made it across the border and were loose in the Republic. I lost the thread of the broadcast when I heard a man shouting over the sound of it.

"I don' see why we're takin' in Corrigan strays on Declan Murphy's say-so, even if he is yer nephew." The voice came from a man sitting at the table, sipping tea. He was Kate's father, Martin, balding, muscular, with a large belly that seemed grafted onto an otherwise thin frame.

"Shut yer gob, ol' man. We have a room, don' we?" Kate's mother, Bridey, was paying more attention to the food she was cooking than to her husband.

"Ma, Da . . ." Kate tried to interrupt, but her parents were too busy bickering to pay her any mind.

"We 'ave a room fer *rent*," Martin grumbled, snapping a paper he had open in front of him.

"It's my unnerstandin' he's already paid Declan somehow, an' we'll get the money from him."

"Ma," Kate tried again, the radio's volume making it difficult for her to get Bridey's attention.

"Maybe in the next life we will. Declan's not exactly good fer it, is he now?" Martin snapped the paper again, making a sound like an exclamation point.

"Ma! Da!" Kate practically shouted.

"What is it?" they both asked at once, finally acknowledging her presence, then noting mine. Martin reacted first.

"Jaysus, see what ya gone and done, Bridey? We've a guest and yer already makin' him feel unwelcome with yer nonsense." Bridey ignored him. Instead, she stared at me, the ladle in her hand dripping broth on the hearth.

"Ya look just like 'im, don' ya?" she asked. I didn't think she really wanted an answer, but I felt awkward saying nothing, so I filled the silence.

"I know. They say I look like my uncle Sean. The one they call 'Mickaleen.'"

Bridey waved the ladle, scattering more broth in all directions, dismissing what I just said. "Yeah, a course ya look like him. 'Ow could ya not? But I meant yer own grandfar Christy 'imself. Now that was a handsome man." Bridey smiled broadly and winked at Kate. "You know what I mean, don' ya, Kate?"

The tips of Kate's ears turned red, but I wasn't sure if it was her parents embarrassing her or the heat in the kitchen after the cold outside. Before she could respond, Martin interrupted with another snap of his paper.

"That's enough. Ya won' talk about Christy Corrigan in my house." Then he pointed the paper at Kate, ready to lecture, "An' you, young lady. Since when do we bring guests in the back door? Did we teach you nothin'?"

"Don't yell at her just because yer still jealous after all these years, Martin," Bridey said with a grin.

"Jealous of what? Christy was an old man an' you were a foolish young girl. Yer lucky I saved you."

"From nothin'. Christy wouldna have had me anyway. He was waitin' fer her to come back around. You know that."

"Iknownaschbledinting," Martin mumbled. I was starting to notice that a lot of Irish men did that. I'm not sure if it was a dialect thing, a holdover from the way things were pronounced in Irish, or if they were just afraid that someone might actually understand what they said and would hold it against them. Kate told me later that she thought it developed over time because the mumble allowed the men to say whatever they wanted without either pissing off the British or their own wives, a kind of secret language for the men, who'd been oppressed by both for centuries.

Bridey wasn't done with Martin yet—obviously she enjoyed tormenting him. "No, you know just about nothin', but you know that. It's always the same with those two. Like there was never anyone else in the world. Inn't that true, Kate?" She turned on Kate with that same mischievous look she used to torment Martin. Kate was staring at her, tense, obviously wanting the subject changed.

"I didna wait, did I? And look where that got me."

"Looks like it's all workin' out now, inn't it?" Bridey asked. I could see the muscles in Kate's jaw tighten as she bit back an answer. Bridey softened her tone. "All I'm sayin' is that Christy waited, and Sean tried to. I'm not sayin' they were right. Wha's that song tha's out now? 'Love the One Yer With'? That's the way to go. No sense wastin' a lifetime if things don' go as planned."

That seemed to diffuse whatever it was Kate was upset about and she took a deep breath, but she couldn't get a word out before Martin interrupted again.

"That explains a lot about you, Bridey. I guess it's a good thing I'm available every time ya get the itch."

"Good fer you, mebbe." She picked up some spices, tossing them into the pot, winking at me. "I like my spices. You know what they say about them, don' ya? Variety an' all that."

"Well, if yer both done, this is Aidan Corrigan, son of Ol' Jim and nephew of Sean," Kate said, trying to end that particular conversation.

"Ya mean Mickaleen. Not Sean," Martin grumbled, glaring at me. I was starting to feel like all the men here held me responsible for everything anyone in my family had ever done.

"They never called him Mickaleen in the States, did they?" Kate asked, moving into the kitchen, picking up utensils and starting to help her mother.

"No."

"Well, Mickaleen's good enough fer us. That's what we're callin' you. A spade's a spade, a Corrigan's a Corrigan, and yer jus' the same as Mickaleen, ain't ya?" Martin snapped his paper again, and I noticed he had yet to turn a page. I don't think he was even really reading.

"His name's Aidan," Kate insisted.

"Mick'aleen's fine," I told her, thinking that giving in would be easier than trying to argue with them, and I wouldn't have to remember to answer to my brother's name.

"He's here for his right of passage. He needs to get out to the island and walk the land." As she finished, Martin stood up and gave me the once over, looking directly at me for the first time.

"So you intend on keepin' the land? Does that mean yer gonna come back and live on it, or are ya just goin' ta run away again?" Martin was direct, if nothing else. His stare made me nervous, like the wrong answer would give him an excuse to beat the crap out of me. I must've hesitated too long, because he looked away in disgust.

"That's what I thought. If you've no intention of stayin', why come back at all?" He looked like he wanted to spit, but before he could Bridey interrupted.

"Martin," she said sharply, clearly a warning. Martin glanced up at her and backed down.

"I've said what I had to say and I'll say no more, Bridey, but you know how I feel about this." Then Martin turned to me, forced into being cordial. "An' you, you know where you can go. Top of the front steps to the left is the bathroom, yer room's across the hall. Ya might want to get cleaned up before supper." He snapped the paper again, dismissing me.

I looked at Kate, who was smiling. She nodded, indicating that it was safe to go. I grabbed my bag and started toward the steps. I was almost there when I heard Martin call after me.

"Be careful on them steps. They was made fer uninvited guests and Tans. The stains at the bottom'll explain why." He never looked up from the paper, but he got the result he wanted. I looked down at the wide wood-planked floor. A large uneven stain about eight feet across was right at the bottom of the steps, between it and the front door. To my eyes, it looked an awful lot like an old bloodstain. Or maybe red wine. Whatever it was, there was a lot of it, and it had seeped into the wood a long time ago, soaking into its core.

My eyes lingered on the stain even as I started up the stairs—and almost immediately fell face first into the treads, barely supporting myself as I caught the banister. My foot had caught on the second step, and as I looked down I realized that it was higher than the first step. In fact, no two steps were the same height. It was as if they'd been designed to trip anyone coming up them. I guess that's what Martin meant when he said they were designed for "uninvited guests."

I heard a snigger of satisfaction from the kitchen as Martin heard me stumble, then the sound of a hand meeting somebody's hard head.

"What are ya hittin' me for? I warned 'im, dinn't I," Martin protested.

TEN MINUTES LATER, after throwing some ice cold water on my face and washing up, I started down the stairs like an invalid, one hesitant step at a time, hanging on tight to the banister. Still I nearly tripped twice. I must have kept it quiet enough, because halfway down the stairs I heard Bridey and Kate talking in the kitchen as they banged around the pots and pans.

"A real keeper. Lookit his eyes an' ya can see jus' who he is, can't ya? If I was forty years younger, I'd be giving you a run fer yer money with that one." Bridey's voice reached me, low but clear. I stopped, wanting to back up the stairs, but afraid to move and end up leaving a bigger stain at the bottom than was already there.

"Don't," Kate answered tensely, scraping a spoon inside a pot for emphasis.

"My bones may be old, but my soul is young. I still enjoy the thought of me and a man like that rollin' in the hay. Makes my thighs warm thinkin' about it," I heard Bridey say. I started carefully backing up the stairs.

"I'm done here. We're not talking about this."

"You were done the minute he walked in the greengrocer's. I'm serious, Kate, don't let him slip away. Get yer head outta yer books and look at what's right in front of you." Bridey's voice had gotten softer and more serious. There was a long silence and I stopped moving again, afraid of making any noise. Then Kate finally spoke.

"It's too soon to even joke about it, Ma." To joke about what? I thought, feeling more and more uncomfortable and out of place. I wasn't sure I was welcome here, and I knew that there were old grudges against my family, but what else was going on?

The pots rattled for a moment or two as the two women fell silent. I could hear them moving, could tell from the rhythms of it that silence wasn't the norm for them. When enough time passed, I started down the steps again, pretending to stumble to let them know I was there. Strangely enough, hearing Kate laugh at my fake pain made me feel a lot better.

Dinner was leg of lamb, potatoes, green beans, and carrots, prepared simply. There was a vegetable soup as an appetizer and fresh baked brown bread, still warm. It was perfect. Kate was gracious, asking about my family. None of them had ever met my mother, although her family had lived in Mullingar, which wasn't that far away, and they seemed to know almost everything about my father, brother, and me—including the names of the girls we had dated in high school. Bridey was nosy and sarcastic, asking how a man of my age and looks managed to be unmarried without being a "poof," but Kate kept her from pushing too far with her questions. At the other end of the table, Martin mumbled. I couldn't decipher a word he said, and everyone else ignored him, so I did, too. It made me uncomfortable, but I figured if he was saying something really nasty, they'd let me know.

About halfway through the meal I saw headlights crawl across the wall as a car approached the house and understood the first thing Martin said during the meal.

"Dammit. The eejit's home." He put his fork down, holding his chest as if to ward off heartburn. I heard the back door slam and then suddenly Patsy filled the doorway to the utility room, glaring at me, then turning on Bridey.

"Ya couldna wait?"

"Ya couldna git yer lard arse here on time? We 'ave a guest," Bridey spat right back but got up and started making a plate. Patsy pulled up a chair next to Kate, sitting down like an overgrown boy, chafing under his mother's disapproval.

"It was Garda business that kept me," he said, staring at me. "We've got word the Provos are in the area raising money for arms and explosives. The British government is givin' us 'ell about it after this *Maidstone* escape." His look was accusatory, as if I'd provided the lard the swimmers covered themselves in to navigate Belfast Lough. I knew it was a veiled threat about the money I'd delivered, but he'd been there, too, as a witness and a cop. He'd be in just as much trouble as I was if anyone found out.

I smiled at him. I wasn't about to be bullied, not by him, anyway. I decided to make nice. "Your mother was just asking me why I wasn't married yet. She wants to know if I'm a 'poof.'" Patsy smiled at that. "I explained that I hadn't found the right woman, but I have my own place and am pretty independent. How about you, Patsy? You still live here at home with your ma? Is she worried about you, too?" Martin snorted, but I wasn't sure whether he was laughing at Patsy or annoyed with me. Patsy went whiter than he was already and looked like he was ready to come over the table at me.

Okay, so maybe I wasn't making nice, but at least I was making conversation. Patsy looked behind me and saw Bridey with a wooden spoon in her hand. A look passed between them and he bit his tongue.

"I help Ma and Da around the farm. I'm a good son. I don' run off and abandon my parents," Patsy said, aiming his words at me as if it were an accusation.

"No such luck," Martin mumbled.

"Patsy rents a room like anyone else would. An' he's serious wit' one of the Walsh girls from over to Athlone," Bridey said in an attempt at peacemaking.

"Which one?" Kate asked with a wide grin.

"Which one what?" Bridey looked confused as she set down Patsy's plate in front of him, his meat cut into neat squares for him, his potatoes buttered and salted.

"Which Walsh girl? If he's so serious, what's 'er name, Ma?" Kate tried to look innocent, but she knew the reaction she was aiming for. Patsy's plate bounced as he stabbed his meat and Bridey waved her spoon at Kate.

"Now you stop that, Kathleen. We don' need any more dirty Irish agitators aroun' this table. Even the Yank seems to be one of 'em." Bridey turned to me, but kept one eye on Patsy as she tried to steer the conversation to a safer place. "Now, Mickaleen, you and Patsy should have a lot in common. Wasn't it you that was goin' to police academy?"

I nearly choked on my meat. "Uh, no, that'd be my brother, Michael," I stammered.

"Why don' you tell Patsy about what it's like bein' a policeman over there. The garda here are a bit envious of your lot. Could learn a bit from them, don' you think?" Bridey smiled at me, and I began to talk about myself in the third person, about going to the police academy in New York City, about all my cases, from working the Columbia riots to being assigned to the joint task force and working with the FBI. I told him all about it, as if I were Aidan talking about me. It made Mike sound pretty good, but it made Aidan sound like a moron with no life of his own. By the time dinner ended, I was tired of hearing about myself and glad the inquisition was over.

That's when Bridey and Kate moved me, Martin, and Patsy off to the parlor with some tea and went back to clean up, leaving us alone. As Kate left the room, she set me up for another excruciating conversation.

"You know, Da, Mickaleen is here fer 'is right of passage. Maybe you two could help him figure that one out," she said, then just walked out. Martin sighed and looked away, sipping his tea, ignoring me. Patsy tried to do the same.

It was absolutely silent for almost two minutes. I had downed my tea and was ready to excuse myself so I could go upstairs when Patsy finally spoke.

"Ya know ya can't walk yer land unless ya can also walk on water, can ya," he said. "How do ya plan on gettin' over to Inchmore?"

"Isn't there a place to charter a boat?" It seemed pretty simple. A lake, water, a boat, money changing hands.

"No. Why would there be?" Patsy smiled.

I looked at Martin, who sipped his tea with a slurp and stared at us as if we were speaking a language he didn't understand. "For people to use them. To make money. Why else would you rent a boat?"

"I dunno 'bout that, but most of the people who need boats around here own them. Who leaves a boat lyin' around in case some eejit comes along without his own?" Patsy asked. I thought he was pulling my leg, but he seemed completely serious.

"If no one rents boats, then how do I get there?"

"I guess you could swim if you like, but the cold this time of year is somethin' awful, inn't it?" Patsy was enjoying this.

"Couldn't I find a fisherman, someone with a boat, someone who uses it and doesn't usually rent it, but might if I paid them?"

"Could ya? Wouldn't ya need to know who to ask?"

I looked at Martin, to see if he'd give me a hint as to whether Patsy was goading me or was really as thick as he seemed, but Martin was mumbling under his breath so low and in such a monotone that he seemed to be humming. I turned back to Patsy, who could at least form words.

"Okay, so who do I ask?"

"About what? A boat? No one I can think of. No one will go out there anymore, will they, Da? They say the place is cursed, don' they? It's dangerous, inn't it?" He looked at Martin for confirmation, who raised his tea and nodded.

"Yer both full a shite." Kate's voice came from the other room. "I can hear ya from the kitchen as I'm tryin' to clean, and if ya think I'm comin' in there to clean up the shite yer shovelin' when I'm done, you've lost yer minds."

"Don' be speakin' like that to yer father, Kathleen," Patsy warned, but Martin looked at her with something like pride as she moved to the doorway.

"It's not cursed," Kate assured me, pushing her hair back.

"No? Who lives there anymore? All of 'em fled or was run off or murdered, wasn't they? Lookit 'is whole family, why don' ya? Every one of 'em from the island is either dead or fled." Kate looked at me as Patsy spoke. She seemed embarrassed by her brother, but I didn't know what he was talking about or why it should bother me.

"There's a difference between a curse and bad memories," she said defensively.

"Not just bad memories, sister, a coupla lifetimes worth of bad memories. You should know. All of it adds up to the same thing. A curse. Bad blood and restless souls. And this one here knows all about that, don' he?" Patsy was staring in my direction.

"Me?"

"Why'd you come back, anyway? You a restless soul? Cursed? What are ya runnin' from this time, Corrigan?"

"Patsy," Kate warned, but Patsy was on his feet now, walking toward me, trying to intimidate me with his height and size.

"Can ya tell me? I want to know, don't I? You think you can tell me without lyin'?"

Patsy was in my face and I was beginning to worry. Was it possible that he knew who I really was? And if he did, what would he do about it? I was nervous, but I'd seen enough criminals tough it out to know what to do. I smiled coldly.

"What is this, an interrogation?" I asked, feigning amusement.

"Why would ya say that?" Patsy squinted at me and backed up.

"For one thing, every sentence you speak is a question."

"Is it now?" Patsy looked at me, then at Kate, apparently with no sense of irony.

"It is."

"And jus' because I ask questions, you feel like you're being interrogated?" he snapped.

"Listen to yourself. Every question I've asked you tonight, you answered with a question."

"Did I?"

"There you go again," I said, doing my best to distract him. "I bet you can't make a statement, even if you try."

Patsy's eyes bulged. I was getting to him. "Can you answer my question or not?"

"I'll answer as soon as you make a statement."

"You think I can't?" Patsy bellowed and Martin snorted. I turned to see him smiling for the first time all day.

"This's better'n *Juno an' the Paycock*. It's *The Eejit and the Amadan*." He nodded to me, either taking my side or inciting me to keep going, I couldn't be sure. "Bet him a pint, boyo. See if my eejit son knows how to construct a proper sentence at all."

"Whose side are ya on, Da?" Patsy whined, offended.

"Ahh, another interrogative. You'd be up a pint already, Mickaleen." Martin winked at me, driving Patsy further over the edge. His eyes bulged and it made his large head look bigger.

"Fine. It's a bet. I'll buy you a pint if you can complete any sentence that's not a question." I couldn't help myself. I got the feeling that somehow this was winning over Martin—and Kate, who was leaning against the wall, trying not to grin.

"I get a pint if I can make statement?" Patsy clarified, and Martin snorted again.

"Two nothin' fer the Yank." I looked at him and grinned appreciatively, but his smirk disappeared. "Don' get me wrong, boyo, I still don' like you much, but right now yer the lesser of two evils."

Martin's attitude didn't really surprise me. I'd seen it in my own family often enough. There's nothing like the Irish for switching sides just to even things out or to make former allies pay for some perceived fault. They can't help themselves. They distrust anyone or anything that has too much power. They've been on the wrong end of that equation too many times.

I've also found that loyalty isn't something freely given by the Irish people. It's earned, every single moment of every day. When they do express loyalty it's to ideals rather than people or governments, which have failed them over and over. Martin wasn't being disloyal to his son so much as he was being loyal to the cultural ideal that preferred a match of wits over violence. It wasn't his fault that Patsy was on the losing end of the competition.

"I'm up by two, but I'll give you double or nothin' if you can say something without phrasing it as a question." I felt safe in goading Patsy, especially now that he'd lost his confidence.

Patsy looked at me hard, then at Kate, to see if I was serious. She just smiled at him and he turned back to me. "You're really serious about this . . . aren't you?"

"Bloodyellealmosadit," Martin muttered, shaking his head.

"You lose," Kate chimed in. Patsy looked bewildered.

"How? I said, 'You're really serious about this.' Didn't I?" Kate shook her head and Patsy looked to me as if I might vouch for him.

"You added 'aren't you,'" I told him, almost feeling sorry for him.

"That was a separate sentence, wasn't it?" Patsy tried to defend himself.

"With the double or nothin' and the last two, you owe the man a good eight pints, Patsy." Martin winked at me, knowing I'd caught his mathematical error and that Patsy wouldn't because he was too pissed off. But he was still too much an overgrown boy to challenge his father, so he turned on me.

"Fine. I'll buy you yer pints, right after you walk yer land, won't I? But you'll need some good luck findin' someone who'll take ya after I let them know what yer here for and that yer in deep with Declan Murphy, won't ya?" It wasn't a subtle threat, but I couldn't help the grin that was on my face.

"Thastenpints, inn't it?" Martin asked.

Patsy didn't look at him and stormed out, his feet nearly cracking the treads of the stairs. I noticed that he moved smoothly up, taking two at a time, never stumbling. Maybe that was the trick, two at a time. Maybe the height averaged out.

"Sounds to me like you'll have more Guinness than ya can handle with all them questions the eejit's askin'. If ya need any help gettin' rid of 'em, jus' let me know, especially since I gave ya a couple. He was too thick to notice," Martin said, as he stood and moved to follow Patsy upstairs. As he passed Kate, he stopped, looked her softly in the eyes and shook his head. Something passed between them—some unspoken permission was given, some unfought battle lost and won—as he gently tousled her hair and started up the stairs.

He took them two at a time as well, but stopped a quarter of the way up, looking back down at us. "Ya might be better off not goin' to the island, Mickaleen. The Corrigans 'ave been gone a long time. Some things have changed and some haven't, neither of 'em any good fer you. I'm only tellin' ya because I care about my daughter, unnerstand?" I nodded, not knowing how else to respond, and then he glided up the steps and was gone.

I glanced over at Kate, but I couldn't read her look. She was staring down at her hands, wringing them in the dish towel. When she finally spoke, her voice was soft.

"You've had a long trip. You might want to get some sleep. You know where your room is, right?"

"I do."

"Breakfast is early. Wake up when ya smell it or you'll miss it," she told me, looking up at me for only a second before turning sharply on her heel and moving back to the kitchen. I sat there for a couple of minutes, wondering how soon I should start looking for a hotel, then went up the stairs. I took them two at a time and never tripped.

The bedroom I was staying in was about average size when it was built, which made it about the same size as a prison cell. You could just stand between the odd-sized bed, which was too short for my tall frame, and the chunky dresser as long as you didn't open the drawers. There was a cold draft from the one window and a seeping dampness in the air, but when I got under the layers of wool blankets, it was all irrelevant.

The mattress was lumpy and hard, but in spite of that, it was the most comfortable bed I'd ever been in. And warm. Some part of me knew it was just because I was tired, but I was drifting off into a state where thoughts didn't really connect to one another and I convinced myself that if I was ever able to go back to the States I was going to market this exact bed and make a fortune.

I don't remember much else until my eyes snapped open. I was disoriented for a moment, unsure of where I was, or what I'd heard, or why I'd even woken so suddenly. I could feel my heart racing and I was beginning to panic, so I reached for my gun, which I always kept next to the bed. My body felt like lead. I could barely move. The thought that my soul needed to come back so that it could get my muscles to move crossed my mind just as I realized my gun wasn't there.

Then I heard the knob on the heavy oak door rattle slightly, and I remembered where I was. The door swung slowly open and she was there, her eyes in shadows, her cheekbones lit by the low hanging moon that peeked in the window. For a second I thought she was going to come in, but instead she looked up the hall furtively and whispered, "I'll take ya."

"Take me?" I asked.

"To the island." I must have still looked confused because suddenly her foot was against the mattress, pushing it. "Get yer arse up. I mean now."

"Now? Right now?" I squinted at her and realized she was fully dressed, with some kind of knapsack in her hand.

"I've learned that you don' wait when ya want somethin'. You never know when you might lose the chance. You want to wait or go now?"

"Sure." I'd do just about anything to be out of this house before I had to see Patsy or Martin again. Especially if they didn't have their morning coffee, or tea, or whatever it was they drank to take the edge off.

She nodded, satisfied. "Then get yer arse out of bed and meet me in the kitchen. An' don' wake up the eejit." Kate turned on her heel and was gone, somehow avoiding all the spots in the hall that made the floor creak. When I followed her two minutes later, I somehow hit them all. The groaning wood sounded like an old schooner in a hurricane, but it apparently wasn't enough to wake anyone.

I remembered to take the stairs two at a time, which was harder going down, and found Kate waiting in the kitchen with a thermos full of tea, a knapsack, and some blankets, listening to the sounds of the house, to make sure no one else was awake.

"You kept me waiting long enough didn't ya?" she asked, then threw the knapsack at me, picked up the blankets and pivoted for the door, all in one smooth motion. She was outside before I could respond, and by the time I caught up she was in my car, in the driver's seat, rolling down the slight incline of the driveway in neutral.

"What are you doing?"

"If I start the engine, they'll hear us. We'll roll to the bottom of the hill," Kate explained, throwing open the passenger's door for me. I jumped in while the car was moving, feeling for the first time like the criminal everyone apparently thought I was. Where had Kate learned these skills? I wondered. Was she with the Provos, too? Or just from a long line of "dirty Irish agitators"?

"Fun, inn't it?" Her question brought me back to the moment and I looked over to see her smiling broadly, enjoying every second of it as she popped the car into first gear and jump-started the engine at the bottom of the drive. She hit the gas hard enough to give me whiplash, taking the turns in the knotted road without slowing down.

"You mind telling me why we're sneaking out? And why your father thinks we should stay off the island?"

She didn't look at me, just sped up. I thought for a moment that she hadn't heard me, but then she slowed down enough to look away from the road for the briefest of seconds. Her eyes met mine, and I saw a sadness there I hadn't seen before.

"I do mind. But we'll talk about that on the way over." Then she hit the gas again and was silent for the next ten minutes.

The road to the lake was a rutted track that Kate abandoned by pulling off into a field a hundred yards before we reached the shore, getting out of the car with only two words over her shoulder to me.

"This way," she said, and started walking with a long stride. It was still dark and I began to wonder what time it really was but couldn't figure it out. I was too distracted by the cold, the ankle-breaking ruts, and watching Kate's athletic body ahead of me, navigating the field like a deer in flight from a hunter.

She reached the shore of Lough Ree a full thirty seconds before I did, and when I came up behind her she was backlit by the moon descending over the water, reflecting off the water's black surface like a mirror. Her pale features and auburn hair gave her an otherworldly look, and I started to understand why people believed in banshees and sprites and warrior queens raised from the dead.

Kate didn't turn when I approached but just kept looking down at the lake. I thought she was looking at her own reflection but then saw through her to what lay below the surface.

It was a half-rotted curragh with an obvious hole in the bottom and a rusted ax lying next to it. It had been there awhile.

I began to question why we were there at all. If I had thought ahead about the cold and the wind, I might not have come. In fact, the only reason I was there was Kate. There was something about her that was tempting. Tempting the way a closed door is tempting when you know there's something you've never seen before on the other side.

"I guess we're not meant to get there tonight. Not if you were intending on using that," I joked, but part of me felt it was a sign. Coming across a sunken boat right before you're about to cross a lake isn't something that inspires confidence.

Kate shrugged. "Ya know whose that is? What it is?"

"It's a boat. Or was."

"It's yer uncle's boat." She turned to me for my reaction, but I didn't have much of one. It didn't surprise me. If the boat came from the island, it probably belonged to someone in my family at some point. Kate turned back to the lake, looking through the wisps of fog to the island. "The night he left he sailed from the island and chopped a hole in the damn thing so he wouldn't be tempted to ever go back. Then he went to the house of his fiancée to get her to run away with him."

"But she didn't go." I knew that much. I would have heard about anyone who made the journey with my father. Over, and over, and over.

"No. She thought, at the time, that he was a traitor who had warned the British and shot Liam Murphy. She wouldn't even see him. She called out her father and brothers and they set after him. If his brother Jim hadn't led them on a wild goose chase, they would 'ave killed him then and there."

"What do you mean my father led them on a wild goose chase?"

"Ya don' know?" Kate seemed surprised, but I was becoming less so. There was lot I didn't know, apparently. She saw my look and went on. "Ol' Jim, he was always playin' the eejit, like he wasna all there in the head. Said it made people underestimate 'im." I was beginning to wonder about him myself. At home he was deaf to all my mother's complaints and got waited on hand and foot because we all worried about him. And now he'd set me up to carry the money over. Maybe he wasn't suffering from Alzheimer's after all. Maybe he was a genius.

"Ol' Jim stayed with the boat when Mickaleen sunk it, knowing they'd come lookin' fer Mickaleen on the island. When they got here, he told them that Mickaleen 'ad gone off to the Tans barracks in Athlone to get protection."

"But he hadn't." I knew this one. I knew how much my father and uncle hated the British. They'd never go to them, not for any reason.

"A course not," she agreed. "Ol' Jim joined Mickaleen on the island, and then they rowed north on the lough an' both made their way up to Belfast. Caught a ship to New York together," Kate said, smiling as if finishing a fairy tale with "a ship to New York" was the same as saying "happily ever after." Obviously she'd never been there.

"But you said he sank the boat. How'd he get to the island and row north?"

Kate smiled again at me, proud that I caught the inconsistency. "The same way we are. Neither Jim nor Mickaleen were eejits." She walked away from me, toward an overgrowth of nearby reeds, found a rope, and started pulling on it.

Another curragh came gliding silently out of the reeds and Kate stepped in gracefully, barely rocking the small curragh. I followed, less delicately, but I didn't get my feet wet either. She let me row. I think she was being sensitive to my manhood, because I was pretty sure she'd be better at it, and I suspected that there were a few times she wanted to tell me how to do it but bit her tongue. Halfway across the lake, I was getting tired and getting the hang of it in about equal measure. I was just beginning to make out the shoreline of Inchmore through the wisps of fog when I saw shadows moving on the island.

Someone was there. I opened my mouth to tell Kate, but she beat me to it.

"It's the wild horses. Nothin' to worry about. They were left behind and have fended for themselves all this time." I watched as they came into focus: a dappled mare, a roan stallion, and a chestnut colt. They were watching us as much as we were watching them, probably wondering if someone was finally coming back to claim them after all these years.

Suddenly I felt Kate's hand on mine, and when I looked up, she was looking me in the eye, the moonlight illuminating her face as if it were daylight. "You need to promise me somethin', Mickaleen. Whatever ya see here, whatever happens, it's between us, unnerstood?" Kate seemed nervous, looking back to the shore of the mainland where we could still see the silhouette of the parish church.

"What could happen here?" I wondered aloud. The worst thing I could imagine would be freezing to death, with Kate trying to keep me warm up until the moment I passed, and I could deal with that. But she knew more about this place than I did.

"The island is only mostly abandoned, Mickaleen. Patsy and my da know it. That's why they tried to warn you away. Why else do you think I'd wake you up at three in the mornin' to go fer a row?"

"The IRA is using the island?"

"The Provos. They need somewhere to hide their little pistols. And Declan thinks it's good craic to put the guns on the land of the county's most notorious traitor—even if he was never really a traitor at all." Kate smiled, apparently finding a bit of humor in that herself. I didn't share their appreciation for the absurd. It felt like the temperature had just dropped ten degrees.

My hands were beginning to blister from the rowing, but the cold was keeping them numb enough that I didn't feel it too much. I glanced back toward the shore of the mainland, now much farther away than the island. The church was the only prominent landmark I could make out. It somehow made me think of my father and the stories he told that I never believed, about rowing to church every Sunday in thunder and lightning storms. I knew a lot of my relatives were still there and could hear the church bells from the warmth of their earthen beds. I wondered how many of Kate's ancestors lay near mine, and the thought made me feel a bit less cold.

Sean

Making excuses about one of his other cousins, Jimmy something, showing up out of the blue and needing his help, Kevin backed out on us and left me to ride alone to Dublin with Anne. Without telling Patsy that Kevin had backed out, we snuck out twenty minutes later and were on the road, taking a shortcut Anne said she knew. I imagined a scenic, relaxing drive through the Irish countryside and got anything but, thanks to Anne's nearly suicidal driving and her nonstop smoking of unfiltered cigarettes. About ten minutes into the drive, with my stomach trying to escape through my throat and my eyes swelling shut, Anne slowed down for the first time since we'd left her driveway.

"Feckin' 'ell. I dunno who's got less of a brain, this arsehole or 'is feckin' sheep," she cursed as she leaned on the horn and opened a window. As she did, the smoke cleared enough that I could see a flock of sheep less than fifteen feet in front of us, covering the road. In the midst of them was a small, crooked man whose limbs seemed to bend at odd angles. Anne leaned out the window, calling to him as if he were deaf on top of all his other apparent problems.

"How're ya doing, Mr. Fitzpatrick? Lovely day, inn't it?" she asked, almost sweetly.

Mr. Fitzpatrick tried to glare, but his eyes were as crossed as the rest of him and he seemed to focus on something off to our left. "You were goin' a little fas' there, weren't ya, Anne? Ya think ya might learned a lesson or two by now, wouldn't ya?"

"Ya would think. But mebbe it only seemed a bit fast with yer sheep movin' so slow. Either way, it's a good thing you were here to slow me down, wann't it?" Anne leaned back in the window, speaking quietly to me, obviously annoyed with Mr. Fitzpatrick. "Bleedin' maggot. He waits until he hears cars comin' to let his sheep cross, I swear to ya."

"Ya could've killed me, Anne. Even if ya didn't hit me, I nearly 'ad heart failure," the old man grumbled.

"My apologies if I scared the shite out of you, an' yer sheep, as I can see that I have from the state of the road, but I was tryin' to show my Yank cousin the beauty of Ireland and not resort to takin' the N6." Anne was smiling and winked at me through the thinning smog.

Mr. Fitzpatrick mumbled something I couldn't understand and then called out. "The bloody N6? You'll end up dead on tha' damn thing. It's an abomination. Let me get these sheep out of the way so you can make up some time." He was obviously passionate about it, suddenly moving the sheep along.

I thought about what Anne had said earlier, about him blocking the road on purpose. "You really think he has nothing better to do than listen for cars and stop them with his sheep?"

"No one will talk to the wanker unless they're stopped an' have no choice. He gets lonely. Ya know how he met his wife?" My blank look was all the encouragement she needed. "He sacrificed a good lamb. Sent it out right in front of her new Volkswagen. The poor woman gets a bloody concussion an' isn't thinkin' straight and feels bad fer killin' the wee lamb, so she accepts the cross-eyed fecker's offer of dinner. Lamb stew, of course. By the time she realized he was responsible fer wreckin' her car an' nearly killin' her, she was pity pregnant."

"Pity pregnant?"

"Yeah. She took pity on him one time after too many bevvies and got pregnant. Pitiful all aroun'. The son's as sweet as his mother once was, an' as dumb as a rock, like his old man. He was hit by a car two years back tryin' his father's old tricks, 'cept he fergot to send the sheep out first." Anne laughed at that, then saw my look. "Stay easy, he lived."

"And how do you know all this?"

"Who do you think hit the dumb bastard? He tol' me the whole thing while we waited fer the ambulance." Anne slipped the car into gear as she waited for the last of the sheep to get out of the road.

"And you took pity on *him*?"

"Whadda ya take me for? He looks like his ol' man fer Chrissakes, eyes an' all. Besides, I have no pity fer eejits. He fergave me anyway. That's why his ol' man hates me. His son's still single and wouldna even sue me." She shook her head as if she barely believed her own story.

"Yer clear. Jus' be careful next time around. This ain't the N6," Mr. Fitzpatrick warned, but whatever else he said was lost on the wind as Anne gunned the engine, racing down the road, spinning up the sheep shit with her tires.

"Remind me on the way back, that shite's slippery and the amadan'll leave it all over the road jus' to be thick." I nodded, making a mental note to watch out for sheep shit left as retribution on the road. I forgot all about it ten minutes later as Anne, doing forty miles an hour, weaved in and out of a herd of cattle giving the finger to the farmer as we passed through. By ten thirty we were pulling into the car park at Setanta Place, and by ten thirty-four Anne had finished the first coffee she'd bought and started a second. After scalding my tongue, I sipped mine carefully as we walked briskly up past Merrion Square and crossed over to what the signs clearly pointed to as Leinster House, home of the Dáil Éireann, the Irish parliament.

We were early, for what I wasn't sure. Anne told me that we wouldn't be able to see Declan for a few hours. I assumed she had an appointment, since she'd said we had to be somewhere at exactly 12:30 p.m. While we waited, she took me on a tour of the Dáil Éireann and Leinster House. I have to admit, it was impressive, from the architecture to the energy, to the sense of history.

Anne kept a running commentary on it all, in typical Anne fashion: "Michael Collins and Cathal Brugha, they were leaders now. Not like this bunch, who steam up the windows with so much hot air you'd think the place was a bathhouse. The best hope we have is that this lot wrestles themselves into headlocks and does a whole lot of nothin'."

Anne went on and on like that, but I noticed that she kept looking around, eyes on every guy in a suit that we passed. She looked like she was either stalking someone or was terrified that security was going to catch her in the building. Given her general anarchist attitude, I started to worry that she might indeed be wanted for some petty antiestablishment crime, and after she ducked behind a pillar to avoid a feeble bald-headed man in a tweed suit, I had to ask, "Do you really have an appointment with Declan or are you just hoping he's here?"

"Shhh. Don' say his name so loud," she said as she punched me. "His appointment secretary said he was in meetin's at the Dáil all day, so of course he's here."

"So you don't have an appointment." How stupid was I to think Anne would do anything the easy way?

"I never said I did. You jus' assumed I did because I said I talked to his secretary. Tha's all I said, dinn't I?" she asked defensively. She was right, of course. I think deep down part of me had known and wanted to go along for whatever ride was in store. If I waited until all the details got worked out, I'd never do anything. I was about to ask Anne what the plan was, when she ducked under the ornate marble staircase leading to the Dáil Chamber, just in time to avoid a petite blond woman in a form-fitting skirt and blouse.

"Don' let that little tart see me. She'll toss us both out. Last time she had me held in a room fer like three hours," Anne whispered. I just stood there, smiling numbly at the "tart," who turned to find me staring at her. I felt like a pervert as I peered from under the staircase, but she just gave me a nasty look and walked away. Needless to say, between Anne's paranoid stalking and her nicotine habit, we never made it through the end of the tour.

We were in the Seanad Corridor and the tour guide was telling us who every gray-haired man in every picture was, including their genealogies, which sounded like something out of the Old Testament. "This is Killian Kearny of the Donegal Kearneys, son of the late Cathal Kearney, who was of course named after Cathal Brugha who was his very own uncle by marriage through the Cahills of Cork city. Now Cathal Kearney's father was, as some of you may know from yer Irish history . . ."

"An Irishman who fought the English? Which of these arseholes don't make that claim now," Anne whispered in my ear. I tried to ignore her, but this time she dug her nails into my arm and pulled me backward. "C'mon. We're out of here. It's almost twelve thirty anyway, and if I hear any more of this shite I'll need my ears cleaned out with toilet paper."

She dragged me down the Seanad Stairway. A security guard yelled that we needed to stay with the tour group, and we started to run as his voice got louder. I almost stopped, but by that time she'd passed through an emergency exit, and I would have been left alone trying to explain, so I ran, too.

I didn't stop until I caught up to her in the middle of the park across the street, Merrion Square. Anne had slowed to a walk as she raced behind some bushes and now appeared to be just another pedestrian, taking a stroll at lunchtime. She must have heard me trying to breathe in her wake and spoke without turning.

"Ya lost the goon squad, dinn't ya?" I turned to look, but no one was following me.

"Yeah. I guess. Why'd you run?"

She shrugged, glancing around the park like she was worried the cops were closing in. "They were chasin' us. Besides, it's twelve thirty. Declan's due."

I followed her gaze, looking for him even though I had no idea what he looked like. "How do you know? Is he supposed to be here?"

"No. This is our last hope. He comes 'ere every day. He's a fag addict." My eyes must've gone a little wider because she grinned at my reaction and sucked on her cigarette. "Ahh, tha's right. It means something else in the States. He's a nico fiend," she explained. "He smokes like a feckin' chimney."

That sounded a bit hypocritical to me, considering how much Anne smoked, but before I could say as much, she tossed down her cigarette and ground it out with her toe, nodding toward the corner of the park where a man in an expensive charcoal gray suit with a royal blue tie had just entered, striding along at a pace as uptight as Anne's, sucking down a cigarette. He had the look of a former marine. His lean muscle and scars were barely concealed by a thin layer of good living that had come late in life. He was wearing the tailored clothes of a politician, but he didn't look comfortable in them.

"There 'e is. I dunno how he survived so long bein' so predictable. The Ulster Volunteer Force must have their collective head up their ass." Anne shook her head, picking up speed as she moved to intercept him. As she did, he suddenly veered off the path and headed in the opposite direction.

"Tha' sneaky shite. He saw me," Anne muttered as she turned to me, giving orders. "Keep followin' 'im. I'll cut 'im off." She disappeared into the bushes. I picked up the pace, trying to follow the man as he headed into a crowd of about fifteen other charcoal gray suits.

I lost him for a minute in the crowd, then started looking for the trail of smoke. I thought I was being clever, but then I realized that following the smoke wasn't going to do me much good. Everyone seemed to be smoking. I paused at the intersection of two paths, sitting on a bench backed by some bushes. I tried looking for Anne, concerned that we wouldn't be able to find one another, but as it turned out I didn't need to worry.

"Ah, bloody shite," I heard a deep male voice growl behind me. I turned to find Anne confronting the dangerous-looking man we'd seen enter the park. She was smiling smugly.

"It's good to see you, too, Uncle Dec. An' sure, I'd love to have lunch with you." She grabbed his arms hard and planted a peck on one cheek.

He reeled back, as if he wanted to push her away, but spoke tersely instead. "Christ, child. We're barely related. Enough with that uncle crap." His voice was low, but it went up a half decibel as his eyes fell on me. "And you brought him?"

I could feel my mouth drying out as it hung open, but I couldn't make my brain connect with my jaw to close it. Up close, I recognized his eyes and the hard set of his jaw. This was Declan Murphy, exactly as my uncle described him, only with a bit less hair and a bit more stomach. He didn't look like a terrorist. Or a killer. He looked like one of my uncles. Except around the eyes. Around the eyes he looked like something more.

"You two could be twins wit' the looks on yer bleedin' faces," Anne said, putting her finger on the moment.

Declan had regained his composure after looking around to make sure no one had noticed him with us. "You'll show me some feckin' respec', Anne. I don' care who ya think ya are to me. I'm a respected politician."

"There's no such thing. Lookit ya, usin' words like 'feckin'' and 'shite' right up in the Dáil. A real man a respect." Anne's words were making his muscles tense. His jaw was clenched, and the blood had rushed to his face.

"Mr. Murphy?" I interrupted, hoping to diffuse the whole thing. "I read all about you in my uncle's journals. About the *Maidstone* prison escape and the battle for Ballymurphy and the awakening on Inchmore when you kille—" I stopped. I stopped abruptly because my trachea was suddenly closing, pinched between his thumb and four fingers. With an ounce more pressure he could've killed me.

"Another word and I'll send you to the next life, boyo, unnerstood?" I nodded as he looked around to make sure there were no witnesses other than Anne. Then he let me go, his eyes never leaving mine. The strange part about it wasn't that he almost strangled me, but that he didn't. There was no animosity in him. He just wanted me to stop talking, and managed to do it quickly, with no questions asked. Finally, when he was sure that I wasn't about to start speaking without permission, he turned to Anne.

"And you, *you* know better. If 'e's 'ere it's only for one reason. You know that, right?" he challenged her.

She just shrugged. What he was talking about was obvious to at least the both of them. "We all want the same thing," she told Declan. "Him more than the rest. Even if 'e don' know it yet."

I hated the way they talked about me as if they were speaking a language I couldn't understand, even if I could, sort of. "Yeah? And what do *we* want?" I asked, imagining I could get a straight answer simply by demanding it.

Declan smirked, apparently amused by the question, and it made me feel like a child. "Peace in our time. All the wild geese come home, an' all the prodigal children livin' happy together. Inn't that right, Anne?" He grinned at her, relishing the punch line to some inside joke neither of them was ever going to explain to me. Then he turned back to me and frowned, looking me right in my eyes. "What'd she do ta yer eyes, anyway?" He spun on Anne, accusatory. "Ya didn't mace this one, too, did ya?"

"Ya make it sound like a habit. I've only maced three fellas in the las' two years, and only one was a garda. His eyes are red from the smoke in my car. He's one a them sensitive types."

Declan nodded, accepting her answer, even though I found it offensive. His eyes just stayed on me, analyzing me as if I were signing up for the Provos and might prove to be an informer. "Sean Michael, is it?" he asked, although

I was beginning to realize that questions from the Irish were not necessarily meant to be answered. "You'd be about the right age, wouldn't you?"

"You know who I am?" I'd always been told that I looked like my mother's side of the family. I didn't think anyone would recognize me as being related to my own father, never mind my uncle.

"Why wouldn't I? I knew Mickaleen himself, didn't I?" he asked as he turned to Anne. "I'm takin' him fer a pint. Why don' you go find somethin' to do with yerself fer a bit. Say an hour. Ya know where to meet us." Declan grabbed my arm, so hard it felt like he was bruising the bone. Was I about to be "disappeared"? I had a vision of my body being dug up in twenty years from an unmarked grave by little kids playing pirates, looking for buried treasure. My only hope was Anne. I could tell that she wasn't going to let Declan do anything to me because she grabbed my other arm just as tightly.

"An' what am I supposed to do without 'im? He's the one flush wit' cash. Dublin's an expensive place now, inn't it," she argued. Damn. Now I was really starting to worry. Was she selling me out for a pint and some bangers and mash?

Declan nodded, as if she were being perfectly reasonable. He pulled out a crumpled wad of bills from a front pocket, shoving them in the hand that reached for them. "'Ere. And thanks fer bringin' 'im to me first. I owe ya."

"Ya bet yer bloody arse ya do," Anne said over her shoulder, already turning away.

"Wait, what do you mean?" I called after her as she abandoned me. "You're leaving me with him?" I was incredulous. What did he mean "bringing him to me first"? Had she just turned me over to an IRA killer so he could get rid of me?

Anne stopped and smiled, enjoying my fear. "Yer fine. 'E's a respected politician, remember? Jus' stay in public places with lots a witnesses and don' eat or drink anything 'e's touched." She laughed and blew smoke at me, twirling away.

I turned back to find Declan grinning at me. "Yer safer walkin' with me than drivin' wit' tha' one, that's fer sure. Has she shown ya her spinning U-turn yet?" The answer must've been written on my face, because Declan laughed, then pulled me by the arm, leading me away from the crowds in Merrion Square and down a side street.

Ten minutes later we were in a small pub, with enough of a crowd to make me feel secure. It only took a few minutes before the feeling faded and I started to worry if everyone in the pub might be friends of Declan. I wasn't entirely sure how we'd gotten there either. We took a half-dozen turns down winding streets and alleys while Declan talked about every murder, street fight, and illicit transaction that had taken place on each corner since the Vikings had shown up and ruined the neighborhood. He was a great tour guide, but his constant patter kept me from paying attention to where I was going. That was probably the point.

Once we got inside, Declan had nodded to the bartender and gone directly to a table in the back. Thirty seconds later a buxom waitress slammed down a black and tan in front of him and a warm pint in front of me.

"If ya wan' it cold, go back where ya came from." The waitress tossed off the remark as she strode away. Anne later told me that my sneakers marked me as an American before I ever opened my mouth, but at that moment I had no idea what she was talking about. All I knew was that I was somewhere in Dublin, where people catered to a man my uncle had called a terrorist and murderer.

Declan waited for the waitress to get out of earshot, sucking on his cigarette in between gulps of his black and tan. His eyes never looked at either one. They rotated from my face to the door and back again. His back was to the wall and he was acting like Anne did in Leinster House, as if he were being hunted, which I guess he had been for more than thirty years. Finally, when he was satisfied that no one was listening or watching us, he spoke over the edge of his glass.

"So. You've read Mickaleen's journal?"

"Uncle Mike's? Yeah, a few times."

He nodded and looked away from me. He was quiet so long, I thought he was going to end the conversation before we started. When he spoke again, he spoke so quietly I had to lean forward to hear him. "Your uncle was an amadan, you know that, right? Writing down all that shite about the past. Don' believe a word of it."

"Why not?" I asked, part of me relieved that it might not be true. Maybe my uncle had slipped a nut and everything he'd written was just the ramblings of a mad man.

"Why would ya? How can ya believe anything he wrote? All that nonsense about him and Kate and Liam an' Mickaleen. All that rambling about 'real' baptisms."

"So it's not true?"

Declan shrugged as if reluctant to call my uncle a liar to my face. He wouldn't say it was untrue, which to me meant that at least part of it was. But which part was it? I had to know, so I started with one question I knew he'd have to answer.

"Did you kneecap Patsy and try to kill him?"

Declan didn't seem to mind the question. After all, he'd been interrogated and tortured by the British, trying to elicit confessions for much worse crimes. He actually smiled, as if remembering the event fondly. "If I tried to kill 'im, he'd be dead now, wouldn't 'e? An' if he's not complainin' about 'is knees, why should you?"

"His limp matches what Uncle Mike wrote," I challenged.

Declan shrugged, calmly waving for another black and tan. "Believe what you like, I guess. You of all people should know what's true and what's not."

"How would I know that?" Had my uncle left other evidence I didn't know about yet?

"After readin' all that nonsense, ya still don' know?" Declan's eyes rested on me for a moment and I gave myself away with my silence. "Ya think it's a bunch of bloody shite, don' ya?" he sneered.

"Mostly," I admitted. "But parts of it feel true. Like I've heard the stories before."

"Maybe as a kid. Around the kitchen table or some such. Yer people always loved a good fairy tale." Declan stopped as the waitress set down another black and tan, ignoring me and my untouched pint. As she went behind the bar, I turned to Declan, trying to imitate his studied nonchalance. "I never even knew my uncle existed until a week ago."

He nodded as if that was the best news he'd hear all day. "Good. Maybe you should ferget 'im again. Trust me, fergettin's the way to go with this one, boyo."

"Why? Because of what it says about you? What it says about Black Friday? Is that why you don't want me to believe any of it?" I pressed. I hadn't come all the way to Ireland to pretend, like my father did, that the past never happened.

"Tha' journal says nothin' abou' Black Friday. Them pages are missin'." Declan said it flatly, without any doubt, daring me to contradict him. He knew exactly which pages were missing, and suddenly I realized why.

"You have them," I said, even as it occurred to me.

Declan's expression remained neutral and his voice got even lower. "How do you know I dinn't burn 'em?"

"Because you wouldn't." It just came out of my mouth, but as I heard it, I knew it was true.

"An' how do ya know that?"

"Because you knew I'd come for them, and you want me to have them." It was hard to believe the words were coming from me, but they were. And Declan wasn't arguing.

He stared at me hard, for the first time not scanning the room. "Ya seem pretty certain fer a kid who says he never knew 'e 'ad an uncle."

I was pushing my luck, but so far it was working. I decided to push harder. "I'll tell you what. I'll make you a deal. You let me see the missing pages and I'll let you have the journal."

"And what's to say ya dinn't make a copy? Ya expec' me to give you evidence people 'ave been lookin' fer since it 'appened? Are ya daft?"

"That's the deal. I promise, no copies will be made."

He looked away, checking out everyone in the room before answering. "Mebbe. Lemme see it first, to make sure it's worth it." Declan held out a hand, waiting.

I was suddenly thankful that I left it in Anne's car. "I don't have it with me."

"You lyin' gobshite. Don' try to pull one over on me. I know you. I know you'd never leave it too far behin'." He was watching for my reaction, but I was getting better at not giving anything away. He tried again. "C'mon, ya eejit—who do you think made sure it got to you in the first place?"

I knew it had to be true. Who else could have sent it? But why would he send a document that incriminated him?

"Your uncle was dead," Declan said. "It was the last thing he asked of me an' I owed him a life or two. I still broke my promise to 'im, rippin' out those pages, but I did what I could do for him."

"What's it say in those pages?"

Declan hesitated, the way some do when they're about to depart from the truth. "Learn from yer uncle's mistakes, will ya? Mickaleen was never right in the head after he shot that poor soul back in the States, and he only got worse after he almost drowned in Lough Ree, so don't go lookin' around where that book points ya, boyo."

I didn't believe him but decided it might be better not to challenge him directly. "Fine. Then just tell me what happened to Kate."

"Jaysus. Ya never learn at all, do ya? You're still hung up on that? You're a hopeless case, you know that, Mickaleen?"

"What'd you call me?"

That stopped him. For the first time he looked uncomfortable. "Ahh, right. My apologies. You reminded me of your uncle just then." He looked away and put down his glass, still half full, raising a finger to the waitress as if for a check. Then he looked back at me, a far-off look of grief in his eyes. "I can't really tell ya much ya don' know, boyo. But what I can tell ya is this: I dunno where Kate went. Not after. You'll have to figure that out on yer own. If ya look in the newspapers, it'll tell you she died, but both you and I know a woman like that, she's doesn't go that easy. I believe she's still out there somewhere." He rose, handing the waitress a few bills as he passed her.

Then Declan walked away, leaving me without a word. Halfway across the bar he stopped and spoke loudly enough for everyone to hear as he looked back. "If she comes back, she'll show up at the old schoolhouse on Inchmore. I've heard rumors that she haunts the place even now. If ya find her ... If ya find her, tell her I've missed her somethin' terrible. An' that I'm sorry, fer all of it."

Then Declan was gone, leaving me lost in Dublin. I drank my warm Guinness out of spite for the waitress and tried to figure out how to hook up with Anne again. I was thinking of ordering another cold pint from the waitress just to get a reaction when the problem solved itself.

"So I hear ya need to get to the island. If ya buy me a couple, I'll get ya there," Anne said as she pulled out a chair and sat down.

"If I buy you a couple we'll never get there alive," I told her, absolutely serious.

"Tha's shite. I'm a pro driver and even better when I'm relaxed. An' ya should see me in a boat. Rent me one an' I'll show ya." Without waiting for a response, she yelled across the pub. "Bridget—get us a couple, will ya?"

The waitress looked up and nodded, pulling a draft. "You know her, too?"

"Went to school with her eejit brother. She's a bit of a tart, but we had some good craic together before that whole trouble I caused with her brother. She blamed me, dinn't she?"

"What happened?"

"Ach, nothin' worth talkin' about. A coupla honest pints and too many sheep in the road. He'll be out of prison in less than a year, so I don' know what 'er problem is. If she . . ." Anne stopped talking abruptly as Bridget approached with two pints. She slammed them down and spun on her heel to leave.

Anne watched her go, then winced as she touched her glass. "Damn. The bitch gave me a cold one." She reached out for my warm pint and switched glasses with me. "Like I said, a bit of a tart, an' stupid, too. She gives us both what we want an' don' even know it." Anne tossed back the warm Guinness with a wicked grin.

Twenty-five minutes and three pints later we were stumbling toward the car park, arguing over the merits of warm and cold beverages. A half hour after that we were on the road, with horns blaring all around us. Five minutes after that I was asleep or possibly passed out. I never thought I'd be able to rest with Anne driving, but between the Guinness and the stress, my mind called it quits.

I woke up suddenly after a good bit of time, feeling the world spin. I thought it was the alcohol until Anne corrected the spin and pulled the car back on the road. As soon as we were running straight again, she turned to me, pissed off.

"A lotta good you are. I told ya to warn me about the sheep shite, dinn't I? Get yer lazy arse up an' help keep me sharp, will ya," she ordered.

I sat up, double-checking my seat belt, and noticed something strange. Maybe it was because she was being careful, or maybe I was drunker than I thought, but Anne was an excellent driver when she'd been drinking. She drove at a safe speed, slowed for all the curves, and even signaled when she was about to turn. It took us twice as long to get back to Portlick as it had taken us to drive to Dublin, but I didn't mind.

AT THE BOAT launch, Anne got out and opened the trunk of the car as I looked out over the lake, trying to pick out which low-lying piece of land was Inchmore. By the time I turned around, she'd managed to shed her clothes and pull on some faded jeans that looked like they might have once belonged to her big brother and an old T-shirt that clung nicely in all the right places.

Anne slammed the trunk and smiled at me. "Ya missed the free show I put on for ya. Pay more attention next time and get yer skinny arse movin'. I'll show you the island."

Before I could respond, Anne was already walking away, moving toward Lough Ree and a clear spot between the reeds that seemed deep enough for the draft of the few small boats that were tied there, gently bobbing off the mud and rocks at the shore. She stepped into the closest one and moved right to the outboard. She pulled the cord and started the engine with one pull, looking back at me impatiently. I wondered what the sentence was for stealing a boat, or even what the charge would be. Piracy? Anne revved the engine and gave me no choice. I had one foot in when she started moving, and rather than fall backward into the mud I pitched myself forward, tumbling into the boat and almost into her lap.

Five minutes later Anne cut the outboard and let us drift toward the shallows as she pulled off her shoes and socks, rolling up her jeans to midcalf. She seemed to have it timed, because she finished rolling both legs as the boat scraped the mud and silt. Before it stopped, she stepped out into the mud, grabbed the tie rope and kept us moving, dragging us ashore. She was efficient and in control, and I think it was in this moment that I noticed she was beautiful. Whether it was the alcohol or the late afternoon sun that torched her pale cheeks, she looked magnificent, her eyes blazing and alive.

I noticed that somewhere along the line, she'd gotten streaks of dirt on her face that highlighted the faded freckles that were part of her beauty. She glanced back for a moment and I looked away from her face, aware that I was staring. My eyes dropped, and I noticed that Anne had splashed water all over herself, dragging us to shore. Her T-shirt was clinging to her and her jeans had become form fitting.

The thought went through my head that she was my cousin. I needed to remember that. Because if lust was one of the seven deadly sins, then lust for a relative was surely an express train to hell. If only she weren't my cousin.

I was jerked back to reality as Anne yanked the rope, forcing me to look up and catch her eye.

"I'm not really yer cousin. Ya know that much, don' ya? I tol' ya that the firs' time we met. I'm not related to ya by blood. Jus' by marriage through Kate. At least that's what they told me."

"Wha . . . What are you talking about?" I stammered, afraid that she could somehow tell what I was thinking. Maybe *she* had the "twitch of the witch." The "knowing."

She wasn't smiling anymore as she held my eye, and I noticed how blue hers were. She squinted slightly, dimming their brilliance. "I wanted it to be clear, so ya dinn't feel so bad about what ya were thinking. I mean its kind of flatt'rin' that you can't take your eyes off my ass, but if I were really yer cousin it'd be a bit obscene."

I tried to deny it anyway. "I wasn't looking at your ass."

"No? Really? Then yer walleyed, are ya? Yer eyes don' point to what yer lookin' at?" She challenged me, and I looked away, feeling my face grow warm.

"Don't be such a git. I don't mind ya lookin'. It's when men stop lookin' that I'll be upset. It's kinda nice, actually. An' it's even nicer to see a man who still knows how to blush. Now come on. I want to get back to the mainland before dark." Anne finished dragging the boat up and held out a hand to help me up, but I was too embarrassed to take it.

"Fine. Have it your way," she said, turning toward a well-worn path through the woods. I watched her until the woods swallowed her in shadow. Then it hit me that if she got too far ahead I might not find her, so I scrambled to my feet and followed her.

The path ran parallel to a small stream lined with brambles that tore at my shins and legs. The density of the trees and undergrowth suddenly made me feel colder and isolated. Within fifteen feet of entering the woods, the lough receded as if it never existed. Even the sound of the water gently lapping at the shore disappeared, hidden beneath the whispers of rustling leaves. I hadn't gone too far when I saw a brilliant patch of sunlight suddenly piercing the canopy of leaves, shining on an open expanse of ferns and weeds that led to what at first appeared to be a free-standing gray wall, because the rest of the building and roof had been overgrown by trees and vines. The old window in the center of the wall still had glass intact, so I knew it had to be a newer building—probably the schoolhouse that had been built for the island residents back in 1927.

I didn't see Anne anywhere around, and I had no idea if anyone lived on the island and would shoot me for trespassing, so I moved slowly toward the building. I knew that when my uncle showed up here, the island was used to store guns and explosives for the Provos. Since there were still people blowing each other up in the north when I arrived, I had no reason to think it didn't now. It bothered me that I couldn't hear Anne up ahead. The island felt too quiet. I grew up in the greater New York metropolitan area, and there silence is not to be trusted.

I knew that Anne had to be somewhere close by, but I was afraid to yell for her. Finally I came around the corner of the schoolhouse to find a gaping black hole where a door once stood. The shadows were too deep to see anything inside, but I thought I heard something move. I leaned in slightly, shielding my eyes, trying to see.

"Anne?" I whispered. There was no response. I leaned in farther and as I did, something warm clamped down on the back of my neck, pulling me down. I opened my mouth to scream, but my breath was taken away when Anne's lips met mine.

Before I could consciously respond, I was kissing her back. Her lips were much softer and fuller than I would have expected, and her breath was sweetly sour with the taste of stale beer and smoke. I could feel the warmth of her skin through her thin T-shirt, as well as the cool spots where her skin was still wet from the water. I remember thinking that I wasn't responsible because I'd arrived less than forty-eight hours before and my soul probably hadn't caught up to my body yet. I could let Anne's hands do what they were doing and not be guilty of anything. Our clothes came off, and I felt the chill air before our skin touched—and then it did.

Somewhere in the middle of it all I felt that I saw Anne as she really was, behind all the bluster and defensiveness and the alcohol and obsessive smoking. Afterward, she was lying on my chest, her body a blanket on mine, keeping me warm. I was stroking her hair and her back, holding her, not wanting to let go. I wasn't even sure she was awake, her breathing was so deep and even. And I felt so comfortable with her in that moment, that I wanted to tell her I loved her.

But even in that moment—even as I thought about telling her how deeply I cared for her—some part of me knew it wouldn't last. It wasn't that I regretted what had happened, and I knew that I could probably spend years getting to know her, loving every moment. She was beautiful on every level, and I knew she would always challenge me. But it would never be complete. It would never feel as if I couldn't breathe without her next to me. It would always feel like she were standing in for someone else. Who that was, I didn't know yet, but I knew she was still out there somewhere, even in those first few moments with Anne. It was romantic and self-serving, and in another context I would have written it off as a fear of commitment, but I wasn't afraid. I just knew, somehow, that I'd never be completely satisfied. I wouldn't know exactly why for a while yet.

Anne stirred in my arms, and I was about to open my mouth and tell her how much I cared for her, when she sat up and saved me from myself.

"Don' say it, okay? Don' ruin the feckin' moment."

"Don't say what?" I asked, wondering if she could somehow read my mind.

Anne still hadn't moved, but now her hand started to run up and down my stomach. "Don' say anyting ya don' mean. I know I'm not her."

"Her who?"

"I'm not yer *sonuachar*, am I?" she whispered.

"I've heard that word before. What does it mean?"

Anne stopped moving her hand and I felt her body stiffen. Suddenly, she was disconnected from me. Farther away. She sighed heavily, then answered, her voice flat: "Your *sonuachar*. The one. She's the one you'll look fer yer whole life if that's what it takes, inn't she?" She pushed off of me then, and stood over me. She paused there, flaunting her body, then turned away.

"How do you know that you're not 'the one'? We hardly know each other, do we?" I asked, even though I knew she was right and that my question was nothing more than a stalling tactic. Maybe that's why the Irish answer questions with questions—it keeps hope alive.

Anne wasn't buying it. "Oh, yeah. We both know the truth now, don' we? I'm not sayin' we ain' good together, but it's not written in the stars, is it?" Anne was looking at my eyes, which I realized as I glanced upward from exploring the rest of her. She smiled sadly as she caught me. "Lookit, no offense, but I knew the minute I saw ya that you'd be a nice ride but nothin' fer the long haul."

I felt used. My vanity was offended. "So this was just for fun?"

"No. Not *just* fer fun. But it was fun, wann't it?" She blew smoke at me and stretched out, lying on top of me once again, holding the cigarette out to the side as if ready to use it on me if I dared to disagree.

"I thought you were Catholic? Don't you believe that sex is sacred? All that?"

"Ah, Jaysus feckin' Christ. Don' you pull that shite on me, Sean. I don' believe in organized religion. It's all a con game to make a few people rich. I deal direc'ly with God and only God, like all the ol' religions did. An' them religions recognized women, too. The Catholic church thinks it's all about the men jus' because their priests are a bunch of self-gratifying wankers. Misogynists, the lot of 'em. "

"You're not serious."

"The 'ell I'm not. Who gives them the right to stand between me an' the

Almighty?" She stared at me and shook her head, disgusted. "Look, you gobshite, it felt good, dinn't it? An' we care about each other, righ'?"

"Well . . ." I began, desperately trying not to put my foot in my mouth, anxious to tell her what she wanted to hear.

"Ya better say yeah, or your bollocks'll be wrapped aroun' yer scrawny neck." She put her hand on my "bollocks" as she said it. Her hands were cold and I shriveled as she touched me.

"Yeah. We do."

"Good answer. An' by doin' it, we got a little bit closer. We trust each other a bit more, don' we?"

"Absolutely." It seemed to be the expedient thing to say.

"Then tha's all it needs to be, okay?"

"Sure, but . . ." I started, too stupid to stop myself.

"But you're wonderin' what 'appens next?" Anne asked, seeing my confused look. "Whatever 'appens, 'appens. Don' make it more complicated than it needs to be."

"But it is complicated, isn't it?" I couldn't let it go. It was definitely complicated.

"Sex is only complicated because we make it that way. If two people agree on what it is, then it's simple. It could be jus' physical, which is nice. Real nice." Anne sat in my lap as she talked, rocking her hips just a bit, demonstrating her point. "Or physical an' emotional, which inn't bad either. An' wit' the right boyo, there's a spiritual bit. Only happens every couple of lifetimes is my guess, but that's the real deal. Ya jus' need to agree on where ya stand an' enjoy it fer what it is."

"And which kind is this?" I asked.

"Two outta three inn't bad, is it?"

"But what about . . ." I couldn't finish. The image of Anne naked with a swollen belly had entered my mind and wouldn't leave. She read my look.

"What? Pregnancy? Kids? Now you ask, ya shite?" Anne punched me. "We're protected. No worries."

"Completely protected?"

Anne stopped rocking her hips. "The way I look at it, nothin's a hunnerd percent. If ya mess around and get pregnant, even if yer jus' friends and all, you have a commitment to tha' child. Ya make it work somehow." Anne was serious. I could tell because she wasn't looking at me. She wasn't trying to intimidate me. She was just telling it as she saw it. "If you bring a soul inta this worl' and you don' take responsibility for it, you're an amadan. Tha's why ya don't take a tumble unless you really got some strong feelings fer a fella, inn't it?"

"You have strong feelings fer me?" I asked, trying to lighten the mood, and she looked down at me, a smile on her lips.

"Don' go fishin' fer compliments, boyo. If modern medicine failed us, I'd be willin' to put up wit ya to raise a wee one or we wouldn't be lyin' here. That's all I'm sayin'."

"I'll take that as a compliment."

"As ya should."

"So, if you like me so much, what makes you think you couldn't love me?" I baited her.

Anne rolled her eyes. "Can't ya just shut up and let me enjoy this while it lasts? And, anyway, s'not me that's the problem, is it? You'd leave me in a heartbeat if..." Anne's voice trailed off, effectively protecting a secret she'd almost given away.

"If what?"

"Let's jus' say I see the path yer on, and I know where it ends."

"What's that mean?"

She shrugged, struggling to explain it. "Sometimes life gives ya what ya need, an' not what ya want. Maybe I'm what ya need right now. An' maybe I'm okay with that, even though what ya really want will show up someday, an' you'll ferget what ya ever needed me for."

"I wouldn't use you like that."

"So ya say. But if what you really want shows up, it'll change the rules. No offense taken. It's the way it's always been." Anne sat up so that we were facing one another. She wasn't self-conscious at all, so comfortable in her own body that she didn't seem naked.

I was about to protest that I wasn't so fickle, but she was staring at me now. Not feeling that comfortable with my own body, I tried to cover myself with the T-shirt that was lying on the floor next to me, embarrassed by the pattern of birthmarks that riddled my chest. The color of dried blood, they were ragged and misshapen and looked like what one junior high classmate called "a shotgun blast of ugly."

"That looks like it hurt," Anne commented as she reached out a hand to touch the largest one—the one over my heart. It was about an inch in diameter and raised and rough, like a scar.

"They don't hurt. They're just birthmarks."

Anne nodded like I didn't know what I was talking about, then pulled her hand away, kissed me quickly, and stood up.

"Now that we've got that out of the way, we might as well do what we came for."

She'd lost me again. I must have had a puzzled look on my face, because she laughed, pulling me to my feet.

"Not *that* ya feckin' eejit. I'm talking about you rememberin' what ya came fer. Rememberin' what happened here. If ya could take yer eyes off my lil' diddies fer a minute, ya might notice that scrawl on the wall behind me." I took my eyes off her breasts and looked behind her.

On the wall was something written in dark reddish brown, like it had been drawn on with a finger. I moved past Anne, remembering what my uncle Mike had written about this place and what happened here. As I knelt down, trying to read it in the shadows, Anne crouched beside me and rested her hand on the small of my back. It was too dark to read, but she spoke the words aloud from memory.

"T. W. is dead, and I remember it all. I remember Liam and Sean and how I almost died. I know that I am Patsy Ryan, and that I am not," Anne whispered solemnly as she reached out to touch the words on the wall.

"T. W.? Is that Trooper Wheeler?" My heart was beating faster, and suddenly the journal I had read was coming to life. It was real.

"Sure enough," Anne said quietly, letting it sink in.

"Why did he stop writing there? He's not *what*? What's it mean?" I turned to face Anne, but her face was impassive.

"Exactly what it says. Come on, I'll show you. It's just as yer uncle described it." She stood, walking out into the sun, her skin shining like white marble in the light.

I followed her out and was blinded by the light for a moment. The soft breeze gave me chills as the hot sun dried my body, leaving my skin taut as the sweat evaporated. It felt good but reminded me that I had perfectly good clothes on the floor of the schoolhouse and that anyone could show up here and find us like this. I was about to turn around but felt stupid letting Anne walk around naked if I was too self-conscious to do the same, so I went to look for her.

I found her leaning against the old stone wall of what was once a small cottage. The wall had started to crumble into the underbrush, with a fallen tree collapsed onto it, now perched right above her head. She was hanging on the trunk and had a sly smirk.

"Yer lookin' in the wrong direction again, boyo," she called out. "Or didja not read that far in yer uncle's journal? 'We buried Trooper Wheeler next to the cottage twenty yards from the school, planting him under the shade of an old tree with our makeshift shovels.'"

I looked down, between her legs, at the exposed roots of the tree that had been torn from the earth when it fell. They had pushed up over time, and between them were what looked like smooth white stones jutting up, with dark spots and dirt clinging to them. As I took them in, I realized there was a pattern to them. They weren't individual stones, they were part of a whole, half hidden by the earth and entombed by the roots. Most were long and thin, but the one closest to Anne, right up against the stone wall, was larger and rounded.

Then I saw the splintered hole where the bullet had exited. This wasn't a stone. It was the skull of a murdered man, a man my uncle had seen killed.

Michael

JANUARY 23, 1972

The sun was still well below the horizon and the moon had disappeared behind a sky full of dark clouds, isolating us on the lake. I couldn't see much beyond Kate at the other end of the curragh and had lost sight of Inchmore. The night was cold but windless, thankfully, and the water was like black glass. The slight rippling sound of the water against the boat hull and the gentle splashing of the oars were so rhythmic they almost lulled me to sleep. The only thing that assured me this wasn't a dream were the blisters forming on my hands.

I kept track of time by watching Kate, trying to read her expression, but it was so dark that she was hard to decipher. It seemed like the island must have sunk into the lake, or we would have reached it by now. Kate didn't seem worried, so I kept rowing, noticing that the night had grown darker in front of us. Then I looked up to see the ominous silhouette of trees and scrub brush right ahead.

It was Inchmore, rising from the waters like some shroud of darkness that was about to envelop us. Although the island looked forbidding and cold, it somehow didn't feel that way. Maybe the trees and brush were blocking the wind, making it feel warmer, or maybe I was just relieved to be able to stop rowing. Whatever it was, it seemed as if Inchmore welcomed us, the gentle slope of its shore beckoning, the leaves of its trees sighing like a soft breath. The island seemed to be alive, an entity of its own.

"To the left, by that line of rocks." Kate spoke for the first time since I'd noticed the island. I pulled hard with the opposite oar, trying to aim the boat, then let it drift straight in.

"No. Row hard through the shallows. Beach us. The water's too cold to wade in this time of year," she instructed, crouching in the front. I rowed hard, straight in. We hit bottom five feet before the shore but managed to glide over the muddy shallows to within a foot of dry land. Kate jumped out just as the curragh came to a stop, a rope in her hand, dragging us up farther on shore.

I tried to stand as she tied off the boat, but I stumbled, catching myself on the edge of the boat. When I looked up, Kate had her hand out to me with a grin on her face.

"Welcome home, Mr. Corrigan," she said as she mock curtsied, with a laugh in her voice. "Do ya like what we've done with the place?"

"I can't see any of it."

"Perfect. Then ya won' notice that the homes are fallin' down and everthin's overgrown. But it's yours. Jus' walk up the track and all aroun' with me. Make yer right of passage complete." And she took my hand, pulling me out of the curragh, holding it as I stepped out—longer than she needed to.

"Stay close to me and keep quiet. I don' think there's any Provos standin' watch, but ya never know. Jus' grab the knapsack and blankets, will ya?" I took my hand away to grab our gear from the boat, but when I turned back, she took it again, pulling me toward the darkness of the woods.

"I know where I'm goin'. I could do it in my sleep. Trust me," Kate whispered, wrapping her forearm around mine, intertwining her fingers with mine. I could feel her warm, sweet breath on my cheek, the heat from her body right next to mine, but I couldn't see a path. In fact, I could hardly see anything. It was a dark winter night on an island where the Provos had arms stored and might have someone standing guard. I knew I shouldn't be there, but I also knew that I'd follow Kate anywhere.

It was an unusual feeling for me. I don't normally trust people. I grew up in a family that kept secrets, with a father who only let them slip when his mind started to go. All my instincts, as well as my training as a cop, were telling me to get out of there, and yet I knew I wouldn't. Where would I run to? Where else would I want to be?

I was following her blindly, and we'd gone a dozen yards, when I heard the sound of heavy breathing, and footsteps—heavy footsteps, at least four sets. I stopped hard and pulled Kate back and down, finding refuge behind a tree. She let out a startled yelp and then she laughed. I tried to quiet her, but she just reached out a hand toward something moving in the darkness.

" 'Ello, boyo. Good to see ya agin. It's been a while, ain' it," she said soothingly as the the clouds parted for a brief moment and I was able to see one of
the horses of Inchmore—the roan stallion—nuzzling his head into Kate's
shoulder. Kate turned to me, still stroking his neck.

"Don' ya recognize 'im?" she asked, but I just shook my head. Kate
shrugged, kissing the horse on its broad cheek. "Well, you two belong together. 'E's a Corrigan as much as you are. Yer da and Sean used to ride his
gran'sire."

One more thing my father never told me. One more bit of family history
forgotten until it showed up in the darkness to surprise me. I put my hand
out to the stallion and he came to me, nuzzling his head under my arm,
forcing me to pet him. "What's his name?"

"Dunno. His owners left without givin' 'im one," she said, accusing the
whole Corrigan clan with her tone.

"And what am I supposed to do with him?"

"Well, give 'im a name fer starters, but make sure it's not some American
shite like 'Silver' or 'Trigger.' 'E deserves a proper name."

"You mean an Irish name?"

"He is an Irish horse, inn't he?"

The stallion snorted in my face and made a throaty noise that sounded
like something mumbled under its breath. Very Irish.

"Ciaran," I said, not really knowing where the name came from. It just
sounded Irish and was better than what popped into my head first, *Focáil
leat.* That was something my father would say to my mother when he was
piss drunk and she was nagging. It usually earned him a couple of days on
the couch. I said it once as a kid to a priest and got thirty Our Fathers and
twenty-five Hail Marys as penance.

"Now where'd ya get tha' name?" Kate asked, looking at me strangely.

"It just came to me." I shrugged.

She stared a moment longer, then looked away, staring at the stallion.
"That was this one's gran'sire's name. Spot on fer 'im, too, as 'e's a dark roan,
inn't he?"

She reached out and stroked the stallion again, then nodded off toward
the small clearing that had become visible as the moon emerged, a sliver

peeking out from the clouds. "What about the others? Ya got any Irish left in there fer them, seein' how ya claim ya don' know any?"

I looked up to where she nodded and saw the chestnut mare and the dappled colt, hanging back, watching us warily, standing so still I hadn't yet noticed them.

"I don't," I answered honestly.

"Ah, shut yer gob an' give 'em names. I don' wanna hear it."

Kate was staring at me, waiting. I got the impression she'd stare all night, and that I'd either give them some kind of names or be here when the sun came up.

"Roisin," I blurted, the pet name my father used for my mother when he was trying to earn his way back off the couch.

"Ahh, yeah. Rose fer the chestnut mare. Perfect. And our dappled colt here?"

"Aislinn," I said, the name coming out even before I thought about it. Kate was staring at me with an odd grin on her face. She seemed unsure of whether I was making fun of her.

"Yer da told ya, dinn't he?"

"Told me what?"

"The names of the horses that passed. The ones he had as a chil'." She nodded to each horse in turn, naming them, "Ciaran, Roisin, an' Aislinn."

I didn't remember ever hearing him talk about horses. As far as I knew he'd never ridden one, never owned one, and didn't like them much. "I don't know. Maybe. They're just names I've heard."

"Well, they're not very original, but I guess they'll do." Kate started walking past Ciaran and he followed her as she greeted Roisin and Aislinn, stroking each of them between the eyes in turn.

"Anyway, Aislinn's a perfect dream, inn't she? On a bright summer's day you'd think she was a vision with that dappled coat, moving in and out of the shadows." The sky darkened again as the moon slipped behind the clouds, but my eyes seemed to adjust better this time.

"Follow me. It feels like it's gettin' colder. We should get inside. We can finish yer right of passage when the sun comes up." Kate turned away, walking across a small clearing to a stand of trees, which, as we got closer, I saw was actually a building with trees and vines growing over and around it. I stopped, looking at it for a moment. It seemed a bit out of place, too new to be here. When I looked up for Kate again, she was gone, but I heard the horses moving around the side of the building, so I followed.

The horses were gathered around an open doorway but parted for me to enter. Inside, Kate was already lighting a match to start a fire in the hearth on the far side of a twenty-by-twenty-foot room with a few boxy windows and a doorway. The warm smell of peat began to drift out as she spoke to me without looking up.

"This was the schoolhouse, built after Sean an' Ol' Jim left. The newest building on the island. It was pretty much abandoned when the last of the Corrigans—yer aunt Mary's son, Cathal, I think it was—decided to go off to Australia and took his seven children with 'im." She turned to look up at me, the soft yellow-orange light of the small fire gleaming in her eyes. "It'll catch soon, but in the meantime get over here with those blankets and keep me warm, will ya?"

I did as Kate asked, unfolding the blankets and spreading them over her. I sat down next to her, unfolding my own blanket, but before I could finish, she'd grabbed me by a belt loop and pulled me closer, so that we were hip to hip and shoulder to shoulder.

I guess I must've looked startled, because she shrugged, put her arm around me, and said, a bit defensively, "I'm sorry if I'm not your idea of an 'Irish lass,' but I'm a bit too old to play coy now, ain' I? I've been married, I've seen a bit of what the world has to offer, an' I'm not about to sit back an' wait fer you to make up yer mind to keep me properly warm. It's too cold fer that."

I nodded, unsure of what else to do. She wasn't. She took my arm and draped it over her shoulder. We sat in silence for a few minutes, watching the flames grow higher, feeling the heat on our faces.

It should have been uncomfortable, but it wasn't. After a moment, it felt perfectly natural, like we'd been sitting here forever, comfortable enough with each other that we didn't need to talk. Still, after a few moments, my curiosity got the better of me.

"Where's your husband now?" I asked tentatively. I knew it might be a touchy subject, but it was a question I had to have an answer to. Kate didn't respond for a moment, and I thought she might not answer at all until she looked down, her eyes focused on something far away.

"Passed on. To the next life, I guess." She said it flatly, without much emotion, and I tried not to be happy with the answer.

"I'm sorry."

"No. Ya shouldn't be sorry. The bloody shites that helped him pass on are the ones tha' should be sorry." Kate was speaking softly, so softly I could barely hear her. I found myself leaning even closer, and felt her respond, pressing up against my side.

"He was murdered?"

"Aye." She nodded, then looked up and caught my eye. Her eyes were moist, sparkling and alive in the firelight. Then she looked away again, creating distance with her words.

"Sam was from the north, Derry. I was seventeen when we met in Dublin. Declan made the introductions. Back then it seemed like Dec knew everybody. He was the big man, a real politician, kissin' the wee ones." Kate fell silent, deciding whether or not she should go on. When she did, her voice was lower, almost a whisper.

"Sam was brilliant. Sweet. He paid attention to the details, ya know? Even two years after we met, he could tell ya what I was wearing, what I ate, and what I drank that first night. He was that kind. It wasn't the first time I was ever in love, though."

Kate looked up at me again, and under the blankets I felt her hand on mine. The silence lasted a long moment and I finally spoke again, afraid to lose this intimacy.

"What happened to him?"

Kate shrugged. "He asked me to run away with 'im. I didn't go because I was an amadan who believed lies I knew weren't true. So I stayed where I was, and a lifetime later Sam came along."

"Sam? Wait . . ." I started, suddenly confused. Who'd asked her to run away?

"Ahh, sorry. I thought ya was askin' about my first love." She gripped my hand tighter, squeezing. "I'm sorry, really. Ya wanna know about me an'

Sam. But there's not much ta tell. I went up there to live with him, in the Bogside." Kate stopped, seeing the lingering confusion on my face.

"Ya never heard of the Bogside? Not the Battle of the Bogside?" I shrugged, unaware. "Jaysus, ya Yanks are an ignorant bunch, ain' ya?"

"Maybe, but could you tell me about the States? About what's going on there right now?" I was indignant. Why do other people always pick on us Americans?

"Where'd ya like me to start? With the war protests, the Black Liberation Army, Nixon takin' yas off the gold standard? Or maybe with the Pirates winnin' the World Series?" I got the point. Thankfully, she didn't seem to hold my ignorance against me and settled back into my shoulder and her story.

"Anyway, the Bogside's just outside the city walls a Derry. Me an' Sam, we'd been up there awhile, tryin' to find our own place to live, but the Orange lads had the housing rigged so we couldn't get anything."

"Wait, what's that mean, 'had the housing rigged'?"

"It's like 'Negroes Need Not Apply' in the States. The Protestants are in charge an' they can get away with it. So they do. They've got all the Catholics kept in one place so that even though we can cast more votes, they get more MPs out of the whole thing. Ya know how it works. I know ya do. I've seen how ya do the same thing to the blacks in America."

"It's not the same."

"Oh no? Ya think stealin' votes and denyin' a person civil rights is about color? They keep all the jobs fer themselves, and they're the only ones allowed on the police so there's no chance we get sympathy there. They segregate us into ghettos. Does that sound familiar to ya? Or maybe ya can't sympathize because yer not black and you've never been a Catholic in Northern Ireland, is that it?"

"I'm just saying it's more complicated in the States. A lot of those civil rights groups have turned to violence and use criminals to intimidate people. They want a revolution."

"An' I don' blame 'em. Do ya think our IRA boys over here are saints? The lot of 'em are mostly criminals. But why are they criminals? Because they can't get good jobs. Because they're hopeless. Because they've got no education. It's the same." I could feel her intensity where she leaned against me. Her muscles were taut, her frustration palpable. I knew if I said one wrong thing, she'd probably bolt and leave me alone on the island. So I said nothing.

I stared at the fire and could feel her eyes on me until she finally looked away again. Then I felt her sink back toward me and heard her take a deep breath. The anger had passed.

"We had no place to live an' they wouldn't hire any of us if they could avoid it." She started into her story again, even more quietly, as if she were gauging my reaction before continuing. "But Sam's whole clan is from Derry, goin' way back. An' at the time his ma was ill, and his sister's husband, Christy, was in Long Kesh 'cause he made the mistake of openin' 'is big mouth to a scrawny RUC shite that was piss drunk on 'is day off."

"RUC?"

"Yeah. The Royal Ulster Constabulary. The police. And they're the same here as in the States. Shoot first an' ask questions later."

I almost interrupted to defend myself, forgetting for a moment that I was supposed to be Aidan, not Michael, but I held my tongue.

"The RUC shite got sober an' had his mates beat the shite outta Christy, then charged him for fightin'. I wanted to come home then, but Sam thought he could change things an' didna want to run away. He started a housing committee with his friends Jim and Eamonn."

"Was that some sort of Republican group?"

"Them? Nah. You'll be happy to know they were nonviolent. My Sam, he was a history buff. Brilliant with that stuff, he was. He studied Michael Collins and Gandhi and even your Malcolm X and Martin Luther King. He was all for peaceful protest—if you can call it peaceful when ya bust into a council meetin' to force the bastards to give houses to Catholic families. But it was just intimidation, not real violence." I was focused on her every word, afraid to move, to break the intimacy of the moment.

Kate snuggled in closer. "Sam organized some peaceful marches through Derry even though the Orangemen in power kept banning them. Him an' his boys defied the ban a course. John Casey even went and painted a sign down on Columbs Street that read 'You are now entering Free Derry,' just to piss them off."

"I think I heard about that."

"Yeah, it was big news, but Sam wanted none of the violence that followed. He was done with violence . . . The night they came for 'im I heard a loud, sharp knock on the door an' then a shout, cut off in the middle by a loud crack . . ." Kate's whole weight fell against me, and she drew in a sharp breath, trying to finish.

"It was Sam's skull that cracked, hit by an RUC baton as soon as he opened the door. Before I could get to him, they were already on me . . ." Kate's voiced trailed off again as she unconsciously touched her jaw line. I could see the hairline scar there where the skin had ripped open, now healed. "Anyway, Sam lasted long enough to see the Derry Citizens' Defence set up an' the Apprentice Boys march on Derry. It turned into a battle that year, with stones an' Molotov cocktails flyin'. Fer the next three days, the city burned. Even the RUC uniforms caught on fire like walkin' torches. Then came the tear gas and the B-Specials—an' finally the Prince of Wales's own regiment. Fifteen hundred Catholics were burned out in one night in Belfast. All of Bombay Street was turned to ashes. Sam died that night an' I left three days later. I left the Bogside an' Derry, I left the Troubles, an' I left Sam in his grave."

Kate sighed, melting into me further, but I was completely confused. What were we doing here? Why was she telling me all this? Why were we here together, keeping each other warm in the middle of the night, talking about her dead husband? Was I supposed to understand? Was I just too dense to read the signals?

"I loved Sam, you should know that. But truth be told, it was never the fairy tale, an' he was never the *sonuachar* I dreamed of." She spoke softly, her eyes never wavering. "He was a good man. He was always there fer me . . . until he was gone." When she stopped, she didn't look away. Now I was sure I was missing the point.

"*Sonuachar?*"

Kate grinned, a sad, lopsided grin. "The one ya see an' jus' know that you've always known 'im. It doesn't always happen, but when it does . . . Ah, when it does. Remember I said I'd been in love before?" I nodded, not sure what she was getting at.

"Right on this very island. He was my *sonuachar* an' I let 'im go. Ya know, when I was younger I'd sneak out here sometimes at night, making a fire like this, dreamin' of the day he'd come back." Kate looked up at me, then away, quickly. Suddenly she pulled away, and I thought somehow I'd missed a cue, but she just stoked the fire, causing the flames to leap up again. Then she moved back, sitting in front of me, reaching back to grab both my hands, pulling my arms around her to embrace her. After a moment she leaned her head back into my chest, twisting around to look up at me.

"After a while, I started to think it might take a lifetime or two to find 'im again. I met Sam and settled fer a good man. But I guess yer fate always finds ya, though, donn't it? Me an' Sam weren't meant to last."

"That's not your fault."

"No, but somehow I always knew I'd end up back here, crossing Lough Ree on a moonless night to get to Inchmore an' this ol' schoolhouse, freezin' my arse off tryin' to keep warm, up against a coldhearted man that I was hopin' could be somethin' more." She was smiling, and suddenly I was getting the message.

"Coldhearted?" I protested weakly.

"An' what would you call it? Ya 'aven't even tried to kiss me yet and I've been throwin' myself at ya all night."

"But you were talking about your husband."

"Who's been dead three *long* years. I've waited long enough. A lifetime."

And then her hand was on the back of my neck, pulling me down to kiss her.

I WOKE UP to the sounds of the horses, snorting and stomping down by the shore of the lough. It was still dark, and the peat fire was reduced to glowing embers that barely gave off heat or enough light to see by. I sat up when I realized I was alone and listened for Kate. I thought she might have gone outside, but I couldn't hear her.

And then I heard something else—the water, its rhythm broken by intermittent splashes. It was the sound of oars, a boat coming in. Somehow I knew instinctually what it was and jumped up. I had to find Kate. Whoever was coming out here before dawn on a frigid night had to be trouble and I didn't want her to confront them alone.

As I stepped outside I could see the moon had pierced the clouds again, and in its light I could see the whitewashed walls and thatched roofs of several small cottages through the trees, brilliantly white in the moonlight.

All four men were wearing similar clothes, khaki pants and some sort of dark jacket, belted at the waist with calf-length boots. I knew immediately that they were Black and Tans, with pistols on their belts and rifles slung across their backs.

Even as I dreamed it, I knew I was dreaming. I even turned back to the schoolhouse and it wasn't there. This dream came before the schoolhouse. I wasn't scared anymore, even though I was sweating with fear and my heart was beating wildly. I'd had this dream before, it seemed, because I knew how it ended, I knew what happened next.

I jumped when I heard the whisper at my side but wasn't surprised, not really.

"Run. Just run, Mickaleen." It was Jim, just woken up, his hair wild from tossing and turning all night. I turned to face him, saying what I knew I would.

"Come with me."

"No. They don't want me. Jus' you. Go. I'll play the eejit fer 'em. Trust me." Jim pushed me toward the other end of the island and the curragh we kept hidden there. Then he ran straight toward the four men, yelling loud enough to wake up everyone on the island.

"The *Tans*! It's the Tans!" I heard cursing from within the cottages as I fled, but as I reached the edge of the woods I turned and saw one of the Tans catch him, slamming him to the ground with the butt of his rifle and smashing it into his head. I couldn't watch. I couldn't stay in this dream, even though I knew he'd be all right. It was too much.

I woke up suddenly, with an image of my father's face in my mind, the welted red scar that ran across his hairline prominent. He'd always told me the scar was from an accident when he was a kid, when he and his brother were playing hide-and-seek. I guess that was true enough, in his own way.

I lay there for a moment, thinking of my father and how I never really knew him at all. The sounds of the horses, snorting and stomping down by the shore of the lough started to filter in, making me aware of the night and its cadences. It was still dark, just like in the dream, and the peat fire was just glowing embers.

Kate was gone, too. It made me nervous and sent a chill through me. If she was gone, there was something wrong. I listened for her outside, thinking maybe she went out for the horses, but I couldn't hear her.

And then I heard it, again, that same distinctive sound, that minute difference in the way the water broke against the shore. It was as if I had lived here my whole life, listening to the sounds of this island. I knew exactly what it was. A boat, landing in the shallows. I also knew that the horses were there, greeting the intruders, making enough noise to give us warning.

I hoped Kate had heard them before I did and fled, though I couldn't think of why she'd leave me behind. As I exited the schoolhouse, I could see my breath as a mist in front of me, coming in short bursts of nervous exhalations. I moved away from the path we had come up last night, on a parallel path, worn smooth and free of vegetation. I was thinking that maybe I could work my way around behind the intruders and get to the boat, but I was hesitant to leave without Kate.

As I made my way down the well-worn path, I felt like the island was closing in on me. Dead branches reached out and touched my shoulder, my face. Fallen leaves whispered loudly under my feet, calling out every move I made. I knew from my dream that I was headed toward the other cottages, even though that made no sense. How could I learn something from a dream? But as I worked my way around a fallen tree, I saw the rough stone wall of one cottage rise up before me. In its grooves and crevices whitewash still clung to the stone, but the rest of it was as faded and gray as the mist. I was about to go around it when I heard something moving.

I stopped. Off through the trees I could see the source of the sound, his red hair giving him away. It was Patsy, Kate's brother. I relaxed a little, sure that he'd come looking for her after finding her missing. Then, just as Patsy turned and looked right at me, I heard a whisper of grass moving behind me. I felt the man's presence before I even turned, registering the sound of a weapon being pulled.

"Mr. Corrigan. If you could please put your hands where I can see them and stop moving, it would be appreciated." I put my hands up slowly, glaring at Patsy for a moment before I started to turn.

When I did, I saw one of the old Ingram Model 11 submachine guns pointed at my chest. I gradually raised my eyes to the less important part of this tableau, the man holding it. He was slightly taller than I was, with hollow cheeks and watery blue eyes that accentuated his thinness. His soft eyes didn't fool me, though. I could tell at once that this was a hard man—cold, calculating, and trained to do exactly what he was doing. His hands were steady, gloved, with one gloved finger cut off. His trigger finger. He was too close to miss if he fired and too far away for me to try to reach him. He was also British, and even if his accent hadn't given him away, his choice of guns, and the fact that he even had one, would have. The garda didn't carry guns. This was going to be complicated.

Behind me, Patsy was charging through the underbrush, sounding like a wild boar. "Garda Ryan. If you will, restrain the suspect," the Brit told Patsy as he came out of the underbrush. I glanced back at Patsy and knew I needed to make a play for time—time to figure out what they knew and if I could talk my way out of this. Was this about the money I'd delivered to Declan? Or was this about James Butler? I wasn't sure which would be worse.

"Patsy, who the hell is this?" I asked, but Patsy hit me in the back of the head, interrupting.

"Shut yer gob. I ask the questions, don' I?" he asked, even though I think it was meant to be a statement of fact.

"Yeah. You *do*." I couldn't help myself.

"Well then, here's one fer ya that I already know the answer to—what's yer real name and why'd ya murder an innocent man?" Patsy was smug, and I was screwed. Even the Brit cracked a smile as he saw my reaction to that question, but it didn't last long. I saw it flee from his eyes a millisecond before I heard the loud click of a magazine shoved home. He started to move, then stopped in his tracks.

"I'll drop ya where ya stand an' ya know it."

It was Kate, inside the cottage we stood beside. Patsy and I turned to see her at the same time, her auburn hair wild, her eyes shining with a mad intensity, holding an Armalite AR-18, an automatic rifle I'd later discover was from the infamous cache that had been smuggled in from New York on the *QE2*.

God, I was learning to love her, even then.

"Move toward me, Mickaleen. Away from these two bastards." I followed her orders.

"Jaysus, Kate, what in the name a Christ do ya think yer doin'?" Patsy asked, indignant but wary enough of his sister not to move.

"Evenin' the odds. What the 'ell are *you* doin', ya amadan? Do ya know what ya jus' done?" Kate was surprisingly calm, never taking her eyes off the Brit, even as she spoke to Patsy.

"I am sorry, miss. There seems to be a slight misunderstanding. Maybe I could explain and we could all calm down a bit, all right?" The Brit was smiling a tight smile, his hand steady on his gun, alert, looking for an opening. Kate wasn't giving him one.

"Patsy, ya better tell yer friend to shut 'is hole and you better start explainin'. What the 'ell is goin' on? What are ya doin' with this wanker?" By this time I was closer to the door of the cottage, close enough to see the wooden crates full of rifles inside.

Patsy sighed heavily, clearly embarrassed that he had to explain himself to his sister in front of the Brit. "This is George Wheeler, Kate, a representative of the British government now, inn't he? They're cooperating with the Garda in an international manhunt. There's a murderer on the loose—"

Kate didn't let him finish. She just snapped the safety off the Armalite. "Ah, Jaysus. The worl' is comin' to an end, inn't it? We're helpin' *them* now? Yesterday ya was ready to blow 'em all up."

"She's not serious, are ya, Kate?" Patsy tried to cover up, looking at Wheeler even as he tried not to snarl at Kate.

"Drop the gun. Slow," Kate ordered, and Wheeler was smart enough to comply. "What are ya, Georgie boy? Security Service? MI5? An SAS trooper in sheep's clothin'?" Kate inched out of the cottage, the Armalite steadied under the elbow of one arm. In her other hand was a second AR-18. She tossed it to me and I caught it on the fly. I thought I saw Wheeler twitch, but he knew he couldn't get his gun back fast enough. He smiled instead, reverting to the tried-and-true English method of fucking over an enemy— polite diplomacy.

"It's irrelevant what I am, miss. I'm just here to cooperate with Garda Ryan and help him effect a detainment of the suspect. Your interference could easily be written off to a simple misunderstanding if you would kindly lower your weapon." Wheeler had barely finished when Kate laughed with genuine amusement.

"Ah, Patsy, you made a balls out of this one, dinn't ya? Damn. It's all bollixed up now."

"That's enough, Kate. Put down that rifle now. An' I don' wanna hear that kind of talk from you. This is Garda business, ya unnerstand?" Patsy's face was crimson red, but whether from anger or embarrassment, I couldn't be sure.

"Then what do ya need a bloody tea bag for? Don' be bringin' one a *them* to *this* place. Yer as dense as a bottle a shite an' I swear to the saints yer out of yer mind, ya feckin' brilliant amadan." As she spoke, Patsy strode toward her, ignoring the AR-18. I lifted my weapon toward his head and he stopped.

"Jaysus, will ya shut yer gob an' listen up, Kate? This has nothin' to do with anythin' else. We got a call at the Garda station about an American fugitive named Michael Corrigan, travelin' on his brother Aidan's passport." He glared at me, proud of himself, then turned back for Kate's reaction.

She glanced away from Wheeler for the first time, for a split second, catching my eye. I could see that she wasn't surprised at all.

"Yeah? So what?"

"So, he's wanted fer murder. He killed a Negro back in the States. A civil rights worker by the name of James Butler." That stopped her. This time she didn't look my way, but her shoulders sagged and her head hung lower, letting her hair fall in front of her eyes.

Patsy was satisfied. He'd gotten the reaction he wanted. But after a moment, Kate stiffened and lifted her head again, gripping the rifle tighter, her finger white with tension on the trigger. "No . . . no," Kate said, almost to herself, in denial. "I listened to shite like this once before and it cost me dear. I want to hear his side of it." I looked at her for a brief second, wanting to explain but not knowing where to start.

"That sounds reasonable," Wheeler said, almost amiably. "You two can chat all you like on the way back to Athlone."

"I meant *now*," Kate said, an icy coldness in her voice.

"Yer actin' crazy, Kate," Patsy muttered, edging toward her. She seemed confused, as if trying to figure out why I wasn't denying all this.

"Me? I'm actin' crazy? You bring in a—what is 'e, MI5?—to this island, an' *I'm* crazy? Ya think it'll all end when ya get rid of Mickaleen, jus' because ya believe all that bloody shite about the Corrigans bein' traitors? An' if he *is* an informer, what do ya think he'll tell this feckin' Tan bastard about Declan." For a moment I thought Kate had gone too far, acted out of emotion, but then I realized she was intentionally provoking her brother. She wanted him to lose his temper.

"Shut up," Patsy growled, but it was too late. Wheeler was starting to notice things—like the crates in the cottage behind me.

"Declan who?" Wheeler tried, obviously making the connection to Declan Murphy, the escaped convict who was known to have relatives in the area.

"Lookit 'im, Patsy. He's not quite such a moron as you thought, is he? Dinn't ya realize he'd want to look aroun'? Maybe find some more of these?" Kate jerked her Armalite up, setting Patsy off. He moved quickly for such a big oaf.

"I said shut yer gob," he growled as he went to grab Kate. I saved his life by cracking him over the back of the head with the butt of my rifle before Kate had a chance to pull the trigger.

He went down hard but was still growling as he hit the dirt, so I stepped back out of his reach. Kate was solid. Her rifle had never left Wheeler.

"Declan who?" Wheeler asked again, a nervous quaver in his voice now. I think he knew then that he might be in over his head.

"Murphy," Kate told him, almost spitefully.

"Ahh, Jaysus, Kate," Patsy moaned. "He'd never have known if ya jus' let us take the Yank."

"Really? An' ya think I'd let a British SAS trooper workin' fer MI5 come here an' *live,* Patsy?" Declan's voice carried easily to us as he stepped out of the woods. He held a Browning P35 HiPower in his hand.

I heard Patsy's sharp intake of breath and turned to make sure he wasn't moving, but I didn't need to worry. Fear had left him breathless.

"Declan, ya don' unnerstand . . ." Patsy began but was cut off as Declan raised the Browning and calmly fired a deafening shot.

Wheeler screamed as his thighbone cracked, the bullet smashing it. His weight bore down on the broken bone causing it to collapse and pierce his thigh, stabbing through his skin as he crumpled to the ground. Declan had hardly moved, only lifting his hand slightly to fire, but the one shot was enough to cripple Trooper Wheeler, who writhed on the ground, holding his thigh as blood pooled around him.

For a moment, no one moved except Declan, who strode toward Wheeler, kicking his gun away and expertly kneeling over him to rip his shirt open. As Wheeler groaned, Declan pulled an SAS commando knife, a seven-inch double-bladed dagger, and sliced off a strip of Wheeler's shirt, quickly tying it as a tourniquet around his bleeding leg. Then Declan smiled, spotting a tattoo revealed when he tore off the shirt—a dagger with a set of wings behind it and a motto: WHO DARES WINS. The motto of the British Special Air Service.

"Nice artwork, Trooper Wheeler. 'Who dares wins.' But I guess that's not always true, is it? At least not today. Not fer you." Declan came off perfectly calm as he chatted with Wheeler, who was in obvious pain. "Looks like a loser of a day, donn't it? And you were so close to bein' a winner. Bringin' home a man wanted fer murder, discoverin' a cache of arms on an abandoned island, and capturin' a wanted terrorist. You'd a been a regular hero, wouldn't ya?"

Declan tied the tourniquet with a yank, pulling it taut. "There. That'll keep ya alive long enough to kill ya properly." Declan looked up toward Patsy, still speaking pleasantly. "An' you, Patsy, what was it the wise man once said? That if you canna learn from history yer a feckin' eejit? 'E was right. And not only that. If you canna learn from history, you *become* history. The stupid get dead faster than the rest of us, don' they, cousin?"

"I was tryin' to protect us, Dec," Patsy blurted, pointing at me. "He's a bleedin' cop, inn't he? On the run from the American autorities an' all. He'd bring them down on us all if we let 'im stay. If we gave 'im up, I thought maybe they'd leave us all alone."

"Is that what ya thought?"

"Yea."

"Then yer a bigger eejit than I realized. Ya need a brain to think, an' yer lackin' the necessary equipment. Don' ya know that informers an' collaborators end up dead?"

Declan had slowly walked closer to Patsy, the Browning held down at his side, seemingly no longer a threat. He was calm, smiling a crooked smile when the Browning kicked back in his hand, the discharge making my ears ring, almost drowning out the horrific snapping crack. Declan hadn't held the gun low because he was done with it. He'd held it low so it'd be at the right angle to break Patsy's kneecap.

Patsy's screams echoed out over the lake, layering themselves on top of the ringing in my ears. I remembered the Armalite in my hands and raised it at Declan's head even as Kate did the same. She drew a deep breath of sympathetic pain for her brother, swallowing the scream on her lips but holding her fire. Trooper Wheeler was rocking back and forth, moaning, only marginally aware that things were about to get a lot worse.

My finger was tight on the trigger. I wanted to shoot him. I wanted to get rid of the problem, but I couldn't. My hands were clammy, sweating and shaking. Declan slowly looked up at Kate and me, his lopsided grin unchanged.

"Put it down, Mickaleen. Ya won' shoot this time an' we both know it. I'm yer best friend here an' ya already owe me a death."

"He owes you nothin' an' you know it," Kate said with tears of anger in her eyes. It wasn't me Declan had to worry about shooting him. It was her. Patsy's screams were fading as he had to catch his breath. His throat was ripped raw from it, and I could hear him pleading in a hoarse whisper, almost sobbing.

"Please . . . Please, Dec. I was . . . tryin' . . . ta help . . . Christ . . . Fergive me . . ." Declan ignored Patsy, his eyes locked on mine. He was right. I couldn't shoot. In spite of what I had just seen him do, his eyes were gentle, familiar.

"Declan. You don' want this on your soul. This ain't necessary, is it now?" Kate was pleading, but her voice was steady, as was her gun.

"She's right, it isn't." I finally found my voice, regaining my bearings. This was no different than dealing with a crazed suspect. We had guns on him. "Christ, we can settle this, Declan."

"Ah, now yer bringin' Christ into it? Don' ya know that's where the problem starts? With organized religion?" Declan looked back at me, his insane grin a little wider. He seemed oblivious to the moans of Wheeler and Patsy. "An' you really think we can settle this, Mickaleen? Is that what yer Christ would think as well? Won't my soul receive eternal damnation? Or do you think I can be saved if I just confess my sins an' say 'I'm sorry' like a good Catholic boy?"

"Killing them doesn't seem like something a good Catholic would do, does it," I tried, hoping he was as radical about his religion as he was about killing Protestants.

"Well, I guess I'm not a good Catholic, then, am I?" As if to prove it, he swung his boot into Wheeler's gut, knocking the wind out of him. "Shut yer gob, will ya?"

I was too shocked to do anything but stare.

"Ya know what this bleedin' country needs, Mickaleen?" Declan asked, breezily conversational. "Less Catholics an' Protestants an' more Christians. *Real* Christians. Ya know what one a them looks like, Mickaleen?"

"I don't see any here."

Declan's laugh was genuine and surprising. At any other time it would have been infectious but not at the moment, for obvious reasons. He caught his breath after a moment, eyes shining. "Ahh, that's where yer wrong, boyo. Jaysus was a rebel, wann't he? Jaysus was a revolutionary like myself."

"Don' start that, Declan. We need to get Patsy to hospital." Kate was inching toward her brother, keeping her gun on Declan, trying to figure out which to deal with first.

"Where he'll tell them what? That he twisted 'is knee playin' football? No." Declan raised his pistol and Kate stopped moving, but his eyes were on me. "She knows I'm right, by the by. She knows as well as I do that crucifixion was reserved fer rebels. Christ couldna have been crucified if he weren't a rebel. If he was killed fer a Jewish crime, he'd a been stoned to death and no Roman soldiers would've been at Golgotha. So it wasn't the Jews that killed him. It was the Romans. An' they did it because he was a rebel." Declan's expression was serene, but his words sounded like the rantings of a sociopath.

"Maybe, but he didn't kneecap his friends and kill Roman soldiers, did he?" Kate retorted.

"You think that informer Judas hung himself in that tree? Don't ya think maybe he had some help? An' ya really think the Romans, after conquerin' most a the known world, didn't know what they were doin'? Jaysus was the bleedin' bastard who told his followers to 'render unto Caesar' what was his. An' he wasn't talkin' about no damn coins like the priests'd have ya believe. He was talkin' about all of it. He wanted the centurions thrown back at the bastard, sent back to Rome on their shields, his laws tossed back in his face, and his bleedin' anal control-freak culture driven into the sea. Jus' like this Brit here today. Let's send 'im back on his bloody shield as a warnin' to stay out." Declan raised the gun and pointed it at Trooper Wheeler's face, done with his soliloquy.

I stepped closer, trying to intimidate him with the Armalite and diffuse the situation. "Nobody needs to die here. I can go with him. I'll surrender."

Declan laughed again, looking at Kate. "Ahh, Kate, you can really pick 'em, can't ya? Another man with a martyr complex." He turned back to Wheeler but addressed me. "Ya think it's that easy now? That you can just surrender? Don' ya think there'll be garda and Brits all over this island before the sun sets?"

"Please, Dec," Patsy was still moaning.

"He was tryin' to help, Dec. He's sorry. He deserves some forgiveness."

"*Fergiveness,* Kate? You know as well as I do that fergiveness ain't free. Ya get what ya give."

"Put the gun down." I stepped forward, Armalite pointed at Declan's head. I had to do something. I didn't want another death on my conscience.

"Put it down or what, Mickaleen? Ya gonna shoot me in the head again?"

Declan had turned toward me, his pistol at his side. He walked straight toward the barrel of the Armalite until it was less than two feet from his forehead.

We were eye to eye, and something clicked deep down in my subconscious. Declan had asked if I was going to shoot him—*again*. He was staring at me, unblinking, as my finger went white on the trigger.

"You knew me the first time you saw me, dinn't you, Mick? You remember a wee bit, don' ya? Kate told me ya answered her in a language you dinn't even know you knew down the greengrocer's."

"My father taught me—"

"Your da dinn't teach you shite. Tell me, you tosser, in that nightmare of yours, the one where you're freezing, lying in wait for the bloody British, what's the lad you kill wearing? Is it an old brown coat two sizes too big? Boots with two different-colored laces?"

I suddenly felt light-headed, like I was floating inside a stranger's body, looking through a stranger's eyes. I tried to focus back on Declan, on what he was saying.

"He lived for a while, dinn't he? Yer bullet took 'im in the forehead, but it didn't catch him square. He lived. And what'd he say to you as you laid there in his blood, pretending to be dead?" Until now, I hadn't remembered this part of the dream, but it came back to me in that moment, vividly. Liam, looking up at me. He wasn't angry. He wasn't even scared.

"He tells you, 'Stay with me. They won't notice. I've got blood enough for both of us.' Inn't that right? Didn't ya play dead there until they passed, chasing Seamus and Cathal an' the rest?" I nodded. He was right and we both knew it. Declan took the Armalite out of my hands and I didn't resist. It didn't even occur to me to try. He stepped closer, so that we were eye to eye.

"Have ya ever seen me in yer dreams, Mickaleen? Have ya ever looked at me straight in the face sayin' my name over and over an' over an' over again?"

They were Liam's eyes. Slightly different in color, and older, but Liam's eyes.

"How?" was all I managed to ask, but it was a bigger question than I'd ever get answered.

Declan laughed. "How? I was there, shot by my best friend because the Shale Ghosts of Mullingar Road made eejits out of two lads who had no place bein' there. The Corrigans were never informers, but only a couple of us knew that. It was an accident, but accident or not ya owe me a death. Yer fate brought ya back here to pay the debt you'd fergotten. Yer fate an' this one. Inn't that right, Kate?" Declan turned to her calmly, but Kate went rigid, uncomfortable, unable to look at me.

"Now is not the time or place fer this, Declan. He's not ready and Patsy's bleedin' out. We can deal with this later."

Declan slowly nodded, relenting. "Put down yer gun an' tend to Patsy's leg. I hit it at an angle, so it's painful, but shouldn't completely make a cripple of 'im."

Kate dropped the gun, going quickly to Patsy, tending to his wound like a battle-trained nurse. My head was swimming, trying to keep up.

"I don't understand."

Declan shrugged, his lopsided grin reappearing. "What's to understand? You're a good Christian lad, and you've been born again. *You* are the resurrection and the life. You are the eternal soul come to fulfill yer karma. Ya jus' don't know it yet."

I started to smile, thinking this was the sense of humor of a psychotic, but somehow it didn't feel like a joke, and it wasn't funny. Declan caught my confusion as he checked the load in his pistol.

"What? Don't ya believe me, Mickaleen? Kate does, don' ya, Kate?"

"Shut yer gob, Declan. Not now," Kate ordered, not looking up from Patsy's leg.

Declan ignored her. "She's come all the way back to Glasson an' Inchmore to wait fer the love of her last life, her *sonuachar,* inn't that right?"

Kate glanced up, not at Declan but at me. The tips of her ears and her cheeks were a delicate pink. Her eyes were watery as she shook her head and looked away again. Declan cocked his pistol, making sure I heard it.

"I know who ya are, Michael Sean Corrigan, accused murderer of James Butler. I know who ya are better'n you do yerself. So let me tell ya what we're gonna do. We're gonna allow Trooper Wheeler here the opportunity to do a little penance so he can be forgiven."

"You're forgiving him?" I was incredulous but relieved. Maybe if I just played Declan's game we could get out of this without anyone dying.

"Of course. Everybody deserves to be forgiven. But there's got to be a penance first. Fergiveness without penance is a crock of shite. Lookit Jesus. He put himself on a cross. Now that's a penance." Declan turned and kicked Trooper Wheeler again. "How about some nails in yer hands an' feet and slow suffocation from the weight of yer own body, Georgie?"

Wheeler shifted, obviously in shock. "Please. You don't need to kill me . . ."

"Scared, are ya? Well, what if I promise that you'll come back? Come back with a clean slate. A fresh start. No tattoos of lethal weapons on yer body. Does that sound good to ya?"

Declan was unbalanced, that much was clear. But the only way to argue with a crazy person is on his own terms, within his own delusion.

"What can he possibly learn by dying?" I asked, trying to figure out a way to keep Wheeler from being murdered.

"Are ya serious? Death is the ultimate teacher. It'll show him that he bollixed up his life."

"He didn't do anything bad enough to deserve the death penalty." I was prepared to defend Wheeler, but Declan wouldn't listen to logic. He just shrugged.

"Hell, Mick, ya don't need to do much. Don' we all get the death penalty in the end? The question is, what's he gonna learn from it? You take this right bastard here, put a bullet in his brain fer comin' over here an' messin' with troubles not 'is own, next time he comes back he'll say to himself, 'Bleedin' 'ell. I better not pull that one again. Last time I tried that bit of shite they put a bullet in my head.' It's a good lesson. A bit extreme, mind you, but it works." Declan moved closer, his finger on the trigger now.

"And what if he doesn't remember?"

Declan sighed, lowering the pistol again impatiently. "We all remember, at least subconsciously. And lookit you. If I'm right, ya have a scar or birthmark on the back of yer head, just like mine, right here on my hairline." He pulled up his hair to reveal a dark birthmark about a half inch across, right on his forehead.

"Trauma leaves scars so deep they carry over to the next life an' sometimes the one after. They're reminders not to screw up again."

Declan turned back to Trooper Wheeler and knelt over him, gently brushing back his hair. For a moment, he seemed genuinely empathetic.

"You remember this death on the other side, will you now, Georgie? I want you to dream of me and remember that it was *you* who came after us. We had no quarrel, you and I—not until you decided to come over here and interfere for the wages your government pays you. I'm only doin' this because I care about your immortal soul."

He pulled the trigger.

The blowback sprayed warm and wet, all over me and Declan. The shot echoed across the lake, and even Patsy's moans were silenced. Declan bowed his head then and spoke so softly I could barely hear him.

"Go swiftly, Georgie. I'll see ya in the next life, and hopefully we'll be friends. I'll owe ya a debt, an' it won't be forgotten. I promise ya."

When Declan looked up at me, his eyes were brimming with tears.

Sean

Like I said when we started this (and I admit it's not eloquent, but it's definitely apt): *Fuck.*

Anne and I were stark naked, standing over the bones of Trooper George Wheeler, a man my uncle had witnessed being murdered in 1972. A week ago I didn't know Uncle Mike existed, and now here I was, standing right where he dug the grave for the British officer Declan had killed.

And if that much was true, what else was also true? Could it *all* be true? I still needed to read the missing journal pages, but I knew it all started here, on the island, and I knew that Patsy's graffiti was somehow related, though I had no idea how. What I *did* know was that standing around naked with Anne and a skeleton was starting to feel a bit awkward.

"What are we gonna do with him?" I asked.

"What do ya mean 'do'? There's no 'him' here, just a bunch a bones." She pushed a thigh bone aside with her foot.

"He's a murder victim."

"He's a victim of circumstance. A soldier shot down in an undeclared war." Anne stepped over his ribs, closer to me, as comfortable standing nude among the bones as she was in her own home. "Or are ya sayin' ya want to destroy the peace process by diggin' up a long-dead issue?"

"He's a person, not an issue."

"A person? Then let's ask him what we should do. Whatta ya think, Georgie? Should we resurrect ya and let ya tell yer tale? Really? Good, then lemme ring up Declan an' fill 'im in on yer plans." Anne looked straight at me as she finished speaking to George's skull, and I got the message. Declan would be charged with this murder. Declan, the politician who was working on the peace process now.

Anne shook her head at me and pried the skull from the dirt. "Alas, poor Georgie, I never knew ya. If I had, then maybe I'd unnerstand why ya'd want Sean here to risk his life fer somethin' that happened before he was born."

"Put that down," I said, yet as strange as all this was, and as much as it creeped me out, Anne looked beautiful doing it. Like some pagan goddess of death and rebirth. God help my next girlfriend, because something about this was striking a chord with me. Anne saw the worry on my face and misinterpreted it.

"Don' worry, Georgie's not here anymore," Anne said. "He's moved on. If I thought he were here, I wouldn't be dancin' aroun' nekkid, would I? I like things one to one. It gets messy with more." With that, she kissed the top of the skull and put it back, turning the skull so the eye sockets looked away from us. "This is just dust, from whence he came an' to which we will all return."

When she stood up to face me again, her face and thighs had streaks of dirt on them where she had rubbed her hands clean. She wasn't smiling anymore. She moved closer, her chest almost touching mine as she looked me in the eyes. For a second, I thought she was going to kiss me again, and my body reacted, but she spoke quietly, almost threatening. "This is between us, Sean. If Declan, or anyone, finds out, yer a dead man. You'll be next ta Georgie boy here."

She turned then, leaving me breathless.

"Where are you goin'?"

"I smell like death and I'm covered with dirt. I'm gonna wash it off in the lake. If you'd take yer eyes off my ass an' watch where ya step, ya can join me. But be careful. There's nettles all through here."

I followed her, but I didn't try to catch up. There *were* nettles, and I still wasn't wearing any clothing.

Something was bothering me about what my uncle had written in his journal about Wheeler dying. Something about the way it was done, and what they were talking about as it happened, didn't make sense. And why had Declan's eyes filled with tears after killing Wheeler? Wheeler was an SAS trooper, a British soldier sent here to fight a dirty war. If Declan was the Provisional IRA assassin Uncle Mike made him out to be, why would shooting Wheeler upset him?

There was too much missing from the journal, too many pages torn out. I knew that if I wanted to figure out what really happened after Declan killed Wheeler, I needed to find out what was in the missing pages. If I could find out what was in those pages, maybe I could find out why the British thought Uncle Mike was working for the Provos, why he maintained his innocence in the shooting of James Butler to the very end, and why he was killed.

I lost my train of thought as soon as I reached the shore and saw that Anne was already in the water, standing chest deep and wringing out her hair. All my higher-level thoughts evaporated into a fresh fog of hormones and, without thinking, I strode out toward her.

I stopped thigh deep, three strides in. The water was cold. Frigid. Lough Ree can be so calm that you forget it's part of the Shannon River system and is fed by ever-moving cold river water, but its icy fingers on your body is a strong reminder. I nearly tripped and fell on my ass as I tried to back up as quickly as I could.

"Damn. That's cold."

Anne was laughing again, the playful gleam back in her eye. With the water making her hair look so dark and weighing it down, she almost looked like a different person.

"Yea. Cold it is. Even yer little thermometer's no longer risin'." She grinned, pointing, in case I missed the innuendo. How could I? Every bit of blood I had was rushing away from my extremities so quickly it made me feel light-headed. "Don' worry, as soon as willie gets wet, you'll get used to it."

I knew she was right, but I wished she wouldn't enjoy my discomfort so much. I eased my way in, determined to reach her, not so much out of pride, but because then my embarrassment would be hidden under the dark waters of Lough Ree.

By the time I got out as far as Anne, I noticed that she looked as if she were wearing makeup. The cold had brought a deeper color to her lips, and her skin looked like white marble with fine cerulean veins. Somehow her face looked younger and her eyes older.

She stopped me from staring by pulling me close. She was warm and it didn't take long for the shivering to settle into comfort. I saw my own reflection in her eyes as I looked down at her and I suddenly felt detached from the whole thing. I was watching myself, with a woman I hardly knew, naked in a frigid lake in Ireland. It felt a lot more like lucid dreaming than real life, as if I were walking around in someone else's body, holding someone else's girlfriend. As in most dreams, pieces of it didn't fit properly. I remember thinking that Anne's eyes were too blue and were missing the slivers of green that belonged there.

They were crazy thoughts. Dream-thoughts. I ignored them, though I shouldn't have. They were trying to warn me that something was wrong.

Anne noticed how distracted I was and made a grab for my attention.

"So . . . What're ya thinkin' right now?"

I forced a shiver to buy myself some time, then answered like a real man. "Nothin'."

"Ya still thinkin' about what we saw back there? Aren't ya satisfied now? What yer uncle wrote was all true. Now ya can enjoy a holiday on him, with no guilt. Ya don' even need to show 'im pictures when ya get back."

I looked away from her, afraid she'd see my doubts. As I did, I heard the sound of an outboard motor in the near distance and saw a speck that must've been a boat leaving the launch at Portlick. It distracted Anne for a moment as well and gave me a chance to change the subject.

"Do you know a lot about what happened back then?"

"A fair bit." I glanced at her, aware that she was being evasive, but now she was looking away, toward the small boat getting closer. "Let it go, Sean. George Wheeler has been dead a long time. It'll do no good to dig him up now."

"But what if what Uncle Mike wrote was true? What if the British were after him because they thought he had a hand in killing Wheeler, and I can prove he was innocent?"

"Even if he didn't kill Wheeler, he wasn't exactly innocent. He still killed that man back in the States, dinn't he? And a diary doesn't prove anything. It's just words on a page. Anyone can lie to himself."

"That doesn't mean the truth isn't in there somewhere."

She stopped at that, pulling away slightly. "Maybe. Maybe hidden between the lines is an inklin' of the truth, if yer smart enough to see it. But a lot more went on back then than you can possibly understand right now."

"Why? You think because I'm an American I can't understand your politics?" I was being defensive but only because she was clearly keeping something from me.

"No. I'd never expect ya to unnerstand our politics unless ya lived it, an' even then ya'd only see the one side. I mean ya don' understand our lives. Our way of thinkin' of things. You're lookin' at it from yer own perspective. Declan an' Kate an' the rest didn't think like you do. They had a different way of seein' things." Anne shrugged, and I noticed that as she watched the boat slowly approaching, she was sinking lower in the water so she was less visible.

"You're talking about all the things Uncle Mike wrote about. You know more about them, don't you?"

She'd pulled away from me completely now and was treading water. "It don' matter what I know."

"You're not answering the question."

"There was no question. You said, 'You know about them.' Not 'What do ya know about them?' "

"So what *do* you know? Do you know what they did to your dad?"

"Yeah. They woke 'im up to what a feckin' amadan he was bein'." Anne swam closer to shore and into shallower water, although she stayed submerged, keeping an eye on the boat in the distance.

"That's not an answer."

"Then ask a proper question. I can't answer what ya don't ask."

"And how am I supposed to know what to ask?"

She looked up at me with a flash of incongruous anger. "I dunno. Maybe try thinkin' fer once before ya open yer gob."

I wanted to shove her under the water and hold her there, but I let the feeling pass and took her advice. I thought about it. I tried to ask a specific question with the little information I had.

"Why would there be tears in Declan's eyes as he killed the SAS trooper? That's what Uncle Mike wrote in his journal."

She didn't answer for a moment, watching as the boat turned farther out toward Inchturk, the smaller island to the north of Inchmore. When she did answer, she was back to her usually obnoxious self.

"See, that's a better question. Good fer you, Sean."

"Does that mean you'll actually answer me?"

Anne glanced after the boat one more time, then stood, revealing herself once more to me. I almost didn't hear what she was saying for a minute, then gradually tuned back in. "Ya know, in the old religions, if ya took a man's life, you were responsible fer everything that followed from it, in this life and the next. If ya were wrong to take it, yer penance would be yer own plus whatever he owed."

"Wait. Stop." I interrupted, trying to remember what I had asked as I watched droplets of water stream over her skin as the sun, low on the horizon behind her, nearly blinded me. "What does this have to do with my question?"

Anne stopped when I told her to, still too far away to grab as the wind kicked up, sending a chill over my body. "If ya don' like my answer, ask a different question. I'm answerin' the one ya asked." With that, she strode toward the shore. I called after her, trying to figure out how to keep the peace with her.

"Fine. Maybe I asked the wrong question, but I just want to understand. I'm trying to do a little research . . ."

"You wanna do research, go make love to a library," she answered without turning back.

"What's that mean?"

"It means that I'm tired, an' its gonna be dark soon. I don't want my da to have to come lookin' fer us. Do you?" She glanced back at me and I started toward the shore. I didn't want to meet up with Patsy in the dark, especially if I was still naked, or worse, if Anne was. I guess that's why she was so nervous about the boat, because she thought it might be him.

As I put my feet back on solid ground, it struck me that maybe Anne was right. Maybe a library was a good idea. Maybe the periodicals from 1972 could fill me in on what was going on when my uncle was here. Maybe I could even find out how he died.

I caught up with Anne just before she reached the path. "Is there a library I could go to? Someplace I could find out all this stuff?"

"Yer serious? I'm standin' here with no clothes on, freezin' my arse off and yer thinkin' about books?"

"Yes. I mean no," I stammered, trying to recover. "I mean, I can't take my eyes off of you and I'd rather spend time with you . . ." It was starting to come to me now. She wanted to be flattered, like any woman. "But I'm thinking if I knew more about Ireland and everything that went on, maybe I'd understand you better, too."

She laughed, a truly amused, heartfelt laugh. "Jaysus, yer cute when yer full of shite, ain't ya?" She smiled, and I couldn't help grinning myself. "I'll tell ya what. You'll get both. I'll take ya to Trinity tomorrow an' ya can be like a real Yank and go drool over the Book a Kells, then do yer research while I drool over the boys down there."

"Can I drive?"

"Are ya out of yer feckin' mind? Ya think I'd trust you behind a wheel?" Anne stepped aside and slapped me on the ass, nodding into the shadowy woods. "Now get up there an' start walkin'. It's my turn to watch yer ass. Maybe it'll keep me warm thinkin' about other things."

I tried to walk with some manly confidence the rest of the way up the path, but it's hard when you're barefoot, naked, and keeping an eye out for nettles. I was less than graceful, wincing as sharp pebbles pierced my feet, and could hear Anne giggling behind me. It was an uncomfortable distraction, wondering what my own ass looked like as I walked down the path, and maybe that's why, when I stepped into the clearing near Wheeler's body, still lit by the sun, I didn't see him at first.

"Well, that's quite a pair, inn't it?"

I squinted in the direction of the voice, and after a moment my eyes adjusted. There, near the fallen trees and Wheeler's bones, was Declan, a pistol in his hand. I stopped, and Anne stepped quickly in front of me, not blinking at the sight of the pistol. Declan just shook his head.

"Jaysus, Mary, an' Saint Joe, what the feck are ya doin' here, Declan?"

"I knew ya couldn't leave well enough alone, and I figured I wouldn't innerfere if Georgie was still planted. But he's not now, is he?" Declan pushed

George's skull back into its proper position with the toe of his shoe, then ogled Anne, letting his eyes linger on her.

"Nobody's gonna know, Dec." She spoke softly, ignoring his look.

"That's right. They won't." Declan stepped closer to us, glancing between us warily. "That's why I went to the other side of the island. So no one would see me arrive an' so I could get some of the belladonna ya planted so long ago. Here ya go, Sean." He reached into a pocket and I flinched as he tossed a twig of some kind at me, laden with bright red berries. "Chew on those."

I caught them, but Declan wasn't watching me. His eyes were on Anne's face. She didn't turn as she spoke, holding Declan's gaze. "Drop them, Sean. They're poison."

I did as I was told. I even stepped back away from them. The last time that Declan had stood here, he killed a man and kneecapped his friend. What was a little poison for a near stranger?

"Poison? Come off it, Anne. Ya know better than that." He looked at me directly now, holding the pistol carelessly. "She's tryin' to cheat ya, Sean. Denyin' ya the rights you were born with. She don' wanna allow ya the full experience. Inn't that right, Anne?"

"Don't do this, Declan."

"Me? Yer the one brought him here of all places. Ya must've wanted this in some way, dinn't ya? Was it a test? Ya wanted to see how he'd react?" He strode closer to me, pointing the pistol. "Go ahead. Just taste one or two, boyo. Tell him, Anne. If he eats just the right amount, he'll solve all our problems, won' he?" It was a challenge of some sort, and I tried to move forward, to see Anne's face, but she was keeping it turned away from me.

"No. It won't."

"An' why not? Why do ya wanna deny him this? So ya can keep 'im fer yerself? How long are ya gonna keep the truth from 'im? Are ya ever gonna tell 'im what ya know?" Declan had my attention now. All those alarm bells I'd ignored when my head was swimming in hormones were ringing now, but Anne seemed oddly calm and composed, not intimidated by Declan at all.

"I'll tell 'im in good time."

Declan snorted derisively, a slow sad smile coming to his lips. "I shoulda known, Anne. Ya always wanted what was never gonna be yours."

"It's mine fer now, and now is good enough." I was starting to feel objectified, but I wasn't sure whether or not they were talking about me. What had Anne lied to me about? Could I even trust Declan that she had lied? If she had, then why was she stopping him from poisoning me? And if she hadn't, why didn't she deny it?

"Sooner or later it won't be good enough. But ya know that, and still ya never change, do ya?"

Anne laughed, and I felt the tension drift away. Somewhere in the subtext they had come to a resolution. "Why should I change? I'm perfect as I am, don' ya agree, ya dirty ol' man?" She struck a pose as she asked, and if I didn't know better, I'd say Declan blushed. He looked away, anyway, and pointed toward the schoolhouse with his pistol.

"Get yer clothes on. Yer leavin'. Now."

Anne sidestepped in front of me, then didn't move any farther. Suddenly the tension was back. "He's with me. I'm not leavin' without 'im."

"How sweet. And useless." Declan grinned, enjoying Anne's brief confusion. "Jaysus, what'd ya think, Anne? That I was gonna kill 'im? No. If I was gonna kill 'im, I woulda done ya both as soon as I saw ya. I jus' wanted to know yer intentions for my boy here. Now that I know, I'll leave him be so I can I see the look on yer face when ya get what's comin' to ya fer this."

"That's comfortin'," Anne responded as Declan strode past her, moving toward me, close enough so that I could smell the Guinness he had pounded back since the last time I saw him.

"Just leave the dead to bury their dead, boyo, unnerstood? Learn yer lesson an' stop messin' with things."

"I'll forget everything," I promised quickly. "Consider it forgotten."

"You think fergettin' is the right thing to do, do ya?" He held my gaze and a chill ran through me even though the breeze had died.

"Isn't it?" I was trying to read Declan's look when I noticed something pass between him and Anne. Anne's lips went rigid and I was sure now that I'd said something wrong.

"He wants to ferget, Anne. Looks like you'll get exactly what you want. Unless I decide to take pity on him."

"Leave it alone, Dec. In his own good time." Anne's voice was tight, and I could see the muscles in her bare back flex with tension.

"In his . . . or yours?" Declan bent over and picked up the belladonna from where I had tossed it.

"Don't, Dec, please. He doesn't even know what he's sayin'. Let him ferget fer now." Anne stopped as Declan faced her down, idly playing with the stem holding the bright red berries. "If ya do what yer thinkin', yer gonna open up a whole lot of history that's better off as history. He's gonna know what ya really done."

"An' why Kate died, inn't that right? Inn't that what ya don' want him to know?"

Anne stopped, saying nothing for a moment. She glanced at me, and I could see that Declan wasn't lying. She was definitely keeping something from me. She turned back to Declan. "It's all the same thing, inn't it? You yerself keep talkin' about this new generation growin' up, an' how they can move on because they can ferget the pains of the Troubles, don't ya?"

"Don't put words in my mouth, girl. The ones who don' know history will sooner or later repeat it. Ignorance is never a good option an' ya know it."

"Really? Fine. Then let's dig it all up. Let's dig up Georgie, too. Let's remind everyone that he died here at your hand." Anne wasn't backing down, and Declan knew it. "Ya know how they are, Dec. There'll be revenge killin's all over again an' they'll start wit' you. Why wouldn't they? Yer the one that put 'im in this grave, ain't ya?"

"Let 'em come. I ain't afraid a dyin' an' you know it."

"Then why are we still standin' here?"

"Because I don't wanna die stupid at the hands of some angry young man with a gun. Not when I'm finally making progress." Declan glanced over at me, shifting the pistol in his hand. Finally he nodded to me and put the pistol away. "We'll ferget it fer now, boyo. Go yer way. But stop diggin' up things that are better left buried. Gimme yer word?"

"All right . . . Sure. It's forgotten. But can I just ask a few questions?"

Anne looked like she was holding her breath, but Declan shook his head, a bit exasperated. "Ask enough questions an' ya might start gettin' answers, boyo. Ya might not like 'em. *I* might not like 'em."

"Let's jus' go, Sean," Anne said as she grabbed my arm, her short finger-nails digging in so I couldn't pull away.

"No. I want to know what he's talking about. What does this have to do with how Kate died? What are you lying to me about? Tell me and I'll stop asking."

Declan choked off a laugh at that and Anne glared at him, pleading with me. "Sean, if he starts answering you, you'll never stop asking questions. Trust me. Jus' leave it be, fer feck's sake."

"I'll tell you what, boyo, if you want to know what happened to yer uncle, you keep lookin'. You . . ." He trailed off, hesitating, seeming to think about the words he was about to choose. "You dig as deep as you like, then ya come talk to me, and I'll verify or deny, all right?"

"How am I supposed to do that?"

"I'm sure Anne will help ya, whether she intends to or not." Declan smiled at Anne, then turned and started walking off toward the far side of the island, calling out as he went, "Enjoy 'im while ya can, Anne. He ain't yers to keep an' ya know it. When he finds out the truth, yer done."

With that, he faded into the shadows. It had grown darker even as we stood there talking, and I was suddenly reminded of how cold and naked I was. As soon as Declan was out of sight, Anne stalked off toward the school-house, forcing me to rush to keep up.

"Are you going to tell me what that was all about?"

"Let's jus' say we've got a history."

"What kind of history? What aren't you telling me?"

Anne whirled on me as she reached the door to the schoolhouse, anger or something a lot like it illuminating her eyes. "Sean, if I can give ya a bit of advice that comes from my heart, shut yer bloody gob an' learn when to keep it shut, all righ'?" She turned away again, grabbing her clothes off the floor, quickly putting them on.

I didn't say anything else, because before she had turned away, I'd seen something that made me tread lightly. A tear drifting down her cheek. I pulled on my own clothes in silence and followed her back to the boat. When I got there she was facing away from me, ignoring me as I got in and started the engine.

She refused to speak to me the rest of the way across Lough Ree, even though it was almost dark and I nearly missed the boat launch. By the time we reached the far shore, there was only a sliver of sunlight on the far horizon. I made the mistake of turning to look at it, thinking that I could get her talking again by commenting on how beautiful it was. By the time I opened my mouth to speak, I heard the car starting.

I ran to get in and opened the door just as Anne put the car in drive. The headlights were askew, so that the one on my side pointed at the sky, and I couldn't see the trees we were brushing past until we almost hit them. I was starting to get a permanent twitch when she finally spoke.

"I need a pint. If ya promise to ask no questions, I'll take ya to the pub fer a bite." It sounded like a concession, almost an apology—for what, I wasn't sure. It could have been for lying to me, it could have been for acting like such a crazy bitch, or it could have been that she was just hungry and didn't want to drive me home first. Either way, if I wanted to get through the night, I knew what my answer had to be.

"I promise. But what about your father? Won't he be worried and come looking for us?"

"God, yer a bleedin' eejit. Dinn't I jus' say no questions?"

Her anger ran through her leg to the gas pedal and we sped up, almost spinning off the road as it turned ninety degrees on itself. She straightened us out, fishtailing the car and throwing up some gravel as she did, but at least it eased the tension in the car.

"No worries about my da, all righ'? As soon as we step in the door that right bastard Frank will ring 'im up an' tell 'im exactly what we ordered an' where we happen to be sittin'. So keep yer hands to yerself under the table, unnerstand?"

"I promise."

I kept my promise, but Anne was quiet anyway, drinking and chain-smoking as we ate. A couple of times I caught her eyes looking like they were about to mist over, but I knew better than to ask why.

After a half-dozen pints for her and two for me, she seemed to relax a bit more. I'd ordered the bangers and mash, since I couldn't bring myself to order nachos my first time in Ireland, and I was just finishing them when I looked up to find her staring at me with a crooked grin.

"What?"

Anne shook her head, disappointed, but still smiling. "That was a question, ya bloody git."

"Sorry, but why—" I caught myself before I finished asking. "You're smiling."

"This inn't a smile, it's jus' not a frown." She kept staring at me for a minute, then pushed her chair back, getting up. "Come on. We better get some sleep tonight if I'm drivin' ya over to Trinity in the mornin'."

I went to follow Anne out, but she waited for me, wrapping her arm around mine, leaning into me for support. She was so openly affectionate that I knew she had to be drunk, or at the very least heavily buzzed.

"I'm driving," I told her as firmly as I could manage.

"Sure enough. It can be your reward fer not *askin'* to drive. An' it's about time ya put yer foot down like a man." I didn't take offense. It's hard to explain if you don't know someone like Anne or the rest of my family, but it's when they're being sarcastic and just a bit nasty that they show the most love. Not in their words—those could be used in a court of law against them—but in their actions and their tone of voice. It's something you learn to live with.

I PULLED UP next to the house as slowly and quietly as I could, but the kitchen light was still on, and as we got out of the car I could see Patsy standing at the door, waiting for us. He was silent as we approached, taking us in, reading the body language and profiling us like the garda he once was. We were ten feet away when Anne stopped, glaring at him.

"What is it now? Ya got something to say, say it." Anne wasn't one to avoid a confrontation, and Patsy was obviously cut from the same cloth. He made her wait, shaking his head in disapproval.

"If I were to say anything, I'd say it's a good thing yer not blood related now, wouldn't I?"

"We were just getting something to eat," I started, panicked that he somehow knew everything we had done today, but Anne interrupted me.

"I dunno, would ya say that? Are ya askin' me or tellin' me?"

"Don't be smart with me, Anne. I'm yer father."

"And now you'll dispense yer pearls a wisdom before us swine. Let's hear it. Whatta ya got?" Neither of them moved for a moment. It was a stand-off.

"What happened to Kevin?"

"Jimmy Coughlin," Anne replied, and Patsy sighed heavily as if there was something about him they both knew. Then Patsy stepped aside from the door, his glare relaxing into something warmer.

"It's better he stayed away, then, inn't it? And as far as my wisdom goes, all I can tell ya is that the nachos are better than the bangers and mash down there, and with six pints in ya, yer damn lucky Sean was drivin' that car when ya pulled in."

"That bastard," Anne said, knowing for sure now that the bartender had ratted her out. She pushed past Patsy in a blur and rushed into the house as Patsy smiled. He'd gotten the reaction he wanted.

"He's jus' lookin' out fer ya now." Patsy followed her in, and I trailed behind, staying out of the line of fire in case anything erupted again.

"Bloody informer is what he is." Anne was moving through the house, kicking off her shoes.

Patsy turned to me and rolled his eyes, a fellow sufferer at the hands of Anne's mercurial moods. "Come on in, Sean. Sit down an' I'll get ya some tea. I'm sure ya can use some relaxation time after spendin' a day with my daughter. Besides, if ya been drinkin', you'll feel better in the mornin' for it."

"He don' want tea, Da. He wants to get some sleep. See the bleedin' Book a Kells in the mornin'."

Patsy was already pouring the steaming tea. Frank must've called him as we were leaving, because he seemed to have it timed. "Ahh, a beautiful work a art that is."

"What do you know about it?"

"Ya don' know everything there is to know about me, young lady. I was an artist in a past life, long before you. I can appreciate the finer things."

"Yea, well, the finest thing I can think of right now is sleep. If you want to drink 'is weak tea, go right ahead, but I'll be wakin' ya up early to get on the road." Anne didn't give me a chance to answer or to excuse myself. I was left holding the cup of tea Patsy handed to me, watching her take the stairs two at a time.

When I turned back, Patsy was watching me watch her, and I could tell from the worry in his eyes that he didn't miss anything. I didn't know what to say, so I sipped the tea to buy some time. Anne was right. It was weak.

"Were ya on the island, then?" Patsy asked me out of the blue. He saw my surprise and nodded to the cuffs of my pants. They were muddy and still damp even after the time at the pub. It was pointless to lie, but I sure wasn't going to tell him anything more than I needed to.

"For a bit. Anne showed me the schoolhouse and the cottages." He nodded at that and took a few sips of tea. I followed his lead, but the silence was excruciating.

"I bet she did," he murmured finally, and I looked up at him, worried about what he might say next. He was still watching me, but his eyes had a far away, almost detached look.

"Don' worry. I know what I don' wanna know, and I don' wanna know any more about what Anne does when she's away from me than I need to. She's a grown woman." He tipped back the last of his tea and turned away from me, rinsing the cup in the sink. He pretended to look out the window but was really watching me in the reflection on it. "I know Anne's a handful, and I want to strangle her almost every day, but I do love her. Ya unnerstand that?"

I nodded, confirming that he was watching me in the window, and he looked down. When he spoke again, it was quieter, as if he was afraid she might hear.

"Yer gonna hurt her." Hearing him say it made me feel as if I'd already done it. I felt guilty for something I had no intention of doing.

"I won't," I promised, but even then I wasn't sure. Patsy, Declan, and even Anne were already treating me as if I was somehow destined to betray her. But how could I possibly hurt *her*? She was the one keeping secrets from me.

Patsy wasn't looking at me, he was scrubbing the teacup so hard I thought the glaze would come off. "Ya won' mean to, fer sure. But ya will. It's jus' the nature of things. Ya don' unnerstand yet, but I'm afraid ya will soon." With that he shut off the water and put the cup in the drain board. "Stay up as long as ya like. I need to find one or two things may int'rest ya. I'll let ya see them when yer ready."

He walked past me, but stopped at the bottom of the steps, his face in shadow as he glanced back at me. "Do yer best to make it easy on 'er, will ya?"

I downed the rest of my tea and rinsed my cup, just wanting to get some sleep, but when I got to the stairs I forgot to take them two at a time and I tripped on the second step. Even the house seemed not to want me there.

When I got to my room, I tried to turn on the light, but the bulb had gone dead. I undressed in the dark and slid between the sheets only to find them already warm. Anne was there. She put her arm around me and whispered, "Sorry fer bein' such a bloody bitch." She lay her head on my chest and my body stiffened.

"Your father—"

"Don' wanna know. Go to sleep already. I'll be out before he wakes up in the mornin'. Try to kick me out an' you'll just wake him up."

She was right. It wasn't worth fighting her, and it felt good to just lie there with the weight of her on me. Her breathing was deep and regular. But I wasn't about to sleep, not with all the questions running through my head. There were so many little things that made no sense. I had to at least get some of it straight or I'd never sleep.

"Anne . . ."

She groaned, but didn't move. "Jaysus, I thought it was women that liked to talk. Aren't ya exhausted already?"

"Yes, but back on the island you told me you can't answer what I don't ask. Which way is it? Should I ask or not?" Anne went still again and didn't answer me, but I knew she was awake. I was going to piss her off again, I could feel it.

"Don't push yer luck, Sean. Just because I let ya drive don' mean I want ya to be manly all the time." Anne seemed to hold her breath, seeing if I were stupid enough to push it, and when I didn't, she sighed, relaxing. A moment later, she surprised me by answering.

"They healed my da on the island. Don' ask me to explain more than that. I wasn't there and can't say. It's meant to be a secret, that's why it was torn out of the journal."

"Do you know what happened to the pages that were torn out?"

"Christ. I'm goin' to my own room so I can get some bloody rest," she grumbled, but she didn't move.

"You said I needed to ask the right questions. So yes or no. Do you know what happened to the rest of the journal?" Anne moved, and for a moment I thought I had pushed it too far, that she was leaving.

"Not all of it," she finally said.

Suddenly I had to know more. I was getting close. I could feel it. I was finally asking the right questions. "Will you give it to me?"

"It's not mine to give."

"Do you know who has it?"

"Some of it, yes, but it's not my place to say who it is. And that's all I'm sayin', Sean, I swear to ya. Now I'm going to sleep, and if ya wake me again, I'll castrate ya. I promise." Her hand drifted down to emphasize her threat.

Anne fell asleep almost immediately, but it took me a while to relax.

When I fell asleep, I dreamt of Inchmore in the winter. Of a sweet-smelling fire in the hearth of the schoolhouse, and red berries on its floor, scattered among twigs, leaves, and other berries. It was so real I'd have sworn that I'd seen it myself.

I woke in the morning to a knock on the door, and as I sat up the door swung open and Patsy stuck his head in. I turned to look for Anne, but she was already gone.

Patsy caught the look, and he knew that I noticed, but neither of us said anything. He just tossed a faded brown envelope at me, hitting me in the chest with it.

"What is this?"

"Wha's it look like?" I looked down at it, peering inside the envelope to see loose pages, like those torn from a journal. "I unnerstand you been lookin' fer 'em. It ain't all there, but there's some."

192 • KEVIN FOX

Anne must've told him. She wouldn't tell me he had them, but she told him I was looking. She was helping me. I don't know why I was so surprised at that, but it was a relief. Thanks to her, I had more of the journal in my hands. I thumbed through the pages as Patsy stepped back out, closing the door.

As I heard it click, I called out. "Wait . . . Thank you!"

From beyond the door, I heard his muffled reply. "Don' thank me yet. Jus' know that I'm sorry fer all I done."

I wasn't sure what he meant but wondered if it might be explained in the pages I held in my hand. I lay back and realized the bed was still warm where Anne had lain, and the smell of her was still on the sheets. I breathed deeply, taking it all in, and then, once more, I started to read.

Michael

We carried Patsy to the schoolhouse and Kate stayed with him there, boiling water to clean the wound, bandaging it, and putting a splint on the fractured bone. He passed out as the splint went on and was pretty easy to deal with after that. Declan was right: the wound he left was pretty clean and not as damaging as you would expect. Painful, to be sure, but not permanently crippling. Patsy would probably walk again.

We left Kate with Patsy, and then Declan and I walked back out to where Trooper Wheeler lay dead. Using two hefty branches we dug a shallow grave and buried him next to the cottage, twenty yards from the school, under the shade of an old tree.

We didn't talk the entire time. I didn't want to set Declan off, and I needed time to think about what to do next. I knew there would be no good end to this whole thing, but there might be a "best" end. Declan had just started kicking dirt over Wheeler's face when he finally broke the silence. "Ya think I'm a bit of a mentaller, don' ya?

I almost smiled. Trooper George Wheeler was dead and his blood was all over me, the man who was burying him with me had just kneecapped his own friend, and he was worried what I thought of his mental state.

"Ahh, I can see it in yer look. Ya think out I'm off my feckin' nut, fer sure. That's all right. Ya jus' don' have all the facts yet. Yer ignerant. I'll get ya straightened out soon enough."

"I've been here less than forty-eight hours and I'm burying a British SAS trooper. That makes me an accessory to murder. I also brought money to terrorists . . ."

"Freedom fighters," he interrupted with a grin. "Better get it right if yer gonna be joinin' the cause."

His lighthearted tone was starting to piss me off. "Call it what you want, but you're terrorists. Killers. And now I'm as guilty as you. I just stood there and watched you kill him. So I've got to ask you, do you see any way out of this for me?"

Declan nodded slowly, seeming to give my predicament serious thought. Then he grinned. "Sure. Ya could go back to the States an' face a murder charge. Oh, but right, they have the death penalty there. Better to face one here. That's good news now, inn't it? They won't extradite ya if yer wanted fer murder here, too."

If I had a real shovel, I would've hit him with it. "You think this is funny?"

"A course it is. All a life is funny if ya look at it right. Course, if ya really want out, just put the ol' AR-18 in yer mouth an' fire away. Come back again. The next life won't be much better if ya bollixed up this one, but at least it's a fresh start. Or if ya don' like the idea of suicide, go home, take the death penalty and go round the game board again." Declan wasn't grinning anymore. He was stamping down dirt on top of Wheeler, pounding it down with his boots. He looked up at me as I stared at him. "C'mon, trus' me. Yer jus' not lookin' at it right." Declan kept stomping on the earth. "In fact, I'd say yer a bit of an ingrate. Ya been here less than forty-eight hours and already ya met yer *sonuachar* and had a nice romantic evenin' by the fire, dinn't ya?" He glanced up at me as he said it and I felt my face grow warm.

"Ahh, I was right, wasn't I? Even a dense gobshite like yerself can see that last night might be worth the trip, can't ya? You don't meet a woman like that every lifetime."

"Leave Kate out of it."

"Sure enough. I'm a sensitive man. Not another word. Though ya do look a bit lovestruck when yer ears turn red like that." I looked up, wanting to be angry, but his grin was innocent and somehow infectious. He wasn't laughing at me but with me, teasing me.

The truth was, despite everything, I liked Declan.

"My ears aren't red."

"No? An' I bet yer shite smells just like my ma's rose garden, too, donn't it?" He was laughing now, as he pounded the dirt down around Wheeler. "Don' worry so much about all doom and gloom, Mickaleen. Yer soul hasn't caught up to ya yet. Kate's right about that much. It's probably still some-where over the North Atlantic. So morally yer probably not even respon-sible. Give yerself a little fergiveness."

"I thought you said forgiveness was a crock of shit."

"I would've said 'shite' now, wouldn't I? An', anyway, I said fergiveness without penance is a crock of shite, not the fergiveness itself."

"How can a dead man gain anything by being forgiven?"

"Ahh, I see. Ya don't think George is gonna learn much from this death, do ya?" Declan stared at me with a disbelieving look. "God, yer feckin' ig-nerant, aren't ya? You really believe people don' come back? You know that most of the worl' believes that we do. Look it up if ya like. Hindus, Budd-hists, Druze Muslims, Hasidic Jews, even Christians all over Europe."

"That's ridiculous. We don't walk around remembering our past lives."

"Says you. Ya know, in Greek mythology, people were dipped in the river Lethe, the 'river of fergetfullness,' so they would have a fresh start when they came back, but like Achilles' heel, not everything gets wet. A course, he was dipped in the Styx, not Lethe, an' I'm mixin' my mythology, but you get the idea. Deep inside your soul, you remember all your lives. All the lessons you've learned." He grinned and did a quick little jig on Wheeler's grave. "Jus' like I remember how to dance. Never a lesson in this lifetime. Ya believe that?"

"You killed that man for no good reason."

"Ya mean besides the fact that we'd all go to jail, the guns would be confiscated, an' the RUC an' the British paratroopers would get away with abusin' an' killin' people like Kate's husband, Sam?"

"So it's okay for *you* to kill people but not them?"

"Good fer you, Mickaleen. Ya hit on the big question straight off, dinn't ya? But let me ask ya this. If ya accept that we all come back and are born again, as I do, and that each life teaches us lessons to lead us back to God or nirvana or the ultimate holiday destination, however ya choose to look at it, ya have to have a different set of moral guideposts, don' ya? Fergiveness inn't free. Ya have to earn it, don' ya?" He was pointing his stick at me, get-ting in my face.

"That doesn't justify killing people."

"I'd say it does. If we let the killers run amok, let the most violent men keep doin' what they're doin', reapin' the rewards fer bad behavior, do ya think they're ever gonna stop? Does Attila the Hun or Genghis Khan or Hitler or Stalin stop rapin' and pillagin' just 'cause ya ask 'im nice? Ya think one a yer sit-ins would work on them? No. Ya gotta teach 'em a lesson. Ya wouldn't let a puppy piss on the carpet, would ya? No, ya rub 'is nose in it so he doesn't do it again. Killin' killers is the same thing. Drivin' out tyrants, defending the weak an' weary. It's a job has to be done," he said as he pushed the last of the dirt over Trooper Wheeler.

"You think killing is the only way to do it?"

"I never said 'only.' I was behind Sam an' his peaceful protests an' all. There's a time an' place fer that. But sometimes, when they're killin' the men tryin' to keep the peace, it's not enough." As he spoke, Declan slammed his stick into the ground, planting it just above Wheeler's head. "Trust me, Mickaleen, when ya believe they come back, it's different. Ya know yer makin' the world, an' the men ya kill, better fer it."

"Better by being dead?"

"Better by comin' back peaceful men." Then he bent over, picked up a short straight stick, and tied it to the one he'd used as a shovel to make a cross.

"And what about you? Shouldn't someone kill you for being a killer?"

"I'm sure they will someday. But it's a risk I'm willing to take if by the time I get back enough of us thick eejits will 'ave learned a lesson that violence is not the answer an' we can have somethin' like peace."

"So you'd want to be shot dead?"

He nodded, trying to get the cross to stay in place. "Isn't that the Golden Rule? Treat others as ya would be treated yerself? I know ya don' believe it, but if it'd help me on my path to becomin' a better human being, yes. Shoot me. Start me over in the next life, teach me the hard lesson."

"And what if none of you learn it?"

"Ahh, but we will. We've infinite lifetimes to recover from our own stupidity. That's the beauty of it all. My soul's on a journey an' if death is a shortcut to bein' reunited with the beautiful perfection that created this green island we live on, that made Lough Ree on a moonlit night, an' romance, an' love, an' is the one who figured out the perfect shape of a woman's arse, so much the better. So if I deserve it, shoot me now. Please." The cross stayed in place and Declan turned to face me, smiling again, self-satisfied.

"You're full of shit."

"Of course I am. But it don' mean I'm not right. Think about it, Mickaleen. What kind of sadistic God makes this beautiful worl' an' only gives us one chance to enjoy it? Not my God. My God, the one I believe in, *that* God would give us all as many chances as we need to get it right. Sure, I'm a dense shite and it might take me a couple a deaths to unnerstand his point sometimes, but I refuse to believe in a God that'd send Georgie here straight to hell an' let me do a jig on 'is grave jus' because he made the mistake of not confessin' his sins this morning." Declan turned to go back to the schoolhouse, still talking as he walked away: "Somebody's gotta stop injustice, Mickaleen. Even if it means ya gotta kill to do it. I won' apologize fer it. It's an eye fer an eye."

"What about turning the other cheek?"

"Yeah, well, the same God said both things, so apparently he expec's us to figure out which to do when. When Georgie boy comes back, I'll offer him any cheek he wants. Clean slate fer 'im. No hard feelin's at all. But in this life, he had to do his penance."

"You're not God, Declan."

His grin was back, as wide as ever. "I'm not? I'd beg to differ, an' I can even prove it to ya sometime, but first you have to accept the fact that yer God, too. Anyway, now's not the time or place fer philosophical discussions. Now that we're finished dancin' on Trooper Wheeler's grave we need to get them guns moved before someone else comes lookin' fer 'im. Let's go."

It was an order. He didn't need to put his hand on the pistol he carried to remind me. It was all in his voice. Still, as I followed him, I couldn't resist pointing out the fallacies in the nonsense he was spouting.

"Whether or not there really is reincarnation, none of what you says makes sense unless people remember their past lives."

Declan was walking quickly, and as I tried to keep up with him I smelled something coming from the schoolhouse, a rich, sweet odor that was both intoxicating and toxic, burning my nostrils.

"They can and do remember. Dinn't you?"

"I have nightmares, that's all. Half-remembered phrases from when I was a kid."

"Don' ferget the convenient birthmark where the bullet went in," he said, stopping at the door to the schoolhouse, avoiding the waft of steam trailing out the door, the source of the odor.

I stopped next to him, peering into the dimness to see that Kate had stoked the fire and was leaning over it, crushing some leaves into a pot of boiling water. Patsy was unconscious across the room, moaning slightly in his half-sleeping state, and the Armalite was leaning on the wall next to Kate, within easy reach. Declan cleared his throat, making sure he didn't startle her into grabbing it.

As she glanced up at us, he looked at me. "If ya don' believe what I'm tellin' ya, maybe you'll believe her. Kate here remembers bein' born again, don' ya, Kate?"

Kate got up, wiping her hands on her jeans and pushing her hair back over her ears impatiently. "Declan, don' be startin' somethin' ya can't finish. We've already got one problem with Patsy, never you mind startin' a whole other process."

"I'm jus' sayin'. People *can* remember. *He* can for feck's sake. It's not like it's bloody brain surgery."

Kate spilled a bit of liquid from the pot and dipped a finger in it, licked the finger for the taste and quickly spit it out. Then she slowly turned on Declan. "Actually, it is. That's exactly what it's like. An' it's dangerous."

"What's dangerous?" I was lost again. Both Declan and Kate were looking at me as if weighing what to tell me. Kate looked away first, moving back to Patsy as he moaned.

"You can remember if you want to, Mick," Kate said softly. "It's not theory. It's not philosophy class."

"Yeah. How do you think a low-class amadan like me knows so much about history? Science? The worl'? I know it from livin' too long. From seeing it happen first'and."

I almost laughed, but Declan was serious. "Great. So not only are you God, but you're omniscient, too? You know it all?"

Declan shrugged. "Me? 'Ell no. I jus' know that I don' know. At least my brain doesn't. My soul might know everything since it's connected to the whole sum of existence an' all, but my brain knows shite. How could it? It's not even the size of a football. The universe is infinite an' ya expect me to fit everythin' about it in this little noggin', handsome as it may be?"

"Can we get back to Patsy, please?" Kate said, glancing at Declan. "He's gonna try to kill ya as soon as he's up an' about, ya know that much, don' ya?"

"An' what do ya want me to do about that? Ya want me to kill yer brother before he kills me? Is that the kinda sister ya are?"

"No. Stop actin' the git and think fer a minute. Patsy needs to know where he stands, doesn't he? He's been told, but he's never gone through his rite of passage, so he remembers nothin' of his own." Declan nodded at that and crossed to the pot Kate had boiling, sniffing its contents.

"What's the right of passage got to do with this?"

"Not 'right,' as in what he deserves, although it is somethin' we all deserve. She means 'rite' like a ceremony. Except she's fergettin' that Patsy's a nonbeliever like yerself. He doesn't want the ceremony." He was staring at Kate now, an unspoken challenge in his eyes.

"I don' see that there's a choice. If he doesn't remember, he's gonna keep makin' stupid mistakes and someone, probably you, is gonna have to kill 'im. I'd rather have 'im alive and pissed at me fer awakenin' him than dead because he was stupid." With that, she held up a handful of berries and leaves, the stuff she had been boiling in the pot that made that strange smell. "I've got everything I need here, except the nightshade."

"Nightshade?" I'd learned about nightshade at the police academy. It's a poison, used as a recreational hallucinogen, that can be deadly.

"Yeah. Ya might know it as belladonna. It's . . . sort of a home remedy." Kate shrugged, trying to downplay the danger of it.

"I know what it is. It's a poison. You'll kill him if you give him too much."

"Trust us. We know. But don' worry. We only aim to *almos'* kill 'im. Besides, nightshade is a plant druidesses an' witches have used for thousands of years. Kate knows what she's doin'. I told ya, she's got the twitch a the witch in her."

"And what exactly *is* she doing?"

Before Declan could answer, Kate interrupted. "Healing his mind an' his soul. We need to get him to unnerstand his place in all this." She was looking down at Patsy's face, which was tense with pain.

"She's right. We need to make him remember his place. It'll be a good lesson fer you too, Mickaleen." With that, Declan turned to leave.

"Do you know where it is?" Kate stopped him.

"It still grows on the other side of the island, right where yer ma planted it the first time. I'll be back."

Declan slid out the door, and I was left alone with Kate and Patsy. I stood in awkward silence for a moment, watching how gentle and caring Kate was toward her brother, who she apparently seemed ready to poison in some strange cult rite. I didn't know what to do. I was feeling lightheaded from the smell of whatever was in the pot, and the scent, mixed with the smoke from the peat, was making my chest feel tight. If I didn't know better, I'd say I was slightly stoned from breathing the steam and smoke, or from a lack of sleep, or both.

We had done some training on cults after I was assigned to the Intelligence Division. A lot of the ones we investigated made claims that their members were special, that they were chosen ones with secret doctrines that gave them special access to some spiritual truth. They controlled their initiates by promising them access to this knowledge and used drugs and threats to make them dependent on the cult, demanding absolute loyalty.

Now, here on Inchmore, I was faced with something that was beginning to look like a classic cult. The access to memories of past lives was held up by Declan as their secret knowledge, they were using hallucinogens to convince themselves the memories were real, and they demanded absolute loyalty or they'd kneecap you, like he had done to Patsy.

At least that's what my rational, professionally trained mind was telling me. Emotionally, I wasn't so sure. I was missing something here. Declan had known what I'd dreamed back home in Staten Island, before I'd ever met him, and Kate was right—I did feel like I knew her much better than I had reason to, and I had spoken to her in a language I never knew before I spoke it.

Pushing aside the argument about cults for a moment, I focused on what seemed to me to be objective concerns. Kate and Declan were about to force potentially lethal drugs on Patsy and I needed to do something to stop them.

"Kate, you know this isn't rational, right? You can't make someone remember a past life. You don't really believe that, do you?"

"I don't expect you to believe anything. You'll believe whatever it is ya choose, no matter what I expect."

"You don't care if I think you're both crazy?"

Kate shrugged, glancing up at me. I saw her eyes and remembered last night. It was then I knew I'd never change her mind. I suddenly felt like the naive one, in over his head. Her eyes were confident and full of sympathy for me. "Look, Mickaleen. I can't tell ya what to think. I personally believe any person that tells ya that ya have to believe somethin' inn't to be trusted. If ya *have* to believe somethin', it's wrong-headed. Ya need to find yer own path, yer own way to unnerstand the infinite. No one else can do that fer ya but you. I know where yer head is at right now. I've been there, so I know I won't change yer mind by talkin'. If you'll just watch and trust me, maybe ya can see things different soon enough."

"You actually think Declan can make Patsy remember a past life with some herbs, berries, and belladonna?"

"No. I think *I* can make him remember." Her tone was sharp, defensive.

"So you *do* believe it?"

Kate didn't answer but just sat looking down at Patsy. After a moment she shrugged and looked up at me, her voice tight with emotion. "Yeah. I do." She stood, moving closer to me, her eyes on mine, hard to read in the dim light. "An' dinn't you believe it when ya walked into the greengrocer's and seen me for the first time? Dinn't ya know we already knew each other?"

Kate was right in front of me now, her face about six inches from mine. Ash from the fire streaked her cheeks, which were red from the heat. Her eyes were shining. I could smell the smoky peat and the herbal mixture in her hair, and somehow I knew I was wrong. About everything. This was what she was supposed to look like, to smell like. This was where I was supposed to be. It was like déjà vu, and I felt like I'd been here before with her.

She held my eye for a moment, and when she spoke, I inhaled the sweetness of her breath.

"You walked in the door and the first thing ya told me was, '*Ta me i gcruachais. Ta me ar strae.*'"

I nodded. I knew what it meant. I remembered it from somewhere. "I need your help. I'm lost."

"That's right. But ya don't know Irish, do ya?" There was a glint of sour humor in her eye and I remember thinking that if sarcasm was an international sport, the Irish'd be world champions. "And what did I say to you?"

"No . . . *Ta tu mall. An bhfuil tú ag lorg duine éigin?*" I repeated what she had said, before I even had a chance to think about it.

"Exactly. 'You're just late. Are you looking for someone?' An' you were lookin' for me, weren't ya?" I nodded, involuntarily. She was right. It was as if I had been looking for her without knowing it. And when I found her, I knew it was her that I'd lost.

"It's not really so hard to believe, is it, Mickaleen? That you an' I were meant to be? That we have been before?" Kate had kept moving closer and her lips brushed mine. Her eyes looked into me, watching for my response. I couldn't hold her stare. I closed my eyes and kissed her.

For a moment, it all melted away as she kissed me back. None of it mattered. And then she pulled away.

"If ya don' believe in that, I don' know what to tell ya, Mickaleen. I can't make ya see it if ya can't after that."

I knew then that I'd believe whatever she wanted if she'd just kiss me again, and I told her as much. "I believe you, Kate. But the rest, how do you expect me to believe the rest?"

Kate's eyes drifted away from mine, her shoulders tensing. "If ya bothered to examine the evidence, Officer Corrigan, you'd see that it's all around ya. But as ya know, 'that which is essential is invisible to the eye,' inn't it? You've got ta listen with yer heart and not yer thick Mick head."

Kate grabbed my hand, pulling me to the door. She pointed toward the cottages, which were barely visible through the undergrowth. "Look out there, at the cottage the guns were in. You and I were in that cottage the mornin' Liam came to get you. The day you shot him."

She turned to look at me, to see my reaction. "Do ya remember that? Or do ya remember when Ol' Jim caught the beatin' that made him a bit daft, coverin' fer you the day the Tans came to the island lookin' for ya?"

"It's not possible, Kate."

"Sayin' it doesn't make it so. Think about all the legends, Mickaleen. Think about our history. How many times have you heard the expression 'he's an ol' soul' or 'in a past life'? How many legends are there that talk about comin' back from the dead? Oisin returnin' from Tír Na NÓg, the land of the forever young, or King Arthur's bein' the once an' future king? It's all there, inn't it?"

"That's myth, not history."

"Then explain to yerself the way ya feel about me, a woman ya barely know. Tell me that ya don't feel like we belong together, like we've known each other forever," she said.

I couldn't say anything. I couldn't deny the way I felt. It didn't prove her point, but it certainly undermined every logical point I could ever make. Kate waited for me to answer, but my answer was in my eyes. I had no arguments left and she knew it.

"For a few hundred years, science has tried to tell us it has all the answers, but for thousands before that, people knew better . . . The ancient Celts believed in reincarnation, did ya know that? So did the Fomorians an' the Firbolg, and the T'uatha Da Danaan, who come before us. They built Newgrange and the passage graves because they knew how to remember."

"You think they built monuments to help them remember past lives?"

"I don't think it, Mick. I know they did. Why do ya think the Egyptians took the trouble to build the pyramids? Why would anyone in their right mind spend so much time an' energy unless it served a purpose? Because they knew it was true. All the ancients knew it."

"If they all knew it, if we all used to remember, why don't we now?"

That stopped her, and she stared out at the island for a moment while searching for the right words to explain.

"Because those of us who remember, who are awakened to who we really are, we're hated by the ones who don't remember. An' I understand why they hate us. If we remember, then we live forever, forever growing old and young again. But the ones who don't remember are lost, Mickaleen. Like you. And they're afraid."

"Why would anyone care what you believe?"

Kate turned on me, a flash of anger in her eyes. "I dunno, why would Protestants and Catholics blow each other up? Don' be such a thick shite. Jus' think it through fer a second. If ya remember the past, an' if yer salvation's in yer own hands, ya don't need to answer to any man. Ya don't need to tithe to any church in order to be saved or bow to any emperor, because when you come back, it's a fresh start. Why do ya think the Romans hated the Celts so much? They couldn't defeat us by killin' us, could they? We jus' came back at 'em again. Not afraid to die. The only way they could defeat us was by killin' our Druids, stoppin' the rite of passage, keepin' us from rememberin' our true selves."

Patsy moaned behind us and stirred. Kate knelt beside him, gently soothing him. I walked closer, looking down at him. The pain was etched on his face and Kate clearly felt it with him. She held his hand, speaking barely above a whisper.

"After the empires tried to kill us all off an' make us ferget, it was the church and the religious zealots, tryin' to control the gates of heaven. They tried to control people by offerin' a shortcut to salvation, givin' their followers a chance to pay fer forgiveness on their deathbeds fer just a donation and a confession after a lifetime of sin. That's not a true confession. Ya need real remorse fer that."

Kate kept telling her story as she moved to the herbal mixture she had on the fire. She took a strip of cloth and soaked it.

"Anyway, they couldn't destroy us all. Some of us can even remember without the rite of passage. They're the ones we say have eyes that see an' ears that hear. They're born with the gift. No one needs to wake them up. It seems to travel in families with redheads. There's somethin' special about them."

Kate wrung out the cloth, then laid it over Patsy's nose and mouth, making him breathe through it. He seemed to settle down and relax as she went on. "Did you know you can find redheads all over the world? Even in Africa an' Japan. An' the word 'Russia' comes from the word 'rus,' which means red, since it was founded by Viking raiders in the first place. Declan thinks the red hair is from the Sea People, our ancestors, traveling the world, givin' people the good news about bein' born again . . . And showin' 'em how it's done, too, apparently."

"Is that what you expect me to believe? That this cult survived because redheads all over the world spontaneously remember the past?"

"Don't be an eejit. It's not a cult, an' the old ways were never lost. Some of it was passed down through families and clusters of us awakened ones, and the rest is right in front of yer eyes, layered into stories an' fairy tales, fer those wit' eyes that see an' ears that hear to remember. It's the *uisce fe talamh*." She stopped as she felt Patsy's pulse, her lips moving silently as she counted.

I knew what the words she said in Irish meant but, again, didn't know how. They were as clear to me as English synonyms. Still my rational mind found it hard to believe. "You're talking about an underground stream?"

She paused, finishing her count, then looked up at me. "Right. Exactly. It's a metaphor. Water under the ground feeds everything, gives life to plants and springs to the surface when its needed. It's knowledge passed down through generations an' it's the resistance to any form of oppression, wearing away the very earth that tries to bury it. You can see it rise to the surface in all the old myths, but to outsiders everything is said in parables so 'they may be ever seeing but never perceiving, an' ever hearing but never understanding.'"

"And you think this proves you've been persecuted for believing in reincarnation?"

Kate placed the cloth over Patsy's face once again, and his breathing almost immediately grew even more shallow. "No, not because we believe in it. Because we can *remember* it. They can't win as long as we remember. What's the worst that they can do? Kill us? Think about what Declan would do if they killed him and he came back knowin' who did it?"

She was lobbing softball questions. I answered even though it was pretty much rhetorical. "He'd shoot the guy in the back of the head, then go after his children."

"Exactly, but not for revenge, mind you—just to teach the man a lesson.

No, killin' us is nothin'. It's when they make ya ferget that yer an immortal soul that doesn't need any help gettin' saved, that's when they win."

"What does that mean?"

"Exactly what it says. We're each our own messiah, Mickaleen. No one can save us but ourselves." She was feeling for Patsy's pulse again, her lips moving much more slowly this time. "I tell ya what a real hell is. It's bein' stuck in this life an' dependent upon some church to save ya. Waitin' on some priest who tells ya that yer a born sinner because Eve ate an apple an' Adam was too weak-willed to say no when she offered him a bite. Them hypocrites with that original sin shite are a joke an' anyone with a brain in 'is head knows it."

The light in the room suddenly dimmed and I glanced up to see Declan darkening the doorway, branches and berries in hand.

"Jaysus, Kate, will ya stop preachin' at 'im? He's not gonna believe a word of it until he does, an' then ya won't need to say another thing. Save yer breath." Declan dropped the branches and berries in front of Kate, then turned to warm himself by the fire.

"I needed to do somethin' waitin' on you. What took so long?"

"I went lookin' fer the right place. He can't be in the cold too long or we might lose him. There's a spot down by the boats that'll do. Not far. Get that nightshade in 'im and let's get it done."

Kate was already crushing several berries in the rag she had laid over Patsy's face, rubbing them into the cloth. She took several others and tossed them into the pot of simmering water, counting them out.

"What are you going to do to him?" I asked.

"What are *we* gonna do?" Declan corrected me. "We're gonna take him to the water and wake 'im, that's what." He glanced at Kate, who held the cloth over Patsy's mouth squeezing the excess water, now laced with night-shade, into his mouth. Patsy gagged and coughed but swallowed it. After she got a few more squeezes in, Kate tied the rag over his nose and mouth, then nodded to Declan.

Patsy's chest seemed to have stopped rising and falling. Every muscle was relaxed, his face no longer tense with pain. I worried that he might already be dead, but Declan didn't seem concerned at all as he stooped over and felt for a pulse at Patsy's carotid artery.

"Grab him with me, Mickaleen. Let's have this done with. Kate, better bring the rifle in case." Declan grabbed one of Patsy's arms, swinging it over his shoulder. I grabbed the other, still worried about what we were about to do. As we carried him out the door, I slowed down. I didn't want another death on my conscience.

"Are you sure he's all right? He feels cold."

"He'll get colder before he gets warmer, but don't worry. You've been baptized, ain't ya, Mickaleen?" Declan asked, struggling a bit under Patsy's weight as Kate slung the Armalite over one shoulder and poured more of her herbal mixture into a second rag to carry with us.

"Of course I was baptized."

"Well, yer baptism was a watered-down load of shite. Did ya know that?" I shook my head as we dragged Patsy along, all dead weight, toward the shore of the Lough. Declan was going to tell me about my load of shite baptism, whether or not I wanted to hear, so I just kept going.

"Ya know what baptism used to be, when it meant something in the old days? It was a real rite of passage. Just lookit the rites of passage all the old religions had—baptism used to be full-body baptism, holding you down in frigid water. Or they'd send ya out in the desert for forty days, nearly starvin' or dehydratin' to death. Then there was sleep deprivation, blood-letting, vision quests an' all the rest. Every one of them rites of passage was set up to bring you to the brink of death and back again."

"That makes no sense. Why would you try to kill someone just to bring them back?"

"Ahh, he's finally thinking. That's the sure sign of a smart fella." Declan winked at Kate.

She stared at me, annoyed for some reason, as if I'd let her down. "Unfortunately it's also a bad habit of eejits and amadans like Patsy. He asks the questions, but donn't want real answers, only ones he's comfortable with. Do you *want* the real answers, Mickaleen? Or would you rather ferget everything?"

"I want to finish this and get out of here."

"I'll take that as a yes." Declan interrupted before Kate could respond, jerking Patsy toward the shore and walking faster, forcing me to keep up. "An' since ya asked, they tried to almos' kill ya because near-death experiences open up a shining path that leads to who ya truly are."

"So you try to kill them to get them to remember?"

"It works. If ya knew yer history you'd be seein' the truth of it already. Ya know how ya read about human sacrifice? Well, that's all just a big misunnerstandin'. In some cultures, after they couldn't remember, they misinterpreted the awakening ceremony. They missed the point that you were only supposed to *almos'* kill the initiate. An' in other cultures human sacrifice was intentional, sending a great soul to the next life so they'd be ready and full grown when society needed them the most. Ya need great leaders in every generation. Too many in one does ya no good." With that, Declan stopped, just short of the water, near a shallow rocky pool. "Set 'im down here, head toward the water. It's time Patsy remembered who he really is . . ."

We gently laid Patsy down, then stepped back as Declan once again checked Patsy's pulse. I could hear him humming or possibly chanting under his breath as he did, the rhythm of it slowing to match Patsy's heart rate. He seemed to finish a verse of whatever it was and looked up at Kate, satisfied.

"He's ready." Before I could move, Declan grabbed Patsy and pulled him forward, shoving his face into and under the cold water, holding him down even as he began to thrash wildly. Declan was chanting something again, in a ritualized rhythm. I moved to stop him by instinct but hadn't taken half a step when I heard the Armalite's safety snap off.

"Leave 'im be." Kate had the Armalite pointed at my chest, held rock steady. "He knows what he's doin'."

I stopped, unsure. Patsy's thrashing grew more intense, but Declan's chant never wavered, even when Patsy's head smashed into a sharp rock, opening a deep gash that turned the water bloody as Declan shoved Patsy's head back under.

After a moment, Patsy stopped struggling and his muscles went slack. Everything settled to silence. Then, quietly, Kate spoke, trying to assure me.

"It's just a real baptism. A rite of passage to awaken Patsy so he can be born again." As she spoke, Declan's cadence changed and I recognized pieces of what he was saying, even though some was in Irish, Latin, and even what sounded a bit like an Asian language.

The bits I heard and understood sounded like "Christ has died, Christ is risen, Christ will come again . . . Travel down the shining path . . . for I am the way and the truth and the light . . ." Declan's voice finally trailed off as he laid his head on Patsy's chest and closed his eyes.

"Is he dead?" I asked. I could see that he wasn't breathing.

No one answered me for a moment and then Declan sat straight up, clenched his fists together and brought them down hard on Patsy's sternum, causing his whole body to arch up, bouncing off the ground. When he came back to a resting position, he coughed, and his chest rose and fell slightly.

"No. Only mostly," Kate finally answered. I looked up at her and she was trying to suppress a wry smile. "Trust us. We've done this thousands of times. He'll wake up fer a bit, then fall back into what looks like death fer three days or so, but he'll be fine. As long as nobody sees him in his current state and tries to bury him. That's happened to too many people throughout history. Buried alive before they had a chance to fully live. That's where ya get yer stories of zombies an' the livin' dead from now, inn't it?"

With that she pushed past me, kneeling next to Patsy, whispering something in his ear and pulling several berries from another pocket, crushing them in the same rag she had brought from the schoolhouse.

Time seemed to drag on, and Kate was repeating herself for the fifth time when Patsy's eyelids fluttered and he managed to focus on Kate. His voice, when it came, seemed rougher than before, deeper, and with a much thicker brogue. He spoke as if his voice was not his own. "Jaysus . . . I'm not myself, am I?" he said.

Kate smiled down at him, stroking his cheek tenderly, cleaning the cut across his face and numbing it with her herbal remedy. "No. Ya are yerself. You'll always be yerself. It's just that now yer more as well."

Patsy nodded, trying to focus on everything around him, his eyes settling on Declan. "You . . . Ya bastard . . . Yer Liam an' Christy an' Finn, ain' ya? Bastards ev'ry one a ya . . . Couldna ya have wakened me before ya took my knee?"

Declan shrugged, unconcerned. "Ya owed me that knee."

"I owed ya more than that. But I wouldna owed ya nothin' if I knew before what I know now."

"It was offered to you. You chose yer path. You didn't believe."

Patsy sighed. "I was an eejit. How could I unnerstand without seein' it myself?" He breathed deeply and sharply as Kate cleaned the wound, twisting away from her, his eyes resting on me as he did.

"Ahh, an' you . . . Mickaleen . . . Welcome back, my friend. God, ya know the shite they say about you aroun' here? An' none of it true, is it?" Patsy smiled sadly, grabbing Kate's hand to stop her from touching his wound again. "Leave it. Let it scar. It'll remind me not to be such a bloody amadan in the future."

"It's the nightshade, isn't it? He's hallucinating," I said.

"No, Mickaleen. I'm seein' clearly fer the first time in my life. Fer the first time in this life, I've got answers, not just questions." Then he closed his eyes and smiled despite his pain. I stood silent for a long moment, trying to absorb all I'd heard, all I'd seen. It looked like if Patsy came around again, I'd owe him a pint or two.

Sean

I was belted tightly into the passenger's seat, next to Anne in her Sierra Ghia, trying to decide if I believed any of what I'd just read, or all of it. I'd read the pages for the second time and could appreciate near-death experiences and seeing my life pass before my eyes in a very immediate way from where I sat, but it was hard to figure out what I thought about the pages. I didn't want to believe some of it, but Patsy's graffiti had been there. *T. W. is dead, and I remember it all. I remember Liam and Sean and how I almost died. I know that I am Patsy Ryan, and that I am not.*

It seemed clear that something strange had happened on Inchmore in January of 1972, but I had trouble believing that it had anything to do with Patsy remembering his past lives and forgiving the guy who'd just kneecapped him. I picked up the pages to read them again when Anne let out a long sigh.

"Feckin' Christ. Ain' ya done with that yet?" She looked at me, annoyed, and nearly rode us into a hedgerow. I stopped reading.

"What's your problem?"

"Ya read it twice already. Can't ya get yer eyes back on the road an' be a proper copilot?"

"You wouldn't need one if you weren't flying. Can't you slow down a bit?"

"Can't ya speed up?" she countered, putting her foot down on the gas out of spite. "It's not really that hard to unnerstand, is it? It's written in English. They gave him a near-death experience. It's as clear as day."

That stopped me. It meant she'd read the missing pages. She was letting me go over it, over and over again, struggling to figure it all out, and she already knew. "You read this before?" I asked, knowing the answer.

"My da had it hidden."

"That didn't answer the question."

She hesitated, feeling the tension radiating off me. "Whatta you think?"

"You still didn't answer the question, but I'm pretty sure that you'd find and read anything that anyone tried to hide from you."

Anne smiled, keeping her eyes on the road for a change, taking my comment as a compliment. "Yer smarter than ya look, ya know that?"

"Well, since you read it, do you believe it?" I asked.

"It don' matter what I think. You wouldn't believe jus' because I did, an' if ya did ya'd be an amadan. Ya need to believe because ya believe."

"That's profound." She was pissing me off. No one in this country seemed to be able to answer a simple question.

"Inn't it? I've a keen sense of the obvious, in case ya haven't noticed." Anne was treating everything lightly, trying to get me to smile.

"If everything's so obvious to you, why don't you tell me what really happened?"

"No."

I could tell by the way she said it that there would be no arguing with her. I sat silently for a minute, looking up only as she slowed down. I knew then that she was being genuine.

"You need to decide fer yerself, Sean. I'm serious. Start by lookin' at the evidence in front of ya. Look at what ya know to be true fer yerself."

"Like what?"

Anne shrugged, trying to think of something. "Like when ya saw me in the airport I guess, ya knew who I was, dinn't ya?"

It was true. She'd looked familiar to me the moment I laid eyes on her. There had to be a reason. "You looked familiar because you looked like a cousin."

"Really? But I'm not even blood related. How do ya explain that? Do all us Irish look alike to you?"

"No. But so what? I overheard you talking and you argued just like my father."

Anne scraped the side of the car on a hedgerow, coming around a turn too fast. I could measure her frustration by the rate the speedometer went up. "Ahh, Christ, yer as thick as a brick, ain' ya," she mumbled. "Lemme ask ya, do ya ever remember dreams that seem like they happened when ya were a different person?"

"Everyone has those. That's the way dreams work."

"Yea? An' why do ya think they work that way? Ya ever have a dream that seemed more real than yer own life? As if you were there?" I shrugged, thinking about the dreams I had about Inchmore the night before. The ones I'd assumed were inspired by the journal.

"That doesn't prove anything," I told her, almost believing it.

"Sure. Sure it doesn't. But do ya ever know things ya never remember learnin'? An' what about all the things ya hear every day? Things that seem like nothin' but ya hear everywhere, like the phrase 'born again.' Or when they say a child's got an 'old soul' or that ya did somethin' in a 'past life.'"

"They're metaphors, that's all."

"Yea? An' where do ya think metaphors come from? The truth is always written in plain sight, even if it's between the lines an' not on 'em. I mean, c'mon, what about all the fables an' fairy tales? What do ya think *Sleepin' Beauty*'s all about? It's an awakenin' ceremony, inn't it? Hidden in plain sight. Brilliant."

"That's insane."

Anne sighed that heavy sigh that anyone from the west of Ireland seems capable of. A sigh so deep the oxygen to their brain has to be cut off. When she started breathing again, she spoke softly, resigned. "Start with Stevenson. Ian Stevenson."

Horns blared, interrupting her as we sped into Lucan, cutting off other cars. I decided it was safer to take her advice and let her concentrate on the road for a few minutes while I tried to read the journal again.

TWENTY-FIVE MINUTES LATER we had parked safely near Merrion Square and were walking toward Trinity. That's when I noticed him. He was maybe a few years older than me and didn't really fit in with the Trinity students. Somehow his clothes seemed more functional and less studiously relaxed. His jeans, scuffed boots, and black leather jacket looked as though they had been worn to do something more than sit in class, and he had that "so black it has an almost blue sheen" hair of the dark Irish. But the thing that was most striking about him was his eyes. I noticed them as he glanced over at Anne, looking at her as if he recognized her. They were almost luminous they were so blue, and they stood out against his dark hair and pale skin. My grandmother used to call eyes like that "the eyes of psychopaths and saints," and in my experience, she was right.

Whichever one he was, psychopath or saint, he made me nervous. I almost pointed him out to Anne to see if she knew him, but then the Trinity campus came into view, and I have to say I was pretty impressed. The buildings were beautiful, the grounds well cared for, and the students disproportionately blond and redheaded and very attractive. One particular redhead distracted me, and by the time I recovered from Anne's backhanded blow to my stomach, the man with the blue eyes had disappeared.

I didn't notice his departure at the time because there was too much else to take in. Everything about Trinity seemed to be built to last as well as to be aesthetically pleasing.

When we got to the library, Anne talked our way in by claiming that I was an American student doing a summer abroad and that "bloody Aer Lingus" had made a bollix of my luggage, so I had lost my college ID and letter of introduction. She was loud and starting to make a scene, and I think they let us through just to shut her up, as long we promised to behave and not use foul language in the library.

As Anne argued, I kept an eye out for security guards while reading an informational pamphlet about the library. It turned out that this was the largest research library in Ireland and had some special status that meant it got a copy of every book published in Great Britain and Ireland—more than one hundred thousand books a year. It had almost five million books in its collection and was actually made up of six separate libraries that held not only books but also periodicals, maps, music, and handwritten manuscripts dating back for centuries.

The most famous of these was the Book of Kells, or "the tourist trap" as Anne put it, an illuminated manuscript of the Gospels in Latin. It was housed in the Old Library, which included the Long Room, a place built for the worship of books that looked more like a cathedral than a library.

It was, I believe, designed to intimidate anyone who stepped through the doors, fairly screaming its message: "Here is all the knowledge in Ireland, but you can never possess it all."

If there was anywhere that I could find out the truth about the past, it was here, in this vast room. I remember thinking as I took it all in that unless I had some direction, finding what I was looking for might take a few lifetimes.

As I had the thought, I remembered Anne's point about the truth being hidden in plain sight, in phrases and in metaphors, there for anyone to see. It was a tempting thing to believe, but I knew that I couldn't prove she was right or wrong unless I could find real evidence somewhere in all the pages of all the books that hovered over me. I knew it was all there for the taking, but there was so much of it, I felt buried under its weight.

"Ian Stevenson." Anne whispered, pushing me toward a reference desk and a haggard librarian.

"Can't we just look in the periodicals? Or find a computer and type in my uncle Mike's name and see what comes up?" I asked, hesitating.

"Yea. And with a name like Michael Corrigan, you'll only find maybe two million references, won' ya?" Anne rolled her eyes at me and stalked over to the librarian, clearing her throat to get attention. She got it, as well as two dozen dirty looks from students in the stacks.

"'Scuse me, miss. My friend's here on a semester abroad from New York and his daft professor has him lookin' up a Dr. Ian Stevenson fer some paper. He's lost 'is voice from that foul air they pump into the planes and needs some serious help." The librarian was looking between Anne and me, suspicious. I nodded, pointing to my throat and shrugging.

She shook her head, a scowl on her face. "A tincture of barberry, eucalyptus, and German chamomile," she said, prescribing a home remedy. "Add raw goldenseal and licorice, and steam it with honey."

Anne was nodding as if trying to remember it all, even as the librarian came over to me and clamped a sweaty palm on my forehead, then she turned to Anne, giving her the orders. "He's warm. He shouldn't be here. Follow me and I'll find him his Stevenson; then take him home and put him to bed, understand?"

"Right. I'll get 'im in bed as soon as we're done here, ma'am," Anne said with a straight face, only winking at me after the librarian turned away and headed for the stacks.

I STARTED WHERE Anne suggested, with Ian Stevenson, a professor of psychiatry at the University of Virginia who set out to scientifically prove reincarnation. Stevenson was rigorous about finding alternative explanations for the knowledge of previous lives, but in the majority of cases, there seemed to be only one: reincarnation. I was about to throw the book down when I came to a section he had written on how birthmarks and birth defects might be remnants of trauma from previous lives. In 35 percent of the cases that he researched, Stevenson found the subjects had a birthmark or defect that matched a wound of the previous incarnation. These cases included children that had birthmarks that matched bullet wounds from a previous life.

I moved farther into the stacks of books and started to take off my shirt. I needed to see the birthmarks that had been called a "shotgun blast of ugly." I was trying to look at it when a pair of cold hands grabbed me from behind and pulled me backward. I made some kind of noise, though not a "little girl screech," as Anne later claimed. When I turned to face her she was laughing so hard she was wheezing and we were getting "shushed" from three aisles away.

"Sorry," she said, catching her breath. "Ya just looked so lonely, touchin' yerself like that. Couldn't ya wait till after?"

"I was reading about birthmarks."

"Jaysus, yer still on bloody reincarnation? I was hopin' you'd haved moved on to bog bodies and passage graves by now."

"Bog bodies? What do they have to do with anything?"

Anne smiled, then turned back toward a shelf where there were a stack of books sitting on the edge. She grabbed three of them and held them out to me. "Here."

She started walking away, leaving them for me. "Where are you going?"

"To find a college boy to buy me lunch. I told ya, I'm hungry." Anne disappeared around the corner of the bookshelves and I followed her with my eyes down to the first floor. That's when I saw him again. Old Blue Eyes. He was sitting at a table reading, but he was still wearing his leather jacket, as if he expected to get up and leave at any moment. He glanced at Anne as she passed him, then looked up to where I stood. His eyes seemed to pass over me without seeing me, but I couldn't be sure. He went back to reading, and after a minute I convinced myself that I was being paranoid. Just because Declan was a killer who didn't want me looking into the past and there was a guy who looked like a killer reading down in the Long Room, didn't mean the two things were related.

I distracted myself from my own paranoia by looking back at the books Anne had brought me. In each one, at a dozen different places, were small tabs of paper. Bookmarks. Anne had tabbed a photo of the Gundestrup Cauldron, an ancient Celtic work of art depicting a column of warriors marching forward to be sacrificed while another column is reborn and marching away from it. She had a dozen other tabs as well, marking passages about the Druid teaching that death was a rite of passage just as birth was another, coming along cyclically in the same way that the seasons passed. The intertwined spirals that were common in their art were symbolic of the immortality of the soul as well as the progression a soul could make in each incarnation.

Of course, she had also marked text referring to bog bodies and passage graves, the megalithic monuments that are strewn about Ireland and are older than the pyramids of Egypt. This particular book theorized that the passage graves were used for awakening ceremonies.

The rituals started on Samhain, a day we celebrate today as Halloween or the Day of the Dead. It was a day on which the souls that had departed the previous year were invited back in a celebration that included fertility rites. It was no accident that by the winter solstice, seven weeks later, a woman would know if she was pregnant or not. Once the child was born, it was believed that he was brought back to the passage grave, where the body of his previous incarnation had been preserved and the child was reintroduced to it in order to spark his memory. That body was then cremated as the new incarnation ceremonially put the past behind them.

The bog bodies were incredibly well-preserved bodies found in the bogs

218 • KEVIN FOX

of northwestern Europe and Ireland. It seems that when the use of a passage grave was impossible owing to an unexpected or sudden death, the bogs would provide for the preservation of a body for the next incarnation to see in order to help retrieve his past-life memories. After a short period of time, the bodies would have been so well preserved that looking at them would have been like looking at one's own reflection. I was a bit creeped out by all of this. Imagine being a little kid and being brought to meet a body. A mummified body, either buried in a bog or entombed. I'm not sure if remembering that the mummified body was actually *me* just a few years ago would freak me out more or less.

I put the book down, looking for something a little less disturbing to read, and found a book on initiation rites. This seemed like a good place to start if I was going to find out if the awakening described by Uncle Mike was an actual religious rite. Looking at the rites of passage old religions used, I saw that many of them used psychedelic drugs and practices meant to induce altered states of consciousness to reveal the "secrets" they taught.

It seems that almost all religions, even the most mainstream ones, have a rite that incorporates elements of the awakening ceremony. Some call it being "born again" and even do it by immersing people in water so they can be reborn. Others, like one in ancient Egypt, would put a person into an underground chamber to experience a death and rebirth. As I read further, I saw circumstantial evidence for reincarnation everywhere, including the Greek myths of Hercules and Orpheus and Demeter descending and returning from the underworld.

Even Pythagoras and Plato believed in reincarnation, and Socrates apparently drank the hemlock just to prove a point—that he was coming back anyway.

It seems that Christianity, like every other religion, was at one time also part of an underground stream of knowledge taught only to initiates who were persecuted by the rest of society. This is what Kate was calling the *uisce fe talamh,* or the water under the ground. As I read on, I realized how pervasive the idea is of secret teachings given only to the elect, even in the Gospels themselves. In Mark 4:11, Jesus says that "the secret of the kingdom of God is given to you, but to those who are outside, everything comes in parables."

In a fragment of the Secret Gospel of Mark, a Gnostic text, Jesus is described as performing secret initiation rites. In the Gnostic text the Secret Book of John, reincarnation is central to the salvation of souls. Written no later than AD 185, the Secret Book of John states that "all people have drunk the water of forgetfulness and exist in a state of ignorance. Some are able to overcome ignorance through the Spirit of life that descends upon them. These souls will be saved and will become perfect." John goes on to ask Jesus what will happen to those who do not attain salvation. Jesus replies that the only way for these souls to escape is to emerge from forgetfulness and acquire knowledge. Even that most rigid and mainstream Christian, Paul, wrote in his letter to the Colossians: "Do not lie to each other, since you have taken off your old self with its practices and have put on the new self, which is being renewed in knowledge in the image of its Creator."

All of this was beyond confusing. And even if it was true, why should I believe it? Was I supposed to believe that I *was* my uncle Mike? And what if I was? What would it change? Would I make the same mistakes this time around?

It was easier to ignore the evidence and go on living my life—but if I did that, would I end up the same way he did? I was damned if I didn't believe, but if I did believe, would it become a self-fulfilling prophecy? I turned to go find Anne, but as I did I noticed a handwritten note on the floor where it had fallen from one of the books I had been reading. I picked up the scrap of paper and looked at it. It seemed to be Anne's writing, and it was a quote from the Gospels: "*Do not give what is holy to the dogs, nor cast your pearls before swine, lest they trample them under their feet, and turn and tear you in pieces.*" I thought back to Anne's earlier statement, "Ya need to believe because ya believe." And if you didn't, apparently, you were swine. Anne knew that I would quit. That's why she wrote the note. But I was only swine if what I'd been reading were pearls of wisdom. I had my doubts. For one thing, if this were all true, why wasn't everyone aware of it?

"It's not exactly hidden, is it?" I heard Anne from the other side of the bookshelves. I looked up as she came around the corner. How long had she been standing there watching me? I held her gaze for a minute, and she saw my doubt. My resistance. "It's in all the history books. It's in the damn Bible. It's everywhere. People jus' choose not to see it."

"And if I don't see it, then I guess I'm the swine?"

"Depends. If ya can't recognize a pearl when ya see one, whatta ya think that makes you?" She stared me down then, challenging me. If I answered her wrong, I felt like it would all end here, right now. I'd never learn any more about what happened to Uncle Mike, and I'd never have to worry about Anne teaching me what she knew about the past.

"I don't know what to think," was all I could manage. Anne nodded, accepting that.

"Ask, and it shall be given you. Seek, and ye shall find. Knock, and it shall be opened unto you." She smirked, enjoying my confusion and discomfort. "Seriously. Jus' ask, it'll be given. Not by me, necessarily, but trust me. The answers come if ya go looking fer 'em."

She stopped then, waiting for me to say something. It was quiet, and all I could hear were the murmuring voices, carrying to me from all over the Long Room. There were no words, only rhythms and intonations. I could hear the rising inflection of so many of them indicating questions. Questions being met with more questions in that quintessentially Irish way. But I was Irish as well, wasn't I? And I wanted answers. Or at least I thought I did.

I decided to ask. The only other option was to do nothing, and that seemed too . . . I don't know how else to say it, but it seemed too final. I glanced down at the book in my hands, unable to meet Anne's gaze.

"What's it like? Remembering, I mean."

She didn't say anything for a minute, just put her hand on my arm, gently. "It's memory, like others. Dimmer sometimes." I turned to face her and noticed the smile a microsecond before she went on. "It's like 'seein' through a glass darkly.' An' seein' through a dark glass is exactly what I'd like to be doin' in the next ten minutes."

She pulled me by the arm, suddenly shifting gears. "Libraries make me dry. Let's go get a pint. We can talk in a pub as well as we can here, can't we?"

As we left, I scanned the library for Blue Eyes, but didn't see him anywhere. Maybe he was out stalking a different victim.

TEN MINUTES LATER we were in the same pub Declan had taken me to, with Bridget the bitchy waitress serving me a warm Guinness and Anne a cold one. We switched glasses, trying not to let Bridget see us do it, so she wouldn't catch on and screw with us in some other way.

Anne raised her glass to Bridget's back. "One thing ya can always count on—the petty stupidity of humanity somehow givin' ya what ya want in spite of their worst intentions." Anne tapped my glass with hers. *"Slainte."*

I mumbled something in return, unsure of how to pronounce *slainte* even though I'd just heard it. I couldn't tell if it was meant to be garbled or if that was just Anne's accent.

"So, are you going to tell me anything?" I asked, after downing a good quarter of a pint.

"Like what? Ya haven't asked a proper question yet. I can't answer what ya haven't asked, now, can I?" She was right. The problem was that I didn't know where to start. There were too many questions.

"If, let's just say, this is the truth," I began. "Even part of it. And if people once knew about it . . ."

"Some people still do."

"Then why doesn't everybody?"

"They don' care to. Most people ain't got the bollocks to take responsibility fer their lives. They want to ask Father Murphy fer fergiveness right before the lights go out an' then go straight to heaven." Anne had downed half her pint and was already waving down Bridget for another.

"So there's no heaven?"

"How should I feckin' know? I'm obviously not an advanced enough soul to 'ave been there, am I? Ya tryin' to make me feel bad?"

"No. Sorry. So there might be a heaven?" I asked.

"Maybe. Maybe when ya get this life perfect an' God is satisfied ya don' need any more chances, ya move up to the next level."

"How come I never heard of this before?"

"Would ya be givin' money to the church if ya knew their story was, at best, a distortion of the truth? No one wants ya to know. It's as simple as that, Sean."

"But why?"

"Ach, the eternal question of two-year-olds and eejits. Think about it. If ya knew yerself, all the way back through all yer incarnations, do ya realize what you'd really *know*? Thousands of years experience. Now that'd be powerful. We couldna lie to each other. Nobody could rewrite history an' distort the truth the way they do. An' we'd be a whole lot feckin' smarter if we knew *now* what we knew *then*, wouldn' we?"

"So you think this is some conspiracy by the church?" They seemed the most likely group, since they had so much to lose if this was true.

"Hell no," Anne snapped. "At leas', not jus' them. It's everybody, an' it started long before Peter and Paul and that lot. It started before even the Romans and the killin' of all the Druids to stop them from awakenin' people."

"I thought the Romans only persecuted Christians?"

"Only the early sects that believed in reincarnation. And the Druids, fer the same reason. It was a challenge to their power. They dinn't want people to have no fear of dying in battle against them because they knew they'd be back in a few years for another battle. Caesar dinn't want to face warriors with thousands of years of battle experience."

"So it started with Caesar?"

"Are ya deaf? Yer not listenin'. It started before history began. If ya look at all the old religions, from India to Egypt to China, it's all there. In China they misinterpreted the reverence for previous lives as ancestor worship. They weren't worshipping ancestors, they were tryin' to tune into the memories of their ancestors, seeking the wisdom they'd forgotten. In Egypt they had the Book of the Dead to guide them through into the next life. It's all there if ya look." Anne was talking fast now, annoyed with me for being slow. "Memory is power. Back then it was the best education ya had. Hell, writin' was only invented after we started to lose our way. After we had to rely on leaving messages to ourselves explaining how to awaken. Before then, we remembered our own damn history."

"If that's true, if people were once so wise they didn't even need writing, then how come there were no civilizations? No architecture?"

She glared at me but finally shrugged. "It's simple, really. Back then, we dinn't leave behind our trash fer whoever came next to clean up. We left the place as we found it, so when we came back, we dinn't need to worry about poison in the water, and pesticides deformin' our bodies. There's no evidence there were great civilizations because they were *great*. We knew how to live with nature without havin' to defeat it."

I must have been getting drunk, because I was finding Anne to be more convincing.

"That's when we started writing, to keep the memories alive even when we couldn't do it ourselves. It didn't work. Turns out it's even easier to burn books than it is to kill people. Even worse, the books were sometimes changed, edited just enough so the rites of passage would fail. People started dyin' in the rites . . . They turned people against us, sayin' we did it on purpose. They accused us of offering up human sacrifice, misinterpretin' the awakenings."

"And now when they find bog bodies . . ."

"They assume the same damn thing. But it was never a culture of death. It was always a culture of life. We took care of the land, because it wasn't our grandkids who'd need it, it was us."

"So how does it work? Is it fate that you come back as basically the same person, acting out the same role?"

"It's more complicated than that, I think. Ya can learn an' move on if ya make different choices. Still, people seem to travel together through lifetimes, helpin' one another or screwin' with each other as much as they can, their lives intertwined. It seems ta be a choice ta move on to other places, with other people. Maybe it happens when you've learned all ya can from the ones ya been with. I sure don' know. Haven't lived enough, I guess." Anne shrugged, seemingly content with not knowing exactly how it worked.

"It sounds good to me. As long as I can learn and move on and not make the same stupid mistakes over and over."

"That's all on you. Stupid or not is still a choice," she said.

Something about the whole philosophy she had laid out appealed to me, even if I couldn't quite wrap my head around it. It was a lot to think about— living lifetimes with the same people, given the same chances to learn lessons and get it right, all of it. I could only imagine the repercussion if we all knew this was true: we'd have an environmental philosophy based on self-interest, justice based on the fact that eventually even the dead would rise to share the truth and face the results of their actions. There'd be no more getting away with murder, would there?

"If you remember past lives, and know karma works, then why have people been killing each other for thousands of years? If we're all in it together, I mean?"

"We were, until we weren't. It ain' about the finer points of religious dogma like they want ya to believe, Sean. That's just the cover story. It's about power an' secrets an' gettin' away with injustice. Today people jus' recognize the injustice and fight over that, but in the beginnin' it was about killin' the memory of what we were." Anne's hand gripped my arm unconsciously, and I could see my own reflection in her glazed eyes as she stared into mine.

"We weren't cast out of Eden, Sean. We destroyed it because we fergot that's where we were all along."

I didn't know what to do. Anne was staring at me as if she expected me to react to that in some way. Part of me thought it was the most profound thing I'd ever heard, and part knew I was drunk and that in the light of day it'd probably sound like drunk talk. Not knowing how else to respond, I leaned over and kissed her.

It felt good, but my head was spinning and the music was assaulting my mind. I had to get away, to clear my head.

I took the coward's way out and headed to the bathroom. On my way I passed Bridget, carrying a tray of empty glasses. I was pressed against her by the crowd, unable to get away.

"Hey, Yank," she said, her warm, alcohol-laced breath right in my ear. "Ya need to listen a minute. I don' know ya, an' don' care ta, but if ya know what's good fer ya, get rid of that one." She nodded toward Anne, who was watching the band and sucking back a cigarette.

"Why? And why do you care?"

"I'm jus' tryin' ta look out fer ya is all. I heard some a that shite she's tellin' ya. I've seen her like. She'll fill yer head with sex an' magic, an' the next thing ya know she'll have ya poppin' pills an' seein' visions. I seen it happen. You'll end up addicted or in jail, fer sure. I swear, I even saw her switch drinks on ya like she was tryin' to drug ya." The crowd eased away a bit, but Bridget stayed right up next to me, her free hand now on my arm, her eyes intense, trying to hold mine as I kept looking away.

"Trust me. It's happened before. To my own brother no less. She'll tell ya fairy tales an' get ya drunk an' shag ya till ole willie's blue. Ya won' know what hit ya. A woman like that sucks a man in, and they end up on the wrong side of the law or dead." Bridget was clearly paranoid, but I thought about how Uncle Mike had gotten caught up with Kate and ended up dead. I thought about how Declan had insinuated that Anne was lying to me. And how, by Anne's own admission, she'd been somewhat responsible for Bridget's brother going to jail.

I nodded to Bridget and pulled away, retreating to the bathroom for a moment of peace. But there was none. A seed of doubt had been planted.

By the time I got back to the table, Anne had downed my pint and another of her own. She'd cursed out the band for being "trite shite" and was more than ready to leave. I was glad to go, since I couldn't hear what she was cursing about over the music and she was getting angrier every time I shouted "What?" at her. I didn't really think anything of her sudden interest in leaving until I saw her glance back into the bar. When I followed her gaze, I was almost positive I saw Old Blue Eyes talking to Bridget, but then he was hidden by the crowd and we were gone.

Outside, the night air was cool and refreshing and we walked the streets, holding hands. From time to time we'd dip into the nearest pub to freshen up our buzz. At least that was what it seemed like. Some piece of my brain was wondering if Anne knew that the guy with the psycho eyes really was following us, and she was trying to lose him. Between what Bridget had told me about Anne and the man with the crazy eyes, I was developing an unhealthy paranoia.

We roamed the streets of Dublin in varying states of drunkenness for

several hours, and although I'd love to tell you what we talked about, I have
no idea.

Spending time with Anne was like being in an extended dream. She
could go from passionate and loving to angry and disdainful with a word,
from drunk to sober when a random thought crossed her mind. I thought
I was hallucinating as we darted through traffic and into Phoenix Park,
especially when we ran right into a herd of fallow deer that darted off like
ghosts. Anne laughed as she saw my startled expression but just followed
them with her eyes into the darkness.

As we approached the obelisk of Wellington's Monument, we stopped to
lie on the grass, catching our breath and looking up at the stars. They were
spinning in the sky and only settled down as I started to sober up. It helped
that Anne pinned them down for me, pointing out where Sirius would be,
and Orion's belt. It was then, as the world stopped spinning, that things
started to come back into focus. It was then that I realized we were sitting
in the middle of the capital of free Ireland under a monument that was dedi-
cated to an Englishman and his conquests. I thought I was pretty smart for
noticing the irony, but when I mentioned it to Anne she just sighed a deep
sigh that somehow combined disappointment and derision.

"It's not just a monument to Wellington now, is it? It's not that simple."

"It never is here, is it?" I could feel the romance and the stars retreating
as Anne sat up to look at me. She was annoyed again and I had no idea why,
but it was clear from her expression that she was about to tell me.

"Have ya paid any attention to what I been tellin' ya at all, Sean? Do ya
even know what an obelisk is?"

It seemed like a trick question. I did know, sort of, but I didn't know what
kind of answer she wanted. "Egyptian?" I tried.

"That's a start, inn't it? But do ya know what it symbolizes?"

I smiled, because I did, actually. I wasn't such a moron after all. "I learned
this in freshman lit. Anything long and hard is a phallus symbol, right?"

She smiled and turned away, glancing back up at the stars as she spoke.
"On a certain level, yes. That's actually true. But even the phallus is a symbol of somethin' else. The Egyptians saw obelisks as symbolizin' power and
stability, resurrection and immortality."

Jesus, we were back to that again? What *wasn't* a symbol of immortality or reincarnation or rebirth? "You're serious?" I asked.

"A course I am. Not only that, but we're in Phoenix Park, right? An' what's a phoenix but a bird that burns up and rises from its own ashes?"

She was right, of course. I should have seen it coming. It was probably the reason we had come to this park—so she could show me how her version of the truth was all around me.

"The phoenix was either a Persian or Indian myth adopted by other cultures, includin' the Greeks an' Egyptians. Doesn't matter either way, 'cause even that name has a deeper meanin' here, because 'Phoenix Park' is a bastardization of this place's real name."

"And what's that?"

"Páirc an Fhionn-Uisce. It sounds a bit alike, but that's not the real reason fer the two different names. *Fhionn-uisce* means 'clear water.' It's where the *uisce fe talamh,* the underground stream of knowledge, rises to the surface to become clearly unnerstood."

I was getting buried in the layers of symbolism, metaphor, and Guinness, and I was struggling to understand. "So you're trying to tell me that there's an Egyptian symbol of reincarnation, layered on top of a Persian one, layered on top of a metaphor for hidden knowledge. But, then, why Wellington?"

"Because he was one a us, of course. The Sea People—the descendants of the people who can remember—are all over the world, Sean, not just here in Ireland. Even the English have a couple of folks bright enough to see the light. Dedicatin' it to the Duke himself jus' gave an excuse to make the stream clear." Anne got up, moving around the obelisk in the dark as she spoke. She stopped in front of a brass plaque that I could barely see in the dim light. Anne nodded toward it. "Read the inscription."

I moved closer, reading slowly to make sure I got it right: "Asia and Europe, saved by thee, proclaim / Invincible in war thy deathless name / Now round thy brow the civic oak we twine / That every earthly glory may be thine."

"The poem's fer shite, but ya can see my point, I hope. I'm not even gonna go into the symbolism of the oak to the Druids or how 'deathless' is a synonym fer everything we're talking about. But surely even an eejit like you can see how this here is really a monument to the hidden knowledge, can' ya?" Anne asked.

A chill went up my spine. I was being haunted by a conspiracy of coincidences. How could all of this be right in front of me and mean nothing until it was pointed out by Anne? Was it really hidden knowledge kept hidden by keeping it in plain sight?

"Maybe it is. I don't know. Right now, none of this seems real." And it didn't. I was too drunk and too far from home.

"Not real? Ya mean like the deer ya thought ya were hallucinatin' on the way in here? Sorry, boyo, but they're real. All of it is. The deer were here even before Wellington. Didja know that the Celts believed deer were guides to the spirit world, to the place where ya became yer true self and learned the sacred truths." She smiled a wicked smile. "Someday, when yer ready, I'll tell ya all about how the mind a God ties it all together fer us."

"The mind of God?"

"Absolutely. In the beginnin' was the 'Word,' when God conceived of all this, right? His daydreams created everythin'. So the way I see it, we're all just stray thoughts in the mind a God. . . . It's all from the mind a God and it's all connected."

"Yeah, really? Well right now I think my 'mind of God' is a bit twisted with all this. I had a lit professor who saw symbols and hidden messages in everything, too, but they sent him off to rehab to fix him."

"To fix 'im? Like they 'fix' an ol' tomcat? Cuttin' off his creativity so that he's well behaved?"

With one phrase she'd cut the balls off of my point.

"Someday ya'll want ta look into how the precession of the equinox and the movements of the planets an' stars are reflected down here, how the seasons and cycles of life give meanin' to the sayin' 'as above, so below.' The universe is all just layers in the same story, from the planets circlin' the sun to electrons circlin' the powerhouse of the cell. Then, when ya know somethin' about layers of meanin', maybe I'll let ya argue with me."

Anne turned away, then turned back quickly, trying to make a point I could understand. "Let's just say fer now that you not unnerstandin' doesn't make it untrue, okay? It all fits together because every one of those stories, every one of those structures comes from the same place."

She paused, but I could hear the words in my head even though she didn't say them.

"They all come from your 'mind of God'?"

"Yeah, it's all connected, but I'm not gonna try an' convince ya of it right now. Yer too ignerant. I could call it somethin' else. I could put it in scientific terms. It wouldn't matter. All the stories describe the same damn thing. If ya wan' me to tell ya about quantum physics, or Einstein's 'spooky action at a distance,' I can, fer sure. But ya won' believe it till yer ready. No one ever does." Anne turned away from me then, striding into the darkness.

"Wait. Anne, c'mon. Where are you going?" I grabbed her arm, but she pulled away and kept walking.

"Home." And clearly without me, from her tone. I hurried to stay in stride with her.

"Look, Anne, I'm sorry. Maybe I'd understand all this better if we talked about it another time. If you're going to start talking about Einstein, it'd be better to do it when I'm sober, that's all I'm tryin' to say."

Anne walked through a gate and out to the street, trying to hail a cab. "Maybe ya better live a few more lifetimes or at least remember a few before ya start tellin' me what's true or not." Anne stopped suddenly, looking across the road, her eyes focused on a couple sitting on a bench in the shadows.

I looked over but couldn't make out what they looked like, their faces shadowed. A cab pulled up as I was trying to see what had made her nervous and Anne opened the door in a rush.

"Get in."

"Sure, but why?"

"Just get in."

I didn't argue. I got in and slid across the back seat as Anne told the cab-driver to take us back to Merrion Square. As we pulled away, the couple in the shadows stood up and moved into the light of a streetlamp. It looked like the guy was Old Blue Eyes. I could see him watching the cab pull away.

When I turned back to Anne, she was staring out the window and wouldn't look at me. We rode that way for a few minutes, and then I felt her warm hand in mine. She still was looking out the window, but she mumbled a half-whispered apology.

"I'm sorry, Sean. Fer all of it. I should know better. I keep fergettin' that ya know just about nothin'. Ya might as well be a complete mentaller yer so thick. But it's not yer fault, is it?" Anne was trying to be kind. I could hear it in her voice. But the more she apologized, the worse she seemed to make it.

"Actually, I should be thankful yer half asleep. If ya remembered any of it, ya probably wouldn' be here, would ya? At least not with me."

I almost asked then what she meant, but I also knew that if I asked, I would have to live with the answer. It could wait until tomorrow. When we got back to Merrion Square, the sun was coming up and the alcohol was starting to seep out of our pores.

We found a cheap hotel and Anne went in to check in. I'd never seen her worry what anyone thought before this, but she wouldn't let me go in with her. I waited by a side door until she came and got me, and then I followed her up a back staircase to our room. Some part of me wondered if she'd stolen the key from the lobby and didn't want me to know, but I was too tired to really care. I collapsed onto the couch and she got in the shower, leaving the door and the invitation open. I was about to follow her in when someone knocked on the door.

I stood up quickly, uncertain what to do. If we were squatting here and I answered, we would be thrown out and end up sleeping in the car.

But then there was another knock, and a gruff voice called out from the other side of the door. "Mr. Corrigan, there's a delivery for you." So Anne had used my name when she checked in. I opened the door before my usual paranoia kicked in to remind me that Anne would never tell anyone our real names without a good reason, but it was just a bellman standing there. Or rather, a bellboy, with a thin scraggly mustache and bad acne, holding a manila envelope.

"Are ya Michael Corrigan?" he muttered, unable to look me in the eye.

"No," Anne called out from behind me, even as the bellboy's eyes went wide. I turned to see the hotel towel barely covering her dripping body. She'd heard the knock and raced out.

"Well, no. I'm not *Michael* Corrigan, but . . ." I started, and the bellboy thrust the envelope at me.

"He said ya might say that. Here. It's yers." He let go of the envelope and rushed away, as if it were a bomb about to go off.

"Damn. How stupid can one Yank be. We're not supposed to be here an' now everyone in the Pale'll know yer in this room, won' they?"

I ignored Anne and opened the envelope. In my hands was a sheaf of ragged-edged pages, full of my uncle Mike's handwriting. More of the torn journal pages had been returned, but by whom? And why? I looked down the hall after the bellboy, but he was long gone.

"Might as well read it now, ya eejit. If they gave it to ya, they're not ready to kill ya yet." So Anne had noticed Blue Eyes as well and had the same reaction to him as I did. Her words weren't exactly reassuring, but she was right—whoever delivered the pages intended for me to read them, and my curiosity wouldn't allow me to do otherwise.

I fell back on the couch, shower forgotten, and started to read. Somewhere in the night, I passed out and ended up sleeping until two o'clock the next afternoon.

Michael

Patsy was dead. If you asked me to swear on a Bible or testify in a court of law, that's what I would have told you. I couldn't see him breathe. His skin was cold to the touch, and he didn't move. I know Kate had said that he'd wake up, then "fall back into what looks like death fer three days or so," but this was a bit much. We'd sat with Patsy for two days now, and if any police had come along, we'd be up on murder charges and he'd be in the ground before he ever woke again.

The night before, Kate told me, "It's all part of it. His mind needs time to adjust, to process the memory. That's what's takin' so much energy even the heat's gone out of 'im." But I couldn't sleep with him lying there, silent and still, where we'd set him down in front of the hearth in the schoolhouse. Kate woke up at one point in the early morning and found me staring at him. She pulled me back down next to her, under the blankets, her arm and leg over me, her head on my chest, keeping me warm. I still didn't sleep. I couldn't, not with her near-dead brother across the room and her near-naked body next to mine. Somehow it wasn't very romantic.

The days on the island had been better than the nights, since we could get out of the schoolhouse and away from Patsy. Kate and I wandered the island hand in hand as she filled me in on the history of our ancestors, who seemed to have lived out some dramatic moment on every corner of this small scrap of land. It was amazing how many places a woman can give birth or a man can have a heart attack or be stabbed or shot over the course of time.

Still, it was peaceful for us, gathering buckets of ice cold water to cook with, watching the sun rise and set, and sitting in the moonlight, with our bodies close for warmth. We talked about the past, avoiding the subject of reincarnation for the most part, and even talked about the future—for

Ireland, for me, and for us. We eventually stopped talking, sitting together quietly, and every so often we'd find ways to draw each other out, entertaining ourselves by finding shapes in the mist that rose over the lake or listening to the sounds of the island. If it wasn't for the near-corpse by the fireplace, it would have been the most romantic two days of my life.

Declan had gone off to the mainland to make excuses for Patsy's absence from the Garda station and to lead whoever came looking for Trooper Wheeler in a different direction. I had no idea how he planned on doing that. All he said to me when he left was "Help Kate with Patsy. I told her to shoot ya if ya try to leave." I didn't ask any questions after that.

It was a good thing I didn't really want to leave, because the one time that I was wandering the island and strayed near the curragh, I thought I saw Kate watching me, Armalite in hand. Even though I didn't think she'd kill me, she *was* the same woman who'd fed her own brother belladonna. Since I had no interest in death, even the "near" kind, I stayed away from the boat after that.

I was on the far side of the island late on the second day, watching the sun sink through the mist when it occurred to me exactly how Declan might set the garda off in a direction that would keep them away from the arms cache and himself.

It was a faultless setup. It made perfect sense. I don't know why I hadn't seen it before—except that I was blinded by Kate. I was already a fugitive, with a solid motive for killing Trooper Wheeler. If I were Declan, I'd set me up, too. There were only a few questions. First, would he risk having me tell what I knew, or would he kill me? Second, if he didn't kill me, how would he get the guns off the island before setting me up? And third, was Kate in on the plan?

I didn't think she was. Maybe it was my just my ego blinding me, but if she was in love with me, I didn't believe she could be planning to betray me. I'm sure that has been the last thought of many men over the centuries, but I knew there was one sure way to find out. I'd interrogate her. If she denied it and was lying, I'd deal with the consequences. But with her or without her, I had to get off the island before Declan came back. It made no sense for him to let me leave there alive.

As I approached the schoolhouse, I could smell something cooking and heard a soft humming inside. It was Kate, singing something half under her breath, the lyrics in Irish. If you've ever heard a native Irish speaker, you'd understand that Irish is a musical language even when it's not sung, and Kate, who sang only when she thought no one was listening, made an incantation of it, a spell that charmed anyone who heard her sing.

I stood just outside the door and watched her for a moment, enjoying the way she moved. Even her simple meal preparations were a dance. I could see why a few hundred years ago a priest might wander upon a scene like this and claim the woman of the house was a witch who entranced him as she knelt over her boiling cauldron. I was about to say something when Kate stopped to taste whatever she was cooking. She must've heard me move, because she turned and looked right at me, smiling as if she knew what I was thinking.

"Ya shouldn't sneak up on me like that. Patsy might wake up an' catch ya bein' a Peepin' Tom."

I'd forgotten about him for a moment, but glanced over to where he lay in the shadows, motionless. "Has he . . ."

"Not a twitch. It's not time yet, though, is it?" Kate tasted whatever was in the pot again and then added more of the herbs she had gathered around the island.

"Maybe we should bring him back to your house. Take care of him the right way." I wanted to ease into the idea of getting off the island while still trying to figure out how to bring up my suspicions about Declan. Kate took it the wrong way.

She turned, glaring at me. "Are ya sayin' I'm not carin' fer 'im properly?"

I backed off. "No! No, definitely not, but Declan didn't say when he'd be back, and the longer we stay here, the more of a chance someone will come looking for Patsy or Wheeler." Kate just stared at me for a moment, then nodded, smiling slightly.

"Ahh, I see it now. Ya think ya figured it out, do ya?" She turned away, mixing whatever was in the pot. "Well, no matter what ya might think of Declan, yer wrong. He'd not inform on ya, ya can trust 'im on that." So much for my planned interrogation. Kate was ten steps ahead of me. At least

I could tell from the way she said it that she believed what she was saying. She spoke without a second thought and with no hesitation. So, although I still doubted Declan, at least I knew she wasn't setting me up.

"Don' worry, Mickaleen," she went on. "He's more hero than villain. He'll do the right thing."

"The right thing? Are you serious? He kneecapped your brother. He killed Wheeler. But you still think he's some kind of hero?"

"That's what I said." Kate still didn't turn to look at me. Her tone was dismissive.

"Heroes aren't murderers."

"No? Mebbe by yer definition, they're not. You think anyone who struggles with temptation is a failure, don' ya? They ain' good enough to be heroes?"

"I don't think heroes need to be perfect. They just need to be close."

"Really? An' how many near-perfect people have ya met in yer life? I know I'm not one of them, so ya better take a good look at me an' go in with yer eyes wide open."

She stood then, walking toward me out of the shadows, the pale sunset coloring her features. "If yer lookin' fer perfection, boyo, walk away now. I can't handle ya walkin' out later. I'm done with that. Unnerstand?" I nodded silently, and she stared me down until she was sure I wouldn't change my mind. "You go on thinkin' heroes need to be perfect and the only ones yer gonna have left'll be dead at least a hunnerd years, an' they'll only qualify 'cause it's too late to dig up evidence about all their failin's."

"So tell me. Seriously. Truly. Is Declan a hero or a villain?"

Before Kate could answer, a low moan came from behind her. It was Patsy. She moved to him quickly, feeling his forehead. He still looked dead to me. His eyes were closed, and not a muscle twitched. He was so still that I thought I'd imagined the moan, but Kate spoke more softly as she turned back to me.

"Declan's tryin' to do the right thing, in spite of the repercussions. He figures even if he messes up, even if he dies, at least he died tryin'—not runnin' away."

It struck me then that I had done the opposite. I had run from a murder charge, even though I wasn't guilty. In spite of the fact that I wasn't sure she was talking about me, Kate's words stung. I tried to deflect, changing the subject back to people who had messed up worse than I had. "So, even if a guy has a drug problem or beats his wife or cheats on his taxes, we should still idolize him?"

"Did I say that ya bleedin' amadan? I'm not sayin' 'e's a saint. Just a man trying harder than the rest." Kate looked back at Patsy, then moved for the door. "Follow me."

I did as told, trailing her out into the crisp dusk air. I followed her to a stone wall that was collapsing under its own weight and sat next to her when she leaned into it. After we'd sat there for a moment, she took my hand and looked right at me. "Tell me about the man you shot."

"Why?" I looked up sharply. I couldn't help it—she'd caught me off guard.

"Ya called Declan a murderer, but ya don' seem to think of yerself that way. Tell me why. I want to know what happened."

I shrugged. Ever since Patsy had mentioned it, I'd known she'd eventually ask me about the shooting. It was a reasonable question.

"I was on a stakeout, watching him. He was trying to outflank me. To come at me from the direction of the sun, so I'd be blinded. When he started shooting, I shot back."

"Really? Then why are ya here in Ireland? Wann't it justified?"

"When I got to the body, there was no gun there."

"And there were no footprints in the snow, either, were there?"

How did she know? I tried to pull my hand away, but she held on tightly. "Who told you?" I asked.

"Declan told me the whole thing before he left, when I walked him down to the boat. He read all about you in the American papers. After ya showed up with all that cash he looked you up." There was no accusation in her tone, just sadness.

"If you already knew, then why ask me?"

"Because you still don' know why ya shot him, do ya? Think about it."

"Pieces of rock hit me in the face. He had to be shooting."

"Then where's the gun?"

"I was hit."

"Yeah, I bet ya were," she said, as if that ended it. She nodded, sincerely, but her answer still sounded like an accusation of some sort.

"What's your point, Kate? 'Cause I'm not getting it."

She sighed, apparently thinking me too dense to understand what she was saying, which it turned out I was, though I didn't know it then. "You were a bit of a hero before all that, weren't ya? A cop, keepin' the world safe from criminals and radicals . . ."

"I never thought of myself as a hero," I said, but of course I had. That's why I joined the force in the first place, wasn't it? To be a "good guy"? A hero?

"Then ya really *are* an eejit. A course ya were a hero. You still are. In spite of the fact that ya bollixed it all up an' ran. That's what I've been trying to tell ya. There are heroes all around us. They're the ones who march in protests and write letters to politicians an' speak out even when they know they'll be mocked, or even beaten, fer sayin' what they think is true. We jus' stopped seein' 'em because we forgot even heroes have flaws." Kate took her hand from mine and touched my cheek, making me face her.

"That's no way to live yer life, Mickaleen. If ya don' make mistakes, ya don' learn nothin'. Yer the same eejit at the end as ya were at the beginnin'. All of us should take on battles we can't win. Fight the good fight an' lose. It's good fer the soul."

I just shook my head. I'd had similar arguments with my father. "If you never have a chance of winning, fighting's not heroic, it's stupid."

"Only if ya believe death is the end." We were back to that, the one thing I wished she would stop bringing up, the one thing that truly made me doubt her.

She crept a bit closer, speaking softly now. "What if heroes weren't perfect? What if they were just workin' toward it, life after life? If a man could live again, he could sacrifice his own life and still be a hero, right?" She wanted an answer, but all I could do was shrug. Philosophy wasn't my strong suit.

"It's not about winning and losing—'cause if death's your measuring stick, we all lose in the end. It's about believing in something so strongly that you're willing to die for it."

"So the good guys never lose, they just live to fight another day?" I said, intending to be sarcastic, but she refused to take it that way.

"Exactly." She stood then, pulling me up, back toward the schoolhouse. "I need to check on the food and Patsy. It'll be time fer 'im to wake soon."

I followed her, but I couldn't leave it alone. "I still don't see how heroes accomplish much if they die."

"No? Most do more than if they lived sometimes. Lookit Jesus Christ, Gandhi, yer Martin Luther King and Kennedy, even Michael Collins. Some of 'em are better symbols than they were men. Dead they're a movement, a shinin' example of what each of us can strive fer. Alive they might've bollixed the whole thing up. What if people found out some a the stupid shite they really did?" She smiled then, as if she had firsthand knowledge of their failings. "Eventually they all come back to pick up where they left off. Real heroes never leave us, Mickaleen. We just don' recognize 'em anymore."

I followed her into the schoolhouse, watching her as she knelt to check on Patsy, then moved to the fire. It would be so easy to agree with her, but I couldn't. Not then. "I don't know if I'm ready to believe in hopeless causes," I told her honestly.

"No? Ya'll leave the hopeless causes to me, huh? I'm supposed to believe in a cop on the run from a murder charge, an eejit whose got himself involved wit' the Provos, is that right? Ya expect me to believe in you, but ya can't believe in me or any of this?"

"I'm sorry."

"No. Don' be sorry. Be honest. I'm not askin' ya to believe in hopeless causes. Because there's *always* hope. I'm just sayin' ya gotta take the long view. Trust that there's more to life than a few glorious bitter years followed by death."

Kate stared into the fire for a moment. When she spoke I could barely hear her. "I'm just askin' ya to have hope fer *us*. Is that too much to ask for? I think we deserve at least that much, Mickaleen." She glanced up at me then, and her eyes were glistening. I knelt beside her, putting a hand on her shoulder, surprised at the depth of emotion I felt. It seemed absurd to have such strong feelings for someone after just a few days.

I didn't know what else to say, so I told her the truth. "Right now it feels like you're the only thing that gives me hope." She looked into my eyes then and leaned into me, kissing me.

"At it agin are ya?" A rough, thick-brogued voice spoke from the other side of the room. Kate pushed me away, rushing to Patsy as I turned to see his eyes on me, sparkling in the firelight.

"I told ya to leave her alone, dinn't I? I won' have her goin' off with no rebel." He tried to sit up, reaching for Kate's Armalite. He had one hand on it as he stretched farther, wrenching his mangled leg in the process. Patsy's face went red with pain and anger and the rifle, thankfully, clattered to the floor out of his reach. "Goddammit. I'll kill ya. I swear, I'll kill ya if ya touch 'er again."

And then his eyes rolled back in his head. His body went slack, and his head would have bounced off the floor if Kate hadn't caught him, laying him back gently.

She stroked his forehead, glancing up at me, focused on my hands. I looked down, following her gaze and noticed that the fireplace poker was in my hand. I must have picked it up instinctively when he went for the gun.

"Easy," Kate told me, motioning for me to put it down. "He means no harm. He's just not here with us. He's still in the past." Then she turned back to Patsy, and whispered to him, "It's only a few more lifetimes now, Patsy. I'll see ya soon."

Kate kissed him on the forehead and held his hand for a moment, but I watched his eyes. That wasn't the Patsy I had seen a moment ago. It was hard not to keep my eyes on him as we ate and later as we talked in front of the fire. Kate drifted off to sleep as I held her in my arms, but I didn't sleep much, waiting for Patsy to open his eyes again, afraid that he'd see me holding Kate and would murder me in my sleep.

Maybe that's why I heard the change in the sounds of the water lapping at the shore. It was a familiar sound—the sound I remembered from my dream, the sound of oars as a boat approached. The same thought from that nightmare resurfaced—whoever was coming out here before dawn on a frigid night was trouble.

I slipped out from underneath the heaviness of Kate's arm and walked out into the night, straining to see by the moonlight to avoid snapping branches or kicking stones. I headed away from the shore and the approaching boat, circling around to get cover behind one of the old cottages. I had just taken up position there when I thought I heard muffled voices, but then the wind shifted and I lost them. A moment later I saw the shadows moving and a lone figure stalked up the path in wary silence, a pistol in one hand, approaching the schoolhouse. I waited, wondering if I had heard voices, and if there was a second man, or even more than two. But no one else appeared.

I slowly moved through the underbrush, wanting to scope out the shoreline while keeping the man near the schoolhouse in sight. It was slow going, but I finally saw the boat, empty, with no one else around. Just the one man, then. I cut across to the path he had just used, getting between him and the boat, approaching him from the direction he least expected.

I was only about ten feet behind him when I heard him click the safety off his pistol and saw him peer into the schoolhouse window. He must have realized I wasn't there, because as soon as he'd looked in, he spun toward the dark woods, pistol up, looking for me. If I'd stayed by the cottage, he would have seen me immediately. As it was, I was behind him, in his blind spot. I leveled the Armalite at his back.

"Drop the pistol and put your hands where I can see them." The words sounded strange coming out of my mouth. I sounded like a cop again, but I sure didn't feel like one.

The man dropped the weapon without flinching, put his hands in the air and slowly turned to face me. He was smiling broadly. He seemed amused that I was holding the rifle on him, but that wasn't the strange part. What was strange was that even in the near darkness, I could see his eyes, catching a random ray of moonlight. They were so blue against his dark hair and pale skin that he looked almost unhuman. He stared for a moment, then nodded as if out of respect.

"Ya must be Mickaleen. I'm Jerry. Coonan. Got the drop on me, dinn't ya? I heard ya was good." He stepped forward, squinting, trying to see me better. "Is that what Kate sees in ya?"

Coonan's ease threw me off. I kept my eyes on him as I moved closer to retrieve his pistol, noticing a small icon on the lapel of his jacket—a phoenix. It was a symbol that I knew the IRA had been using because my father had one, a gift from one of his cousins. I had found the gift to be ridiculous at the time, believing he had no real contact with the IRA. Clearly I hadn't been seeing what was right in front of me. The old man wasn't as out of touch as he seemed.

I picked up the pistol as I caught movement from the schoolhouse, and Kate appeared around the corner, still half asleep. I didn't intimidate her, either. "Put it down, will ya, Mickaleen? He's not here to harm anyone, are ya Jerry?"

The blue-eyed man winked at me as he answered Kate. "Me? I'm the most gentle man ta ever walk the face a the earth, ain' I?" And he grabbed Kate, giving her a bear hug. If I hadn't seen her smiling, I would've shot him, but she clearly knew Jerry Coonan and liked him. "It's good ta see ya, Kate. It's been too long."

I waited for Coonan to put her down before asking, "Who is he?" I tried not to sound worried or jealous.

"I'm 'er brother-in-law, ain' I, Kate?" Coonan responded, looking at me for my reaction. I'd almost forgotten that Kate was a widow and found it hard to imagine her married to anyone. After the last few days it felt like there had never been anyone but me, a naive sentiment, but it was the way it felt.

"He was . . . is . . . my husband's brother." I could tell Kate had tried to soften the blow, but it only made me feel more like an outsider.

"What she's tryin' ta say is that she *was* my *dead* brother's wife, an' now that an appropriate mournin' period is passed, she's free to be out on an island wit' the likes a you." Coonan ducked as Kate swung at him, and even in the darkness it looked like she might be blushing.

"Ya gotta be quick on yer feet around this one, Mick. She's dangerous, I'm warnin' ya. She's the one who encouraged my brother ta be a man a peace . . ." Kate's fist connected with his arm as Coonan looked toward me, and he winced. His tone was light, but there was an accusation in the subtext, and Kate's punch was fair retribution. He rubbed his arm. "Yer not a man a peace, are ya, Mickaleen? She's not makin' that mistake agin, is she?"

"Don't, Jerry. Don't do this," Kate said, almost under her breath. Coonan's strangely luminous eyes flicked toward her, but then quickly moved back to me—and beyond me.

"Ya got nothing to worry about, Jerry. Mickaleen's not the peaceful type, are ya?" I spun around as I heard the voice, pulling the rifle up, ready to fire, only to find Declan emerging from the trees across the small clearing.

"Sorry. Dinn't mean to startle ya. I just wanted to work my way around and make sure there was no one else here . . . It looks like we're all getting along, though, don' it?" Declan smiled sardonically, reading the tension between Jerry and Kate. "Let's go inside and talk."

Declan nodded toward the schoolhouse and Kate moved to go inside, followed by Coonan. I hesitated, still wondering whether Declan planned to set me up. He saw my look and smiled. "Ya still don' trust me, do ya?"

"Is there a reason I should?"

Declan glanced after Kate and Coonan, already inside the schoolhouse. "None ya can remember," he said, lowering his voice. "But there's one thing ya do know. I could've shot ya in the back just now and left Patsy here to say he killed ya after ya ambushed him and the trooper. Patsy'd do it, too. He knows I'd kill 'im if he didn't."

He was right. It was an elegant solution to his problems. The only thing I didn't understand was why I wasn't dead already.

"And why didn't you?"

"Because I don't shoot my friends without good reason, a course." He laughed, finding himself amusing. "I'm gettin' chilled standing around here, Mick. Can ya bear to put the rifle aside fer the moment so we can go inside?" Declan nodded to the Armalite, and I realized I had it pointed in his direction. I lowered it and Declan moved past me, into the schoolhouse. I followed him into the warmth to find Kate leaning on the hearth and Coonan by the fire.

"How's Patsy?" Declan asked.

"Close. He stirred an' recognized Mickaleen as Seamus, then went out again." Declan nodded, looking closer at Patsy, kneeling next to him, but

Kate wasn't worried about Patsy just then. She was still staring tensely at Coonan.

"What's he doin' here, Declan? Not that I'm unhappy ta see 'im, but inn't it a risk? His face is known."

Coonan answered before Declan could, cutting him off. "I made 'im bring me. I wanted to see this Mickaleen myself and to warn all of ya." He turned back to Kate, serious now. "It's startin' to get techy up in Derry, Kate. Three days ago, while Dec was down here gettin' the cash fer the next shipment an' dealin' with Patsy's bloody mess, yer old friends marched on Magilligan." Kate seemed to shrink away from Coonan, putting one hand on the wall of the schoolhouse to steady herself. Whatever the news was, it was obviously bad.

"Magilligan?" I asked, losing track of the conversation, but trying to keep up.

Kate looked up at me, filling me in as much to delay the news as to keep me informed. "It's a prison camp up north. They're keepin' political prisoners there. The march was to protest internment." Slowly she turned back to Coonan, needing to know the rest. "How many dead?"

"None. A few almos' dead, but almos' don' seem to count when it comes ta dead, does it?" Kate sighed, too relieved to be mad about the sarcasm. "The paratroopers fired rubber bullets and beat on the lot of 'em with their batons, but the officers called 'em off before they could kill anyone."

"You seem disappointed," I said, and Coonan nodded, admitting that he was.

"The world won' pay attention to almos' dead people now, will they? Give us a few dead fer real and those'll make more of a difference than a thousand sent to hospital."

"Ignore him, Mickaleen. Jerry thinks the sooner blood is spilled, the sooner people will wake up to stop it." Kate threw him a disapproving look, then went on, "The blood's been flowin' fer almost a thousand years and no one's stopped it yet."

"The more blood the better. No one's gonna stop it by walkin' on the beach and shoutin' nursery rhymes at armed soldiers." Coonan spat the words out. It was an accusation, and it took Kate a moment to recover.

"If things are so bad up there, what're ya doin' down here? Go get yerself killed already."

"We need to move the Armalites," Declan interrupted, and Kate whirled on him, eyes wide.

"What? You're not thinkin' about bringing them to Derry, are ya? Ya'll give the bastards an excuse ta burn down the Bogside if they find out they're up there."

Coonan traded looks with Declan, who answered, clearly in charge. "No . . . they'll not go north yet. But someone's goin' ta come lookin' fer that trooper and we don' want 'em findin' the guns when they do. It's goin' to get worse before it gets better, Kate. Ya need to know that. There's another march planned next Sunday in Derry."

"Great. An' are ya plannin' on bein' there to incite another riot? Maybe this time you'll get someone killed."

"Here's hopin'," Coonan chimed in, then flinched as if expecting to be hit, but Kate just glared at him. Declan shook his head, agreeing with neither of them.

"There's no chance of that now, is there? We weren't invited. In fact, we were told to stay away so they'd have no excuse fer violence. It's a peaceful protest. They don' wan' anythin' to incite the Orangemen. If it looks like we done anythin', we'll give the bastards an excuse to burn the Bogside to the ground."

Kate sighed, obviously relieved.

"It's a mistake, I'll tell ya, even though ya don' wanna hear it," Coonan muttered. Kate glared at Coonan, now squatting to warm his hands over the embers of the fire as he continued, "Sometimes thin's need to get worse to get better. People need to see the bastards fer who they really are. Even Sam agreed with me an' ya know it."

Kate's eyes flashed at the mention of her dead husband's name. "Sam never thought gettin' innocent people shot was good public relations, did he?"

"Maybe that's why he got 'imself killed, God rest 'is soul. He knew somebody 'ad to die to give life to the movement." The fireplace poker was smashing into Coonan's forearm before I even saw Kate move, but Coonan was fast. He grabbed the poker and twisted it out of her hands, turning it on her, ready to swing, even as I raised the Armalite to his head. I think I would've shot him if Declan hadn't stepped right in the middle of all of it.

"Enough," was all he said, but it was said forcefully, despite his low tone. "No one wants anyone to die, Kate. But you know as well as I do that if they burn people out, or attack us without reason, we'll have more support than we can handle. Those people'll come runnin' to us fer protection. Sooner or later, the Orangemen or the British will drive us to all-out war, an' it's a war they can never win. They've been tryin' on an' off fer eight centuries."

Kate was clearly angry and it didn't look like she was going to back down. No one moved for a moment until Coonan finally glanced at me, seeing the rifle pointed at his head. He grinned and dropped the fireplace poker. "I'm likin' yer new man, Kate. Quick enough to react but disciplined enough not to shoot. We could use a few more like him."

"If you want to be a martyr, I can help you out," I told him, and Coonan laughed then, hard. Even Declan grinned, but Kate wasn't ready to relax.

"Yer all out of yer blasted heads. You ain' won it either in all this time. Ya can't fight all of 'em. You don't have the weapons. Ya think a few crates of rifles can stop the British army if they decide to burn us all out?"

"Yer fergettin' about the black stuff, ain' ya?" Coonan growled defensively, referring to the fertilizer-based explosive developed by the IRA. "We can blow up half a Belfast an' they won' see it comin'. We can destroy their whole bloody colonial infrastructure. All their fancy weapons are nothin' next ta the terror of Belfast Confetti fallin' three times a week."

"The black stuff? Yer serious?" She stared at Coonan, who smiled and nodded, enjoying her reaction. "Well, I hope yer the one usin' it. Maybe it'll knock some sense into ya in yer next life, cause that's where it'll blow ya to."

"Not no more. We got it stable. We're gonna set it up in cars an' walk away long before it goes off."

"Really? An' what happens when some wee child wanders by? What happens when *yer* the one killin' innocent people? Who will the people turn on then?" Kate turned to Declan to gauge his reaction, but Declan looked down, unable or unwilling to meet her gaze.

"This isn't the killin' of the Ulster Volunteer Force men or paratroopers, is it now? This is about innocent people."

"Jaysus feckin' Christ, Kate, can ya be more naive? Isn' it as simple as shite? Sooner or later, they gotta get tired a people dyin', don' they?" Coonan ranted, frustrated. "When there's enough blood on the ground, no matter whose it is, people will realize there's got to be a better way."

Kate stared at him for a moment, holding her temper as her face grew red. When she spoke, her voice was quiet, controlled. "Some of us know it now, ya bloody arsehole. How many more people need to die before *you* get it? How many more brothers do ya need to lose?"

Coonan stood, moving toward Kate. I glanced at Declan, but he stayed where he was. He was going to let them have it out, as long as it didn't get violent. "Dyin' ain't our problem, is it? We'll be back and we'll remember. But even if they come back, they won' remember shite. They've got no one to awaken them, an' it's the rare breed that remembers on their own, inn't it? We can win by dyin'. They can't."

"It's that simple to you? You'll send people—yer own people—to a bloody death, just to make a point?"

"So what? Death don' matter so much to us as them, does it? What matters is the next life. Ya think I wanna come back an' have this same blasted shite goin' on? When is it gonna end?"

"Maybe when you end it," I said without thinking, wanting to diffuse the tension.

Coonan turned slowly to look at me, like he'd just remembered I was in the room. "Ahh, the Yank speaks. Whatta you know about it? Ya know nothin'. Remember nothin'."

I shook my head. This wasn't just about Ireland. The same battles were being fought all over the world . "In the last few years I've seen plenty of civil rights marches, and Martin Luther King got way more done with peaceful protest than Malcolm X and his revolutionaries."

"An' still yas shot both of 'em to death. I'm afraid yer missin' the point, Yank. Ya still treat Negroes like second-class citizens over there, don' ya?"

"What he's sayin', ya eejit, is that if ya believe we're given a second chance at life, we're supposed to use it to make things better, not killin'," Kate interrupted. "Turn the other cheek. Lead by example."

"So ya say. I tried that fer a few lifetimes an' I keep comin' back to this shite. I'm tired a dyin' fer a cause. I say an eye fer an eye. I'll do my fergivin' in the next life, after they learn a lesson for once."

Kate turned away, giving up on arguing. Declan nodded to Coonan. "All right, are you two done?" Coonan looked away, and Kate glared.

"Good. We're not gonna settle this here anyway. There's a time fer livin' and a time fer dyin'. Fer fergiveness an' fer vengeance. And right now we need to be ready fer whichever one comes our way, so we need to get rid a' the Armalites." Declan turned to Coonan, giving orders once again. "Go get the cattle boat an' prepare the graves. It's two in the mornin' now and we'll need all the time we have before it's light."

Coonan nodded and moved out into the darkness without hesitation as it hit me what Declan had said: "Prepare the graves." I felt my hands tighten on the Armalite I held, but Kate was already confronting Declan.

"What graves are ya talkin' about, Declan?"

Declan just shrugged, enjoying her unease. "Don' worry, Kate. They're not fer you. Any of you. You'll stay here with Patsy, fill him in on what's happening when he wakes, that's all." Then he turned to me, already walking out the door. "Come with me. We need to start movin' the rifles."

"Declan . . ." Kate called after him, not satisfied with that answer. He turned back, trying not to grin.

"Don' worry, Kate. I won't kill him. It ain' necessary this time. At least not yet." Then he winked at me. "Besides, he's still holdin' the rifle, ain' he? I'd be an amadan to tell 'im my plans now, wouldn' I? Now c'mon, Mick." With that he turned, walking off into the shadows. I glanced at Kate for guidance, but she looked as nervous as I felt.

"Be careful," was all she said. As I stepped into the night, I wondered what the hell that meant and kept the rifle close. Declan was already on his way to the cottage where the rifles were stored, and I rushed to catch up. I didn't want him getting his hands on one before I got there.

IT TURNED OUT that I didn't need to worry, not then at least, not yet. When I got to the cottage, Declan was already picking up one end of a heavy crate full of Armalites. He had no hands free to shoot me. Given that, it only seemed fair that I take the other end of the crate. I swung my rifle over one shoulder and grabbed the crate, which was heavy but not unmanageable.

Over the next hour, the crates got heavier and my palms started to bleed as we carried crate after crate of Armalites down to the shore, at a point where the water was the deepest. Declan planned on having Coonan pull the cattle boat he was "borrowing" in as close as possible so that we could slide the crates right on. The crates were awkward, and the Armalite kept slipping from my shoulder. I finally propped it up against the stack of crates near the shore, making sure that each time we returned with more crates that Declan's hands were full and that I was close to it when we did set the crate down. I'm sure Declan noticed my caution, but he ignored it, no doubt confident that I had nowhere to run and that he could kill me in his own good time. After all, if Coonan was getting graves ready on the far shore, there was no sense in killing me here and carrying the body the whole way back. It'd be easier to shoot me later, after I'd served his purpose.

We'd just laid the last of the crates down, stacked four high on the dry grass, when we heard the heavy drone of an outboard motor. Out on the lough, I caught a glimpse of the cattle boat cutting through the mist, a flat-bottomed craft with high rails, moving slowly toward us. I watched it for a second, then turned quickly as I heard Declan move behind me.

He had the Armalite over his shoulder and was smiling. I'd let the boat distract me for a moment, and now I had no gun.

"Is there a reason you don't trust me with a rifle? Should I be worried?" I asked, tired of wondering.

"It's not that I dinn't trust ya, Mickaleen. I think the problem is that ya don' trust me. I think yer nervous, and nervous men and rifles are a deadly combination, so I'm jus' gonna keep it safe fer ya." I couldn't argue. He was right. I was nervous and jumpy and felt like pulling a trigger just to have the tension broken. I also couldn't argue because he had the gun. It made the rest of my decisions that night rather easy.

Loading the cattle boat went quickly. Coonan was a sinewy mass of muscle underneath unkempt clothing and could manage a crate by himself, slamming them down on top of one another so hard I hoped he wouldn't set off the ammunition in some of them. Twenty minutes after he let the gate down on the boat, it was going back up, the boat noticeably lower in the water, all of the rifles on board.

The crossing was slow, and a cold wind cut through the night. The image of the ferryman bringing the dead to hell across the river Styx came to mind as I stared out into the darkness and mist, trying to make out the church graveyard we were headed for. Coonan stood in the back of the boat, guiding it as intensely as Charon, the fierce-eyed ferryman of Greek myth, and I could almost feel him staring at the back of my head, causing the hairs to rise. Or maybe that was just the wind.

I stood in the front of the cattle boat, both Coonan and Declan behind me. I kept waiting for the sound of a rifle, wondering if I'd hear it before the bullet hit my brain, if I'd feel anything, or if it'd be so quick that I'd never know. I remember thinking that I should vault over the high rails of the boat into the water, but where would I swim to? Both Declan and Coonan knew the area better than I did, even if I could outswim the rifle shot. So I didn't try to escape, and I never turned to face them, either of them. It wasn't "bravery in the face of death" or anything like that. I just didn't want them to see the panic in my eyes. I hoped that if I pretended it wasn't going to happen, it wouldn't.

It didn't. When the boat scraped bottom at the far side I was surprised that I was still standing, until I noticed that we were still almost forty yards from the gravesites. It suddenly made sense why I wasn't dead yet. They'd wait until all the work was done, then shoot me. That meant I still had time to outsmart them.

I threw the gate down and turned to grab a crate, only to find that Coonan already had one in his hands and was passing me on the way to the churchyard. Declan nodded to me to grab the other end of the crate he had, and as we picked it up the Armalite slipped off his shoulder and smashed him in the knee. Good, I thought. Let him see how it felt for a change.

The churchyard was crowded with monuments and grave markers. Many of the family plots were outlined in stone and covered in loose white gravel. As we approached with the first crate, I could see that Coonan had already cleared the gravel from several plots, including two that bore the last name Corrigan. He grabbed one of the shovels sitting at the edge of the graves next to a wheelbarrow and threw it at me, barely giving me time to catch it.

"Dig four feet down and put the earth in the 'barrow. Dump it in the lough when yer done. We'll get the rest of the crates," Coonan ordered, nodding toward a handcart he'd brought along.

As Declan and Coonan went back to the boat, mumbling and muttering in low voices, I started to dig, wondering if I were digging my own grave. If so, I thought, with a bit of gallows humor, then at least the stone would say Corrigan on it.

I was about three feet deep into the first grave when Coonan and Declan dumped the last of the crates at the edge of the hole.

"As soon as you're about two crates deep, put 'em in the hole, then cover 'em up with the gravel. No one will know the diff'rence." Coonan told me, grabbing the handcart as if to leave.

"An' where do ya think yer goin'? There's another coupla graves to dig, inn't there?" Declan asked, grabbing the other shovel. Coonan shook his head, looking out beyond the graveyard to where the shadows danced as clouds passed over the moon.

"No. That's on you. I'm not temptin' the spirits any more. I've done enough fer the night." His eyes stayed on the shadows for a moment, then drifted out toward the mist rising off the lough. "It's too close out here. Too close by far. I'm done." He turned away without another word, toward the church and a car that sat to the side of it, walking more quickly than he had all night.

Declan watched him go, then shook his head. "I guess there's only two shovels anyway, inn't there?" He hopped into the hole I was in and started to dig, humming something under his breath. It took me a moment to figure out what was going on. Why would Declan let Coonan leave, and why would he help me dig? He could make me do the whole thing myself if he wanted.

I watched Coonan get in his car, sending gravel flying as he sped away. Finally, I had to ask, "Who's in charge here, you or him?"

Declan looked up, surprised, as if had never occurred to him. "I am. I mean, I guess I am, but it don' really matter. I couldn' make him stay regardless. Jerry's a bit particular. Unbalanced, ya might say. Ya don' force him to do what 'e don' wanna do."

Declan kept shoveling. I didn't know what to say, so I kept going as well. After a minute, Declan looked again. When he was sure Coonan was gone, he spoke, quietly, as if he were still afraid someone might overhear him. "Have ya noticed the man's eyes, Mickaleen?" How could I not notice them? They seemed to glow in the dark.

"Yeah. They're blue." I didn't want to say much more, but I agreed there was something off about Coonan.

"They're more'n blue. They're the eyes the *Duine Matha* curses men with. You know what I mean, yeah? The Good People. Fairies." Declan was whispering and it felt like I'd suddenly stepped into some Irish ghost story. Declan wasn't laughing.

"Fairies, huh? Then why's he so scared of ghosts?"

Declan nodded grimly. "I think those bloody eyes see more'n yours or mine." He crossed himself, then went back to digging. I almost looked around to see who was watching, who was going to come out of the shadows laughing at me if I bought into all this.

"You're serious? I thought you believed people came back from the dead. Now you're going to tell me you believe in ghosts, too?"

"Believin' in one thing doesn't stop the other thing from bein' true now, does it? Some make it back, some don't, fer whatever reason." He glanced around nervously, as if waiting for a ghost to appear. "Why do ya think I'm diggin' up a Corrigan grave? I know all a ya who come back now, don' I?"

"You really believe that?"

"Ya ask that like ya think I'm an eejit, ya know that?" Declan stood up and stopped shoveling, clearly offended. "Don' ya unnerstand the difference between 'believe' and 'know,' boyo? I don' *know* everythin', so I accept that there's a shite more maybes than I'd like."

"Like what?"

Declan shrugged, tossing more dirt into the wheelbarrow. "Like maybe there's ghosts, maybe not. Maybe we meet the ascended masters after we die, and maybe we pick our next life and the lessons we want to learn, or maybe it's all just fate. Like it's yer fate to empty this damn thing while I take a break." He climbed out of the hole, waiting for me to empty the wheelbarrow. The short break only raised more questions for me, and when I got back Declan was finishing a cigarette, watching me as if he knew I'd have come up with a few more things to ask.

"So you don't believe what the Catholic Church tells you, and there's not a book like the Bible for whatever it is you believe? No Pope or priest or Druid leader?" I was pushing his buttons and I knew it, but I wanted to keep him talking.

"No. None of us are stupid enough to think we know it all. We decide fer ourselves." He tossed a shovel at me, and we started digging down into the second grave as he kept talking. "An' besides. The ones of us who're awake, we remember what happens when people start believing they have the 'One True Faith.' People start dyin'. Burnin' at the stake an' all that."

"Then what makes you so sure you're right about any of it?"

"Because *I* remember. Maybe not everybody does, maybe some can't, but I know it's true because I've been there. People come back, Mick. Otherwise, there's no deeper meanin' to any of this." Declan was digging rhythmically, stabbing the earth with his shovel, as if the questions were making him tense. "Tell me, if ya don't believe in reincarnation, where is Georgie boy right now? Heaven or hell? What's yer lovin' God do with a man who kills other men for a living? Tell me that, Mick."

"The church says if he confessed his sins . . ."

"Jaysus, don' tell me ya believe that shite," he interrupted, annoyed. "He says 'Oops, sorry about that bullet, boyo,' an' that makes it okay? Where's his penance? Where's the consequences for his actions?"

"I'm not defending it, I'm just trying to understand."

"Good. Because ya can't defend it. If you're sorry, it doesn't matter if ya killed three hunnerd people, but if ya shag yer one true love before marriage an' yer not sorry fer doin' such a beautiful thing, yer goin' straight to hell. Does that make sense to you? Does it?" Declan stood, staring at me, waiting for my answer.

"No." I kept shoveling, knowing that the last time Declan got philosophical with a guy it was Trooper Wheeler, right before he shot Wheeler in the head. Still, I couldn't help adding, "But I don't think there's anything wrong with a little forgiveness."

"A course not, an' sometimes it's even free. In fact, it's better to fergive fer your own health instead a harborin' the poison a resentment, but ya shouldn' count on it and ya gotta fergive with caution." Declan must have been in great shape, because he kept digging as he spoke, and the hole was almost deep enough to start loading the crates in.

"What the hell does that mean, 'forgive with caution'?"

Declan looked at me. "Isn't it obvious? Fergive the sinner but not the sin. That's all I'm sayin'. If ya fergive too easily, a man isn' held accountable. He canna learn from 'is mistakes, an' he'll keep gettin' the same lesson over an' over again."

"So, if you believe we all come back, how come most don't remember?" I asked.

"Some don' wanna. They wan' a fresh start, to get away from their harpy wives and whiny brats. An' who wouldn'? But most aren' born with the memory jus' like they're not born with the gift a speech. They got the ability, jus' not the know-how. They could remember if they knew how. And they'd be better off for it, too."

"Better off?"

Declan was moving crates faster, letting gravity take them to me. "They can choose to run from their past or learn from it. Pay fer the sin, an' then it's forgotten. Ya learn yer lesson an' move on."

"So what are you here to learn?" I had to ask. He was standing above me as I stood in a grave with my last name already on it, preaching to me about God and resurrection. I was hoping he was here to make sure he finally learned the fifth commandment—"Thou shalt not kill."

Declan stopped with a crate in midair, hovering over my head, annoyed. "If I knew what I was here fer, would I be diggin' graves wit' you in the middle of the blasted night? Jaysus. Don' look at me as if I got all the answers. I don't. No one does, or they wouldn' be here, would they?" He tossed the crate down. I slowed it down with my chest long enough to deflect it onto the others as he turned to grab the next one. "Besides, my lessons ain't yers. Decide what the feck ta believe fer yerself."

The next crate came over the edge more gently but slipped from my grasp, smashing into the coffin so hard that it cracked. I heard a noise from inside. Maybe it was just something shifting, but I jumped, almost climbing out of the grave, until I heard Declan laughing above me. "Don' worry about them in there. There ain't no bodily resurrection. Jaysus wasn't talkin' about raisin' up half-rotted bodies an' bones. He meant that he'd raise up the same soul in new bodies."

I nodded, sliding back in, pretending that I didn't just have the "shite" scared out of me. As the next crate came at me, I stacked it on top, seeing that it was almost level with the ground. "The gravel will barely cover these. Are you sure you don't want to dig deeper in case somebody looks?"

"Hell no. We may need to resurrect these dead soldiers after next Sunday. Even without us there, Jerry may get what he's lookin' fer. The Prods an' the Brits are lookin' to find a way to keep us in our place. If they don' have an excuse, they'll make one, trust me." Declan slid the last crate over the edge and I lifted it onto the stack, effectively wedging myself between it and the earthen sides of the grave.

"Now, before we close up this 'ole an' finish our business here, do ya have any more questions, Mickaleen?" I looked up at him, standing over me, the Armalite over his shoulder. I wondered if I could pull him off balance before he got the weapon into his hands. He'd waited until all the work was done, and now would be the time to kill me if that was his plan. But as we had been speaking, I'd realized that burying me wouldn't be the best move for him. If Declan was setting me up to take the fall for murdering Wheeler, he'd want my body found. So I did have a question.

"Just one." I hesitated, feeling weak for having to ask. "Are you gonna kill me?"

His face, in the shadows, seemed to contort, and I tensed, ready to try and grab his leg to set him off balance if he went for the rifle. But then Declan bent double, trying to catch his breath as the sound of laughter echoed off the water. He was laughing so hard he was wheezing and I suddenly felt like the "eejit" he seemed to think I was.

"Is that a no?" I asked, climbing out of the hole.

"Jaysus, yes. No, I mean no. I have no current plans to kill ya."

"Why wouldn't you? I have evidence that can get you arrested or killed. You can blame me for killing Wheeler if I'm dead." It made some sense, not that I wanted it to. Declan shook his head, still amused.

"Damn. Ya always were a practical bastard, weren't ya? But yer takin' the short view. I still have use fer ya, plenty more I can blame ya fer besides killin' Wheeler if I wan'."

"So you'll use me until you're done with me?"

"Ahh, Christ. Ya really don' unnerstand, do ya?" He'd stopped laughing and his look changed to something like pity, which pissed me off even more. I was missing something here, and no one seemed to want to make it clear. Declan handed me a shovel and started to shovel the gravel back over the top of the Armalites. I joined him in silence for a moment, and then he stopped, as if considering a difficult option.

"Maybe it's time. Maybe ya need to learn a bit more of where ya come from, an' why I couldn' kill ya." I stared at him, not understanding, but he just nodded to himself, making his decision. "I'll get Kate to take ya, an' show ya some real ghosts, Mickaleen. Maybe then you'll unnerstand."

" '*Real*' ghosts?"

"Yea. Sure, the Shale Ghosts of Mullingar Road. You've met them before, ya just don' remember." With that he looked out over the lough. While we were working, the moon and stars had faded, and now the first rays of the sun were hitting the mist, turning a black and white world multihued and vibrant. "Yeah. It's time ya saw the light. But right now we need to get movin'."

Declan turned back to the gravel, shoveling rhythmically, not saying anything else until all the rifles were buried.

PATSY WAS AWAKE by the time we got back, though his eyes were glazed from some herbal remedy Kate had cooked up to help dull the pain. He could speak, and even sit up without moaning. As we entered the schoolhouse, Kate was handing him a bowl of something that smelled both foul and hearty, an odor somewhere between liver and onions and cabbage soup. Patsy looked up from it as Declan's shadow fell over him.

Both men just stared at one another for a long moment, and I waited for the outrage as Patsy confronted the man that kneecapped him. It never came. Instead I watched Patsy's eyes slowly well with tears and he struggled to mutter, "Thank you."

A slow smile crept across Declan's face as he nodded, putting down the Armalite he still carried. "Don' mention it." Then he went to get himself a bowl of whatever it was Kate had cooked up, the issue apparently now settled. After a moment, Patsy cleared his throat and tried to wipe his eyes inconspicuously.

"I'll only ask ya one favor, Dec." Declan turned to look at Patsy. "Next time, afore ya take my knee—put me through the rite first, will ya?" I noticed then that his brogue seemed to be thicker, no doubt a lingering effect of whatever he'd been through.

"The rite was offered to ya. Ya always felt like it was superstition and old wives' tales."

"Maybe I did. But isn't it yer moral responsibility to care fer feebleminded eejits? Inn't that what I was?" Patsy started to laugh, but it quickly became a pain-filled moan.

"Still are, if ya ask me." Kate admonished, shoving the bowl back at Patsy. "What's done is done. Eat yer food and shut yer gob. It's the only way you'll get better." She offered him a spoonful of the thick, goopy stuff and continued as he ate, "As soon as yer strong enough, I'll take ya home."

"Jaysus, an' make me live with Bridey?"

"That's yer ma, no matter who else ya remember her as," Kate chided him.

"An' what a 'mother' she is," Declan said.

Kate's eyes flashed at him, but she turned back to Patsy, still spoon-feeding him. "She's yer ma an' she loves you. Fer all her faults an' all her self-servin' lunacy, she's always done the right thing in the end. Jus' be glad she's not a young woman anymore."

Declan, sobered by Kate's harsh look, nodded his agreement. "She's speakin' the truth, Patsy. Bridey'll take care of ya. Whether ya like it or not, an' she'd probably enjoy it more if ya dinn't like it. But she's not as bad as she once was. She's slowed with age. I'll take ya home to her as soon as yer able."

"You? An' what's wrong with me?" Kate snapped.

"Ya have to go with Mickaleen."

"Go where? Where would I go when he's laid up like this?"

"Mickaleen needs to go to Mullingar. Or at least as far as the killin' field," Declan said softly, and I almost missed the part about the "killing field."

"What do you mean kil—" I started, but Kate held up a hand, stopping me.

"Quiet, Mick. Ya have nothin' to say in this right now." She turned to Declan, coldly. "An' neither does Declan. There's no reason fer him to go out there now. Not so soon. I won' take 'im."

"It'll be warm enough today fer a bit of rain an' should be cold enough after dark. I don' know when the weather'll next cooperate," Declan said evenly, as if it were a foregone conclusion that Kate would do as he instructed. I tried to make sense of it, but what the hell did the weather have to do with ghosts or karma or a killing field?

Kate hesitated, looking me over as if I weren't there, something in her eyes that I couldn't read. Finally she sighed one of those Irish sighs that takes all the breath out of the room and nodded to Patsy. "And what about the gimp in the corner? Who'll manage him?"

"I can manage myself, thank you," Patsy said indignantly.

"I'm jus' worried about getting ya off the island before Jerry comes back. Where'd he get to?" She was grilling Declan now, taking stock of the whole situation. "The one point that Mick's got right here is that this whole thing will blow up on somebody if it ain' handled right. Jerry knows about Wheeler, an' if he wants to make an issue out of it, all he's gotta do is tell people where they can find a dead SAS soldier. He'd just as soon blame Patsy as Mickaleen."

"Why would he do that?" I asked, trying to see their side of the logic.

"The Brits ain' supposed to be here, and a dead one, especially one murdered by a police officer of the Irish state, well, that might draw the Republic into the conflict, wouldn' it?"

"And isn't that what you want?"

"No . . . not most of us anyway. We want our rights, maybe even a united Ireland, but almost no one wants an all-out war. We'd destroy everythin' we were tryin' to save." Declan set his jaw and nodded toward the door. "Go. I'll keep Jerry in line. And leave Patsy to me. I need to fill 'im in on his alibi fer the last few days anyway. He needs to catch up after 'is trip down memory lane."

He and Kate held a look for a moment. "You'll need to leave soon if ya wanna get there before it gets too cold." Finally Kate nodded, grabbed her jacket, and started out the door, expecting me to follow.

"Kate," Declan called out as she reached the threshold. "Be careful goin' out there. I'm not sure who might be watchin' fer ya with Patsy among the missin'. An' if ya see Jerry, tell 'im he does nothin' before talkin' to me." Kate nodded and slid out of sight, into the mottled patches of sunlight outside. I followed her. I couldn't think of any other option.

KATE DIDN'T SAY much on the way across the lake and seemed to resent being forced to leave her brother. I wasn't sure where I stood with her, and my few attempts at conversation went nowhere. About halfway across I tried again.

"What's Declan mean when he says 'the killing field'?"

"He means the field where people got themselves killed," she answered, without turning to look at me. It was a conversation killer for sure. She obviously didn't want to talk.

As we landed on the far shore, I tried again as I climbed awkwardly out of the curragh. "It's nice to get some time alone with you."

I got no response. I started thinking that maybe I had to raise the stakes and let her know I'd been thinking these last few days about moving on. Trooper Wheeler might have told someone he was coming with Patsy to get me. And especially now that Declan and Jerry knew who I really was, it was probably time to make my escape.

"Seriously, Kate, any time we can get is good, with all of this going on and me trying to stay ahead of anyone finding out who I am. I don't know how much time—"

"Shut yer gob," Kate snapped. "Don' talk about time or leavin' or any of the rest of it, unnerstood? Ya know nothin' about time or leavin'."

She was starting to piss me off. What had I done to deserve her anger? "I know I don't want to be here when someone finds that body. I left my whole life behind."

"No, ya didn't." Kate stopped next to her car, covered in dust where we'd left it four days ago. She turned and looked at me. "Ya never really leave nothin' behind, don' ya know at least that much?" Her green eyes flashed and every muscle tensed and I suddenly understood why the Celts had warrior queens—because there wasn't a man alive who could tell them no. I certainly didn't have the guts to interrupt her.

"Everything ya do, every choice ya make, every other soul ya touch, ya carry all that with ya an' it makes ya who ya are. There is no runnin' from yerself, an' that's God's honest truth." Her anger seemed to ebb out of her with each word, and by the end of her rant, she seemed more sad than mad.

"What did I do? Why are you so upset with me?"

A surge of anger ran through her again, but it was a quick one—a flash of feminine anger familiar to every man who's ever been in a relationship. The kind of anger reserved for any man too stupid to read minds and know what he's done wrong.

Kate opened the driver's door and leaned on it, pointedly avoiding looking at me. "Ya did what ya always do. Ya ran. An' now yer talkin' about runnin' again. Makes it start to feel like it's me yer runnin' from." She turned fully away from me and started to get in the car, but I grabbed her arm.

"I'm not running from you." I pulled her from the car and hugged her, but her body was tense. "I won't run at all if that's what you want, I'll stay till they find me. But I'd rather you run with me."

Kate looked up at me, pale, as if I'd somehow said something worse. "Stop talking. Please. You don't know what you're saying." She pushed me away, getting in and slamming the door. She stared at me, waiting for me to go around and get in.

I circled the car. As soon as I got in, even before I could close the door, she was spinning the car around.

"What now?" I asked, starting to lose my patience.

"Nothin'. You'll see. Or ya won't. Jus' don' ask me nothin' else until after yer out there. After ya see what it is Declan wants ya to see." Kate cut the wheel, fishtailing as she pulled out onto the main road.

I stared out the window, feeling like I was on my way to my own execution. A few interminably silent miles later, we passed an overgrown track on the side of the road and I caught a glimpse of a battered and rusted old 1960 MG MGA. Leaning on the hood was Jerry Coonan. I'd have sworn it. I was sure I saw his eyes as we raced past, and he watched us go, a smirk on his face.

I twisted the rearview mirror so I could look to see if the car had pulled out to follow us, but even as I did it Kate twisted it back.

"I'm drivin'." She was still tense, still keeping me at arm's length.

"There was a car back there—" I started to explain, but she interrupted again.

"Yea, an' even in rural Ireland we allow more'n one car on the road at a time, don' we?" Kate glanced at me, then quickly looked away again, and I suddenly wondered if she knew that it was Coonan following us. Maybe she'd even arranged it with him and Declan.

I thought back on the phrase Declan had used for where we were going. The killing field. Maybe Declan didn't kill me earlier because he wanted me far enough away so that it couldn't be traced back to him. Why else was he sending me all the way out toward Mullingar? I turned all the way around in my seat to look behind us. The MG had pulled out but was quickly lost as we swung around the twisted curves in the roads. Still, if it was Coonan, and if he'd set this up with Kate or even Declan, he already knew where we were going.

"Yer gonna strain yer neck like that. Relax. Enjoy the scenery. Be the tourist yer supposed to be." Kate's tone had softened a bit. She nodded toward a decrepit farm just ahead of us. "See that farmhouse?" I knew she was trying to distract me, but I stayed sideways in my seat so I could keep glancing back. Kate pretended not to notice and kept talking.

"In the '98 rebellion, the British took fourteen local lads, put 'em up against the wall and shot 'em all. Ya can still see the bullet gouges in the stone." She slowed down, apparently so I could see gouges underneath the whitewash but I had no idea if that was the natural stone or the result of rifle fire.

"After the French sent the Brits off on the Castlebar Races and set up the Republic of Connaught, the three boys who lived in that cottage with their widowed ma ambushed one a the local lords. The oldest fired 'is rifle point blank at the bloody bastard, but his powder 'ad gotten wet an' it misfired. If not fer the dampness those three woulda been sung about to this day. As it ended up, they hung each of them, not a one of 'em older than fifteen, an' the youngest barely twelve, right in front of their ma on an old tree that once stood in front of the house. She cut it down that night herself with an ax."

I nodded, wondering whether there was a point to Kate's story, or if she was just passing time.

"They say she saved the wood from that tree and the family kept it in the barn until the Tan War. They finally gave it to a group a rebels who used it to burn down the barracks in Mullingar." Kate's eyes lit up for the first time in hours, and I marveled at the ability of the Irish to hold grudges for generations. Imagine saving firewood for all that time, through harsh winters and hard times when it could bring in cash, just to use it to burn out a group of men who happened to wear the same uniform as the men who killed your sons twenty years before. Then imagine, eighty years after the fire, that the local population savoring the story for its ironic justice, thinking that saving firewood for generations was not only sane but admirable.

Still, the stories kept me from worrying too much about what I was walking into. Kate gave me a blow by blow tour of the whole county, including its history. I couldn't tell how truthful the history was, as it was always told with a dash of what my father called the "Irish salt." "History," as my father put it, was just "his story" and everyone had a right to their own story.

I listened with half an ear as Kate kept talking and I kept looking for Coonan. "Durin' the Easter Risin', there was a young woman of about sixteen, lived up that way. Maureen O'Hanlon. On Easter Monday she was outside her house an' was singin' in Irish. A patrol of the Royal Irish Constabulary 'appened by an' caught 'er singin' in Irish, which under the penal laws and Statutes of Kilkenny was punishable by death up until 1831—and was punishable by caning even then. The constables raped the girl an' burned 'er house down, with her in it. No one even knew who did it until sixteen years later, when a former constable come back to visit after the peace set in, and a sixteen-year-old girl set the bed he slept in on fire, burnin' him alive. Ol' Maureen remembered 'is face in her next life an' gave 'im back exactly what he'd given her."

"The young girl that lit the bed on fire was the same girl they burned sixteen years before? She was reincarnated?"

I looked at her face and noticed the grin was gone. Some other, more subtle emotion had replaced it. I found out later that it was Bridey herself who was accused of killing a former RIC officer, in 1934, by lighting his bed on fire. She was acquitted and the story was forgotten by everyone except those immediately involved.

"No one can force ya to believe anything, Mickaleen. But if ya believe there's a God, then why not believe in one that gives ya a second chance?"

"Fine. You want me to take this seriously? Then explain to me how it's a second chance for anyone who's born blind or crippled?"

"If ya ever read yer Gospels, you'd know. The blind man don' have to be payin' fer his sins. He could be learnin' a lesson he chose to learn, or volunteered fer. Maybe the blind man wanted to learn what it felt like to be dependent on others. Or maybe he needed to develop patience. No one ever learned kindness without understandin' pain, or fergiveness without knowin' the bitterness of bein' hurt. As my ma says, ya can't learn to ration food at a feast, can ya?"

"What happens if you kill yourself? Do you get to start over again?"

"Ya don' come back to a better place if ya put a bullet in yer own head, boyo. Ya don' destroy a gift ya been given an' expect to be rewarded fer it. That's like quittin' in the middle of the game. You'll have to play the same hand all over again."

She was about to go on but cut it short as she spun the steering wheel and slammed on the brakes, trying to make a turnoff I never saw until we were almost on it.

Suddenly we were on what could at best be called a track—two muddy ruts and dead weeds in between, just off the Mullingar Road. Once the wheels were in the ruts, the car ran rather smoothly up the track. The ruts seemed to have been worn smooth by hundreds of years of use. As we rolled forward, the light seemed to seep out of the sky, the low-hanging sun disappearing below the tree line and the shadows so long they covered everything like a blanket of night.

Once we'd moved into the shelter of the trees and the Mullingar Road had disappeared around a bend, Kate seemed to relax a bit, even though she kept glancing in the rearview mirror.

As the car rolled out into an open field and glided to a slow halt, Kate turned to look at me, then silently opened the door and got out. I followed her but stopped as I looked over the rough, overgrown field.

This was the killing field, lined with stones piled up to form a rough wall and with trees that crowded over the wall. It was isolated, beautiful . . . and I hated it. It was cold, colder than I'd felt it anywhere else in Ireland, and the breeze made the hair on my neck stand up. I wanted to get back in the car and get out of there.

Instead, I watched as Kate climbed over a short stone wall and headed toward the rocky hill that rose up over the lower field offering a view of the valley below. As she stepped from the shadows of the trees into the light where the sun still hit the barley, Kate turned to face me, and it seemed that the sun was shining just for her, a spotlight bringing out the reds in her hair and the flecks of green in her eyes.

"What're ya waiting fer?" she asked, but her tone was more frustrated than playful. She knew what was going to happen here, or at least what Declan expected to happen, and she wasn't looking forward to it. And if she wasn't, neither was I.

Kate turned and walked toward the rocky outcropping that looked down over the Mullingar Road in the distance, and I slowly closed the car door. It was then that I heard the drone of an engine racing up the Mullingar Road. It seemed to slow as it approached, then faded abruptly to silence. I looked up at Kate to see if she'd noticed, but she was staring down the hill at a stand of trees in the near distance.

I kept listening but couldn't tell if the car had gone by or if the driver had cut the engine to hide its approach. I could visualize Coonan gliding to a stop on the road below, getting out and stalking us as we sat here watching the sun set. If Declan had arranged it, he'd know right where to find us, out in the middle of nowhere.

I kept listening, but I couldn't hear anything except the breeze through the trees, making the branches groan as if they might snap at any moment. I looked up to see Kate settling in on top of a large slab of rock, a gnarled tree hovering overhead, its roots crawling out through the hard soil like fingers grasping the edge of a grave. The sunset framed her, and in spite of my worries about Coonan, there was nowhere I wanted to be more than next to her.

If someone was going to kill me, maybe this wasn't such a bad place to go. I started walking toward her, annoyed that the dry, brittle grass made so much noise under my feet. As long as I was moving I was going to have a hard time hearing anyone approaching. Something about this place made me alert. There was an electric charge that rode on the cold breeze and carried familiar smells of dampness and rotting leaves, and a rich earthy smell that reminded me of someplace else.

Maybe it was that cabin outside Wellsboro. It was a day like this and in a place like this that I shot James Butler. I remembered the cold, the sharpness of the air, and the smell of the woods. That's why I was uneasy. That had to be it. Still, there was something else about this place, some eerie familiarity. Even the rock Kate sat on looked like one I'd seen before, although the trees all around were wrong. They looked too big. It was possible my father had photos of this place from years ago, from his trips back. He grew up in this area, knew hundreds of places like this.

I reached the rock Kate sat on. Its surface was still damp, and in the rapidly cooling air, ice crystals were already beginning to form. The driest spot was right next to her and I used it as an excuse to sit close, thigh to thigh, for warmth. Kate didn't look up as I settled in next to her, but she did move closer and took my arm.

I could see the Mullingar Road below us, over the tops of the trees, and knew I'd be able to hear any traffic from below. This small promontory was a great vantage point for watching the comings and goings of anyone traveling between Athlone and Mullingar, but it was also isolated. I could imagine sitting here in another century, watching British soldiers ride by on horseback as the sun set, then racing off for home to warn everyone before night fell. I felt myself starting to relax.

Then the breeze picked up, cutting through me and rattling the trees, causing the branches to rustle and groan. Dead leaves whispered from the ground and I knew that if Coonan had followed us, I'd never hear him coming. I'd never see him through the thick shelter of the trees and never be able to get to cover from this spot, exposed on a slight rise in the middle of an open field. This place might be fine for watching the road, but if anyone knew you were here, it was a death trap. I glanced around behind us quickly, suddenly nervous.

"The sunset's beautiful, Kate," I started, wondering how soon I could convince her to leave or at least take cover somewhere less exposed.

"But?" She turned toward me, eyes narrowed, with something a bit dangerous behind them. "C'mon. I hear it in yer voice. Ya got a question, ask it."

"Fine. Why are we out here? And please, no riddles or philosophy or answering questions with questions. I really need a straight answer."

"Why should I bother? You wouldn't believe a straight answer now, would ya?"

"That was a question. Not an answer."

"Do ya think I'm an eejit? I know a question when I ask one."

"Yes, but do you know an answer when you give one?"

Kate stared at me for a moment, revealing nothing, then turned away. "Fair enough. Yer here so you can meet the ghosts. That's as straight as it gets."

I looked away, frustrated, wondering if I should just get up and walk away. I watched the sun as it set, and the first few words to a long-forgotten poem came to mind. For some reason I knew that if I could remember the rest, or even the title, it would somehow make sense of this moment. I know how the poem began: "Now goes under, and I watch go under, the sun / That will not rise again," but that was all I could remember. It really wasn't cheering me up very much.

"That's a metaphor or something, right? Ghosts?" I had to keep talking. I was missing something important here, and even though Kate was just plain old pissing me off by not coming straight out with it, I didn't think she was trying to upset me. I think she was trying to tell me something I couldn't quite grasp. I knew that. So I kept talking, hoping I could catch a glimmer of what it was.

"An' what if it wasn't? What if they're real, the ghosts? Or what if it didn't matter if they were real or not, as long as ya learned the lessons they taught?" Philosophy again. Great.

"You can't learn from something that's not real," I told her firmly, though even I could hear the doubt in my voice.

"No? Then tell me, did ya ever learn from a fairy tale? A parable? Neither of 'em are real, are they? Fiction is just the lie we make up to reveal a greater truth, ain't it?"

At times I hate the Irish. I hate their word games. I especially hate the ones who believe in things unseen that are more real to them than the world is to me. I hate feeling like a child who's watching shadows and images on a wall while the others see three-dimensional beings that cast the shadows.

I started to pull away, to get up and go back to the car, but before I could, Kate took my hand. She was gentle, but there was no way I could pull away. She spoke quietly, her voice in harmony with the rustling leaves, a whisper among whispers.

"Whatever we believe in *is* real, Mickaleen. That's one truth ya can't argue with. Hypnotists and philosophers have proven that time an' again. Ya can die of a heart attack as much from an imagined ghost as a real one, an' yer placebo can cure yer disease as well as an expensive medicine if ya only believe."

I wasn't going to argue with her. I'd accepted the fact that to argue was pointless. She'd win every time. And the truth is, I wanted her to win. I wanted to believe in something. I always had, I just couldn't let myself. I was too worried about being conned.

Kate was watching my eyes, and she must've seen that I wasn't going anywhere, because she pulled me closer, putting an arm around me.

"Stay just a few more minutes. It's almost cold enough."

And once again, I was left behind, following her blindly toward something I couldn't see. "Cold enough for what?"

"Fer the Shale Ghosts to make themselves known," Kate said, and I knew that I might as well play along. She wasn't going to tell me anything she didn't want me to know. Besides, maybe I was just being paranoid. It's been known to happen.

"Fine. But if I'm staying to see the ghosts, why don't you at least tell me who they are."

"They're not really a *who,* an' I never promised you'd *see* them now, did I?" Kate replied. It was true. She hadn't said I'd see them, only that they'd make themselves known. The specificity of her language pissed me off. It was like talking to a lawyer all day, or my father, with his obsession about asking the right questions even when you couldn't possibly know what the right questions were.

"What I can tell ya is a little history," she said. "It involves the Shale Ghosts, in a way. Ya see that tree line down there?" I looked to where she nodded, at the trees that I felt I had seen, probably in a photograph, back when they were less tall.

"Back in '21 there was a group of our boys, a flyin' column, down there. They were lyin' in wait fer the Black an' Tans to come through on their way to Athlone. It was a winter day, like this one, an' gettin' colder. Up on this rock right here was their lookout, a young man petrified that he'd miss seein' the Tans in time or that they'd send scouts through the woods and discover the ambush." I knew exactly how he felt, exposed, like I did, waiting for Coonan to appear out of the woods. Maybe it was the empathy I felt for him that made me start to realize why I was here and why this place felt so familiar.

"Was my uncle Sean one of them? My father?" I asked, already knowing deep down that one of them was.

"Yer father wann't here. He was too young," Kate answered, looking down, avoiding my eyes. "Yer uncle wouldn' let him come."

"And what is it you expect me to remember? Is this about Declan?" Declan and all his bullshit about my dream of Liam had made me paranoid, but only because everything he said *felt* true. It felt true because deep down, I knew this place. I could feel my heart racing, my legs tensing, ready to run. Panic was setting in and I couldn't say why.

Kate saw it in my eyes and gently stroked my back with one hand, gripping my arm with her other one. Her voice was soothing and warm, holding back the biting wind.

"It doesn't matter what Declan said, does it? An' I don' expect ya to remember anythin'. You'll remember what ya remember. But jus' close yer eyes and listen to this place, listen to the sounds that've always been here." I could feel my muscles loosen as she spoke. I listened to the dry leaves muttering, to the trees groaning, and I could taste the acrid cold as it filled my nose and throat, burning like it did before. Kate kept talking, her voice part of the fabric of this place.

"Imagine it as it was, as ya see it in yer mind. Feel the cold."

I was trying, but even as I struggled to see the place in my mind, with my eyes closed, something else intruded—someone approaching through the trees. I heard it. I saw it as if my eyes were open, catching glimpses of his faded jacket. If it was Coonan . . .

I opened my eyes, but there was nothing there, just the trees, different than I'd seen them with my eyes closed. Kate squeezed my hand, gently pulling me back.

"Close yer eyes, Mickaleen. See without 'em fer a minute. Somethin' went wrong here. Can ya feel it?" I closed my eyes and lost the image of the place as it had just been, seeing it instead as it may have been, years before. Still with my eyes closed, I listened as Kate went on: "Five boys died in this field on a cold morning in 1921. There's people who say on certain winter days ya can still hear the gunshots and them cryin' out in pain. Others say the Shale Ghosts were here long afore them boys died and that the ghosts is what killed 'em . . ."

"Liam," I heard myself say. I didn't mean to say it. I would have sworn I didn't say it, except I heard myself. I opened my eyes, not needing to imagine anything anymore. It was all right in front of me. "Liam was here, wasn't he? This is where it happened? I stood up, looking down the hill through disjointed time, seeing the trees that were then and the trees that were there now, seeing the jacket he wore moving through the trees, seeing him in my mind and memory.

"It was here, wasn't it?" I turned on Kate, demanding an answer. "That's where he came running from." As I stood and moved from Kate's side, a sudden wind ripped into me, and my ears burned from the cold. It felt ten degrees colder. She didn't say a word but nodded solemnly. This was the place I'd dreamed of. "Right from those trees."

I could see it all in front of me, a temporal double vision, blurry and over-laid, shifting back and forth. And then I heard it again, movement in the woods. I strained to find it, but I was too disoriented. Was it the movement of memory or something more ominous? I couldn't trust myself.

That's when it happened. Again. I heard the echo almost at the same time I heard the shot and saw Kate flinch as a shard of rock flew up at her face. At my feet the rock exploded, cutting a gash in my jeans and gouging the skin beneath. I reacted without thinking, pushing Kate backward and covering her with my body as splinters of rock flew up around us. I didn't think she'd been hit and had no idea of where the shooter was, but he must've had a bad angle because he hadn't hit me yet. He was firing fast, bullets tearing into the rock all around me. Then a shard flew up, catching me on the cheek.

"I can't see him," I told Kate, "but we have to get out of here. As soon as I move, run for the car and start it." I was going to run downhill, making myself more of a target, giving her time to get away, but I stopped as I heard a strange sound.

At first I thought it was Kate crying, but then I realized she was laughing. Laughing with tears rolling down her cheeks, gasping for air. "I'm sorry, Mickaleen, but there's no one there. It's just the Shale Ghosts."

I sat up, confused, still looking for the shooter even as the rate of fire slowed down. I couldn't see anyone and couldn't hear anything other than the wind and Kate's breathy laughter. It was a desperate laugh, the kind that comes when the tension is too high and it needs to be released. She took pity on me then, seeing my bewilderment.

"The rock all around you, Mick, it's brittle shale." Kate caught her breath, stifling her laughter. "The water seeps into the cracks and crevices, then expands as it freezes. When it expands far enough—"

"It cracks the rock and sounds like gunshots," I finished for her, suddenly putting all the pieces together for myself. And then more pieces fell into place. James Butler. The cold, and the snow, melting and refreezing. My God. What had I done? Suddenly there was a roaring in my ears, like an ocean of waves coming in to roll over me, the blood in my ears pumping so loudly I was almost deafened. I felt light-headed and faint, and Kate's voice seemed to come to me from far away in time and space.

"That's why yer uncle Sean thought Liam was shootin' at him. That's why ya thought James Butler had a gun. Ya got hit with the rock."

Kate was right. It was the shale. The ghosts. It all made sense now. "Not real gunshots at all," I managed to mutter.

"No, but ya believed they were real, and because ya believed, they had the same effect, didn't they?" I looked at her blankly, too overwhelmed to realize that she was back to proving her point. I barely heard her as I looked

270 • KEVIN FOX

down the hill to the spot where Liam had lain as he died. I knew exactly where it was and how long it took to get there that day. I walked toward the spot just as I had walked toward James Butler's body, hesitant and on edge.

The moment and the memories were getting tangled together and torn apart as it all came back to me. The echo of the gunshot almost overlapping the sound of his skull cracking as the bullet went in, like brittle branches snapping. There was so little blood.

I'd shot my friend. Liam. Declan. I recognized both of them, although they were both the same and different in my memory, as one. He was the one who lay there with my bullet in his head, looking up at me in shock and pain. He wasn't angry. He wasn't even scared. His eyes met mine as he struggled with the words. "Stay with me. They won't notice. I've got blood enough for both of us . . ."

I sat down in the barley, sinking into the tendrils that rose from the earth, right where I remembered sitting in my dream. I could feel my muscles go loose, my heart racing as it all came back to me. Suddenly I didn't have the strength to sit up anymore, and I lay down, like I had so long ago, absolutely still, my chest straining as though it wanted to burst.

In my mind, I was lying in my friend's warm blood once again, feeling it pool under me as the Black and Tans raced past, chasing Seamus and Cathal and the rest of our ragtag column. Shooting them in the back as they ran. Shooting Frank and Michael, the O'Connell brothers, as they tried to get away. I could see it all from here, each of them falling not ten feet from me, almost synchronized. Even in death, they were so similar, I couldn't tell which was which.

I remember seeing Seamus through the tall grass, stopping at the stone wall farther up the hill. He took cover and fired back at the Tans from behind it, and as he did I saw him look right at me. He caught my eye and could see that I was alive, only pretending to be dead. I saw the judgment in his luminous blue eyes as he peered from under a ragged mess of dark black hair. Seamus knew I was alive. He knew I was faking it. He knew that I was a coward.

I knew then that I couldn't face him. I couldn't face any of them. I'd shot Liam. I'd lain in his blood and watched as the O'Connells took bullets to their backs. Still, I didn't move. I couldn't move until the silence returned, and then, after a bit, the sounds. The trees moving in the wind, their groaning branches in harmony with Liam's dull moans.

I sat up slowly, kneeling over Liam, and was surprised that he was still alive. I noticed that his eyes were fluttering, and that somehow hurt me even more, because I knew I couldn't save him. I could see him struggling to keep his eyes open, and finally he did, fixing his gaze on me.

"Go," he said raspily, "before they come back." His voice drifted lower and I heard the gurgle of blood in his throat. Still he made the effort to speak. "See ya . . . nex' life . . . Finish it, please . . ." He was begging me. His speech was slurring and he was losing the ability to think, but his eyes said it all for him. He knew he was dying or, worse, living as if he were dead. We both knew that bullets can scramble your brains, ricocheting off your skull without killing you, leaving you mumbling and moaning, shitting yourself and wishing you'd died.

I shot him again. It was what he wanted, but it also somehow released me. I knew he'd go on to the next life and not suffer anymore in this one because of me. He never would've been whole again in this one.

"I guess ya remember it now?" Kate's soft voice centered me, bringing me back to the present. I looked up at her in the growing darkness and almost didn't recognize her, the way you sometimes don't recognize people out of context. Slowly I felt myself come back together. It was almost the way she described jet lag, as if my soul had gone elsewhen and I had to wait for it to catch back up to my body. As I gathered my senses, I slowly nodded.

"I shot Declan."

"Ya mean Liam." She took me in her arms, holding me as she whispered softly, "An' I know. Twice. On purpose the second time."

"How do you know?" How could she possibly know? No one was here except my uncle Sean and Liam that day. Kate backed away, looking at my eyes, catching the look of doubt there.

"Declan told me a few years back, after his own rite a passage." She held my eyes, trying to look past them, through them, trying to read something more there. "Ya remember anythin' else?"

"What else is there?" I asked, wondering how it might get worse.

"Everythin'. There's more to a life than just a death now, inn't there?" Her brow was creased with worry, and I thought of her statement earlier, about being afraid that I'd remember *her*. "Do ya remember what happened after?"

"No, but you do, don't you?" That was the truth of it, I was sure. She was afraid I'd remember what she already knew. "What is it?"

Kate pulled away, hesitating. Then she squeezed my hand, looking down at the ground where Liam had died. "Do ya remember what ya said to me as we got in the car to come here?"

"I told you that I wanted to run, but not from you, that I wanted you to run with me."

She nodded. "That was it. But what ya didn't know, what ya couldn't know, was that after he left here, yer uncle Sean went to see his fiancée." Kate couldn't look at me, and as the frigid wind picked up, her eyes started to tear. "You can think of it as you comin' ta see me, but things were different then. We were different . . . Anyway, Sean told m . . . her, Erin, his fiancée, that . . ." Kate hesitatied, trying to recall the exact words. "He told her that 'as long as you run with me, I won't be running away from anything, I'll be runnin' to something. Our future.' "

I could have finished those sentences for her, I seemed to know them so well. It had grown even darker as we stood there, but I could see the dim light shining off the wetness on her cheeks. Kate knew what happened with Liam, and she knew the exact words my uncle Sean had said to his fiancée, Erin, over fifty years ago. I knew them, too. Because we were both there.

"I didn't go with you. I'm sorry." Even though I remembered it all, it still felt as if it happened to someone else. It was like a long-forgotten memory, both alien and familiar, no different from the memory of my grandfather's funeral when I was six.

"They thought you were guilty because I didn't go with ya, that I knew you were guilty an' wouldn't go because I blamed ya fer Liam an' the O'Connell brothers. But I didn't. No, I never thought ya did anythin' wrong, I promise ya. I didn't go because I thought ya'd stay fer me. I thought ya might not run if I dinn't go. That ya'd stay an' fix it."

"And I . . . my uncle Sean. He ran anyway."

Kate nodded and finally turned to look at me. She was crying, and I couldn't find the words to apologize for something I hadn't done, at least not in this lifetime. I held her instead, appreciating her warmth as the night set in even colder. She was muttering into my shoulder. I pulled away slightly, trying to understand what she was saying.

"It jus' repeats itself, until ya learn. Ya keep gettin' the same lessons over an' over. Ya can't keep runnin', Mickaleen. Ya gotta stop runnin' from ghosts."

I looked down at her and shook my head. "Is that my lesson? Or is the lesson that you should run with me?"

Kate shook her head, thinking about that for a moment. "I don't know." And then she looked up at me, a lopsided grin on her face. "Maybe the lesson is that ya should never sit on shale in the cold?" And Kate laughed again, even as the tears still clung to her cheeks. I heard myself laughing with her, unable to hold back, just glad that we were both here, alive, together. Kate laughed so hard she made herself hiccup, and that made us both laugh even harder.

"Damn. I've no whiskey," she managed to say.

"Whiskey?"

"It cures my"—a hiccup interrupted—"hiccups." We laughed until we were both out of breath.

"I have another cure," I finally told her, and kissed her, holding her through five or six more hiccups, trying not to laugh. Somewhere in the midst of it all, the hiccups went away, and by the time I stepped back to look at her again, it was completely dark. It was then that I felt safe asking her what I wanted to ask her the first day I saw her in the greengrocer's.

"Do you think there's such a thing as love at first sight?" I asked.

She laughed again, a genuine burst of laughter that she quickly stifled, trying to explain so she didn't hurt my feelings. "I have no feckin' idea, Mickaleen. I'm sorry, but I don'. I've known ya so long, an' been through so much, that rememberin' the first time . . . it's irrelevant." I could feel her warm breath on my face, and I knew she was right. It didn't matter. "Sometimes I wish I dinn't remember, so I could feel somethin' like that again, but what I'd lose is all those lifetimes with you an' it wouldn' be worth it."

"So you remember us, and I don't. It doesn't seem quite fair."

"No, it's not. But ya know what really pisses me off about all this death an' dyin'? It keeps interruptin' a perfectly good relationship." Kate kissed me. After a moment, she pulled away.

"I wish I could tell ya more, Mickaleen, but memory is the most personal thing we got, an' ya can't just have mine. That's my story—it's what gives everything meanin' fer me. You need to discover yer memories on yer own. Ya need to feel 'em the way ya felt 'em before. Memories without yer emotions have no meanin'. They're just a list of dates of births and deaths. Some of it will come back natural to ya now, but to really remember, you'll need the rite."

That stopped me for a moment. Kate knew more about me than I did, more about us, more about everything we'd been through, and she wasn't going to tell me what it was. As an investigator, it always bothered me to know that I didn't know something, that the facts could be hiding a completely different truth or agenda. "What else don't I know, Kate? What else should I know?"

"Like what? What do ya need to know?"

I thought about it, but where do you start with lifetimes worth of questions? I started with the place most investigations start, with a dead body. "How about we start with Declan—Liam, I mean. He asked me to kill him, so he wouldn't come to New York to kill Uncle Sean, right?"

"Yer thinkin' like a detective again." She was right, I was thinking like a cop, and I had new evidence now. I'd remembered more details, had more suspects in my internal lineup.

"It was Seamus, the one who was here, wasn't it?"

Kate's face gave her away, and the slight hesitation, her eyes averted from mine gave me the answer before she spoke. "No. Don' lay blame. I won' tell ya who because it was all a mistake. They thought ya betrayed them, givin' away their position to the Tans on purpose."

I thought about the story I'd heard so many times from my father about how my uncle Sean had died in the alley behind his bar, and how his last words were *"Ni dhiolann dearmad fiacha."* A debt is still unpaid, even if forgotten. He didn't owe the bookies. He felt that he owed his life for what happened here in the killing field that day. I knew now that was what he meant, because I remembered it. It all came back to me as I thought of it, the long locked doors in my mind creaking open on rusty hinges, unlocked by Kate and the Shale Ghosts of Mullingar Road. How many other doors would open if I thought about the past?

I wasn't sure I wanted to know. The memories that were coming weren't that pleasant. As I stood there with Kate, I was immersed in the past, remembering my uncle's death, which was my own. I could feel the uneven pavement of the alley under my feet, could smell the stale cabbage and alcohol from the night's St. Patrick's celebration and could feel the warmth of the rising sun on my cheeks from where it peered around the corner of the alley. I even remembered the silhouetted figure blocking it out suddenly and calling me by a nickname I hadn't heard in almost twenty-five years . . .

"Mickaleen?" he asked, and I started to answer with a voice that was both mine and my uncle Sean's, unable to see his face with the rising sun in my eyes. I saw the pistol coming up, and I knew it was Seamus. Too late, he stepped forward, and I saw those eyes.

I turned to Kate. "He came at me out of the sun. I didn't see him in time. It was Seamus."

"Maybe that's why ya had such an irrational fear of Mr. Butler sneakin' up behind ya," Kate offered, and I suddenly knew it was true. They both came at me with the sun at their backs.

"And Seamus and Jerry Coonan are one and the same, aren't they?"

"Ya can't blame Jerry. That was a lifetime ago, and he thought ya were a traitor. He did what he thought was right. Declan only told us after Seamus shot ya, after he went through the rite an' remembered."

"How'd he find me? How'd he find my uncle Sean? After twenty-five years?"

Kate stiffened in my arms, and when her voice came it was barely audible over the breeze. "It was my fault." I pulled away a bit to try and see her eyes, but she looked away, toward the dimming brightness of the western sky.

"Sean kept sendin' letters to Erin fer years after he left, but I ignored them. I dinn't know what really happened until Declan finally remembered, years later." Her voice trailed off, and I thought she was done for a moment, but then she looked back at me, tension at the corners of her mouth as she spoke. "Then one day I got a letter an' nothin' was in it but a poem. It was his way of sayin' good-bye, of fergivin' me. I remember every word of it. 'Now goes under, and I watch go under, the sun,'" she said, looking up at the western sky.

"'That will not rise again,'" I finished for her. It was the poem that was going through my head earlier. The one I couldn't really remember. Or maybe I had been remembering it from longer ago than I could possibly imagine. Kate was somber again, looking into my eyes, the darkness between us slipping away. Her words were a physical thing now, washing over me with the sweetness and warmth of her breath.

" 'Today has seen the setting, in your eyes, cold and senseless as the sea, / Of friendship better than bread, and of bright charity . . .' " Kate went on, then stopped, losing track of the words. "There's more, an' if I say all of it you'll have me cryin' again. But the part that I've never gotten out of my mind, after all these years, is the end. 'Now goes under the sun, and I watch it go under. / Farewell, sweet light, great wonder! / You, too, farewell—but fare not well enough to dream. / You have done wisely to invite the night before the darkness came.' " Her voice cracked, and she took a deep breath before going on. "A month later, Sean was dead, murdered outside his pub in New York. It was like he knew that he was movin' on and was fergivin' me before he went."

"There was more to it than that," I told her, recalling more of the poem now, the part that hit me hardest. "You're leaving out the most important part of that letter. The third verse goes, 'I would have sworn, indeed I swore it: / The hills may shift, the waters may decline, / Winter may twist the stem from the twig that bore it, / But never your love from me, your hand from mine.' "

Kate squeezed my hand and wiped her eyes with the other hand, nodding. "They found you because ya sent that to me. Seamus found the letter and followed the postmark to New York. He dinn't know where to go from there, so he went the first place we all go when we need to find a pair a loose lips."

"The bar," I concluded.

"Yea. It was fate that it was Corrigan's Tavern. Out of twenty Irish pubs in the postal code on that envelope, that was the one he walked into."

"The name didn't help, did it?" Kate nodded, agreeing. "You're right. I shouldn't have run. If I'd stayed in the States this time, I could have explained why I shot Butler. If I'd known about the shale . . ."

"But ya did run, an' there's no goin' back now. Yer fate'll find you wherever you go. An' no matter how far ya run, there ya are, face to face with yerself."

She was right. I'd made my decisions and I was stuck with them. Still, I had to ask. "I can't go home again, can I?"

Kate shrugged, a soft smile on her lips. "Whether ya remember yet or not, Mickaleen, ya are home."

Sean

My uncle was innocent. The pages of his journal that the bellboy had shoved into my hands proved that much. Or at least they proved that he was mostly innocent. He did flee prosecution and was probably guilty of at least negligent homicide, unless there's such a thing as "mistaken self-defense." He'd also killed Liam on purpose with his second shot. But he didn't actually murder anyone. Still, I guess being "mostly innocent" is like being "mostly dead" or "slightly pregnant." The fine line that makes all the difference seems to disappear when you look at it in the wrong light. All I know is that whatever the subtle legal distinction, it made a big emotional difference to me. The intention of the act was different, and if the law didn't take that into account, then it was the law that was flawed.

All of this was going through my head as I stared at the chipped and peeling paint on the ceiling of the hotel room Anne and I had shared the night before, listening to the pipes bang as she took another shower. She'd woken up in a mood, annoyed that I'd fallen asleep while reading, and she had taken her energy out on me in an aggressive and exciting way, but when she was done, she'd pushed me aside and said she needed to shower so she didn't smell like a "sweaty Yank wanker."

I was lying there, spent, in the afternoon sun that fell through the sheers on the window when Anne came out of the bathroom, already dressed. I hadn't moved. "What're ya now, some kinda cripple? Get yer lazy Yank arse outta bed, an' let's get a move on." Anne reached out and tore the covers off of me.

"Go where? Why? What's your problem?" Why would we go anywhere? Now that I knew my uncle was innocent, it was over. I'd proven what I'd come to prove. Anne, however, was still on a mission.

"Jaysus, yer dense as shite, ain' ya? Them pages ya been huggin' all night, where'd they come from? Who knew ya were here?"

"I don't know," I answered hesitantly. I hadn't thought too much about it. "No, a course ya don' know. Tell me, genius, who would give 'em to a bellboy, 'stead of handing them over himself?" she asked, "An' why did ya see the same fella all over the damn town yesterday? The one with the eyes of the Duine Matha?"

"You saw him, too?"

"'Course I did. I'm not the one here who's blind and deef, am I? Get yer things. We kept him waitin' long enough that he's probably gettin' tired, but if we wait much longer, he'll be comin' in to see if we slipped out. If we go now, maybe we can catch 'im off balance." As she spoke, Anne had finished getting dressed and was pulling on her shoes. I looked at the clock. It was almost four in the afternoon. If he'd been waiting for us to come out all day he *would* be tired, but when had she thought this all through? Had she thought about it all night? And if she'd known all along we'd have to run, why didn't she leave me time to get a shower?

"Can't I get a shower? Or room service at least? I'm starved," I pleaded, not seeing how ten, maybe fifteen, minutes could make a difference.

"Oh, that's brilliant now, inn't it?" For once I felt like I had an idea that she appreciated. She grabbed the room phone and started to order as I got up to get a shower. As I reached the bathroom door, she covered the phone and called out to me.

"What do ya think yer doin'? Dinn't I jus' say we gotta go?" And I was back to being the "eejit" again.

"But you just ordered room service. I have time to get in and out of the shower before it gets here."

"Jaysus, yer an amadan, ain' ya? I did order room service, but not fer you. Anyone watchin' will assume we're gonna be here to eat it now, won' they?" Anne waited for an answer, and even though I knew it was a setup, I answered anyway.

"Umm, that's what *I* assumed."

"An' if they're out there waitin' on us an' hungry, they'll take advantage of the time it takes fer room service to show up an' go get a bite themselves, right?" Anne laid it all out for me, but I was paying more attention to how manipulative and sneaky she was than her actual plan. Where'd she learn all this stuff? And what other paranoid thoughts did she harbor?

"So we're not getting food?" I had to at least make that much clear to my stomach, which was growling at me.

"No. We're getting out," she answered, even as she threw my pants at me, followed by my shoes.

Two minutes later we were walking out of the hotel's delivery entrance with black plastic garbage bags over our shoulders and the white smocks of the hotel staff over our clothes. We'd cut through the kitchen and out the back door. No one even looked at us. On our way down the back stairs we'd made a historic compromise: as soon as we were out of Dublin we'd stop to eat as long as I'd let her read the new pages. She guided me through the first few minutes as we got onto the N1 and then onto the M1 going north, telling me to stay on it straight for at least a half hour.

"Wait, what about stopping to eat?" I asked.

Anne barely looked up from the torn and tattered pages the bellboy had given me. "I said as soon as we're outta Dublin. The first acceptable place to eat is at least a half hour now, inn't it? Unless ya wanna get off, and that's jus' not a good idea this time a day. We'll run into all kinds of traffic now." I should have realized that she was giving in too easily.

"I'm still hungry."

"Don' be such a wanker. It's mind over matter. You know what tells ya yer hungry or not?"

"My stomach," I answered, knowing even before we started arguing that I'd lose.

"Wrong, boyo. The stomach just sends a signal to the brain, and the brain tells it that it's hungry."

"Right. So if your thoughts can change the world, think me up a sandwich."

"Sure. I did that twenty minutes ago when we ran through the kitchen." Anne reached into her purse and pulled out a sandwich I'd noticed on a cart in the hotel kitchen as we made our way through. She handed it to me with a grin. "Here. Ya can thank me later."

I looked at the sandwich. Turkey club. I took a bite. Perfect.

I wanted to ask her to think me up a drink as well, but before I could say anything, she pulled out a Guinness and a bottle of Coke. I took the Coke. She clicked her Guinness on my Coke, muttered "*Slainte*," and went back to reading as I ate.

ANNE GAVE ME directions as we got off the highway, calling out turns ten seconds before I had to make them. Finally, she guided me to a deserted road surrounded by farm fields. I'd slowed down, waiting for more directions, but she just pointed to the side of the road, near a hedgerow.

"Park there so I can finish readin'. We need to wait till dark anyway."

"Dark? Why?"

"'Cause they won't let us in any other way. Now quiet. I'm tryin' to concentrate." I knew that was bullshit. Anne could read while having a full conversation. She didn't need to concentrate, she just wanted me to shut up.

"Do you mind telling me—"

"To shut yer bleedin' gob? No, not at all." She kept reading but after a moment sighed, almost as if she felt bad for treating me that way. "If ya reach behind yer seat I've got some emergency spares. They're warm, but you'll live. Take a few an' relax."

I wasn't sure what she was talking about until I reached back and felt the bottles there. She was right, they were warm, almost hot, from sitting in the car, but after a few sips I got used to it. In fact, the Guinness was less bitter warm than it was cold. It went down more smoothly. After a half bottle, the air in the car was getting stale, and I was getting impatient, so I rolled down the window. Somewhere in the near distance I could hear the low growl of diesel engines, trucks or buses from the sound of it, and when they faded, a scattering of loud voices carried across the fields. Strangely, even at this distance, I could tell that they weren't the mumbled melodic Irish voices I'd started to grow used to. They were harsher, louder. German or American, if I had to guess.

But where were they? And where were *we*? We'd finally stopped moving long enough for me to think, and it dawned on me that I was in a foreign country with a girl who was thankfully not blood related to me even though my father had called her a cousin. I was in the driver's seat of a car, drinking my second Guinness in five minutes, parked on a sad excuse for a road, waiting for it to get dark so I could sneak in someplace, and I didn't even know where that place was.

A week ago, I'd have been figuring out a way to get the hell out of here. But tonight I was totally calm. I didn't feel lost anymore. As much as Anne scared me, I trusted her to keep me on the right path. If only I knew where we were headed.

I'd been staring off into the fields for a few minutes when I realized that the light had faded and it was nearly dark. I no longer heard Anne turning pages next to me and when I looked over at her and she was grinning at me.

"Welcome back, boyo. Ya done daydreamin' now that ya finished off my spares?" Anne nodded at my feet. Four empty bottles lay there. I guess I had lost track of time.

"Sorry."

"Don' be. I always have a backup plan." Anne reached behind her own seat and pulled out a plain brown bottle. Easily forty ounces plus.

"Home brew. Poteen. An ancient recipe," Anne told me as she opened it, then offered me some.

It was unlike any alcohol I'd had before. The taste was peculiar—sweet at first but with an acrid, bitter aftertaste. I expected it to burn on the way down, and it did, but not harshly. It was warm, thick, heavy, and vaguely licorice-like. "Damn. That's good."

"Special recipe. Jus' fer you." Anne leaned over and kissed me. We spent the next few minutes alternating between drinking and fooling around until I looked up and noticed that the moon had risen and was illuminating her eyes and hair, making her look almost spectral. Once again, time had sped along at a strange pace. The poteen bottle was empty, sitting on the floor. I didn't remember finishing it. In fact, I didn't remember drinking any more than the first sip. It must have been more potent than I imagined.

Anne was watching my eyes as I tried to take in the bottle, the sudden onset of night, and the light of the moon on her skin. She smiled at me, but it was a grim smile. A prepared smile. "Looks like yer ready. We better go." And she opened her door, stepping out into the night, forcing me to follow her.

As I hit the night air I could feel it invading my lungs, warming me from within and without, and I realized that I was completely and utterly intoxicated. Strangely, there was nothing "toxic" about this intoxication. I didn't feely clumsy or light-headed or confused—just clear and complete, every sense tuned in perfectly to the night.

It was a quiet night but not silent. In fact, it was full of subtle sound, harmonious, and almost musical. The breeze was a soft swaying rhythm and insects hummed and buzzed like a string section as the the deep bass of cows lowing accompanied them somewhere nearby. The sounds of diesel engines were long gone and there were no voices for miles. The quality of light was also intriguing. The moonlight seemed to make the air thicker, and I felt as if I were floating through it, able to swim three inches off the ground, gliding across the blue-green fields, following Anne.

As I thought about it, I tasted the air, tasted the pungent pollen mixed with the rich soil full of oxides and iron. I could feel the grass bending under my feet, springing back, brushing across my calves. Even through my jeans, I could feel the dew drops land and cling to my skin, leeching heat and dissipating it into the night.

I remember thinking, what the hell was in that poteen? but then the thought drifted off like a wisp of smoke, and in spite of the fact that I couldn't hang on to a thought, I'd never had more clarity in my life.

I followed Anne through a path of moonlight on the field, awed by how the moon seemed to lift us up off the ground, guiding us. I felt an energy in the air and followed the moonlight to a wall of sparkling white quartz that shone as if lit from within. Somehow it made sense to me that the moon had led us here, to this quartz, the source of the energy I'd felt.

The wall of quartz was actually a facade, one that I'd seen recently in a book. We were at Newgrange, the five-thousand-year-old passage grave. With all the visitors gone, it looked as though it had just materialized in a farm field, and in the moonlight the triple spirals carved into the stone stood out in grave relief.

I stopped in my tracks, taking it all in, feeling as if there were a fierce wind at my back pushing me forward and a gentle hand holding me back. I didn't notice that I was immobile until Anne rounded the entrance stone and peered back at me, annoyed.

"The guards will be comin' back some day ya, eejit. Move it." And then she disappeared again. I followed her this time, climbing over the ropes set up to block out the tourists, and walked into the blackness that had swallowed Anne.

And then the world was gone. I know a lot of people think that they've seen complete darkness, but most of us really haven't. To comprehend complete darkness, you'd need to be buried alive. That's what it felt like as I stepped through the entrance of Newgrange, trailing my hands out to both sides so I could feel my way down the passage.

I could hear Anne ahead of me and followed the sound she made. Then the passage got broader and I was on my own, trying to walk in a straight line. I soon discovered it wasn't that hard. I could easily follow the path, worn smooth over centuries, not just because it was worn by so many feet, but because I was like a street car on a cable, guided by a low thrumming of energy, the kind of silent energy you feel in old churches or temples.

And sober or not, I could definitely feel that energy here, which made sense if this place had been some kind of shrine for a couple of eons. One of the books I'd read at Trinity said that this place had been used for ritual sacrifices and to help speed along the journey of the soul. On Samhain, the Day of the Dead, the souls that had departed were welcomed back to inhabit the new children who would be born the following year.

"This was the place, Sean," I heard Anne whisper somewhere ahead of me. "We met the first time here. On Samhain. You and me, durin' the rite. God, what a way to meet, wann't it?" I felt her hand take mine, pulling me farther along the passage, quickly, as if she could see every obstruction in the dark.

"And then we came back, jus' like this time, except then it was solstice, and we invited another soul to come back an' join us. He was our son, already inside me." It took me a moment to realize that Anne was talking about *us,* in a past life. A very long ago past life.

The energy of the place turned frigid, and I was suddenly sober. I pulled my hand from hers. "Wait. Stop. What are you trying to tell me?"

"Ahh, Jaysus. Enough with the drama already. There's nobody inside a me now, other than maybe one or two demons." Her voice carried in distorted whispers throughout the chamber and I imagined a demon lurking in the dark.

"That's a relief."

"Right. Better demons than a baby. Yer a man all righ'. Anyway, the point of this place was to try to invite yer lost loved ones back. They used this place an' others like it fer thousands of years."

I was silent for a moment, listening to the slow heartbeat of the stones, feeling the life in this place that should feel dead. "I know. I believe you. But why doesn't anyone else know? Why is there no record of it?" Anne started to slow down as we approached the end of the passage, and her voice took on a different quality, as if it were echoing in and out of more crevices before it came back to the both of us in hushed tones.

"There is a record. You people don' know how to see it. Like I said in Phoenix Park, it's all around ya. Yer jus' blind as a deaf bat. Too thick to ask the right questions."

"How can I ask the right questions if I don't even know there are questions to ask?" I'd been taught all my life to listen, but in the last two weeks I kept being told that I didn't know how. "Do you expect me to just ask whatever stupid question pops into my head?"

"Why not? Dinn't anybody ever tell you there are no stupid questions? I bet ya been taught yer whole life to listen but never to ask questions." As she spoke we moved forward, and I felt a change in the air as the passage grave receded around us and the air grew less dense. "The truth is always in the unasked questions, Sean. Why do you think the Irish ask so many?"

"Fine. I'll ask. Why do you believe in reincarnation and all of this? And how can you live in Catholic Ireland and go to church if you do?" As I spoke, I suddenly felt light-headed. Standing at the center of the cruciform shape somehow made the whole structure spin. Maybe it was the alcohol, but I thought I could see the knots and spirals cut into the stone walls in spite of the dark and would swear that they were all spinning.

"Not a bad question fer a start but about as shallow as they come, don' ya think? Truth is, they teach us all about this stuff in Mass every Sunday, if yer really listenin'." There was a lightness to Anne's voice, a playfulness as it spun off the stones, seeming to come at me from several directions at once. I felt like I needed to sit down but didn't know where it was safe to sit.

"Mass? When?"

"Ahh, now yer gettin' the hang of it. Jus' keep askin', an' I'll keep tellin'. Does this sound familiar? 'I say unto you, except ye be converted, and become as little children, ye shall not enter into the kingdom of heaven.'"

"That's in the Bible?" I asked.

"*Jaysus*, yer a poor excuse fer a Catholic, ain' ya? An' here I'm supposed to be the apostate. Jaysus said it himself." I lost track of what she was saying for a minute. I thought I saw the darkness moving, torchlight flickering on the walls. I heard a deep thrumming sound as if the rocks were vibrating, and I started to wonder how much I'd really had to drink. I didn't feel sick. In fact, I felt great. Just a bit out of it. I tried to focus on Anne's words to pull me back. "Jaysus tells ya himself that ya need to live more'n once to get it right, don' he? Except he dinn't mean ya need to act like little children. He meant ya need to become little children."

I stumbled, dizzy, trying to regain my balance by holding on to Anne. "But the devil can quote scripture too."

"Sure. But only an ingnerant mentaller with his head up his arse can't tell the difference." She took my arm firmly, pulling me toward where I knew the central stone basin lay, the one in which they'd found the cremated remains of a human being. "Why don' you sit a moment. Rest." She pushed me gently and I stumbled back, my hands catching the lip of a large, smooth concave stone.

"That's one quote out of context," I said, thinking that I was sitting on a surface that hundreds, if not thousands of dead and dying men and women had spent their last moments on. I ran my hands over the stone, wondering how much blood had seeped into it, like water into shale, waiting to explode the rock from within when the moment was right.

"You wouldn' know context if ya held it in yer hands, but fine. Ya want more proof that the truth has been right in yer face yer whole life? Never mind the myths an' fairy tales. Let's stick to what ya supposedly know. How about this: 'Whoever welcomes a child like this in my name welcomes me.'" Anne was right on top of me now, her breath warm in my ear as she knelt over me, unbuttoning my shirt. "The good man meant it literally. How many times did he tell people he'd be back? He promised over an over that he'd rise an' come again." Anne pulled off my shirt now and then pulled off her own, her hands traveling down over me. I tried to push Anne away, but I had no strength in my arms. It felt as if the stone I was on, now touching my bare back, were stealing all of my energy.

Anne was still quoting scripture. "'I tell you the truth, no one can see the kingdom of God unless he is born again . . .'"

"How do you know all this?" I slurred, trying desperately to figure out what was wrong with me. I was starting to panic. This wasn't just being drunk. My arms and legs were starting to go numb. I couldn't feel my hands. Anne was obviously unaffected by whatever had intoxicated me.

I could hear my heart beating loudly, but even as I listened it began to slow down. What if it stopped? I knew that few human remains had ever been found in the passage graves, but there were some. I could feel Anne taking off her clothes, then moving to take off the rest of mine. I felt the hard smooth stone beneath me, surprisingly warm, as I struggled to speak.

"What . . . are you . . . doing?"

"Don' worry. I'll be right beside ya till you come back to me," she said soothingly. I thought for a moment that she meant to kill me and would wait for my next life. "I won' let ya die jus' yet. But I want ya to feel what it might be like to pass into the next life," she whispered, as if she were giving me a gift. I could hear myself breathing, surprised that I wasn't panting, that my heart was slowing down rather than racing. My mind wanted to panic, but my body wouldn't cooperate.

"Just sink into the stone. Let yer flesh absorb its energy. Don' resist, Sean. Let it pass its memories to ya." Anne's voice seemed to match the cadence of my heart, and I found myself breathing in sync with her as I held her hand, feeling the pulse in it.

And then I saw it. It started in her chest, I swear, just a dim glow, but soon I could almost make out the outline of her body in the dark.

"Is it getting light in here?"

"No, Sean, yer just learnin' to see again. Yer eyes are adaptin' to see more of the spectrum. It happens in absolute dark. We each one of us exudes energy. Our nerves are powered by electric impulses. Our hearts are blood pumping electromagnets. An' in absolute darkness ya start to tune into those frequencies. It's my aura yer seein'." She explained it all like it was simple science. "Of course the nightshade doesn't hurt, either. Nightshade always helps ya see in the dark."

"You . . . poisoned . . . me?"

"No. I gave ya what ya needed. The sensory deprivation, the loss of yer sense of self. It all helps you focus. Just hold on to me, flesh to flesh, so ya don' lose yerself an' go mad," Anne said as she held me close, both of us naked in the dark, in a five-thousand-year-old tomb. I soon lost all sensation in my body, feeling nothing, tasting nothing, and seeing phantom sources of energy. Anne kept talking, and I tried to focus on her words, letting her lead me so that I didn't fall through one of the spinning spirals that seemed to be sucking me in from all sides.

"I'm doin' this fer you, Sean, not fer me. Ya need to remember some. Just a bit."

I could hear the tears in her eyes, see the colors in the outline of her body change as she spoke. The hallucination was vivid; never had I seen anything like this. Anne, or whatever it was I was watching, was floating, changing, a kaleidescope of color.

"You saw him, Sean. The one with the eyes of the Duine Matha. He's come fer what ya took from him last time. Ya owe 'im a life, an' more." Her words reverberated from every corner of the chamber as I tried to latch on to what she was saying.

"More?" I managed to ask, wondering what more than a life he could want.

"Jus' try an' remember what ya stole from him. If ya give it back, maybe he'll spare yer life." She held me closer, gently but firmly, whispering in my ear. "I need ya to remember that much an' no more. Please, no more, or I'll lose ya. But if ya remember enough, I can save ya from him, an' maybe you'll stay with me just a bit longer . . ."

Her voice was floating away from me, seeming to drift down from the corbeled ceiling. I knew she was still holding me, but I couldn't feel her anymore.

"Remember, not so long ago, on a warm summer night. There was a truck . . ." Anne was gone then, and I was alone in the dark, but it was a different kind of dark. A dark with the stars above and a lake off behind me. No, not a lake, a lough. Lough Neagh. Somehow I knew that, even as I took a gas can from the back of a box truck and pulled some matches from my pocket. From somewhere beyond my reasoning, I could still hear Anne, guiding me through this memory.

"You took what belonged to him. Remember it, Sean." As she spoke, I grabbed large duffel bags from the back of the truck and tossed them on the ground, opening them to see British pound notes with the queen's face all over them. Cash. A lot of it. I poured the gas on the bags, watching myself as I got ready to torch it all. Anne's voice kept me in the passage grave even as I stood by Lough Neagh. "I know I can't keep ya forever, but I just want to keep ya safe with me a little while longer. Remember so ya can give it back..."

I lit the match and the cash went up in flames so bright they blinded me, so hot they singed the hair on my arms and made me step back. "Jus' remember where ya put what belonged to 'im, an' if ya remember any more'n that... well, then, remember that I knew ya first, and we were together long before ya ever knew her."

The colors of the flames danced like the aura Anne projected, and she spoke to me from within the heated inferno. "I loved ya first. She took you from me. Remember that an' let me have this moment, just a moment, with ya," Anne whispered. The flames died down as her voice did, and I went to the back of the truck, glancing inside to see wooden crates full of rifles and grenades. Several of them were marked M14. I got in the truck and rolled down the windows, then started the engine. It was too loud, piercing the nearly silent night, drowning out the roar of the flames. I knew that I needed to hurry, so I pushed down the clutch and slid it into gear, then drove straight at the water.

Water gushed in as the truck's momentum took it farther out into the lake. I felt the water's chill fingers grabbing my legs as the truck sank, quickly and efficiently. I climbed out the window even as the cabin flooded, and I swam away, toward the shore, ready to warm myself by the fire I'd lit. As the engine hissed and sputtered, dying, the flames spoke to me again, in Anne's voice. "Jus' tell me what ya did with what ya stole, Sean, an' I'll get him to leave ya be." I pulled myself out of the lough, dragging myself up against the weight of the water, watching the flames form the shape of Anne. I collapsed on the stones at the edge of the lough close to the fire, as close as I could get, feeling her warmth wrap around me. I'd burned a fortune in cash and destroyed a cache of weapons and I knew he'd kill me if he found out, but I didn't care. I smiled, trying to get the words out, hoping that if I gave her the words, the fire would keep holding me and would keep me warm.

"I burned it . . . I burned the cash. Sank the rest," I muttered, and the flames raged higher, then abruptly died down, dimming. And then they were gone.

It was dark again, and colder.

I could still feel the smooth warmth of Anne next to me, her arms and legs around me, her breath in my ear, coming in short quick bursts. And then she whispered, almost in anger, almost below the threshold of my hearing. "Ya burned it, ya bleedin' eejit? Do ya know what he's gonna do? Kill ya to start, inn't he?"

The room was no longer spinning, and once again I couldn't see anything, couldn't feel anything, except the stone beneath me and Anne around me. If I weren't naked in a passage grave in the middle of the night, I'd have said everything had gone back to normal.

Then it struck me what had just happened and that I *was* naked in a five-thousand-year-old passage grave, which may well have been used for human sacrifice, and that Anne was telling me the psycho with the blue eyes was coming after me to kill me. That is, if she didn't do it first.

"You poisoned me," I said angrily, turning to look at her, even though I was blind in the darkness now.

"Ahh, Jaysus. Don' start that now. Poison's a strong word, inn't it?" She pulled away.

"Belladonna's a poison. It can kill you." I was getting myself worked up as my head began to clear.

"Are ya dead? No. Then I dinn't poison ya, did I? All I did was get ya to remember." Anne moved away from me and I lost my anchor.

"I didn't remember shit. I was hallucinating. Because you *poisoned* me. And you did it to make me believe in this stupid cult thing of yours." I'd

290 • KEVIN FOX

started to yell as she moved away from me, afraid that she was going to leave me alone in there.

"Cult thing?" Her voice came to me from a few inches away. I hadn't even been sure she was still there until she spoke.

"We're in a passage grave. We're naked in the middle of the night using psychotropic drugs. What else would you call it?" I demanded, and got a response that I didn't expect. She giggled.

"A turn-on," Anne said, even as I felt her hands reaching out for me again. I wanted to push her away but was still worried about her leaving me alone. I wasn't about to let that happen and there was one sure way I could stop her.

I held on to her and did what any other twenty-one-year-old male suffering from the lingering effect of drugs would do. And Anne was right: it was a turn-on. I started to worry that there was something wrong with me. Mentally, I mean. Physically, it all worked. Hours later, when it was almost morning, we crept out, our clothes in our hands. We ran across the dew-covered fields as the eastern horizon glowed a dull red.

When I saw the sun rising over Newgrange, the hair on the back of my neck stood up and a chill went through me that wasn't from the dew on my skin. For the first time, I thought that maybe I hadn't been hallucinating, because I'd seen that sunrise before, over that horizon. A hundred times before. Words ran through my head, and even though I knew where they'd come from, it surprised me how well I remembered them: "I would have sworn, indeed I swore it: / The hills may shift, the waters may decline, / Winter may twist the stem from the twig that bore it / But never your love from me, your hand from mine."

Anne's hand was in mine as we ran across the field, but I knew that hers was the wrong hand, and that this wouldn't last, even as the poem continued to hammer at me from inside my head. "Now goes under the sun, and I watch it go under . . ." As the words echoed in my mind, I realized that the poem begged a question. A question Anne kept pushing me to ask. If the sun goes under, doesn't it also rise?

I wasn't sure what the question meant, but I knew it needed to be asked.

Michael

I woke up to the sound of someone rushing up the stairs of Kate's parents' house, taking them two at a time. If they knew enough to climb the stairs that way and not trip, they were friends. They had to be. I hoped. I sat up just as the door was shoved open and slammed into the plaster wall, sending white powder drifting to the floor. If it wasn't a friend, I was in trouble, still tangled in the sheets.

It was Declan. He stood there, looking down at me coldly, but I could see that he had expected to find Kate here as well. He said nothing, his eyes red and bloodshot, as if he'd been on a drunken tear for the last few days. I wanted to ask him what was going on, or get angry at the way he burst into the room, but something about the way he looked told me that whatever I'd say would be wrong. He needed time. I held his look until Kate appeared behind him, her hair wild from sleep, still in her nightdress.

"What's goin' on, Dec? Whose voices do I hear downstairs at this hour?" Now that she said it, I heard them, too, a murmur of strident anger running through the house like an electrical current. Declan didn't look at Kate as he answered. He was still looking at me.

"The bastards are killin' people in Derry. Thirteen dead, most no more'n boys. I'm gonna need yer help," he stated flatly.

My help? For what? I wanted to ask, but Kate had grabbed him by the arm, twisting him around so she could see his eyes. "What happened? Who's killin' people? When?" she demanded.

Declan finally looked at her, his eyes unfocused, still trying to absorb the impact himself. "The paratroopers. They were shootin' at men with white flags, includin' Father Daly. He was just tryin' to carry the dyin' to safety."

"Shootin', why? Is Father Daly dead?" Kate's voice grew tight, her grip on Declan turning her knuckles white.

"No, thank God." Declan was mumbling, staring off as if seeing it happen. "But Jackie Duddy. An' Paddy Doherty. They shot him while he was on his knees tryin' to crawl to safety. An' Jim Wray. They shot him once and took his legs, and as he called out he couldna feel 'em, they shot him again and finished him . . ." His voice trailed off and I realized that his eyes weren't red from too much alcohol. They were welling up as he said each name.

"Were you there?" Kate asked, more gently.

"Bernie McGuigan, wavin' a white handkerchief as he tried to get to Paddy. They put one in the back of 'is head." Declan wasn't hearing Kate. He was just reciting the facts, as if speaking them would release them from his head.

"Were you *there*, Dec?"

"No." Kate flinched at his palpable anger. "I said I'd stay away, dinn't I?" Declan responded harshly to Kate's seeming accusation. But Kate wasn't backing down. It struck me suddenly why she was asking—the killings were senseless if they weren't provoked. And if the Provos weren't there, why'd the paratroopers shoot?

"Jerry. Where was Jerry?" she pushed.

"With me." I could see the confusion in Kate's eyes. If the British could just shoot people down at a peaceful protest, what options did that leave? She looked away from Declan and staggered over to the bed. She sat heavily on it as her legs buckled beneath her.

"It was a peaceful march, wann't it?"

"As peaceful as they get in Derry. I'm sorry, but I'm tellin' ya, Kate, we weren' there. Not a one of us. A course they said we were. Claimed we was throwin' nail bombs." Declan's eyes had dried, but his face and ears were going red as the rage built up again.

A single tear streamed down her cheek. "But then *why*? You stayed away so they'd have no excuse."

"Looks like they don' need an excuse no more, donn't it?" It was Jerry Coonan, standing in the hall behind Declan. He peered into the room, staring at Kate, perched on the bed next to me. "They kill us and make up any lie they want."

"How many soldiers were killed?" Kate asked, ignoring Coonan.

"None."

"Wounded?"

"Not a one."

"That should prove it to everyone," Coonan interrupted. "If we were there there'd be plenty of 'em dead. But we weren't."

Declan nodded slowly and spoke quietly. "We know that, but the world don' know. They'll believe whatever they're told, same as always, won't they?"

"So tell them your side." I spoke for the first time, and everyone stopped to look at me.

"Ahh, from the mouths of babes," Kate said, trying to make the best of it. "But he's right, inn't he? If we keep the peace, the whole worl'll see what they're doin' an' force 'em to change."

"From the mouth of a feckin' eejit is more like," Coonan spat. "If we don' retaliate, an' soon, they'll jus' keep shootin'. No one's gonna stop 'em but us."

"And then they'll retaliate, an' it'll just get worse, won't it? We've gotta get the world to see what it is they've done. What else can we do?"

"Kill us some a them an' teach 'em what it feels like."

"Kate's right. The whole world will be on your side if you can show that they murdered innocent people," I said, keeping my eyes on Declan, who was sitting back and watching, an eerily neutral expression on his face.

"Yea, an' you should know, right? The whole worl's comin' after the United States because yer out shootin' niggers, ain' they?" Coonan prodded me. I felt my adrenaline surge but kept control. I didn't want to start a fight now.

"Things are changing over there," I said in an effort to deflect my anger.

"Oh yeah? Tell that to the nigger you shot. Your new man's a murderin' liar, inn't he, Kate? Is he playin' the role of a peaceful man jus' to get in yer pants or is he—"

Coonan shut his mouth, or rather, I shut it for him as I hit him, slamming his head back into the door before I could stop myself. His fists came up quick, but I'd gotten two shots into his face and cut my knuckles on his teeth before he could take a swing. As he did, Declan elbowed him in the gut and grabbed me by the throat, shoving us apart.

"Jaysus feckin' Christ. Like we don' have enough troubles already? Yer like are the reason Ireland's divided. 'Cause the Irish are divided. If we ever got our shite together an' stopped fightin' amongst ourselves we'd rule the feckin' world."

Coonan pushed Declan's hand aside but backed off, clearly not the alpha in the room. "Don' blame this on me. She's actin' the merry widow, ain' she? An' he just waltzes back over here an' thinks he can pick up where he left off." Coonan was glaring at me, but I caught Kate out of the corner of my eye. The "merry widow" comment had hit home.

"Go downstairs," Declan ordered Coonan, who, with a last glare at me from his spooky eyes, turned and left. Declan waited until he was gone, then turned back to Kate and me. "The two a ya, get dressed. Then ya might want to explain where ya been the last few days. Coonan's not wrong to worry about informants, an' his experience with you inn't what ours was."

Before I could defend myself, Kate interrupted. "Ya really thinks he wants to know what it is we been doin'? Because I think he's already got a pretty good idea an' that's why he's pissed in the first place."

"I don' need the details, dear, jus' account fer where ya been an' let's put it behind us, shall we?"

"Sam's been dead three years, an' he didn't even like him when he was alive, so what's his problem? I have a right to move on, don' I?"

"His problem ain' with you. An' it ain' because of any fond memories of Sam, that's fer sure. It's with him." Declan nodded toward me, and I knew he was right as he said it. "Jerry don' trust 'im because a last time."

I remembered Seamus's eyes on me at the killing field. The same eyes Coonan laid on me every time he looked at me. Coonan hated me because he thought I'd killed Liam and warned the Tans. He hated me for something I didn't do.

"Jerry settled that last time 'round," Kate said flatly. "It's done."

"Sure enough. But that doesn't mean he's gonna trust Mickaleen, does it?"

My nerves were getting frayed talking about the past—a past I wasn't sure I believed in, even though I'd caught glimpses of it. I was struggling to explain it, wanting to believe, but afraid it would mean that I'd lost my sanity if I did. And right now I was just angry at everyone for assuming they knew me and all my motives. I turned on Declan. "How about you? Do you trust me?"

"If I dinn't trust ya I wouldn' a come here lookin' fer ya. I need yer help, don' I?"

"Doin' what, exactly?" Kate asked.

"Settin' things right. Ya can't stay on yer brother's passport very long, but I know people who can get ya a new one. I know a priest that fer the price of a good meal will find yer baptism papers and even confirm ya." He smiled reassuringly.

"I knew one like that back home. He'd swear to your alibi for a pot roast," I said, thinking of Father Finn, my mother's favorite leech.

"Sure, there were a lot of fat fathers even during the famine, weren' there? Anyway, it'll get you set with new papers. There's enough Corrigans around, no one'll notice one more or less. We can even give ya yer name back. I know three Mick Corrigans myself, so one more'll make it even."

"And what do I need to do for it?" I asked, knowing I wouldn't like the answer.

"The Armalites. We need them in Derry. No one'll question an Ameri can too close."

"Yer insane," Kate muttered, shaking her head.

"What'd ya think they were for, Kate?"

"You'll start a war. An' you'll bring him into it." She didn't even glance my way, treating me as if I wasn't there to speak for myself.

"I'm not startin' nothing. This war's been goin' on longer than even you can remember. An' he's been involved fer as long as either one a us. If he backs out now, I can't answer for what Jerry'll do to him." Declan spoke calmly, but the threat was clear. If I didn't join them, I was a traitor. "Get dressed. When ya come down, I want to know where ya been the last few days, an' who ya were with."

Declan walked down the hall and we listened to his heavy footfalls on the stairs before either one of us spoke. Kate drifted to the doorway, making sure they were all gone.

"Yer gonna help him, ain' ya?"

"What choice do I have? Help Declan and get a new identity, or wait until I either get caught or get killed by Jerry Coonan?"

She nodded, expecting that answer, and then was quiet again. I didn't know what else to say, so we sat there, awkwardly, until she finally looked up at me.

"I'll do the talkin' about where we been. Unnerstood?" Her voice had an edge to it, and despite the question in her tone, it was an order. Not that there was anything to hide, except for the fact that we'd had three perfect days alone, never once thinking about our troubles. We'd left the killing field and had headed south, talking and driving until we came to Cashel late that night. I did all the talking then, signing us into a small inn as Mr. and Mrs. Aidan Corrigan from the United States. We woke up late the next day and walked around the famous Rock of Cashel.

We moved on from there to Killarney, once again playing the American couple. We held hands as we walked around the lake and Ross Castle. We even held hands over the simple meals prepared by old women in the pubs and homes converted to small restaurants. A local boy rowed us across Lough Leane and told us the history of the area, filling us with tall tales about the "Devil's Punch Bowl" and the origin of Magillicuddy's Reeks.

The nights were spent exactly as one would imagine, except maybe a little more sedate. Ours was not the heated passion of a brand-new relationship, but a slow smoldering that had reignited. It didn't feel rushed. It felt like we were doing what we'd always done, just being together, relaxed, satisfied, sleeping in each other's arms and shifting in synchronicity, like one person in two bodies.

Not one of the people we met ever doubted that we were married. In fact, an old woman at the place we were staying in Killarney approached me the day we left, just as I carried our one bag out. I was waiting for Kate to pull the car up, and her smooth, smoky voice startled me as she spoke.

"You look too young to be married so long, son."

I turned to see a wrinkled crone with a sparkle in her blue eyes, sitting in a ragged chair. "Excuse me?" I said.

"Ahh, a Yank. I'd not 'ave guessed from the look a ya. An' married to an Irish woman so long. Ya must be a patient man."

"What makes you think we've been married so long?" I couldn't help ask. It was exactly how I felt about Kate—as if I'd always known her.

"It's the silences. An' the way ya touch 'ands when ya think no one's lookin'. How yer always doin' for her before she even knows what it is she needs ya to do. How long ya been married?"

"Longer than I can remember," I said, smiling to myself.

"Well, don' ferget this part of it. This time. My husband's been gone now two years, an' I been livin' here in purgatory, like half a me is gone. I'm just waitin' so I can find 'im on the other side, because I'm just about done livin' without him." Then the old woman looked past me, seeing Kate outside the door. "You better go, son. She looks like the jealous type, an' I'll not be gettin' between what the two a ya 'ave got."

I turned to see Kate staring at me, a smile on her face. When I got in the car, she asked me, "Were ya tryin' to pick her up?"

"She was like ninety years old, Kate," I protested, though I couldn't deny that I'd seen what Kate had also seen—that the woman's eyes were ageless.

"She *was* beautiful, though, wann't she," Kate said, completing my thought. I glanced back over my shoulder at the woman and saw that it was true. She was beautiful, in a way I didn't know how to describe. So I did what I always did when I was unsure, I changed the subject.

"Where to next?"

"Home. Tomorrow's Sunday. My da will be upset if I miss Mass."

I hadn't even known what day it was—hadn't thought about anything other than Kate for three days—but Kate's words brought the whole world back to mind. I thought about my own family and the fact that I was traveling on my idiot brother's passport, and that at any moment I could be stopped by a garda, arrested, and sent home to face the death penalty. After all of that, and all the sex, violence, and talk about past lives, she wanted to go to Mass?

"You're serious about going to Mass? But you don't believe in any of it."

Kate shrugged. "I want to spend time with my parents, and if ya ever really listened at Mass, you'd hear a different message than what ya think yer hearin'."

We did go to Mass the next morning, although I had a hard time understanding anything. I thought the priest was speaking in Irish until I realized he just mumbled like a true Irishman. Since I couldn't understand most of what he said, my mind began to wander. I took in all the men in their suits, hats clipped to the pews in front of them, Mass still a very formal affair here in Ireland. It struck me then how odd it was that God seemed to require you to dress like you were going to a funeral when you came to visit. I glanced over at Martin, who stood ramrod straight, a rosary in his hands, clicking the beads as if they were a metronome to time the Mass. Kate's mother, Bridey, was next to me, her arm touching mine throughout the service, and every time she stood or knelt, she'd grab me for help.

If she weren't Kate's mother, I'd have sworn she was flirting. I tried to ignore her, taking in the church, and that's when I noticed the baptismal font and thought of the "holy" water within it. There it was again, the underground stream that seemed to rise up everywhere when you started paying attention. As I thought of Patsy's near drowning on the island in a faux baptism, I caught a piece of what the priest was saying.

His recitation, thickly accented, sounded like "Chrisisdid … Crisisrisn … Crisiscommagn," but I'd heard the words often enough to realize he was actually saying, "Christ has died, Christ is risen, Christ will come again." For the first time I actually listened to the meaning, rather than just the words. After that, I started listening more closely, using the thousands of masses I'd attended but never listened to as guides to try and translate his mumbling. As they were recited, several portions of the Mass suddenly became clear to me, and given what I'd learned in the past few days, they were surprisingly subversive.

As the congregation intoned, "God from God, Light from Light, true God from true God, begotten, not made, one in Being with the Father," I thought of something Declan had said, that each of us was made from God. Wasn't that the same thing as saying "one in being with the father"? And didn't it apply to all of us?

I kept listening as the priest droned on. "We look for the resurrection of the dead and the life of the world to come." It was strange hearing these prayers from a new perspective, really hearing them again after so many years of simply reciting them by rote and giving little thought to their meaning. When the priest got to the Our Father, it became even more clear.

By the time the priest got to the "He who eats this bread and drinks this cup will live forever" part, I was pretty convinced that the entire Catholic Mass was heretical. My mind was reeling. It was all there in the Roman Catholic Mass. The priest hadn't said anything I hadn't heard before, and yet it was all new to me. I was still putting the pieces together as I walked home in the cold wet air when I unconsciously took Kate's hand. Bridey must have been watching for it, because as soon as her daughter's warm hand was in mine, Bridey wedged herself between us and glanced up at me.

"Ahh, Mickaleen. My ol' legs are tired. Would ya mind if I leaned on ya fer a bit?" I glanced at Kate, who just shook her head, annoyed and a bit amused. She nodded and I let Bridey lean into me. Martin pulled ahead of us, walking more briskly, and Kate picked up her pace to catch up to him, whispering something in his ear. For the rest of the walk home, Kate and Martin walked in silence. Bridey didn't say much either, but as we got close to the house, she stopped, making me look down at her. Clearly she had something to say, but waited, watching until she was sure Martin was beyond hearing.

"Is everything all right, Bridey?"

"No, I don' think it is. I know it's not my place, Mickaleen, but this is all goin' ta end badly. Ya know that, don' ya?"

I did. Deep down, even then, I knew. How could it not, with the Troubles and murder charges and all the rest piling up? Still, part of me felt that if I could ignore it long enough it might all go away. But Bridey surprised me, going on, "It's Kate's the problem, ya know that, don' ya? Always has been. The two a ya together are too much in love ta see that ya gotta pay dear for that much happiness. If ya don' go now, you'll break her heart an' it'll all go bad agin."

"What are you talking about?"

"Why don't ya run? Switzerland or somewhere like it," she said, and then I saw her logic. I wouldn't run without Kate. It hadn't even occurred to me.

Bridey read my thoughts. "You two 'ave always been like that, livin' out the same doomed fairy tale over an' over. But she won' go, Mickaleen. An' you need to run. There are other's that'll love ya jus' as much, I promise ya."

There was a pleading in her eyes, but there was also a hopelessness. She knew as well as I did that while I could run anywhere, if Kate stayed, I wouldn't leave her.

"I can't."

"I thought ya might say that." She let go of my hand and started toward the house but turned back as she reached the door that Kate and Martin had already gone through. "Ya can stay as long as ya like, but try not to flaunt yer relationship in my house, an' next time aroun', when this ends as it must, try to remember my warnin'—an' my promise."

Then she was gone, inside, and I was left alone, trying to figure out what she was talking about, hoping she was wrong about the way all of this would end.

A FEW HOURS later, after a meal of roast beef, baked potatoes, peas, and carrots that Bridey had made in silence, ignoring all of us while Martin mumbled under his breath and glared at me, Kate finally lost her patience with her parents and asked me if I wanted to go out to "walk the land." Part of the problem was that both Martin and Bridey had been kept in the dark about what had gone on with Patsy and only knew that he had taken off after coming back from the island.

As we left the yard and headed up the hill so Kate could show me the view, which she claimed went as far as the Atlantic, I reached to take her hand. She pulled away, glancing back nervously at the house. I saw Bridey there, in the kitchen window, staring out at us as we left.

"You're worried about what your mother will think?"

"No. Well, yes. But not the way ya mean. Ya don' unnerstand her."

"No, I don't. Maybe you can explain her to me."

Kate smiled slightly, but it was not a smile of amusement. "No, I can' explain her to you. Not yet . . ." Her voice drifted off and she glanced back through the gathering trees toward the house. Bridey was still in the window, still watching us. "Do you think she's beautiful?"

The question startled me. I'd never thought about it. Bridey seemed old to me, probably almost sixty. I looked back again and caught her in profile, her graying hair catching the late afternoon sun. Actually, she was beautiful. This was the second time in as many days Kate had asked me to look at an older woman and see her beauty, and the second time I was surprised by my response. I could still see the wrinkles and all the flaws, but I also saw everything else that was there and everything that had been there. It was all in her eyes.

"I can see where you get your looks from, if that's what you mean. Bridey must've been beautiful when she was young."

Kate frowned. She knew that I was being evasive. "She still is, an' ya know it. But she's a sad woman, if ya dinn't notice. Fell in love once a long time ago but lost the man to another woman." Kate looked up at me as we entered the shadows of a stand of trees. I couldn't see her eyes here, but I could feel them on me as she went on. "Made my ma a bit cold, a bit defensive. I always wondered how anyone could fall in love with anyone else after they'd loved her."

I tried to imagine Bridey thirty years younger. Had I never met Kate, she would have been a real temptation. She had a certain spirit, a confidence and a sensitivity underneath her harsh exterior that you could feel in her gaze . . . But she was no Kate.

"He could only fall in love with someone else if that someone else was you," I said, trying to distract Kate with flattery, but she just looked away.

"Nothin' changes, does it?" she asked, incongruously, as we emerged from the trees to an open field at the crest of the hill.

I figured out later that she wasn't talking about the view, but in that moment the view was all I could think of. It felt like I could see forever and, on a clear day, beyond it. We were facing west, and the sky was a thousand shades of mutable reds, oranges, and yellows, all framed in a deepening blue as the sun inched toward the horizon through scattered, far-off storm clouds. In the near distance was Lough Ree and County Roscommon, peppered with farms and cottages, looking the same as I imagined it had for a few hundred years, at least from this distance. Farther out I was convinced I could see all the way to Galway Bay and beyond.

And the beyond was the strange part, because somewhere out there, on the farthest horizon, was an island of emerald green that looked as if it were almost floating on the ocean. It had to be an optical illusion. Maybe what I was looking at wasn't the Atlantic but Lough Corrib, and the island was the land beyond it. But that didn't make sense either, because the land beyond Lough Corrib, if that's what it was, should've taken up the whole horizon.

"What is that out there?" I had to ask; I had to know. It was not a place I could put on a map, but it looked like someplace I'd want to see if I could find it.

"I was hopin' ya'd get to see it tonight. It's not always there. Depends on the weather, an' ya know how that changes aroun' here, don' ya?"

"Is it real?"

"Depends on what ya mean by 'real', don' it?" Kate said. "Aren' you one a them that goes by science an' thinks it ain' real unless you see it? Well, ya see it, don' ya?"

"Maybe I'm getting past the whole seeing is believing thing."

"Not likely. Yer an Irish male. Change one letter an' it's 'mule.' The mind-set's about the same." Kate walked away, toward one of the low stone walls that ran across the edge of the trees. I followed her and she slid over to share her warm rock with me. She took my hand and moved a bit closer, although given the wind and the chill in the air, I wondered whether it was for intimacy or just comfort.

"I've come up here a lot over the years. It's a good place to be alone an' to think."

"I could see that," I said, hoping she didn't mind me sharing her private place.

"God, I loved this place as a chil'. Especially after I started rememberin', an' before I really woke up." I held my breath. It was the first time she was talking about her own experience of remembering, and I didn't want to stop her. I wanted to know everything about her. But Kate hesitated for a long time, carefully weighing her words. When she finally spoke, she kept her eyes on the horizon and away from mine. "Bridey's the one who noticed how much time I was spendin' up here, an' as much as she hated to do it, she's the one who gave me all the letters Erin left behind."

"Erin? My uncle Sean's fiancée?"

She nodded as I tried to process everything she was revealing to me. "Apparently Erin used to come up here, and Bridey'd follow her when she was a little girl. Erin's the one who told Bridey about Tír na nÓg, the Land of the Ever-Young." Kate finally looked at me, then nodded toward the horizon. "That place ya see out there." I glanced up at the horizon, looking right into the sunset, trying to see the ephemeral island, glimpsing it, then losing it in the glare.

"Bridey found Erin up here one day, lookin' out there and cryin' quietly by herself, an' that's when Erin told Bridey her Sean had gone there, to the land across the sea, to the west. She told my ma that he'd be forever young there, forever happy, and that one day she'd find him, when they were both young again in Tír na nÓg."

"But that didn't happen, did it?" I asked, wondering why the Irish stories always seem to end in tragedy.

"Says who? Things happen in diff'rent ways, that's all." Kate stared off into the distance, melancholy, then took my hand in both of hers, stroking it softly, and I realized she was talking about us, and her belief that we were Sean and Erin, young again. When she looked up again, her eyes were glittering in the sunlight, moist with emotion. "What's wrong with dreamin' about a place where death don' keep interruptin' a perfectly good life?"

I searched for something to say, some way to keep the moment going, but I didn't want to upset her. "Maybe it only interrupts so we can be young again," I said.

She grinned. For once I'd gotten it right. "Now yer talkin'. Romance ain' quite the same with stiff hips, is it?" Kate turned back to look into the sunset, and when she spoke again, I could barely hear her, her voice riding on the breeze. "Maybe if we could all jus' remember who we really are, we'd realize we're already in Tír na nÓg."

It certainly felt like it at that moment, alone with Kate on that hilltop. I don't know how long we sat there in silence, warming each other and watching the sun set, but it was long enough for the sun to disappear below the horizon, dissolving the apparition that was Tír na nÓg, the dreams of heaven burning off like mist and dispersing on the night air as the moon rose.

We walked along the moonlit path back to the house, holding hands. When we got there, we traded a look and, out of respect for Bridey, let go. We thought we'd have all the time in the world to get back up the hill, but the next morning Declan came knocking, and he expected us to account for all the time we'd spent together.

What could we tell any of them that would satisfy them and make them believe we hadn't sold out their cause? No matter what we told them, Coonan wouldn't trust me. By the time I was dressed and ready, Kate was back in my room, also dressed. She'd pulled her beautiful hair up into a quick ponytail, and her soft sea blue eyes had turned cold and hard.

"I'm the one talkin' down there. Just leave it to me and don' let Jerry Coonan get to ya, unnerstood?" She held open the door, nodding for me to head down the stairs first. I didn't mind her being in control, but the fact that she felt she needed to be in control left me wondering just how much jeopardy I might actually be in. I was so worried about it that I forgot about the uneven stairs and almost tumbled down them, catching myself on the railing.

"Ahh, tha's brilliant, inn't it? Yer recruitin' that eejit to help ya?" I heard Coonan mocking from the front room downstairs. "He's a real stealth oper'tive now, inn't he? Can' even get down the stairs without feckin' it up." I was about to defend myself when I heard the slap. I managed to make it down the last two steps in time to see Bridey confronting Jerry Coonan.

"I'll not have that bloody language in my house, you unnerstand me, Jerry?" Jerry wanted to laugh, but knew better and just nodded. Then Bridey turned to Kate and me, putting us on the spot.

"So let's get it outta the way, shall we? Where were the two a ya the last few days an' what exactly were ya doin'?" All eyes were on Kate and me, and I wanted to answer, but somehow the way Bridey asked it made it clear that this discussion was between a mother and her daughter. As uncomfortable as it might get, she'd taken the power away from everyone else in the room by asking the question on everyone's minds. Obviously, Ireland was still more conservative than the States, and the "sexual revolution" hadn't made it over here yet. Despite the fact that Kate had been married before, they all seemed concerned with propriety, and Bridey was especially judgmental in her attitude.

But apparently Kate knew just how to handle her mother. "We were tourin' the churches of Ireland, Ma. On our knees in every town from here to Killarney, weren't we?"

"An' makin' offerin's to the only virgin left in Ireland, I bet, is that right?" Bridey countered.

"I was married fer three years, Ma. I don' need ya to give me the lecture or talk to me about somethin' ya haven't seen yerself for a good forty-five years."

"Very nice. Talkin' to yer mother that way. And to think I gave up my own innocence to bear the likes a you an' yer brother who's off doin' God knows what right now. What'd *you* give it up fer? Married fer three years, an' no grandchildren."

The battle-hardened males in the room all had their eyes on their shoes, afraid to get caught in the cross fire between the two women. Even Declan and Coonan were suddenly acting deaf and blind. Only Martin, seated in his chair and hidden behind a newspaper, dared to speak.

"I think it's time fer all a ya to go. My life's mis'rable enough as it is without ya gettin' her goin'," he said in a perfectly placid voice.

"Shut yer gob, Martin. They can leave whenever they like. I'm jus' tryin' to answer the question Jerry here needed answered, ain' I?" Bridey's eyes flashed as she turned to glare at Kate. "An' it seems obvious to me these two haven't done much talkin' in the past few days 'cause they was busy wit' other things, inn't that right, Kate?"

Kate glared right back, walking calmly down the rest of the stairs. She stopped in front of Declan. "I think it is time to leave now." I hesitated, waiting to see what Declan and Coonan would do.

Bridey went right on ranting.

"Good riddance. Take yer new man wit' ya. The two a you are so damn happy wit' each other yer about to bring out the curse a the Good People on us."

"Ya have a real way with guests, don' ya, Bridey," Martin said as he finally put the paper down, and got up from his chair.

"Twice blessed is twice cursed. Same fer this house as fer the whole bloody country."

Martin ignored Bridey, going to hug Kate in the only public display of affection I would ever see him give—and probably only to piss off his wife. "Take care of yerself, Kate. Ya know that yer welcome here anytime. An' so is anyone ya bring with ya. Inn't that right, Bridey?"

Bridey's eyes were on fire. "Did ya hear me say any diff'rent?"

Martin shook my hand, but I kept my distance from Bridey, unsure of what would happen. As soon as we were safely outside, I turned to Kate. "She really doesn't like me, does she?"

Kate just smiled. "Most of that was an act for the fellahs, but a bit of it was real, sure." She stopped then as Coonan caught up to us.

"Yer both headed to Dublin first with Declan. Take yer car, Kate, since we know that no one's lookin' fer it. I'll meet ya outside a Cavan with the crates from the graveyard. Jim Quinlan'll be drivin' one a 'is trucks fer us." Kate nodded, heading to her car, but I stopped, having recognized the name.

"Wait. Quinlan? The one who ran me down when I first got here?"

"He's a helluva driver when he's sober. We might need 'im if things get dicey at the border. I once saw him drive right through a barrage a bullets an' he didn't flinch at all." Coonan smiled, grabbing Declan's keys as they passed each other, leaving me to wonder just how bad of a spot I'd gotten myself into.

FEBRUARY 3, 1972

The funerals of eleven of the victims killed on Bloody Sunday were held on the second of February, so it took us a few days to get organized and move the load of Armalites. The funerals were held in the Creggan area of Derry, which had turned into an occupied territory. In Dublin 90 percent of the workforce stopped to respect the victims, and almost one hundred thousand marched on the British embassy. In the end the crowd attacked the embassy with stones, bottles, and petrol bombs—Molotov cocktails. The building was burned to the ground. Needless to say, Declan's friends were busy, and the first time they were available to assist us was on the third.

They looked like they hadn't slept in days as they helped us load the truck that now carried the Armalites, but they were motivated, and by 11 a.m. that day we were headed toward the border, with Declan driving the truck up toward Clones and the rural border area west of Monaghan. According to Declan, it would be the easiest place to cross. The line between the north and the south was so convoluted in that area that on the map it looked like the Republic had herniated its border and spilled over into Ulster. Declan was counting on both the confusing lay of the land and the remoteness of the crossing to help us.

In the truck Kate was uncomfortably seated between Declan and me, the diesel's stick shift between her legs. The Armalites were carefully hidden beneath the load in back, a load we were hoping the British wouldn't want to move. Behind us were Jim Quinlan and Jerry Coonan, armed with a couple of Armalites of their own, ready to drive straight at the British border guards with guns blazing to get us out of there if anything went wrong. Farther behind was Patsy, still looking a little glassy-eyed and stunned from his ordeal on the island and still speaking with a thicker brogue than I remember him having before. He was there to drive the getaway car if it all went wrong, with the thought being that if we were stopped on the Republic side, he could identify himself as garda and get us safely away from the scene.

It looked good on paper, but Coonan was a bit too eager to try out his Armalite, and Jim Quinlan had tipped back a few when we stopped for lunch in Cavan. As we skirted the border near where the N54 crossed below Clones, I got a glimpse of one of the more heavily fortified crossings, complete with barbed wire and the British armored vehicle they called a Saracen. This was beginning to feel suicidal, especially since Declan didn't seem to be worried about dying. He was convinced he'd be coming back again to fight another day.

"Are you sure this'll work?" I asked, hoping he'd admit some doubt about his plan and that maybe Kate could talk him out of it.

"Not at all," he admitted cheerfully. "But I know that the Brits don' like bein' told what to do, so I bet if we beg 'em to search us, they won't."

"That doesn't seem like much of a plan."

"Ahh, ya don' remember how stubborn these bastards are then, do ya? Jus' treat it like the joke it is, Mickaleen, an' you'll be fine." Kate said nothing.

She just hummed softly to herself—a tune I half remembered. I was starting to wonder if I was the only sane one in the car.

"A joke? Really? Which part is funny?" I asked.

"All of it. Life. It's a game, inn't it? It's got a set a rules, a start, and a finish. If you lose, you die. Do not pass go, and do not collect two hundred quid. You go back to the beginnin' an' have to start all over. That's all. A game." He shrugged as if it really were that simple.

"I'm wanted for *murder* back home. If they catch me, I'm going back there to face charges, and we've got the death penalty in the United States."

"I know. Savages, the lot a ya. But no worries. We're jus' crossing an imaginary line, imagined by the Brits. What's the worst that could happen?"

"Well, for one, Coonan could start a firefight and get us all killed." Declan's eyebrows went up and he nodded as if he hadn't thought of that.

"True enough. But he's more afraid a dyin' than you or I. He's a coward at heart, afraid of the unknown. It's what makes him so angry all the time." Declan turned to face me and must have seen that his words weren't making me any less edgy. "Relax, Mick. I've done shite like this a thousand times, an' only been killed a half-dozen times doin' it. Inn't that right, Kate?"

Kate rolled her eyes. "Don' put me in the middle a this. I wann't there, was I now?"

"Ah, yeah. She's been a pacifist forever now, hasn' she? She thinks she can do more by dyin' nobly and shamin' the other side into submission than by killin' 'em." Declan was grinning, teasing Kate.

"Your way seems to be workin' out so much better, does it?"

"Mick's on my side on this one, dear. He's died fightin' the good fight more times'n I have, haven't you?"

I shook my head, not wanting to admit that he might be telling the truth. "Do you really expect me to believe everything you tell me is true? To believe that I'm on your side? Or hers?"

"Of course ya should believe us. Why would we lie?" Declan looked truly shocked at the accusation.

"Why wouldn't you?" I asked. Lying was such an essential human trait, I couldn't imagine someone who knew the past so intimately *not* lying about it in order to serve his own interests.

"Well, I guess I would lie if it served a purpose. But only if I was sure you couldna remember the truth, otherwise ya'd catch me, wouldn' ya?" I thought about that for a minute. It was true. If they all remembered the past, *personally* remembered it, they couldn't rewrite history. Things could only get distorted if we couldn't remember the past and it could be spun and twisted.

Kate took my hand. She seemed to sense what I was thinking. "That's the problem between us and the ones who can't remember. There's no way to earn their trust. For us, history is what it is. For them, it's the distorted lies they read in books a hunnerd years after everyone that was there up an' died."

"But we know the truth," Declan interjected. "We *remember* the truth. An' when we try and tell it, they don' appreciate us muckin' aroun' with their precious history. Every time I try to tell someone, they up and shoot me."

"Are you sure it's because of the message and not the way you deliver it?" I asked, positive that Declan had always been, in every lifetime, a pain in the ass.

"C'mon, even you know that they shoot anyone who disturbs their little image of the world, Mick. Lookit Gandhi. Or Kennedy. Or even Jaysus himself. If ya wanna know about the danger a preachin' ta the masses, jus' ask him if ya ever see 'im. The stories he could tell . . ." Declan shook his head, as if he actually remembered the man.

"You're trying to tell me you knew Jesus Christ?"

"Don' believe a word of it, Mick. He's havin' one on ya. He dinn't meet the man."

"An' how would you know? I dinn't meet yerself until two go-rounds later, did I? And dinn't the man himself say he'd come agin? Who are you to say he dinn't?" Kate rolled her eyes, but Declan didn't see it. He was too busy watching the road ahead. I could see him becoming more alert as we approached the border, his eyes scanning the roadside and the other cars in traffic. It was a hyperaware state I'd seen before in criminals and drug dealers whenever things were about to get dangerous.

"I'm not sayin' he dinn't. I'm jus' sayin' I'm not sure ya ever met the man himself," Kate challenged him. It was then that I realized the banter was partially for my benefit, to distract me from what we were about to do, and partially for their own. If they were busy going back and forth, they didn't have as much time to worry about things going wrong.

"An' how could I avoid meeting 'im?" Declan asked. "The man likes to be center stage, don' he? Keeps tryin' to change the hearts an' minds a people that ain' ready to hear it when he could move on if he wanted. Bit of a masochist, if ya ask me." Declan braked harder as the Volkswagen in front of us slowed down on a turn. It was the first time I'd heard him say anything about moving on.

"Could he avoid coming back if he wanted?" I asked. They'd talked about people being more "evolved" before, as if I should know what that meant—was this it?

Declan didn't answer, distracted by what was ahead as we came around the final bend and could see the border crossing. Chain-link fences topped with razor wire and an armored car outfitted with a machine gun made it perfectly clear that this line wasn't imaginary to the British. Kate answered for Declan, trying to distract us from the threat of the border. "Ahh, 'e wouldn't know. He's never gotten that far." Kate's answer seemed to bring Declan back to the conversation. He pulled up behind the last car in line and turned to face me.

"True. Ya might be better off askin' St. Kate here. She's more morally developed than I am. All I know is what Jaysus and a few others like 'im told me—that we can move on to a more aware an' enlightened way a livin'. But Kate's right. I never seen it myself, an' they're few an' far between, those who have come back from there to say where it is they been . . ." His voice trailed off and I followed his eyes to what had caught his attention. The first car in line had just been surrounded by soldiers, guns pointed at the men inside.

The British soldiers were yelling orders we couldn't quite hear through the windows, but we watched two young men slowly start to get out of the car, hands above their heads. The two men were tripped and shoved to the ground before they could get halfway out of the car, and the soldiers immobilized them as the rest of their squad proceeded to search the car.

"If this goes wrong, maybe we'll all get to see what comes after," Kate said in an effort to be lighthearted. Her joke fell flat, even with Declan.

"I know what comes after fer me. I'll be right back here again. Over an' over until I find a way to make my peace. Live or die, I'll finish it out." Declan felt under the seat, and for the first time I noticed the handle of a pistol, hidden just below him.

"How about we go for 'live'?" I asked, trying to stay calm. I could feel my heart pumping so hard the veins in my neck were twitching in rhythm.

"No worries, Mick. Nothin' to get yer knickers in a knot about," Declan said in a controlled voice. "The border and death are jus' both bumps in the road, and crossin' one's no worse than crossin' the other. Different levels a pain, maybe, but pain fades in time. An' besides, they can't really kill us."

"They have guns," I pointed out. "Guns kill." Even as I said it, the two men the Brits had pulled from the car were being half dragged, half marched to a small building off to one side. I could see blood on one of their foreheads as the other stumbled, trying to resist.

"Can we change the subject now? We're movin' up in line an' we're supposed to be relaxed, enjoyin' ourselves. We don't want to be all worked up when we have to talk to them now, do we," Kate pleaded, her eyes on the soldiers, waving the next car forward.

"Sure we can. As soon as I make my point for Mick here. Guns can put a nice hole in yer head, Mick, true enough. But they can't ever *really* kill us. They can separate our souls from our bodies and send us inta the next life in a bloody hail a bullets, but that's the worst they can do to us."

"You're not helping my nerves."

"That's a shame. It helps me a lot. It's like sayin' a little prayer fer myself. From God I came an' to God I shall return."

"You keep on telling yourself that. I'm just hoping I'm not getting returned to sender just yet."

I wasn't really joking, but Declan laughed.

"There ya go. Looks like 'is sense a humor's comin' back. Jaysus had a sense a humor, too, did ya know that? Wouldn' know it from the way they write about 'im, but 'e did. A regular fella. All that Jaysus is 'God' crap Paul added later. We're all part of the same Trinity."

Declan stopped as he popped the clutch and shifted the stick between Kate's legs, moving up in line. There were only two cars ahead of us now.

The first car we saw getting searched was pulled over to one side, its seats being torn out.

"So I'm the 'Son of God,'" I asked, intending to be sarcastic.

"Sure. Ain' we all?" Declan interrupted as he moved the pistol from under the seat to under his thigh.

There was just one more car to go, and it looked like an ancient crone of a woman was driving it.

I watched the soldier who was examining the crone's papers as Declan put out a hand.

"Gimme yer stuff. It's time." He put out his hand as he popped the clutch one more time, gliding up to the waiting soldier and his squad, their guns ready.

As we rolled to a stop, I noticed that the pale-faced soldier had bags under his eyes and red splotches from where a dull razor had scraped his face bloody. His blue eyes were watery and clouded, exhausted by the suspicion he held in check as he put out his hand, waiting for our documents. He didn't say a word as the rest of his small squad swarmed over the truck, looking at everything on it and underneath it, distracted as they ogled Kate.

Declan smiled at him as he handed the papers over, leaning out the window and acting like this soldier, barely out of his teens, was his new best friend. He spoke conspiratorially, as if trying to keep me and Kate from hearing. "Hey, boyo. Can you do me a favor? My Yank cousin's over fer the tour. Scare 'im a bit if ya can? Give him the whole experience."

The soldier ignored Declan, going through his checklist of questions as he checked our IDs. "What're ya carryin'?"

Declan laughed at the question, nodding toward the open back of the truck. "Can' ya smell it? A load a shite it is."

"And why are you bringing it across the border?" the young soldier asked in a regimented monotone.

"Apparently the shite don' smell over there, and my other cousin needs some good smelly shite fer his farm." Declan needled him.

"Is that so?"

"Yeah. He tells me the shite on yer side a the border smells like roses. Good fer ya, I say, but bad fer the potatoes." Declan leaned out the window again, still playing a part. "C'mon now, boyo. I'm only tryin' ta get ya to put on the whole show fer my Yank cousin. I mean no disrespect, but couldn' ya give me a bit a the rough stuff?"

The soldier ignored him, stepping up on the sideboard to get a better look at me, holding up my ID as he did. "Are you really a U.S. citizen?"

"In from New York," I said, making sure it came out an authentic "Nu Yawk." He nodded as soon as he heard the accent and handed my ID back in the window.

"Don't let this wanker fill your head full of stories. We're only here to prevent trouble." With that he stepped back down off the running board to wave us through. "Go on ahead."

"What? Can' ya at least search the truck? Give 'im a show of it?" Declan protested.

"You could have an atomic bomb under that, and I wouldn't search it, sir. We're not here for your entertainment."

"Yer kiddin', right? Last time through they had me dump my whole load." Declan's voice was rising and the soldier was starting to get annoyed.

"Get moving. Now. Before I have you all arrested."

Declan stared him down, but Kate put a hand on his arm to calm him down, playing her part perfectly. "Let's just go. C'mon. We all know 'e's just bein' nice to give us a hard time."

Declan shook her off but slammed the truck into first gear, as if disgusted with the soldier for not searching it. He drove slowly through the razor-wire-topped fence, watching the mirrors to see if the British soldiers were going to change their minds. As we rode over the speed bumps, I swore I could hear the wooden crates of Armalites banging around under the manure, but in the mirror the soldiers had moved onto the next car. We were in Northern Ireland with a truck full of rifles, headed for Derry. I wondered how long it would be before one of Derry's residents loved another one enough to shoot him, just to teach them a lesson.

A few hours later, we were approaching another roadblock of British soldiers, just outside the Bogside in Derry. We had switched to a small sedan outside of Enniskillen, transferring six Armalites over with the intention of ferrying the arms into the Bogside a few at a time so we wouldn't arouse suspicion. This roadblock was more makeshift, with a Saracen blocking the street and some razor wire rolled out. Beyond it, we could see the roadblock thrown up by the residents of the Bogside, which was far more formidable. They'd almost entirely blocked the road with burned-out cars, piled-up bricks, and wooden stakes.

On top of the Bogside residents' barricades were a small group of boys and even a few girls yelling at the British soldiers. The soldiers were ignoring the kids and trying to ignore the stones that periodically pelted the side of the Saracen. I slowed as I approached. I had planned to do so anyway, but the several automatic weapons pointed at my head, with more added every few yards, provided extra incentive. Finally I stopped and rolled down my window, staring down the barrel of a paratrooper's rifle.

"Where do you think you're going?" the sergeant asked. I could see his stripes, so similar to the ones we used in the United States.

I knew my part. Declan had coached me endlessly. "My name's Aidan Corrigan. I'm a United States citizen—my father works for the U.S. State Department and asked me to come over and check on my cousins. He said to tell whoever stopped me that they should call him directly in Washington. I have his number here—" I reached for the paper with the actual main number of the U.S. State Department, but the sergeant reached for his weapon nervously, stopping me.

"Keep your hands where I can see them."

"Sure. Whatever you say." I put my hands back on the wheel. The sergeant seemed ready to turn us around when he was stopped by a voice from inside the Saracen.

"What's going on there?" A captain emerged, glaring at me as he spoke to his sergeant.

"He's an American, here to see his cousins."

"Jesus bloody Christ. An American. That's all we need. Turn him around. It's too dangerous in there." The captain motioned to the soldiers, but the sergeant hesitated.

"His father's with the U.S. State Department."

I spoke up, knowing that now was the make-or-break moment. "I'm just trying to find out if my cousins are okay after all that craziness last Sunday.

I can't seem to reach them by phone, and after everything I saw on the news . . . well, I'm worried."

"No worries for your relatives. They don't have phones in the Bogside." The sergeant smiled and his men joined him, as if they were personally responsible for making sure no one had phones.

"Yeah. Animals can't use 'em," said a dull-looking paratrooper with so little chin he almost looked like British royalty.

The captain silenced his man with a glare, then looked over at Declan and Kate. "Who are these lot with you?"

"My other cousins. From down in Athlone. I brought them with me because I heard these IRA types are suspicious. I didn't want to get shot." I tried to sound naive, which isn't difficult when the listener is British. They have a seemingly inborn sense of superiority. I was counting on it. "But, really, my father won't like me getting stopped. His number in Washington is right here, and he spoke to Mr. Whitelaw just yesterday, and Mr. Whitelaw assured him that—"

"Whitelaw?" the captain interrupted. "He spoke to your father?" I nodded, and I could see the wheels turning. He didn't want to make that phone call.

"Well, I don't think it's such a wise idea to go into the Bogside, cousins or no. We can't protect you in there. There's no police. No law."

"I can't tell my father no. You can if you want." I offered the number, but he just looked at it, then turned to the sergeant.

"Let him pass. Maybe we'll get lucky and he won't come back out." The sergeant nodded and stepped aside.

I put the car into gear and rolled forward, just as a group of masked gunmen emerged from behind the next barricade with their own mixed bag of guns ready. I started to slow down again, but Declan muttered fom the back.

"Keep drivin'. They're friends." I saw him motion with one hand out the back window, and the men in the masks stepped aside. As we drove through them, they greeted us.

We cruised past the corner of Lecky Road and Fahan Street, past the hand-painted sign on the gable end of a set of row homes that read YOU ARE NOW ENTERING FREE DERRY, and I tried to take it all in.

Derry itself looked like it was anything but free. It was being torn down from the inside out as if under siege. The buildings were in bad shape and the cars looked like they'd been resurrected from the junkyard and put back on the street. The people, however, looked like they belonged to another, more refined time. The older men all wore suits. The children, for the most part, were clean and respectful. All the women were in dresses and skirts. It was nothing like the States, where men had given up wearing suits except for business, where young women wore jeans as a statement, and children ran a bit wild.

As we drove farther into the Bogside, I started noticing something strange. Almost everyone—man, woman, and child—was crying. Not bawling but squinty-eyed, with tears staining their cheeks. Then I started to see young girls, ghostly and pale . . . No, not pale. Their faces were covered in something powdery and white, the tracks of their tears more visible because of it. My own eyes started to burn and well up, and my throat tightened, causing me to panic. I was getting a bit disoriented and I wanted to turn the car around. But before I could react or even think to ask what was going on, Kate put a hand on my arm and gently explained.

"It's the CS gas. It's heavier than air, so it gathers in the Bogside at the low points, waitin' for time and the wind to blow it away."

It made sense in a twisted way. It also made the entire place strange and unnerving. Smiling women and singing children had perpetual tears in their eyes, as did the angry and defiant young men. The Irish character that I'd seen and never understood my whole life was suddenly on the surface and visible here, tears and laughter so intertwined they were inseparable.

"The bloody British keep pumpin' it in." Declan added. "They know it causes miscarriages and they're tryin' to kill us off by killin' the next generation as well. Some of the women think baking powder helps, so they cover the children's faces in it."

"*Does* it help?" I asked. My eyes really burned.

"It makes them feel like they can do somethin' about it, so I guess it does in a way. But ya don' see them girls cryin' any less, do ya?" Declan shrugged, pointing to a small two-story brick building ahead of us on the right, what we'd call a row house in the States. I swung the car in to park out front and noticed that Jim Quinlan and Jerry Coonan were already standing in the doorway.

As I got out, Coonan fixed his crazy eyes on me but spoke directly to Declan.

"Yer aunt says yer welcome ta stay as long as ya want, but she's gonna stay with yer cousin Mary fer the time bein'."

"She wasn't upset with me now, was she?"

"She knows it's fer a good cause. You were a hunnerd percent right on this place. The rear entrance gives ya access ta Chamberlain Street, and there's an alleyway on one side. Plenty of ways out," Coonan said as he glanced toward the center of Derry, worried. "The only issue is that Jim here heard from his sister that they got snipers up there on the Derry walls, watchin' us all the time, jus' waitin' fer us to move so they can put a bit a lead in our heads."

Declan looked up at the walls and waved with one finger erect, smiling. "Good. It'll keep us on our toes. Did you talk to Brian Sullivan about his garage?"

Jim Quinlan nodded, pointing farther up the street. "Just around the corner. We can keep the car there and use it to unload all our merchandise."

"Show Mickaleen where it is. He'll be the one driving," Declan told Coonan, who didn't seem to be particularly happy about that. Neither was I, because if I was driving, I knew it meant that I'd be going in and out of those barricades over and over, and it was at the barricades that you were most likely to get killed.

"Come on. We'll walk on the other side of the street. I think the snipers have a better angle on this side," Coonan told me, then crossed the street quickly. I couldn't help glancing up at the Derry walls, wondering whether I should make a run for the Dublin Airport and take my chances with a jury of my peers in Pennsylvania. A death sentence was beginning to feel like more of a sure thing here than there.

IT ALL LASTED a little more than two weeks. Every other day I would drive out of the Bogside, out of the no-go area, to the Protestant-controlled city center to get groceries. Then I went down to my "uncle's" farm just outside Nixon's Corner for fresh fruits and vegetables and whatever else I, as the rich American cousin, needed to pick up for his poor relatives. Underneath the groceries I hid a half-dozen rifles that I'd picked up from the farm along with the apples and potatoes. Kate joked that I carried all the staples of Irish life: food and firearms.

The British soldiers on the cordon got used to seeing me come and go, and although I knew they thought I was a bit daft for not going home to New York when I could, they also didn't bother me. No one wanted the American government looking too closely at what was going on in Derry. There were too many Irish Americans in politics, and Teddy Kennedy had already caused enough grief over Bloody Sunday.

I was coming in with my sixth load of Armalites after being waved through the cordon at the price of a half-dozen apples to the paratroopers when I saw Jerry Coonan and Jim Quinlan standing outside the house Declan and Kate and I were staying in. The usual procedure was for me to unload the groceries, then drive around the corner to Sullivan's garage where I kept the car. There Coonan and Quinlan would unload the rifles inside, where no one could see. If Coonan and Quinlan were here at the house, something was wrong.

"What happened? Where's Declan and Kate?" I asked, worried.

"Lord Widgery's startin' 'is show down in Coleraine. Dec and Kate are inside with one a the witnesses to calm 'er nerves," Coonan said, staring at me as if expecting me to call him a liar.

"He told us to help you unload here an' at the garage, and then Jim's gonna drive 'em all down there."

I shrugged. I didn't trust Coonan, but if Declan was in a rush, I could use the help. I'd just opened the trunk when I heard a brief buzzing whistle and then the rear window of the car shattered almost at the same time as I heard the far-off crack of a rifle. The noise startled me, and I stared at the window confused even as Coonan tackled me, sending me to the pavement, scraping my hands and cheek on the glass-covered ground.

"What the fuck?" I muttered, reverting to my own natural vernacular.

"Bloody bastards is playin' with us again," Quinlan growled from the other side of the car, scanning the horizon for the shooter.

"Is he on the walls?" Coonan asked, squinting into the distance.

"I dunno. I can't see shite."

A loud pop caused my whole body to twitch and Quinlan to scramble to the opposite side of the car. A bullet had punched a hole in the fender two inches from his head. At least now we knew the general direction the sniper was shooting from.

"I bet the cowards think it's funny, watchin' us take cover like rabbits as they sit over there in hidin', shootin' at us," Coonan grumbled, trying to spot the sniper's vantage point.

"They think them damn signs are true, that IRA stands for 'I Ran Away.' We'll show 'em soon enough." Quinlan's speech was slurred, and I realized he'd been drinking already.

"No. We'll show 'em now." Before Quinlan or I could stop him, Coonan was on his feet, tossing groceries out into the street in order to get to the Armalites underneath. I heard him jam in a magazine before I realized that he was serious, and I had barely gotten to my knees by the time he opened fire.

The chattering of the gun was deafening this close, and he wasn't easing off. He fired at the Derry walls and at anything in the distance that seemed like a target. Tiny puffs of dust showed where the bullets hit, and I could hear people in the street shouting their encouragement.

There were no visible targets, just Coonan's impotent rage being funneled through the barrel of that gun. The smarter pedestrians had already fled the street, and some old women were leaning out windows, shouting down the teenage boys who were encouraging Coonan. Then his rifle jammed. For a moment, it was blessedly silent. It occurred to me that maybe the sniper had decided Coonan was too crazy and dangerous to play with. We all knew that the Brits were trying to keep things quiet after Bloody Sunday.

All the hopeful thoughts went out of my head as the next bullet struck the car just above my head. From the angle of it, it was clear that there was more than one sniper. They had us triangulated. We had to move.

"They have us. *Run!*" I pushed Quinlan ahead of me, leaving Coonan behind, trying to get to the shelter of the narrow alleyway next to the building behind us.

Quinlan made it. I didn't. I felt a hot pain stab through my calf and my right leg went out from under me halfway to the alley. Cement chips hit me in the face as bullets struck the sidewalk around me, and I knew I had to keep going. I pushed and dragged myself around the corner, feeling another sharp punch to my shoulder as I went, as if someone had hit me on the back with a sledgehammer.

And then the wall was between me and the snipers. It chipped and sprayed dust as the bullets hit. I don't know if the brick dust had gotten in my eyes or the lingering CS gas was doing its job, but my vision had gone blurry, and everything looked distorted. I could still hear everything perfectly, however—Coonan cursing, starting the car even as bullets shattered what was left of its windows; Quinlan yelling for help in the back of the house; people running toward me, from the same direction. And then I heard Declan's voice, behind me, and the pavement beneath me began to hum.

"They're comin'. The army. With Saracens."

"Carry him. Get him *up*! We have to get him out of here," came Kate's voice, the panic bleeding through.

"We can't, Kate. They'll catch us all. We gotta go." I could see the hazy silhouette of Declan standing over Kate, right in front of me now. He was right. If they carried me, they'd all be caught.

"Go, Kate. Please," I begged her, but I was mumbling so badly I sounded like an Irishman.

"They'll kill him," Kate said, not making me feel much better about the whole thing. She was trying to convince Declan.

Then it struck me. The Brits might rough me up if they caught me, but what would they do to Kate if they caught her? I was an American, not just a mere Irishman from the Bogside. That might keep me safe, but she had no diplomatic protection.

"Kate. They can't just kill me now, can they?" I asked, trying to convince her to run, hoping she wouldn't remember that they might figure out I wasn't really Aidan. That they might send me home to the good state of Pennsylvania, where I was just as likely to be killed.

"Kate, please. I won't make it if I have to worry about you."

The Saracens growls were growing louder. I could hear the good people of the Bogside cursing at them, then the woosh and shattering glass of the petrol bombs raining down from the Rossville Flats.

"Kate!" Declan shouted. "Either we go now or they get us all."

Kate nodded, then reached inside her jacket and took something out, placing it in my palm. "Here. If the pain gets too bad, take this."

I dropped it. I didn't want to take anything to end the pain. I wanted to get back to her as soon as I could. I looked up at Declan, begging him, "Carry her, Dec. Make her go."

"Take it!" Kate forced the small gumdrop-shaped object into my hand, and I took it so that she'd leave.

"I won't kill myself," I muttered. "I won't go . . ."

"It won't kill you. It'll just take away the pain and help you deal with what they give ya. It's what I gave Patsy." She kissed me then, hard, and finally stood to go, whispering as she did, "I love you. I'll be waiting fer ya."

"Kate!" Declan grabbed her arm, dragging her up the alley as gunfire erupted out on the street, slowing the Saracens. "Take them!" she yelled back to me, already moving away. The pain seemed to burn brighter the farther away she got, and I swallowed the berries. When she saw me do that, Kate finally turned and ran on her own. I heard her go, her feet slapping the asphalt, while the Saracens closed in.

I was alone for a moment, the approaching engines and gunfire my only company. I almost closed my eyes, just to rest for a bit, but a soft voice from a window on the alley above me called out.

"Are you okay, mister?" I struggled to open my eyes, and although she was blurry and tear-stained, I saw a redheaded girl with a ponytail, hanging out her window across the alley. She couldn't have been more than seven, but her eyes were ancient. The phrase "old soul" went through my mind, and suddenly I felt the panic leave me. She was watching me.

Either that or whatever Kate had given me was starting to have an effect, because the pain, although still there, felt like it was happening to someone else's body. Maybe the girl wasn't even real but a belladonna-induced hallucination. She looked like someone I'd once known, but I couldn't quite place her.

"Don' close yer eyes, mister. Don' invite the night. Jus' keep talkin' to me an' you'll be okay." She seemed accustomed to giving orders. Her voice was so sweet, so familiar. I hadn't seen her in so long that I couldn't remember her name, but she was my friend, here when I needed her.

"You look like someone I know," she told me, echoing my own thoughts.

"I know."

"But listen to ya. Yer a Yank. How do I know you?"

"You don't," I groaned, trying to keep my eyes open, feeling the warmth of my blood pool under me, soaking my shirt, knowing that as it spread, my life was seeping out of me.

"Sure I do. My name's Ciara. Don' ya know me?"

I wanted to answer her, but I felt like I was being buried in mud. I couldn't move. Could hardly breathe.

"I'm gonna go get my da," Ciara said, worried that I didn't answer.

I struggled to speak. I couldn't let her do that. "No. Go. Stay away," I warned, but she hovered in the window as I heard doors slamming at the end of the alley and angry shouts as boots hit the pavement. Ciara leaned farther out the window, lowering her voice.

"Don' worry. I won't let 'em hurt you. Even if you were one a them and not a Yank, I wouldn't let 'em hurt you." Then she looked up the alley and leaned back in, even as I heard the sharp clipped tone of a British soldier.

"I told ya I hit one a the bastards."

"Good for you. Now finish him," came a second soldier's voice.

"No," ordered a third. The sound of the boots moving toward me slowed and the soldiers went silent for a moment. I couldn't understand why they wouldn't shoot me until I heard the third man go on, "Get the girl out of here. I want to talk to anyone inside who might have seen anything."

I heard two sets of the paratroopers' footsteps moving toward the front of her house, and watched as the little girl calmly faced down the British officer above me.

"He's an American," Ciara said calmly, as if she were used to people being shot and debating with a British officer about whether they should be murdered or not. If she'd lived in Ireland for more than one lifetime, maybe it was a common occurrence for her. Not for me. My muscles were trembling and I was trying to move, but I was getting cold and knew I was going into shock.

"Is that true?" he asked, kneeling over me. I needed him to believe it. My survival depended on it.

"I'm here to visit my fucking cousins. From New York," I said, stressing my accent.

I could see him shake his head in frustration and turn to the paratroopers behind him. The last thing I heard was him cursing in beautiful and articulate English, without a mutter or a mumble. "Motherfucker. You wankers have done it now. What a bloody mess you arseholes have gotten me into. Get him to hospital. Now."

Michael

I never made it to the hospital, or even "to hospital," as they say over here. I started to lose myself as the paratroopers picked me up roughly and literally tossed me into the back of a Saracen. My head bounced off the floor, briefly taking my mind off the pain from the gunshots. I could hear the little girl, Ciara, yelling at them and was vaguely aware that she kicked the shortest one before he backhanded her and sent her sprawling on the concrete. I tried to get up, but although my muscles tensed, they didn't get me far. I felt like both my body and mind were mired in mud, and I was drowning. Breathing took concentration. The pressure on my chest was made worse by the pain that shot through me every time I managed to get some air in my lungs. Then the doors closed and the Saracen lurched forward and I was gone until they opened again.

As the doors opened and light streamed in, I heard voices, clearly British. "Are you positive? No, let's keep the Americans out of it for the moment. They'll just extradite him before we can talk to him." I tried to see who was talking as two paratroopers grabbed my arms to drag me out, but my vision was blurry and I could barely lift my head.

"Let him be who he pretends to be for the moment. We can always say we were unaware of his identity later. Besides, no one will care. He's a murderer. We can use him for whatever we want and still ship him home afterward." The voices grew more distant as I was dragged through a heavy steel door that clearly did *not* lead into a hospital. God help me. The Brits knew who I was, and they wanted me for something more than murder.

"Get a doctor in to sew him up. He's of no use to us if he's dead," was the last thing I heard before I was dropped on a cot inside a cell. The pain shot through me and knocked the wind out of me. For a moment it felt like the air had turned to cement and was crushing my rib cage. I tried to focus on the flat gray ceiling above me, but it kept going dark.

When it finally settled into something I could focus on and recognize, I saw that it wasn't a ceiling at all. It was the sky. It was a dark blue night sky with almost no stars because it was full of light pollution. Framed by redbrick buildings, as if I were lying in an alleyway on my back, the sky was a narrow strip of infinity, a path out of the hole I was in, a hole that smelled like stale alcohol and wasted cabbage.

I sucked in a painful breath, trying to remember who and where I was when Jerry Coonan suddenly appeared above me, smiling, a pistol in his hand. Although his name was Seamus then, I recognized him by his eyes. They were just as blue and just as intense as if he were of the Duine Matha himself. I could feel myself bleeding here, too, the blood pooling under me and drenching my shirt. There was more of it this time, and somewhere deep down, I knew that I wouldn't make it. He'd killed me. Seamus, or Jerry, or whoever he was this time, had killed me.

I wasn't upset. I felt like I'd known it was coming, and that not only was I ready, it was past due. There was only one thing I hadn't gotten to finish and felt compelled to try. "Seamus," I managed to say, trying to get his attention before he left, "one thing, please." Seamus stopped and turned to look down on me. He was satisfied now that he knew I was dying.

"I'll not deny a dyin' man. If ya have somethin' to ask, ask it. I'll give ya my fergiveness."

"No. Not that. I don' need that," I told him, knowing even as I said it that it was a mistake. "I jus' need ya ta tell Erin I'll look her up. I won't ferget. Tell her I love her."

Seamus's face clouded over. "Erin? Yer still stuck on that? Well, ya'd be better off askin' fergiveness, because ya should know this, Sean. She's the raison I found ya."

I didn't understand. Had Erin told him where I was? Did she still think I'd killed Liam in cold blood? That I'd betrayed my best friends? Seamus smirked, annoyed, then propped my head on my coat and put a flask of whiskey to my lips.

"Yer actions got more than one person I loved killed, Sean, so if I see ya in the next life, I canna answer fer mine. Yer a traitor an' a coward. I hope this teaches ya a lesson, but if it doesn', I'll do it agin," Seamus said, matter-of-factly. Then he placed the whiskey by my head, within reach, and walked away.

I started to fade then, but it wasn't the end, it was another beginning. The beginning of my journey back, my remembering. The drugs that Kate had given me were starting to take effect, and whether they were activating hallucinations based on stories half remembered or actual memories, I had no idea. In this peculiar dream state I was seeing pieces of images, distorted as if viewed through dark glass, reflected and misshapen. Bits and pieces of lifetimes, out of context in a highlight reel of memories.

There was one common thread: Kate. It was aways Kate. Kate or Erin or Maureen or Moira, or any one of a hundred names I'd known her by. Sometimes she was with me a whole lifetime, and sometimes it seemed like I'd search a lifetime to find her. I saw Bridey singing in Irish as she waited for me so long ago, before they burned her house down with her in it. Maureen O'Hanlon. That was her name that time.

The dreams went on, tearing me apart emotionally but at the same time taking away my physical pain. The pain was nothing compared to what I'd been through over the years, and even though it could kill me, I knew it would never again destroy me. Not as long as I could remember who I really was. It was no longer a question of belief or *if* I had lived before. There was no cult or religion involved. I didn't need faith, I had memory, and as I remembered, I lost all sense of time and place.

After what seemed like several dozen lifetimes, I was back among the living. I could tell because the physical pain returned, sharper than ever. I was in total blackness with a hood tied over my head and my hands tied behind my back. I think what brought me back to awareness was my arms being wrenched up over my head and fixed to a hook above and behind me, at such a height that my toes could just barely touch the ground to prevent my shoulders from snapping out of their sockets.

But it wasn't close enough to the ground to prevent the sutures in my shoulder from slowly sawing their way through my flesh as they ripped loose. I knew that if I went flat-footed, the sutures would tear free and tendons in my shoulder would snap. As long as I remained on my toes, it was just immensely painful. As intended. My throat was parched and I could feel the weakness that came with not having eaten in a few days.

"Welcome back," said a familiar voice—the only voice I was going to hear for several days. It was a man they called "the captain."

"I . . . need . . . water," I croaked, assessing that asking to be let down and treated according to the Geneva Convention was probably out of the question.

"Certainly," the captain answered. "As soon as we're done here, Officer Corrigan, I'll give you all the water you want." I heard water being poured somewhere close by and would have salivated if I could have. "Can you hear that? I have a pitcher right here. Delicious."

"You know I'm an American," I rasped.

"We know who you are, Michael. A racist murderer and an Irishman, although these days it seems redundant to call you both, doesn't it?" I could almost detect his grin as my legs twitched and shook from muscle fatigue. They started to give and the tendons in my shoulders pulled a bit farther apart. The pain sent adrenaline down to my legs, allowing me to stand again. At least for the time being.

"Do you know who we are? Have your Irish relatives filled you in on the horrors of internment yet?" the captain asked, almost conversationally.

"No, but I'm learning."

"No, I don't think you are. Not quite yet. There's so much more you need to understand. We're trying to keep the good citizens of this country safe, just as you were trying to keep your country safe from radical black revolutionaries."

"He shot at me," I gasped. "At least I thought he did." The captain just laughed.

"Isn't that the excuse we all use? They shot at us *first*? And maybe they did. But that's not really the point, is it? The fact is that our reports say that *you* shot at us. You're a fugitive who shot at British troops. No one would blink an eye if you turned up dead, would they?"

"I had no gun."

"Ahh, so you know your part. Go ahead and play it. 'I had no gun.' Isn't that what they said about the man you killed as well?" I couldn't answer him. It took all my concentration to stay up on my toes so my sutures didn't rip open. And besides—he was right. I heard him stand up, could feel him move closer, so close I could head butt him if lowering my head wouldn't tear my arms from their sockets.

"Come on now, Officer Corrigan. You're a man of the law. You know how this works. You help me, and I can help you. We can work together here."

"Is that why you aren't sending me home?"

"Of course. Why would we?" His tone was smug. He held all the cards and knew it. "You're an experienced officer. You've even worked to root out subversive groups back in the States. It would be a waste to send you home and see you convicted of murder because you were a politically convenient sacrificial lamb, wouldn't it?" I didn't answer. I knew where this was going and couldn't see a way out.

"As a gesture of my goodwill, I'll give you a hand. Step forward and up." I heard something scrape the floor and put one foot forward—there was a small box there. I stepped up onto it and relieved the pressure on my arms as he went on, "Maybe we can help each other. You can use your skills here, and when it's all said and done, we can give you a new identity."

"As long as I work for you?" I asked, knowing the answer.

"Exactly."

"Feck off." I almost laughed as I said it, but it was cut off as he kicked the box out from under my feet and my arms jerked upward, ripping muscles and ligaments as I tried to catch myself. I screamed in pain, my ears ringing.

When I ran out of breath, the captain calmly continued. "The stubbornness must be in the blood. I'll come back after you've rested. Maybe then you'll be more reasonable."

I heard him cross the room and heard the cell door shut behind him. I hung there for what seemed like hours but was probably only a few minutes before my legs gave out and I collapsed, pulling both arms from their sockets, tearing all the sutures free. I passed out to the sound of my own screams.

WHEN I CAME to the hood was still over my head and I had been lowered to a point where I could stand flat-footed, but as exhausted as I was and as tender as my shoulders were, it didn't help much. The captain had one of his men give me water when I asked for it, pouring it directly onto the canvas hood they had over my head, making it hard to breathe. It was so drenched in water that I felt I was drowning and I panicked, thrashing about until the pain in my shoulders outweighed my desperation and I passed out again.

The next time I came to, they said nothing, just moved around me in silence, striking me with random blows that I couldn't avoid. I never knew where they were coming from or when, and that lack of control was torture. Flinching was painful.

I lasted two days, although that might sound like I was stronger than I was. Most of that time I was unconscious or screaming my head off.

I found out later that while I was unconscious, Britain had announced that it was assuming direct rule of Northern Ireland. My tormentors were now the law and order in this country, for better or worse.

MARCH 1, 1972

Between the treatment of my original injuries and the interrogations that followed, I had been gone from the Bogside for over a week. The captain, whose real name I never knew, gave me a cover story to tell Declan and the others, which included a glowing description of the health care given to an American citizen who had been accidentally caught up in the Troubles and was then set free to be reunited with his family. It sounded like absolute bullshit to me, and I knew it would sound like "shite" to Declan as well. I couldn't do it.

At the risk of my life, I was determined to tell him the truth.

The captain accompanied me in the Saracen up to the barricades and I walked through them in silence, not knowing if the masked men on the other side would shoot me on sight. There was Declan, waiting. On either side of him were Coonan and Quinlan, looking like they were hoping to be appointed to the firing squad. I walked up to them, glad that this was all taking place in the open, in the middle of the street. At least there were witnesses. Maybe they wouldn't be so bold as to shoot me dead right here.

"Where have you been?" Declan asked, direct as ever.

I laid it on the line, trying to speak low enough so that only the three of them could hear. "With a British captain, promising him that I was going to tell him everything I saw and heard from all of you." Before I finished, Coonan had a pistol out, pointed at my face. Quinlan had his hand on his gun, too. But Declan hadn't flinched.

"Go ahead, shoot me. Sooner or later either you will or they will. That's why I'm not playing games, just telling it like it is."

"Why? Why would ya tell us this when ya know we'll kill ya for it?" Declan challenged me, and I knew that one wrong word and he'd let Coonan put a bullet in my head.

"I'm just telling you the truth. They tortured me, and I said what I had to say to get out of there. Now I'm here. If I told you anything different, you'd call me a liar and shoot me."

Declan smiled at that and nodded. "True enough. But the truth don' set ya free, Mickaleen. That lot'll kill you or send you home if you don't live up to your end of the bargain. You'll have to inform on us, and then I'll have to kill you."

"So let's kill 'im now, right," Coonan urged.

"It's your choice. I know I have to tell them something, but half-truths and well-placed lies may do us more good than harm if I work this thing out properly." Declan stared back at me, not giving anything away.

"Ya can't trust 'im, Dec. He's not one a us," Coonan pushed.

"I'm an asset. Trust me. Bad information is worse than none at all. I can tell them things too late to do anything about it and lead them down blind alleys to set them up. Trust me, I've seen it done by professionals. These are soldiers, not cops, and they're in over their heads. I can lead them around by their noses." I stopped myself then. I was starting to sound like I was pleading instead of selling my position to him.

"Are ya sure? If they were MI5 . . ." Declan's voice trailed off, doubting whether or not I was capable of playing both sides.

"*If* they were. The one captain might have been trained, but he's arrogant, making stupid mistakes. He thinks torture will buy him the truth. He thinks you're all uneducated thugs and will back down if he just kills enough of you," I said, knowing that would set off Coonan.

"We answer blood with blood. He doesn't know 'is history," Coonan spat.

"No, he doesn't," I agreed.

"So we can use you to screw with them all, can' we?" Declan grinned.

"That's my plan."

"Put the gun away, Jerry," Declan said in an even tone.

"Can' we kill 'im jus' ta be sure," Coonan asked, staring down his barrel at me with those crazy eyes.

Declan stepped in front of the pistol, between me and Coonan. "I've known Mickaleen a long time, and I've even watched as 'e put a bullet in my brain, but I've never known 'im to be a traitor. If I'm wrong, I'm sure I'll pay fer it, but I'm not wrong."

"An' what if ya are?"

"I'm not. Even if he don' know it yet, I know it. An' now that we know he's not dyin' today, go tell Kate 'e's back," Declan ordered.

Coonan hesitated, but Quinlan grabbed his arm, saving him from Declan's wrath.

"Where is Kate?" I asked, worried about her and what she'd been through the last few days.

"She's raisin' hell down at hospital, demandin' to see every man with a gunshot wound. Or maybe she's back at the RUC barracks screamin' bloody murder. I was beginning to think they let you go because they were tired of her yellin' an' carryin' on."

A half hour later, in the dirt- and dust-encrusted yard behind the flat on Rossville Street, we were reunited. In spite of the burning pain in my arms, I held her as tightly as I could.

We stood there together for a long time, until it began to rain. It was a cold, bone chilling rain, but it took the place of our tears and stopped the burning of the CS gas, clearing the air and stripping us of all the grit and grime that clung to our souls. It was a beautiful Irish rain, as harsh as it was pure, cleansing us like it had cleansed Ireland of so much blood for so many centuries.

The rain felt timeless, like the rain that had fallen in so many lifetimes. I think that's why we stayed there, even as we shivered and huddled for warmth. We wanted time to stop, because we both knew that if it kept moving the way it was, we were going to have a perfectly good love affair interrupted by death, too soon.

MARCH 18, 1972

I'm not sure why I'm writing this anymore, except that now that I see where everything is headed, these might end up being my notes for the next time around. That is, if I can find some way to make sure they get back to me. I might send them to Dr. Sorenson, and Doc, if you're reading this, hang on to these pages. I'll try to send someone after them who can verify what I think you were trying to prove with me. I know you'll keep it scientific and not lead the witness, but please, if someone comes to you, steer him in the right direction and let him know that he needs to follow up on what happened to me, and all that I've found out about us.

It's been a while since I've written, partially because I developed a habit as a cop of not incriminating myself and partially because I hadn't felt the need to explain any of what I'd done. Now I think I need to clarify things for whoever might come after. I need to explain why I'm about to give the captain information about the workings of the Provisionals.

I don't mind writing about any of the things I've done except this one. But I had to do it in order to save lives. I never compromised Kate or Declan, and I never would. Declan is more than a brother to me and in fact has been a brother in the past. And Kate, well, we've been children together, had children together, cared for each other through all kinds of sickness, and have even had to hold one another as the life passed out of our bodies. When you've lived so many lives together, you're not really separate anymore but truly become as one. I could never betray her, but the Provisionals are just an organization of people, some good, some bad. By betraying the bad, I don't think I've betrayed the organization or its goals, but some might see it that way. If they find out, I'll be dead before anyone else gets a chance to read this.

My decision to give the captain accurate information began with the bomb that went off on March 4 in a restaurant in central Belfast. Two people died, and 136 were injured. Declan was furious because public opinion turned against the Provisionals in the aftermath, and the bombing hadn't been sanctioned. He confronted Jim Quinlan first. Quinlan was supposed to have transported a load of the black stuff to the Ballymurphy estate in Belfast with Jerry Coonan but had shown up with only half of the load. He denied any involvement in the bombing but told Declan that Coonan had disappeared for a few hours just before. When Declan challenged Jerry Coonan, Coonan denied that he had anything to do with it.

Then, on March 9, another bomb went off prematurely, leaving four Provisionals, including Jim Quinlan, dead. Coonan couldn't deny knowing about that one, but he shifted the blame to Quinlan, claiming he was behind both bombings.

I didn't believe him and told Declan so. I thought Coonan had set Quinlan up and knew the bomb would go off early in retribution for Quinlan telling Dec the truth about the March 4 blast. Unfortunately, with Quinlan dead, there was no way to prove anything, so Declan ordered Coonan back to Derry to meet with him in our flat.

Coonan sat at the kitchen table across from Declan, looking meek but unapologetic. I sat in the corner, taking it in as Coonan tried to shrug it all off.

"Look, Dec, I know how ya feel, but I wasna exactly disobeyin' orders here. The fellas in Belfast don' wanna be seen as cowards. They wan' retribution fer Bloody Sunday, don' they? Have ya seen the writin' on the wall? The signs that say 'I Ran Away'?"

Declan didn't answer, letting Coonan suffer in the hanging silence. After a moment he called Coonan out. "Yer tellin' me this was sanctioned by the fellas in Belfast? If I call an' ask 'em, that's what they'll tell me, is it?"

"Now how would I know? Quinlan was the one doin' all the talkin'." Coonan sidestepped the question smoothly, laying it all on Quinlan. Declan nodded. It was pointless to push this way—he'd never get the truth without Quinlan.

"Why don' ya tell me what went wrong," Declan said, his tone innocent.
Coonan avoided the trap. "Well, I wasna there now, was I? But the way
I hear it, Jim was rushed. I heard that it went off premature because there
was some MI5 movin' in on 'im." Coonan glanced at me out of the corner
of his eye as he said "MI5," trying to get Declan to make the connection.
Declan ignored the insinuation and Coonan was forced to continue his
half-assed explanation, laying it all out this time, since Declan hadn't taken
his hint earlier.

"Personally I think the problem with both situations, on the fourth and
this past time, is that we've got an informer in our midst. Nobody needed
ta get hurt, but when things get rushed, they go bad."

"An informer?" Declan asked, forcing him to be specific.

"Sure 'nough. Why else would Jim screw up so bad, twice?"

"Because he was an alcoholic who shouldna been messin' with the black
stuff in the first place. You were supposed to be there," Declan told him
bluntly.

I couldn't help but chime in, annoyed that Coonan was putting the blame
on a dead man. "Or maybe it's because he wasn't the one messin' with it, and
whoever it was wanted to kill as many people as they could. Wasn't it you
who said 'the more blood the better'?" I hadn't even finished when Coonan
was up out of his chair, fists clenched, coming at me.

"Ya accusin' me of somethin', Mickaleen? If anyone here's an informer,
it's you, what with that cozy affair ya got goin' with that Brit captain."

Declan just watched as we stared one another down, finally asking the
question on both his and Coonan's minds. "What have you told them,
Mick?"

"Nothing about any black stuff or things goin' on in Belfast. I've been
here in Derry."

"That's convenient, inn't it?" Coonan smirked, but Declan wasn't buying
it. He knew me too well.

"I want ya to stay in Derry fer a while, Jerry. Let things settle down." He
waved toward the door, dismissing Coonan. "Now if ya don' mind, Mickaleen and I have some things ta sort out."

Coonan smirked, getting up. "I bet ya do." He grinned at me, thinking he'd won.

Declan watched him until he went out the front door, then spoke quietly. "Well, he's settin' ya up, inn't he?"

"I didn't do anything, Dec."

"I know, but it's his word against yours, and yer a Yank who spent a lot of time with the Brits a few weeks ago. Some would kill ya jus' fer that. They don' know that ya got any reason ta be loyal to the likes a us." Declan seemed worried and distant, preoccupied with staying three moves ahead in Coonan's game. Coonan clearly had a home field advantage and it didn't look good for me.

I saw the way some of the people in the neighborhood were looking at me after that, even the ones I'd come to know over the last couple of months. Coonan was spreading rumors, but there wasn't much I could do to stop it. I was a stranger, and this was his hometown. Derry had become a lonely place except for Kate and the neighbor girl, Ciara. She kept me company when Kate wasn't around and would tag along sometimes even when she was.

As strange as it seems, except in the middle of explosions and gun battles, life was fairly ordinary in the Bogside. An old Quonset hut behind Mary O'Day's house was set up as a bar and christened Mary's Tavern. Kate and I spent our evenings there, but in the afternoons we would always take a walk, and more often then not Ciara would join us. I think she knew that Kate and I had a habit of stopping by the ice-cream man, who still came around every day and had the bullet holes in his van to prove it.

Ciara got a vanilla cone every time, and then she, Kate, and I would sit on the curb enjoying our ice cream as Ciara filled me in on all the neighborhood gossip. It was during one of these times, about four days after the sit down with Declan, that I found out what Coonan was up to from Ciara.

"Hey, Yank. I got some good news fer ya. I almos' fergot ta tell ya," she said.

"Good news for me?"

"Sure. They're tellin' people ya might not be the dirty informer." She smiled, her face full of ice cream, and I have to admit, I was relieved. "They got the real one, they think, up at the hall."

My chest tightened and the relief was gone. I knew there was no "real" informer and that Coonan had just made it up to distract from the fact that he was off blowing things up without the sanction of the Provo's leadership. "What do you mean? Who?" I asked, hoping he hadn't set up anyone I knew.

"Some boy from the neighborhood. I heard me da say Jerry Coonan was gonna get an informer one way or another, and if you was protected he'd take the first one that looked good enough ta shoot." Ciara spoke simply, as if it really were that simple.

"Are ya sure that's what he said, Ciara?" Kate interrupted, pale and tense, one hand squeezing my forearm. She knew what was going on as well. Coonan was covering his tracks.

"Sure enough. I remember it exact. Once I heard yer name, I paid extra attention." She flashed a grin at me.

"Maybe we should get up to the hall," Kate said quietly to me, starting to get up.

"You really think he'd shoot someone just to cover his own ass?"

Kate nodded solemnly, pulling me up off the curb, suddenly tense and rushing. "Jerry Coonan would shoot someone just to make his pistol lighter by one bullet, never mind coverin' his arse." I started after Kate, headed up toward the hall, as Ciara scrambled to her feet.

"Wait. Where are ya off to? Ya said ya'd play some jacks."

"Next time, sweetie. Next time. Promise. Just go home for now," I told her, worried that she might try to follow us.

"That's what ya always say, inn't it? Next time. Go home fer now," she called after us, but she sat back down on the curb, finishing her ice cream.

Three minutes later we pushed past one of the young neighborhood guys who hung around Coonan and went into the hall. It was dark and quiet, but at the far side Coonan was standing over a boy of about sixteen, who was tied to a wooden folding chair, his forehead bleeding, matting his long hair and dripping into his eyes.

"What's going on here, Jerry?" Kate called out before his man at the door could stop us. Coonan looked up but didn't answer Kate. He only had eyes for me. He seemed to have been expecting me.

"Ahh, I was hopin' ya might stop by, Mick. An' ya brought the bloody Morrigan with ya, wunnerful." He pulled the boy's head up by his hair so he could look at us. "Jackie O'Connell, meet Mick Corrigan."

"What are you doing to him, Jerry?" Kate demanded, moving closer and only stopping as Coonan's man raised his pistol toward her.

"Take it easy, Kate. Jackie spent a few days up in Girdwood Barracks last week, right before poor Jim got himself blown to bits, dinn't ya, Jackie?" Jackie didn't respond, just moaned, so Coonan forced his head to nod. "Jackie also happened to be Jim Quinlan's next-door neighbor. They shared one a those thin walls ya can hear everythin' through."

Jackie tried to pull away from Coonan, and I could see that the boy was obviously in pain and scared.

"I dinn't tell 'em nothin'. I dinn't know nothin'."

"Let him go, Jerry," I told him, catching his eye. We both knew this was a farce, and this poor kid was just a pawn.

"Let him go? An informer?" Coonan picked up his hand, a pistol in it now. With his other hand he pulled the kid's head back and pointed the pistol at it. "Are ya sayin' it wann't him? An' if it wasn't him, Mick, who was it?" He stared at me hard, his threat clearly implied.

"Finc. You want to shoot someone, Jerry, have some balls and shoot me. Don't blame some teenage boy who never did anything to you."

"So, is that an *admission*, Mick? Are ya sayin' yer the informer?"

"I'm saying there is no informer and you're playing a game to cover your own ass," I told him bluntly, hearing his man behind me take a sharp breath, expecting violence. Coonan was cooler than that. He smiled grimly, still playing out his game.

"If there's no informer, how did Jim get himself blown to bits?"

"Maybe *you* can tell us," I pushed, and Kate gently touched my arm. A warning.

"Me? Tell you? An' fer what reason? I don' see anyone but an admitted informer questionin' *my* loyalty now, do I? An' ya know what we do ta informers, don' ya?" He pressed the gun to the kid's head, turning the question on him. "You know, don' ya, Jackie?"

"It wasn' me. I swear. It musta been him," Jackie pleaded, desperate.

"See? Now even Jackie thinks it was you, Mick." Suddenly I saw what Coonan was up to, even as the door opened behind Coonan's man and several young Provos slipped in. I glanced at them, all the angry young men who just wanted payback for Bloody Sunday and were willing to follow anyone who'd give it to them. Even a psychopath like Coonan. "Do ya have any proof, Jackie? Did ya maybe see my man Mick talkin' to Jim Quinlan jus' before he left fer Belfast?"

Jackie took the hint, telling Coonan what he wanted to hear. "I did. I saw 'im. They were talkin' about the black stuff. I swear."

"He'd say anything with a gun to his head," I interrupted, knowing how this would sound to the rebels Coonan had somehow orchestrated into being here.

"I know. That's the way informers are, inn't it, boys?" Coonan finally addressed his audience and got the murmurs of agreement that he expected in return. "An' if he'd give it up so easy here, among friends, think about what he might say up at Girdwood Barracks, inn't that right?"

"*No!*" Jackie yelled, desperate.

"Somebody got Jim killed, Mickaleen. Was it you or Jackie here? You said ya had no idea what he was up to. Is that true?"

"Yes, but—"

Coonan didn't let me finish. "Then we have our answer, don' we?"

"*No!*" I screamed even as the gun jumped in his hand and a fine mist of blood and bone sprayed over the hardwood floor. I was so close to him that the shot deafened me for a minute, and as Jackie toppled sideways he seemed to do it in silence.

My ears were ringing, but I heard Coonan as he calmly put his gun in his waistband. "Now if we have any more problems, we can be sure it wasn' Jackie that informed, can' we?" He smiled at me and motioned to his pack of awestruck followers, striding out the door without a backward glance.

I stared at Jackie for a long time, seeing his face, relaxed now, at peace. He deserved better. He deserved a life. For the first time, it occurred to me that I hoped he had a better one next time around and that if I met him again, I owed him something. I owed him because I didn't stop Coonan. I didn't answer the question right. I didn't take the bullet myself.

If I had never run from my responsibility for killing James Butler, maybe Jackie would still be alive. This wasn't fate. This was my fault. If what Kate had told me was true, my decisions and my choices could have changed the outcome. If I'd learned the last time that I couldn't outrun karma, I wouldn't have left the States, and Jackie wouldn't be lying at my feet in a pool of blood. But I hadn't learned my lesson. I had run. Again. And once again, someone had died because of me.

"We have ta go." Kate was pulling on my arm, a touch of desperation in her tone. "Mick, c'mon. We have ta go now."

"Somebody has to take care of this boy." I couldn't move. Couldn't just leave him there.

"I'll tell Declan. He'll send someone. But you can't be here. You can't let it appear that you had anythin' ta do with this," she pleaded, and she was right. I let myself be led away, but only because I knew at that moment that I had to live long enough to kill Coonan. If I didn't, I was sure he and his crazy eyes would kill us all.

Two days later, my worries about the no-warning bombs causing a backlash showed some evidence of being right. William Craig held a rally in Ormeau Park in Belfast that was attended by sixty thousand Protestants, not all of them militant. When he shouted that they needed to "liquidate the enemy," he was met by resounding cheers. Clearly, things were going to get worse before they got better.

Two days after that, on March 20, there was another no-warning car bomb on Donegal Street that left six dead and over one hundred injured. It was rumored that a hoax led people toward the bomb rather than away from it, causing more injuries than necessary. Clearly, it was something Coonan would do, even if he didn't set it himself. *The more blood the better.*

I had to do something, but what? I was distracted thinking about it, and walking home with Kate from Mary's Tavern that night, I was edgy. I kept waiting for Coonan or one of his guys to come for me. I was jumping at shadows, waiting for them, or waiting for the sniper's bullet from the Derry walls to find me.

"Maybe we should go," Kate said suddenly, reading my mind.

"Go? As in run?" I asked. Hearing it spoken out loud, it became clear to me that running wasn't an option. It was crazy. I'd tried running before, always with the same result. "I don't think running's worked out so well for me, Kate."

"Well, it's fight or flight, inn't it? They seem to be yer only choices." She shrugged, as if she'd already known I wouldn't run.

"And what will you do if I choose one or the other?"

She pulled me closer, hanging on to my arm tightly. "I won' make the same mistake again, Mickaleen. Whatever ya do this time, I'll be right next to ya."

That's where she stayed the rest of the night, neither of us sleeping, trying to figure out how to make our lives last as long as we could before being interrupted once again by death.

APRIL 15, 1972

It took until today, but this morning I made contact with the captain and let him know where Jerry Coonan would be. Coonan was supposed to take the sedan from Sullivan's garage and go back to Belfast alone, relaying messages for Declan and picking up some Armalites on the way. I watched him as he spoke with Declan, then walked up around the corner to Sullivan's garage, and then I went to one of the few phones we had and dialed the number the captain had given me.

I felt sick. I felt like a true informer, even though I knew I was helping to stop a murderer who was using a cause to hide his psychopathic crimes. The captain tried to reassure me, but I could hear the bloodlust in his tone. He knew who Jerry Coonan was and couldn't wait to take him out of the picture. It occurred to me that I might be sending Jerry to be tortured worse than I'd been, and perhaps even killed, but in the end I'd either be responsible for killing him or responsible for the deaths of the innocents who would become the victims of his bombs.

I was hopeful that by the end of the day Coonan would be imprisoned, and I wouldn't have to worry about more people being killed. After I hung up the phone, I walked back out to the street. I wanted to be out there and visible as much as possible so that I could establish an alibi, no matter how weak it was.

That's when I saw the O'Connors, Kevin and Sean, driving the sedan that Coonan was supposed to be in. Two young and ambitious brothers, they ran a butcher shop in Derry and sometimes borrowed the car to bring back meat for their neighbors. They were past me before I could stop them, turning the corner, driving out of sight. Coonan must've known. How, I don't know, but he was supposed to be in that car.

I started to move. Maybe I could get down to the barricades before they got out. Then I saw him. Jerry. Already at the corner, leaning on a wall, watching the barricades that were out of my sight line. He glanced back up at me for a moment, smiled, and waved. Less than two seconds later I heard the screech of tires and gunshots. The screams and broken glass seemed to come just after that, and then more gunfire.

I sat on the curb and threw up in the gutter, not needing to see what had happened in order to imagine it. The captain had no intention of arresting Jerry Coonan. He was going to assassinate him. Instead, he'd murdered the O'Connor brothers. I was sure of it. And I'd sent them right into his trap. It was my fault.

I looked back down to the corner, but Coonan was gone. I guess he'd seen enough. In my mind's eye, I could see it, too. The shattered windshield, the blood sprayed across the seats, and the paratroopers striding closer to the now motionless car to carefully put one more bullet in their heads. I was only wrong about the details. The British, not wanting any more bad publicity, had plainclothes SAS men execute the O'Connors. The O'Connors also actually survived the initial gunfire, running from the car only to be shot in the back in a nearby alley.

I found out later that when the captain arrived to gloat over the dead, he saw Kevin O'Connor's face and turned to the SAS men and screamed at them. "You stupid bastards. You shot the wrong fuckers!"

It didn't stop him from claiming that the O'Connors were Provos, however, and it didn't stop the Provos from using the O'Connors as another reason to kill more people in retribution.

I was still sitting there on the curb a few minutes later, halfheartedly hoping for a sniper's bullet to give me a chance at a better life next time when Declan walked up the street from the barricades and silently sat down next to me. He just sat for a few minutes, saying nothing, the silence as much a form of communication as words between two people who'd been friends for so many generations. After a while he sighed that West of Ireland sigh and put a hand on my shoulder.

"Welcome home, Mick," he said without irony. "Just like old times, inn't it?"

"How'd he know?"

Declan shrugged. "He's a bloody bastard. A lot of people want 'im dead. He's in the habit a takin' precautions. Or maybe he got lucky. Nobody knew you were gonna do it but you, right?"

"I didn't even tell Kate."

"Good. That's good operational procedure. Tell no one and no one can tell." He went silent again for a few minutes, but I could tell he was choosing his words carefully and was as aware as I was that a lot of eyes could be on us as we sat here in the street. Finally he spoke, straight to the point. "The Army Council has been listenin' to Jerry, Mick. He's sowin' seeds a doubt about yer loyalties."

I nodded. I'd assumed as much. "He's crazy, Dec. You know that. You saw what he did to Jackie O'Connell."

"I saw what he done. But he's tellin' 'em that yer out ta kill 'im and that yer informin' on the lot of us. This thing here makes it look like he's tellin' the truth, crazy or not."

"What do you expect me to do?" I asked, knowing he wouldn't have brought it up without having a plan of some sort.

"We should get over there an' have ya meet the lads face ta face. You'll have ta give 'em somethin'. Make the boys in Belfast look good," he said. It wasn't a suggestion but a warning. This would be a test, and if I failed, I'd be a marked man.

"And how do I do that? How do I make them look good?"

"Set yer captain up. Give 'im information that's not so good so we can take out a military target fer a change."

I nodded. It made sense. It would prove my "loyalty" and keep me from getting killed. And no innocents would be killed in the process.

"Will it solve my Coonan problem?"

Declan shrugged. "It'll keep ya from gettin' killed fer a bit, I would think, wouldn' you? An' maybe ya can take out those feckers that shot the O'Connor lads instead of arrestin' 'em."

I looked up sharply at that. Was someone listening in on the phone? "How'd you know they were supposed to arrest them?"

"Don' be so paranoid. I jus' know because I know you, Mickaleen. Ya coulda set Coonan up to be killed, but you'd have him arrested instead because yer a bit soft. Always have been." He smiled sadly then. He seemed to know that being soft would always be my fatal flaw. Then he got up and walked away.

As he left, he passed Kate, who I realized now had been watching us, waiting for Declan to leave. She came and sat by me in silence until we both saw Ciara approaching, watching us warily.

As we looked up at her she spoke, hesitantly. "One a those days, inn't it?"

I nodded, and she sat down, taking my nod as an invitation. "I know how ya feel. I went to brush my teeth this mornin' and my loose tooth fell out. I was so surprised I swallowed it—see?" She grinned for us then, and Kate and I couldn't help but smile.

Life goes on. And on, and on. And most days that's a good thing.

MAY 14, 1972

It worked perfectly. I played on the captain's ego, telling him the Provos thought they were untouchable inside the no-go areas of the Ballymurphy estate and that they were going to torch the buses they hijacked so they could roast marshmallows and get drunk while laughing at the British troops who couldn't seem to stop them. I even warned him that it would be a trap.

"They'll burn them right beside the BTA center. They know that you'll come in after them. You'll be lookin' for them to come at you from Ballymurphy itself, but they'll be on the other side, behind you," I told him confidently.

Two hours later the King's Own Regiment was racing up the road toward the two hijacked buses and jumped out of their vehicles. They'd opened the doors toward the Ballymurphy estate, assured by me that the attack would come from elsewhere. They were wrong. Six soldiers were injured before they could retreat, racing down the Whiterock Road to the Royal Victoria Hospital. There would have been more casualties, but the Provos manning the guns that day were laughing too hard at the inability of the Brits to shoot straight.

I was called to a meeting—or a "celebration," as Declan put it—two days later on the thirteenth of May in the back of the bar at the Whiterock Junction in Belfast. It seems that the Provo leadership in Belfast was happy to have struck back at soldiers and not civilians for once and wanted to figure out a way to use my conduit into British intelligence again.

Coonan was invited as well, since the meeting was supposed to be an overall strategy session. We'd be deciding whether to continue to spill as much blood as possible and risk alienating supporters or to more carefully choose targets for maximum impact and minimal blowback. Declan, Kate, and I arrived a few minutes after five to find the bar almost full, with men and some women watching England against Germany in football. I noticed that the front windows had been cross-taped to stop the glass from becoming shrapnel in the case of a bombing, but that wasn't unusual in this neighborhood, or anywhere else in Belfast for that matter. Neither were bombs.

We were almost at the door to the back room, where the meeting was to be held, when it felt like someone had smashed into me from behind, sending me sprawling into Declan and pushing him through the door into the back room. When I landed, he was under me and Kate was on top of me and we were all covered in splinters and debris. The bar behind us was a madhouse of bleeding men and shattered tables and bottles.

My ears were ringing, dampening the moans and cries, but through the front window I saw flames and a burning motorcycle that rested on top of a young man. Several of the bodies scattered about the bar weren't moving. Declan pushed past me to help the injured. His movements inspired me to action, although there wasn't much I could do other than helping a few of them get outside.

I know it will sound strange, but the bartender kept serving alcohol, and an attempt was made to get the television working again even as the ambulances began to arrive. It was only after they loaded their passengers up that things got more complicated.

As the first ambulances went to pull away, gunmen started firing down from the apartment buildings, the flats on the ridge in Springmartin. As soon as that happened, the army, which had only just arrived, fled, and the rescue workers scattered. By the time the IRA got their guns and tried to return fire and protect the wounded, the army had joined whoever it was up there shooting down on us, most likely the Ulster Volunteer Force.

Declan was shouting orders, telling his men to commandeer some buses to block the line of fire from Springmartin, but that took a few minutes—time that cost the wounded dearly, since we could get none of them to the hospital. I tried to stem the bleeding for a few of them, using my shirt as bandages. I was ripping off my own sleeve when Declan approached, his eyes on fire and looking ready to kill someone. At first I thought it was directed at me.

"Where is 'e? Have ya seen 'im?" he demanded.

"Who?"

"Coonan. Bloody Coonan. He was the only one that hadn't shown up yet, wann't he?" All I could do was nod. The insinuation was clear. Someone had told the Ulster Volunteer Force that we were meeting at the bar, and when. It wasn't a random act of violence. We were targeted. Maybe Coonan had gone rogue. Maybe was just choosing to be allied with the more militant men that the Provisionals had spawned. Or maybe it wasn't him at all. But either way, it didn't look good.

"Don' leave. An' whatever ya do, if ya see Coonan, go the other direction. We need to settle this once an' fer all." With that he walked away, straight across the street, ignoring the sniper fire as if he were somehow immune to bullets.

A little while later Declan had his buses blocking the line of fire, and I sat leaning against the wall of the bar in the rain again. It felt good after the heat and mayhem of the last few hours. I could still hear gunfire in the distance, but it felt like the worst had passed, at least for the night.

Kate wandered over, and I realized I hadn't seen her in a while, losing her in the crowd as she helped the injured.

"Sometimes it seems like the sun never shines here, doesn't it," I said, trying to hold on to the relief I felt at seeing her, whole and beautiful, without a scratch on her.

"It makes you appreciate the sunshine," she responded as she sat down next to me, the rain slowly soaking through her long hair. "But ya gotta learn ta appreciate the rain as well. Appreciate water in all its forms. It's an amazing thin'. It can move mountains and yet it's never hard or harsh. It can be small enough to rise to the heavens and fall again to quench the thirst of the earth. Hide underground in streams until it's ready to burst forth and join a larger stream to become a wild ragin' river." She looked up at the sky, letting the misting rain wash over her face.

I couldn't appreciate the rain, not now, not with the streets still covered in blood. "Yeah. That sounds lovely. And how Irish of you to see the beauty and ignore the reality at hand."

"I'm talkin' about the reality at hand, you're just not listenin'."

"Sometimes water just lies there, Kate. Then it becomes a stagnant, poisonous pool."

"Ya sayin' Belfast is a stagnant pool?" she asked, amused that I'd bought into her metaphor.

"This place isn't changing. Hasn't changed for as long as I can remember. Every man who's ever lived here thinks he's the lord of the earth, and it's his right to rule over all the others," I said, thinking back to a time when it was the Northmen invading from Belfast Lough and not the British.

"Lord of the earth, is it? Well, that bloody attitude started with one little misinterpretation, dinn't it? Tha's why I'm against writin' on principle. It gets misinterpreted," she said.

"What gets misinterpreted?"

Kate smiled sadly, quoting from memory. "God said, Let us make man in our image, an' let him rule over the fish of the sea, and over the fowl of the air, and over the cattle, and over all the earth, and over every creeping thing that creepeth upon the earth."

She shook her head, disgusted. "But call it 'rule' or 'lord' or 'have dominion,' it's all still wrong. The real word used, in its original context, meant 'caretaker.' We're supposed to be caretakers of the earth, not lords of it. Another brilliant distortion a the truth, inn't it?"

I nodded to the Provos firing up at the Springmartin and the gunmen hidden in the flats. "Maybe you should tell all of them that."

"They won' listen. They don' remember the truth like we do. They don' remember that we're here to serve God's creation, not master it. Sure, like the water, we can wear down the mountains and cut channels to the sea, but we should be nourishin' the earth, not destroyin' it."

It all sounded so simple coming from her, so clear. Why hadn't I seen that before? One word changed in one book, for whatever reason, and the whole outlook of humanity could have been changed forever. It was like that old joke about the monk who goes into the Vatican library and comes across a very old text. He reads it and comes out an hour later in shock, running to the Pope to tell him that there's something he has to know. When the Pope asks what it is, he says, "It says 'celebrate,' not 'celibate.' "

Of course, the story is not really funny, but unless we question what's been written and twisted around forever, the joke will be on us.

Sean

JULY 14, 1996

"You really think the guy with the crazy eyes is looking to kill me?" I asked Anne as she drove toward the border near Clones, her driving as maniacal as always.

"Do you remember how much of 'is money ya burned?"

From what I remembered of the dream, it looked like a lot. Bags of it, and British pounds no less. Each one of those was worth a good bit more than a dollar. "I could tell him where the truck is," I offered. "Where I dreamed it was, anyway."

"Right. All nice an' rusted at the bottom of Lough Neagh. Lotta good it'd do him. Or you." Anne shook her head, goosing the gas as she hit one of the rare straightaways.

"How can he be upset with me? I didn't do anything. It was my uncle Mike." It wasn't fair. Really. Even if Uncle Mike was guilty as charged, it wasn't *me* who'd stolen his money. Not in this lifetime, anyway.

"There's no diff'rence to him. Ya know that, right? What is it the good Catholics use ta justify it? 'For I, the Lord your God, am a jealous God, punishin' the sins of the fathers to the third and fourth generations'? Somethin' like that. Call 'em incarnations, though, an' ya get the picture. An' Crazy Eyes figures he's got two or three more times to kill ya afore yer even."

"That's ridiculous. I don't even believe in any of this. I can't be held responsible for something that happened before I was born."

"Sure ya can. Because it's not a matter of what *you* believe, it's a matter of what *he* believes." Anne glanced in the mirror, as if worried he might be following us, then at me. "No, yer gonna have to solve it the same way ya did last time."

"What'd I do last time?"

Anne glanced at me again, obviously unwilling to answer. "I'll tell ya later."

"I died last time. That's it, isn't it? It ended when I died." I pushed her, trying to get an answer, but for once her eyes were on the road ahead. There was a border crossing up ahead and I could see the cars backed up, stopped by razor wire, machine guns, and the soldiers who looked like they wanted to use them.

"Stop bein' such a nancy-boy, will ya? It ended before ya died."

"Thank God." Then it struck me, she still hadn't really answered my question. "How? How did it end before I died?"

Anne smiled, and even before she spoke I recognized it as her sadistic smile. "Coonan was blown to bits by 'is own car bomb." I felt sick, because something about that answer rang true, as if I already knew it. As if I was somehow responsible for it.

"It was an accident, right?" I asked hopefully.

"Well, that's not what Declan thinks, but what does 'e know? Nobody was there but you and Coonan, right?"

"I was there?" I was. I knew I was in my gut. "I burned his money, sank his truck, then blew him up?"

"That's one theory." Anne was smiling, proud of me. Nice for her, but I was the one he had come back to kill.

"Christ, he's really gonna kill me, isn't he?"

"It's not like he doesn' have good reason now, is it?"

"Can we stop him?" There had to be a way to stop him.

"Sure."

Finally. I felt some of the stress release. We could stop him. Then Anne finished her thought.

"We can stop him the same way ya done last time."

"What? You mean by blowing him up?"

"No. *Setting* him up." Anne hit the brakes, gliding to a stop three cars back from the border and the British soldiers stopping the cars. She turned to me, trying to calm me down so I didn't make a scene as we crossed. "Look, if he wanted to kill ya, you'd be dead already. Must be he thinks ya come back fer the money an' yer gonna lead him to it—so lead 'im somewhere."

"Is that why we're goin' to Derry?"

"He knows it's not here in the Republic, but we're not goin' all the way ta Derry jus' yet. We might have ta go there eventually, since that's where it started last time, an' that's where it's prob'ly gonna have to end, but first stop's Enniskillen."

"Why there?"

"Ya went there after ya stole 'is money, an' it's convenient fer the people we 'ave ta meet."

"Who are we meeting? IRA gunmen?"

"Jaysus Christ, shut yer gob, will ya? We're at a border crossin', fer Chrissakes." Anne's eyes scanned the soldiers, checking to make sure no one was paying any more attention to us than necessary. Her paranoia was infectious, and I could feel myself start to sweat. "Jus' relax. Ya want ta find out what happened to Mickaleen, right? So I'll make some innerductions to the people that knew him. That guy—the one who was Jerry Coonan—he'll be watchin'. He'll think yer goin' after 'is money and follow us. And then we can set 'im up."

She stopped, then pulled forward again, and I suddenly felt like I'd been here before, even though it wasn't as I remembered it. The buildings now were more permanent, the fences firmly planted in concrete footers, and the small tower with a soldier and a machine gun weren't here last time I passed through with Kate and Declan.

Maybe this was like an acid flashback, a reaction to whatever it was that Anne had given me at Newgrange. Maybe she'd brainwashed me and implanted false memories. Why else would I be remembering things that happened to my uncle? The only problem with this theory was that it was just as far-fetched as the idea that I was remembering my uncle's life because I *was* him.

I was indulging my paranoia when Anne spoke quietly, barely moving her lips.

"Yawn."

"What?"

"Yawn. It'll make them think yer bored, waitin' in line. Nobody yawns when they're nervous or full a adrenaline."

"You really think I'll fool anyone?"

"Jaysus, jus' feckin' yawn, will ya?" she said through gritted teeth as she pulled forward and rolled down her window, handing over our ID to the soldier waiting for it.

"Where are you headed, miss?" The soldier leaned in the window, glancing at everything inside, including me. I found now that I'd started yawning, I couldn't stop.

"My cousin's over from the States. Givin' 'im the tour. Lough Erne, Giant's Causeway, the whole she-bang."

"My condolences," he said, then turned to me. "Too much craic in the Temple Bar, son?"

"Crack?" I asked, startled, thinking he was accusing us of having drugs.

The soldier smiled again. "I guess you are from the States, aren't you? Where are you from back home?"

"New Jersey," I blurted, wanting to tell him whatever he wanted to hear.

"Again, my condolences." He turned back to Anne, handing back our IDs. "How long are you staying?"

"One night at the Killyhevlin Hotel."

"Enjoy yer stay." He stepped back, waving us through. I was quiet until the crossing was behind us, then the panic started to build.

"You really think this is such a good idea? Going back? What if I meet people who knew my uncle Mike and want to kill me for what he did? Or what if they don't believe I'm really him and won't tell me shit?"

"Relax. Yer the prodigal child, returnin' home. Don' worry so much. I'll tell 'em that ya are who ya say ya are," she said, checking her mirror to make sure the border crossing was out of sight before speeding once again.

"The prodigal child? Isn't that the one where they kill the fatted calf?" Why did every reference Anne made seem to involve a death.

"Ahh, right, I keep fergettin' that ya don' remember. Your version a that story is all fecked up, inn't?"

"I don't know. You tell me."

"The good son gets screwed the way they tell it to ya in church, don' 'e?" Anne looked at me to see if she was right. Of course she was.

"The prodigal son goes out and screws up his life and they throw him a party when he comes home broke and messed up."

I'd always thought that was a stupid story. There's not a soul in the world

352 ■ KEVIN FOX

who'd choose to be the good son in that story. Work your ass off for the old man and then the idiot brother gets the party.

Anne was smiling. "That wann't the original point a the story. In the real parable, the prodigal son, he goes off an' makes a complete bollix of 'is life. He gets shot in the head, hung as a thief, or some such. He's dead as dirt. But then the ol' man has another son, an' it's the prodigal son reincarnated. A sweet little innocent baby boy who's got a fresh start. That's who they throw the party for. The baby boy that's got a fresh start, all sins from 'is past life forgiven."

"I think we *should* be forgiven for what happened last time around, don't you?" I asked anxiously.

Anne laughed at my transparent worry. "Let's hope Coonan agrees, right?"

"Are all the stories like that? Twisted, I mean?"

"Most. But the truth is everywhere ya look, if ya weren' as thick as three-day-old dog shite. It's in half the damn stories in the Bible."

"Like where?"

"How about Joseph an' his coat a many colors?" she asked, incredulous that I hadn't questioned this story before. "His coats are his bodies, boyo. His skins a diff'rent colors. He had a many-colored coat because he remembered his past incarnations and 'is jackass brothers dinn't. They was jealous, right? But when 'is bloody brothers tossed him down the well they killed the little shite an' he was raised up again."

As much as I hated to admit it, my college literary criticism professor would have admired Anne's analysis of the story. As he would say, "The logic is internally consistent."

It suddenly struck me that Anne wasn't just a better talker than I was, she was also smarter. Or at least she remembered more. I glanced out the window noticing the curbs of the small town we were slowing down to make our way through. The sign said NEWTOWNBUTLER, and every curb in town was painted red, white, and blue, the colors of the Unionists. The Republicans would have painted them the orange, white, and green of the tricolor, just to let "eejits" like me know what kind of town I was in. The bus stop also had a flag hanging from it—the Red Hand of Ulster. We were clearly in a Protestant stronghold.

That's when I noticed a silver Isuzu Trooper jeep parked on the street.

Inside, a man was adjusting his mirror—as if to look at us. I don't know why it caught my attention, but it did, and as we passed the jeep I turned to look at the driver.

It was him. Seamus or Coonan, or whatever name he went by this time around. He had those same eyes, locked on me. I turned to say something to Anne, but she already knew.

"Yeah, I saw him, too. It's what we wanted, inn't it?"

I wasn't so sure. We didn't say much more for the rest of the trip, both of us constantly looking back to see if he was still following, until we finally reached Enniskillen and the Killyhevlin Hotel.

ON THE BANKS of Lough Erne, with its peaceful, flat surface marred only by the boats of fishermen and German tourists, the Killyhevlin was a perfect spot for us to get away to. It was romantic, and beautiful . . . and I had a feeling that we should leave as soon as we arrived.

Anne checked us in, picking up a message at the desk before we even got our bags out of the car.

"He's already here. Waitin' in the bar," she told me, pivoting in the middle of the lobby to head that way. I was tired and hungry and wanted a shower, but Anne had already made her decision.

"Of course he's in the bar. Where else would he be? Doesn't anyone in this country ever meet any place else?" I called after her, getting dirty looks from some of the women in the lobby.

"Quit yer whinin', Guinness is good food," she said as she walked into the bar and out of sight.

When I caught up, I found her at a dimly lit table in the corner, where a man of about sixty sat alone with his drink. He looked nervous and withdrawn, but he smiled at something Anne said, then laughed.

"I got Declan's message all right, an' that's why I'm here. It's a relief to tell the truth. I've been waitin' a long time for this."

"Waiting for what?" I asked, stepping up to the table, wondering what Anne had gotten me into. The man glanced up at me, taking in my features carefully. Then he smiled a grim smile and offered me a hand.

"You must be Sean. Pleased to meet you. Yer uncle Mick . . . well you know. He was a good man." I shook his hand and Anne pushed me into a seat.

"Sean, this is Pat Gavigan," she explained, but the name meant nothing to me. Gavigan saw my blank look and helped me out.

"Ciara's da . . . I was, I mean." He stumbled over his words, his face getting red.

"The little girl. With the ice cream?" I asked, putting it together.

"That's the one."

Then what he'd said finally hit me. Was. He'd stumbled over the words, even after all this time. "What do you mean, 'was'?" I asked, but even as I did, an image flashed across my mind of Ciara running to open the door of a car, smiling. And then she was gone and all I could see were flames. I didn't even realize that I had lost myself for a moment until Gavigan's voice brought me back to the present.

"You mean ya don' know?"

"I know a bit, but not all of it."

"Then ya know a bomb took 'er, right?"

"Oh God." I remembered now. I felt like I was going to be sick, facing her father again, seeing the pain still there in his face.

"Yeah. Yer uncle blamed himself. Said she'd not be dead if not fer him." Gavigan shut up as a waiter approached, a habitual paranoia revealing itself.

Anne kept it simple. "Two Guinness, one warm, one cold."

The waiter nodded and left. Gavigan waited for him to be out of earshot, then went on. "But he made sure the bastard who killed my daughter suffered the same fate she did. Good thing he did. I couldna done it myself. Not after Long Kesh."

"What happened at Long Kesh?" I asked.

"About a year before Ciara was killed they had me in Long Kesh, and the things they did to me there, the things they made me do . . . They made me swear off any kinda violence. After that I became a pacifist. That's one of the reasons that bastard Coonan hated me an' my family so much."

I knew what they could do to a man, but it amazed me that torture had made this man swear off violence when it made so many others more violent. "What'd they make you do?"

"It's of no consequence. Let's just say they thought it would break me . . . You know why it didn't?" he asked, and I could see a smoldering rage in his eyes, a rage that gave him the power to keep his hatred bottled up. "I'm an awakened man. You unnerstand that, I know. I have eyes that see an' ears that hear, and I know the truth about life. They could break my body, but they never touched my soul. I kept tellin' the bastards I loved them and that I understood they were just young souls on the wrong path . . ." Gavigan laughed at the memory, and I began to worry if they'd broken his mind while they were at it.

"Did that work?" I asked.

"Sure. It pissed them off to no end. Got them angrier and angrier. And it made me laugh. You want to defeat any man, Mick, just laugh at him an' tell him you love him. It denies him the fight he's lookin' for. You did the same when ya left to get married."

"When *I* left to get married?" I swallowed hard. I knew what he meant, but the way he said it so casually startled me.

"Sure enough. My sister told me. She lived up that way where they were hidin' out."

"At the Rock of Boho?" I asked, remembering where it all ended.

"Yeah. At her sister Mary's place. She had a niece up that way, too. I heard ya lived a nice normal life fer a few months before it all caught up to ya. I always thought that was good. Ya both deserved some peace. More'n you got, tha's fer sure."

"Did you see . . . them again?"

"Never, not before I got the call from Declan about you showin' up again."

"When Declan called did he warn you that Co—" Anne stopped, mid-sentence, looking up as our drinks arrived.

"At a loss fer words, love? That's so unlike you." I looked up to see that our waiter was not standing there with our drinks. It was the man who was once Coonan. The one with the eyes of the Duine Matha. "I hope the order's right. One cold, one warm, same as always."

"We don't have your money," I said without thinking.

"Ahh, Mickaleen. Good ta see ya, too. It's been a lifetime, ain' it? I tol' my cousin Kevin ya'd be speechless when ya saw me. I convinced the sap we were old friends an' that he should let me surprise ya. He told me right where ta find you two. Even pointed out where ya burned his manual.

Strange, though, there was no journal burned there. I'd have found some leather bits, wouldn' I?" He smiled, pulling up a chair and winking as he introduced himself. "Jimmy Coughlin this time 'round. Suits me, don' it?" Then he turned to Gavigan, all attitude. "You look familiar, don' ya?"

Gavigan looked as if he was about to try to strangle this man, but I knew that's what Coughlin wanted. He could kill the old man in self-defense and get away with it. No one would believe that Coughlin deserved to be attacked for killing a girl who died before he was born.

There was one way to diffuse the situation. If I could convince Coughlin I knew where his money was and that I hadn't burned it all, maybe he'd let us live long enough to find out where it was. I could at least stall him. So I lied.

"I know where your money is. I didn't burn it all," I said, but was actually glad that I had. The thought of him using the money to kill any more children was unbearable.

"Jaysus, yer a feckin' eejit, ain' ya? Do ya know what yer sayin'," Anne gasped.

I kept the farce going, hoping she would catch on. "He'll find out sooner or later, won't he?"

"Didja ever think a lyin', ya amadan? He's never gonna let ya go till he finds it now." Anne *had* caught on, confusing the issue to make my lie seem more like the truth.

Coughlin looked from Anne to me, seeing the real fear in our eyes. Finally he smiled. "No worries about that, Anne. It's too late fer that. Money's easy ta come by with a gun in yer hand. Revenge is worth more than money."

"Ya can't just kill us here, in the middle of a bar, can ya, Jimmy?" Anne challenged him, sure of herself here in public.

Coughlin stood, shrugging. "Sure I can. But I don' need to be here when it happens, do I? I just wanted to make sure that he *was* here an' knew who it was that killed him this time." Then he walked away. He was at the door of the bar when it hit me what he was doing and I jumped up.

"Get out," I barked, pulling Anne up out of her chair.

"What the hell, Sean," Anne griped, still not getting it.

"I've got to stop him," I told her as I started out after him. "Go. Get out the back. Now."

She still wasn't getting it, so I raised my voice, hoping the crowd in the bar wouldn't panic and go the wrong way. "Dammit, Anne. There's a bomb. Get out of here now!"

Other patrons were already moving, having been trained by generations of violence to react first and ask questions later. Anne hesitated, but I didn't wait to see if she took my advice. I ran to try and catch Coughlin. The last thing I remember is rushing out the front doors of the Killyhevlin, looking for Coughlin so I could get hold of the detonator and stop him from setting it off. I caught sight of him across the parking lot, but it didn't matter.

It didn't matter because twenty feet in front of me was a silver Isuzu Trooper sitting low on its axles, laden with explosives. Coughlin smiled and waved at me from across the lot, the same way he had the day the O'Connor brothers had died, as if he was still two steps ahead of me, playing with me and enjoying every minute of it. I knew what was coming a fraction of a second before I heard an audible click from the Isuzu, and then I was hurled back through the glass doors, hit first by the concussion, then the shrapnel, a thousand burning projectiles piercing my skin . . .

FIRST THERE WERE the crackling flames, then the sirens—high-pitched, like the ones I'd heard in foreign films. Then came the voices, muttering and mumbling at a fast pace. The pain was next, all over, all at once, the sharp and burning pains edging out all the dull and throbbing ones. I wanted to pass out again, just to escape the pain. I screamed then, loud and long, forcing all the air out of my lungs, unconsciously trying to get rid of it so I might regain the blessed blackness that kept the pain at bay. It was almost all gone when I felt a cold hand on my cheek and something soft and bitter dropped into my mouth. I almost choked on it as I heard Anne, whispering in my ear.

"Swallow it. It's belladonna. It'll ease the pain." And then her hand jerked away, even as I gagged on the berries, unwillingly choking them down.

"What're ya doin'? What'd ya give 'im?" I heard a gruff male voice demanding as I started to realize that I could see blurry images through nearly swollen-shut eyelids. A dim silhouette that hovered over her own had pulled Anne away from me.

"I didn't give 'im nothin'. Why don' you do yer job and get 'im somethin' fer the pain?" Anne argued. I could see a paramedic kneeling over me as I sucked in air, feeling it burn all the way down into my scorched lungs. I tried to scream again, but nothing happened . . .

Then everything got brighter, as if I were staring into the sun, getting closer and closer to it. But it wasn't the sun—I could tell because the light was brighter, but cool, not hot, and it was draining the heat away from my burning skin. I felt like I was floating, the ground and the glass there no longer digging into my back. The pain was still there, but it was somehow separate from me. I felt it, in my body, but it was like a remembered pain that wasn't affecting the "real" me, the me I was at that exact moment. Whatever it was that Anne had given me, it seemed like it was working.

Then the paramedics were lifting me, closer still to the light. I traveled toward it as I heard voices coming from the other side. Children's voices, singing. I remembered that day so clearly. A day that I had lived in another lifetime . . .

Michael

It was eerie, hearing the children's sweet voices. The dew was fresh on the grass, but the smell of ash and burning tires still filled the air from the bombing the night before. It was a new song they were singing, one I hadn't heard before, and the words belied the innocence of the voices. They sang of men interned, and tanks and guns, of sons taken from their families and beaten bloody in the streets of Belfast. They sang of being guilty of the crime of being Irish, and they sang about that guilt with pride. I wish I could remember the words, or the name of the song, but even though I can't, the mournful emotion it provoked has never left me.

Maybe I can't remember the lyrics because they kept getting interrupted by the chatter of the Lewis Gun that Declan was firing up toward Spring-martin to keep the snipers at bay. The kids tried to outshout the gun, but it was no contest. The gun kept interrupting the song until Declan finally turned toward the kids and threatened to open fire on them if they didn't get the hell out of harm's way. They did, retreating behind a building, but shouted the words even louder to make up for the distance from the action. That was when several of the men I was supposed to be meeting with the night before—the men who were part of the Army Council—approached Declan and started a conversation that left him red in the face.

I saw him shaking his head and then throwing up his hands, giving up and turning the gun over to one of the many "Jims" who were part of the Provisionals at that time.

I saw him looking up and down the street, since I was outside the bar, helping to clean up the mess. His eyes fell on me and I knew then that whatever his conversation had been about, I was involved and it wasn't good. I stared as he walked over to me, grabbing my sleeve and pulling me toward what was left of the back room.

"We need ta talk."

"So talk," I said, and pulled away, annoyed that those men sent a messenger and didn't come to talk to me themselves if there was a problem.

Declan shrugged, looking around to see who might overhear. Satisfied that we were alone, he put it bluntly: "Coonan's in the clear. I don' wan' ya messin' with 'im, unnerstood?"

"In the clear? What's that mean?" I demanded, feeling every muscle in my body tense as I stood among the ruins he'd created. At least *I* was sure he created this mess, even if no one else was.

"It means that he says he was on 'is way to warn us but got held up at the barricades. The lads believe 'im and it's best you do as well," Declan said, conspicuously leaving out what he believed.

"Pardon the expression, but are the lads a bunch a feckin' eejits?" I asked, glancing back to see if they were still out there.

"They know what they're doin'," Declan said, reading the disbelief on my face as he tried to explain. "He gets a certain kind a job done, an' they need mentallers like him ta do the dirty work, don' they?"

"Do they? Do they really need more bloodshed?" I asked, suddenly sure that they'd let Coonan kill me rather than dare to stop him. "This is some war you're runnin' here, Declan. The crazies are runnin' the asylum. You're all following different agendas."

Declan smirked. "Yer not the first ta notice, an' you'll not be the last. It's the problem with us Celts. We're individuals. We don' fit in no hierarchy. We don' take orders well. We can' be controlled. That's how we sacked Rome twice against the greatest military pow'r there ever was. They couldn' predict us 'cause we had no single plan, we had thousands of individual plans . . . An' that's why they'll not stop Coonan. He's wild, but he's a fighter. He might win somethin' fer 'em."

I was stunned. The leadership of the Provisionals was willing to let Coonan kill innocent people on the off chance that it might pay off some-day? "So you're okay with Coonan killing whomever he wants to?"

"I never said I was okay with it. I said it's the way it is an' always has been."

"Then it should change." It had to change, I thought. If we kept match-ing a bomb for a bomb the whole island would be ash soon enough.

"It's not that easy, boyo. It's not the way we are, as a people. It's in my bones that while I might not actually be better than the rest of the world, the rest of the world is sure as hell no better than me. And it's the same fer all of us. It's a hereditary disease—an inability to follow orders that leads to messes like this."

"A hereditary disease. Really? What's it called?"

"Bein' Irish." Declan grinned, breaking the tension.

"Very funny."

"Yea. An' sadly true. Trust me, I don' like it anymore'n you do, an' we may have to take our own initiative wit' Coonan soon enough, but don' do anythin' fer the time bein'."

"Why not?" I challenged, wondering how long Coonan would let me live if I did nothing.

"Because there'll be a meetin' a the minds a bit later. Yer ta be invited. There's plans in the works fer a big push. Fer peace maybe or maybe fer step-pin' it up. They want ya there fer balance, Mick. It's a good thing."

"Balance?"

"They know what ya think an' they been talkin' about it. Some want ta burn Belfast to the ground, but others think we should be talkin'. Maybe even callin' a cease-fire to let things cool down a bit. It's all hangin' in the balance now, inn't it?" Declan's voice seemed to distort and blur, losing its edge as another voice intruded.

Sean

"It hangs in the balance. His blood pressure is low, brain function is minimal. Almost as if he's in a coma." I heard a doctor talking. I was back in the present, trying to open my eyes, but I didn't need to.

I could hear them around me, wounded and moaning, probably bloodied and lined up on stretchers. Nothing had changed. I'd seen it all before . . .

Michael

I saw the priest try to run out and reach the car that the snipers had pinned down. Two seventeen-year-old boys had tried to get the kids out of the car. Both boys now lay in the street dying, one with a sniper's bullet in his head, the other with several in his chest. I tried to stop him. Father Fitzgerald, I think it was. He was with an older man and a fourteen-year-old kid. None of them would listen.

The priest and the older man ran out into the street, trying to help, and both men went down within seconds. I grabbed for the boy but it was too late, he'd run after them.

The sniper cut him apart before he ever reached the two men. I could see them all lying there in the street, bloodied and moaning, dying. Even if I could reach them, I knew that they'd be dead before they ever saw a hospital.

This needed to end. It needed to end soon. I had gone to Declan's meeting and another after that, but minds never met. All I had learned from the meetings was that Coonan somehow had an almost endless supply of money he was using to buy explosives and arms, supposedly from some bank robbery he had pulled off with Jim Quinlan before he died. Of course, with Jim gone, Coonan had all the cash and was lording it over the Army Council, promising weapons and financing if they steered things his way.

He wanted blood and he was getting it. Almost every other day, there was news of another death. A fifteen-year-old boy in the Bogside, a soldier home on leave visiting his mother, a store owner sweeping the street outside his greengrocer, and a sixteen-year-old boy who took up arms to avenge him.

Gun battles took place at least twice a week, with the Ulster Defence Association firing on Nationalist areas, and when the IRA defended them the British army opened up with heavy machine guns and snipers.

It seemed every time the cooler heads started talking about peace, Coonan and his ilk would shoot someone or blow something up to incite the old hatreds and keep everybody's blood hot. In the two weeks between June 27 and July 9, fifteen people were killed in sectarian shootouts. The IRA cease-fire Declan had managed to push only caused the violence to spike. No one wanted a cease-fire if it meant compromise. The peace delegation went to London on the seventh, but the only thing they'd succeeded in doing was getting more people killed.

It was turning into a civil war. The Nationalists were patrolling their own neighborhoods, the de facto government on a local level. On July 9 the Loyalists declared that Dee Street was no longer part of the state but under their rule. Then the floodgates opened. A Catholic family tried to move into an empty flat in Lenadoon that the Loyalists felt rightfully belonged to one of their own. Provocation led to tension and finally to a British soldier breaking the cease-fire. Four hours later, I watched the priest, a fourteen-year-old boy, and the man I would later learn was the peaceful father of five, get shot to death trying to help a wounded innocent pinned down by sniper fire.

At 3 a.m. that night I found Declan in the pub with the bearded guy from the Army Council and Coonan, all of them angry and ready for vengeance. Coonan was drunk, talking loudly, not even aware that I was approaching as he went on about one of his plans.

"Twenty-five, thirty of 'em, all at once. At bus stops and stations. I'll take the money I got and get the stuff from the American fella from Vietnam, and we can do a second round a week later. They kill one a ours, and we'll burn a city down. Sooner or later they have to surrender."

"And what if they kill more of ours than we do of theirs?" I asked. Jerry spun on me and smiled.

"Yer a bloody coward, Yank. Afraid to stand up fer anything."

I don't know what happened next, but I exploded. Before I knew it I had punched Coonan in the face, feeling his nose crack under my knuckles. He went to the floor like a sandbag and I started to kick him in the ribs, wanting to shut him up for good. In my head was the image of that fourteen-year-old boy, cut to pieces, one hand still reaching out to help a priest and a father of five.

"Who's afraid to stand up now, Coonan? Stand up if you can! Stand up!" Declan was on me then, and the bearded man with the gentle voice had my arms pinned.

"Hold on there now, boyo," said the bearded man, pinning my arms tighter than I thought he'd be capable of, skinny as he was.

"Get him out of here," said Declan. He was leaning over Coonan, who was still on the floor.

"He had it comin', Dec."

"Where do you want 'im?" asked the bearded man, still holding me.

"Out of here. Out of Belfast. Unless you want him dead."

The bearded man nodded and shoved me toward the door. I went willingly. I was tired of Belfast anyway. I went back to Derry.

It was a mistake.

Sean

As I opened my eyes, I saw her. The same smile, the same eyes, the same pattern of freckles across the bridge of her nose. She was a nurse's aide or something from the look of her, around my age, her cool hand on my wrist, taking my pulse.

"Shh, close yer eyes. Yer fine. I'm just makin' sure yer still breathin'." She smiled down at me. "You've had a bit of a time of it, but haven' we all at some point."

"I . . ." I started, but my throat was sore and the words wouldn't come.

"I know," she said, her voice soft and soothing. "When yer feelin' better we'll get ya some ice cream an' ya can tell me all yer troubles." Then she winked, and as she turned away, I managed to get out one word before I returned to the past. "Ciara."

Michael

"Ya look like hell, Yank." It was the first friendly thing I'd heard since getting back to Derry.

I'd been back two days and had barely seen Kate. She was busy working on some new protest strategy with a group of women, something about a "dirty protest." Since she was busy, I'd been spending more time alone, trying to figure out how to get out of Ireland without dying first.

I looked up from where I sat in the dusty yard of the flat on Rossville Street to see Ciara in the alleyway, smiling at me.

"If ya buy me some ice cream, ya can tell me all yer troubles," she said, offering the perfect antidote to my depression. Ciara could always lift my spirits. In spite of the chaos around her, she exuded hope and joy.

"I'll buy you the biggest one they got." I reached for my wallet, then realized I didn't have it on me. "My wallet's in the car. I'll have to go get it."

"I'll git it," she said, running off.

I got up to follow her and was just coming out of the alleyway as I saw her open the door to the car. I heard a click—and then I was blinded by flame.

I can't keep the memory in my head long enough to describe it. It's horrible to say, but I was relieved when the screaming finally stopped. Ciara was gone. The Ulster Defence Force, or maybe even Coonan, had tried to get me and they'd gotten her by accident. Either way, she was dead. A joyous, perfect little girl, dead. Burned to death for my sins, because I ran from a murder charge instead of facing the justice I deserved. After they took her away, after Kate had held me for hours, I went back in the flat and locked the door to the bedroom.

I had a pistol. I had a solution. I thought about it long and hard, but in the end I knew it wouldn't change anything. You can't run from karma. I knew I had to break the pattern and face whatever was coming, but how? I lay there, waiting for inspiration, living in a sort of hell, hoping I'd find a way to fix everything I fucked up.

Ciara was gone.

By then I understood that she was not gone for good, that her soul lived on, but it made no difference. She'd been taken from me. She'd been put through horrific pain because of me, the innocent casualty of a war that had gone on too long. A war that had gone on because most of the people involved in it didn't remember their history, instead they only read about it. They learned nothing from it, because as far as they were concerned they hadn't lived it. And 90 percent of them wanted to grab everything they could in this life, killing each other in the process, because they didn't believe they'd get another chance.

I knew better, and yet I still wanted to kill someone for what they'd done to Ciara.

I sat there in the dark for three days, wondering if the person I should kill was myself. On the morning of the third day, there was a soft knock at the door.

"Go away," I muttered.

It didn't work. "It's Kate." Then the doorknob rattled and I was blinded as light streamed in. Two silhouettes filled the frame.

"An' me," Declan said, stepping in. "I got here as soon as I could."

"We all did," Coonan chimed in. He walked in, just behind Declan, eyes falling on the pistol in my right hand, the three-day growth of beard on my face, and the empty whiskey bottles. I raised the gun weakly and it occurred to me that killing him might lift my spirits, but he started to talk before I could shoot him.

"Look, Mick. I'm sorry. I want ta put the past behind us. I know what it's like ta lose someone ya love." His crazy eyes suddenly looked soft and almost tender. Maybe he wasn't responsible for Ciara. "Ya want vengeance, don' ya?"

I stared at him for a moment, trying to read his intentions. He looked as if his eyes were welling up, and I couldn't pull the trigger on a crying man.

"I'm willin' ta help. I'm willin' ta let bygones be bygones . . ." He paused, a glint of something else in his eye. "If yer willin' ta help me in exchange."

The gun came back up, I could see his eyes down the barrel.

"You should listen, Mick," Declan said softly.

"How? How do you expect me to help?"

Coonan stepped farther into the room, making his pitch.

"Ya might know, I got some money from a job I done a while back, and an opportunity to buy some land mines from an American, but I'm too high profile to do the exchange myself right now."

"We'll have everything we need to even the odds with the Brits and the Loyalists," Declan explained. "We need someone to make the trade. Someone who's free to move around."

I was starting to see a light at the end of the tunnel. Was this a way to fix everything I'd fucked up? To earn my penance?

"Yer a British informant and a Yank. They'll let ya go places I can't." Coonan could barely contain the excitement in his voice. He was right. I could lie to the British, tell them anything I wanted. I could buy arms and explosives. I could teach whoever killed Ciara a lesson they'd remember for a few lifetimes.

I agreed. Two nights later, Coonan and Declan had laid out the plan for what would become known as "Bloody Friday," including all the bomb sites and timing. All I needed to do was to pick up the munitions and deliver them to Belfast. The truck Coonan and Declan had arranged for was waiting for me on a farm outside Derry, already packed with the money I needed. As I got into the car Kate was using to drop me off at the truck, she handed me a piece of paper, then pulled away from the curb without a word.

"What's this?" I asked, unable to see it clearly in the dim light. Kate reached up and turned on the light and I looked back down at a photograph. My chest tightened and I couldn't breathe at all.

It was Ciara, lying dead in the street. Bloody and alone, her face burned almost beyond recognition.

"Where did you get this?" I demanded, grabbing Kate by the arm, rougher than I'd meant to.

She didn't complain, just spoke through clenched teeth, holding back her own anger. "Coonan had it. Declan caught 'im tryin' to sell it to some American newspaper. He tried to defend himself. 'Blood is blood,' he said, and then he laughed." I could see the tears glistening on Kate's cheeks. "Ciara's death gave Coonan the excuse he was looking for to escalate the war. That's all it was fer 'im."

Sean

The pain was coming back with the memories, but I could welcome it now. Maybe this was my purgatory for what had happened to Ciara. Maybe I needed to feel what she did in those last moments. The terror of the explosion, the flames, the burns, and the shrapnel tearing and burning its way through my skin. I deserved this. I guess I deserved it for what I did to Coonan later as well. I could accept the pain, because I knew it was my penance. Maybe when I came out the other side, I could get back to the things that I loved in life.

I could hear the soft murmur of voices in my room now. Anne and the nurse's aide, arguing about something.

"He's not a blood relative," I heard the nurse's aide tell Anne.

"Fer feck's sake, neither am I. He's an MP, at least."

"I was told, given his history, that we shouldn' let 'im in."

Declan. They could only be talking about Declan. And I understood why they might have a problem trusting him. After all, he was the one who'd let Coonan loose in the first place. He was the one who had agreed to the plan.

Michael

I decided as soon as I saw the picture of Ciara that I would go through with the meeting and get the explosives and M14 land mines that Coonan wanted me to buy, but I wasn't about to buy them and feed more money into a corrupt system.

I stole them. I shot the guy I was meeting, tied him up, and told him that Coonan had set him up. Then I stole the merchandise and kept the money. I drove directly from the meeting to Lough Neagh, where I burned most of the money and sank the munitions.

I knew what I was doing—I knew that I'd signed my own death warrant—but what choice did I have? I couldn't be the cause of more innocent people dying.

I hoped to get back to Derry before Coonan and Declan discovered that I'd betrayed them. On that I wasn't so lucky. As I pulled up to the flat on Rossville Street, Kate bolted from the house with a bag in her hand and was pulling open the passenger's door even as I stopped.

"Keep driving," she told me as she climbed in. I hit the gas, but we'd only gone about twenty feet when I heard a metallic thud on the car and then the rear window shattered. I looked up to see Coonan in the middle of the street, firing a pistol at us.

"I can explain," I started to tell her, but she held up a hand, stopping me. "It doesn' matter what ya did, Mickaleen, or even why ya did it. They're gonna go ahead with it anyway this Friday. They're gonna blow up all a Belfast. They'll use the black stuff if they don' have what ya took."

I nodded, knowing that I probably hadn't stopped much of anything, and now I'd gotten Kate involved. We were approaching the barricade leading out of the Bogside, and I could see the masked gunmen moving into position to stop us. I put my foot to the floor, crashing through the barricade as they opened fire.

All the windows shattered and the car doors were riddled with lead, but we made it. The British didn't even try to stop us. Maybe they figured it was a good thing if we were killing each other, or maybe they figured if the Provos were shooting at me, I must be a friend.

As the bullets stopped flying, I looked at Kate, who was pale and shaking.

"It's time to run, Mickaleen," she said bluntly.

"I can't." It wasn't even a choice anymore. Everything I'd ever run from followed me. "I need to talk to Declan. I need to stop it. Where's he going to be? Where's Coonan going?"

Kate looked away for a moment before answering and I could barely hear her when she did. "Belfast. They're both goin' ta Belfast in the mornin'."

I MADE PHONE calls to my British captain and the Public Protection Agency from a pay phone on Castle Street and then made sure that Kate headed out the Crumlin Road so she could meet me at Woodvale Park when I was done. The stuff I was carrying in my bag was heavy, but I took a black taxi out the Shankhill Road and had him drop me a half a block from the flat Declan was renting. I made my way around the back, leaving the bag near some garbage cans, hoping no one would come along and touch it while I was inside. If they did, it'd be a nasty surprise for the both of us.

Once I ditched the bag, it was easy enough to get inside and up the flight of stairs. I knew Declan wouldn't be expecting anyone to arrive without warning, as the whole neighborhood would have been on the alert if strangers, Loyalists or otherwise, had shown up. And they wouldn't have come alone in a taxi. A man in a taxi seemed harmless, because if the taxi left, there was no escape route, but I didn't care if I didn't have a way out. There was only one way out in the end and I knew it.

I paused at the top of the stairs, my ear pressed against Declan's door. Behind it, I heard his voice, tight and tense.

"We've only got enough for twenty-one sites," he said. I didn't know who he was talking to, and I hoped it wasn't more than one person, but it was too late to turn back now. I pulled out the pistol Kate had given me and tried the handle on the door. It was unlocked. I gently pushed it open as Declan continued. "But twenty-one will sure as shite make an impression."

"And when does it stop?" I asked from the doorway, surprising Declan and the bearded man from the Army Council. They both turned toward me, taking in the gun in my hand. Neither blinked an eye as I went on. "We keep killing each other, generation after generation, always thinking the other side will give up, but they don't. So when does it stop?"

"Mr. Corrigan. Good to see you again," said the bearded man, like the politician he'd someday become, smiling as he tried to figure out how to work this situation.

"Just answer me that one question, Dec. When does it stop?" I said, not getting distracted.

"When they give up," Declan answered, ignoring the gun in my hand as if he were continuing a conversation we'd started a long time ago.

"It's been a thousand years . . . That's the problem with karma. Someone has to break the cycle. Someone has to be willing to let go."

"Let it be them. Let them give up when they realize we won't. If somethin's gotta change, let it be them," Declan stated, as if it was that obvious. And it was, in a way.

"I don't want to wait that long. I don't want to live another life dying young and losing everything, losing Kate . . . we both know that to end this cycle, something's gotta change. That's why I called in warnings. It has to end here. Now."

"Ahh, damn. Ya don' know what ya done, do ya?" the bearded man said. "If ya called in warnin's, we'll look like inept arseholes. You'll have proven William Whitelaw's bloody point."

"No, not me. You and Coonan. You'll have proven the point that we're getting what we deserve. That we're killers. Worse than they are. After Derry and Bloody Sunday, you could have beaten them. You were better than them and the whole world knew it. Now what will you prove? That they were right in the first place? That we're no better than animals?" I was clenching my jaw, trying to slow myself down and to stay calm. "You could have chosen a path to peace instead of this."

"Peace?" Declan shook his head, unconvinced. "Ya know when we'll have peace? Only when enough people believe we will an' not until then."

"What does that mean?"

"It means this world yer lookin' at is created by what all them out there are thinkin'. Only they can agree to change it. An' maybe Coonan's right. Maybe if there's enough blood, people'll get sick of all the violence an' start believin' peace is the only answer."

"Maybe you need to lead the way, Dec. Show them what to do instead of what *not* to do. No matter how many of them you kill, they'll keep coming back, and it'll go on for another thousand years. When are *we* gonna learn? When are we gonna change our own fate?"

Declan opened his mouth to say something but was cut off by a voice from the bottom of the stairs. "Declan! Come on! We gotta move." It was Coonan. I turned toward the door without thinking and the bearded man took advantage of the moment to hit me with the chair he'd been leaning on. I dropped the gun but didn't move to get it, since Declan already had his own pointed at my face. I waited for the impact as I saw his knuckle go white on the trigger, but he just growled at me in a low voice.

"Ya better get out. Now. The only raison I haven't killed ya already is because of Kate."

"I owe you a life. Take it," I dared him, almost wanting it to end.

"No. Ya don' owe me one like this. Just get out. We'll need someone to take the blame fer all this anyway. I'd rather let the damn Brits have ya than face the wrath of Kate."

"C'mon, Dec, dammit," Coonan yelled again, and I heard his feet starting up the steps. I didn't have time to argue with Declan, so I ducked out the door.

In the hallway I noticed the door to the second flat, recessed around the corner. The alcove provided just enough room to hide for a moment as Coonan reached the top of the stairs and marched into the flat with Declan and the bearded man.

"Jaysus, what the bloody 'ell are ya still doin' here? We need to get outta Belfast. Dinn't ya hear that somebody called in the bomb threats? An' who do ya think that was, ya amadan? Ya wanted ta tell that feckin' eejit Mickaleen everythin' an' this is what it got us. He informed on us again."

I started toward the stairs, hoping that Coonan was distracted enough not to notice me slip by as I heard the bearded man, calm as always, answer. "Don't concern yerself, Jerry. There's a simple solution. We just need to counter the warnin's."

I made it to the stairs and started down as I heard him dialing the phone and talking to someone on the other end, his voice full of guilt and fear. "Yes, I have information about the bomb threats that were called in. They're all lies. Jaysus, they're tryin' to get more people killed. They gave ya the wrong locations. I swear. I can't have this on my conscience."

The son of a bitch was going to send people *toward* the bombs, not away. I stopped for a moment so I could hear him better.

"Please. You have to tell them that they're running toward the bombs. Get them back to where they were," he went on, then abruptly hung up. I heard Coonan laugh, appreciating his own performance.

"There we go. This might even work out better. Send 'em runnin in all directions."

I started moving again, going down the steps as quietly as I could. Outside, I retrieved my bag from next to the garbage cans, then calmly walked around the corner and found Coonan's car. It was unlocked, which saved me the risk of him seeing the bag under the car. I opened the back door and put the bag into the backseat, then crossed to the corner and waited.

It wasn't long before he came out, moving fast and smiling. I let him get in the car before I detonated it, hoping to make it quick for my sake, not his. Unfortunately, I wasn't as good at making bombs as he was, and he managed to get out of the burning car, full of glass and metal and in flames, screaming and running, then dragging himself through the street before he finally collapsed, a dark black smoke rising off the deep orange flames that covered his body. I felt sick but reminded myself that Jim Quinlan and Ciara had both died the same way at Coonan's hand. It was just karma.

When I finally tore my eyes away and looked up at the windows of the flat above the bar, I could see Declan standing there, not looking at the bombed-out car or Coonan, but staring straight at me.

That was the last time I saw him and the last I saw of Belfast. I met Kate at the edge of Woodvale Park fifteen minutes later, and we ran. Again. We were gone before the bombs exploded. There was nothing left for us in Belfast, or Derry for that matter. We would have left Ireland entirely, but there were too many people looking for us.

Kate's sister, cast out of the family for marrying a Protestant farmer, was our best hope. Because she'd been disowned, I'd never heard her name until two days ago when Kate and I discussed where we could run to. In a way it didn't surprise me that Kate had a sister, another example that if the Irish don't want something to exist, it doesn't. The proof of our state of denial was in the propaganda Declan and the rest were selling, telling themselves that Ireland had never been conquered in spite of the British army that was shooting at them.

It works to our advantage sometimes, though, because as far as anyone who'd met Kate as an adult knew, her sister had never existed. Her home was the perfect place to hide.

Sean

I woke up on morphine, barely able to feel my body, but clear-headed. My first thought was that I needed a pen. I broke into a cold sweat worrying that I might forget all that I had remembered before I had the chance to write it down. In my mind, I knew every detail would be important because every detail, every mistake I made, had led me directly to this point. If I could write it all down, maybe I could understand how I got here and where I might find her. Kate. She had to be here somewhere.

It wasn't that I wanted to write it all down. I *needed* to write it all down. When I saw the sweet nurse's aide who I could only think of as Ciara, my first words to her were, "Please. A pen. I need a pen."

I had just begun to write when I felt someone staring at me from the doorway. Before I could look up, she spoke, softly. "Yer uncle risked gettin' himself shot doin' jus' that very same thing."

Anne. I hadn't thought of her at all since I started remembering Kate, letting my memory fill in the blanks of the journal. She was staring at me with a wary expression. I couldn't tell whether she was unsure that she was welcome or unsure that she was glad that I was going to be okay.

"He risked getting shot doing what?"

"That obscene thing yer doin' with yer hand."

I looked down at the hand in my lap, holding the pen, and wondered what she meant. "I was just writing."

"Exactly. *Writin'*. Ya got some bollocks on ya, don' ya?"

"What's wrong with writing?"

"It's a cheap substitute, don' ya think?" Anne said as she slowly entered the room, moving toward the bed.

"Substitute for what?"

"If ya can remember, ya don' need ta write. Didn't ya notice that none a the great societies permitted writin'?" she asked, leaning over the bed rail. She kept talking, trying to buy time to steal a glance at what I'd written. "The Egyptians only allowed pictures, because they could be open to interpretation, an' the druids, damn, those bastards woulda burned ya in the wicker cage if they caught ya writin'."

"That makes no sense. Why?" I shifted the page away from her.

"Because if the ones who don't remember read it, an' they think it's the truth, it's a problem. Even the best writin' can only be an opinion—one way a lookin' at what happened. Say ya described a murder, right? Well, if yer the murderer, it's justified, a great act of necessity when ya write about it. When yer the victim, it's pure cruelty. It's all biased, no matter how it's done. Writing is shite." Anne looked straight down at the paper in my hand, but the angle was wrong and she couldn't see the word.

"But how else can people learn if they can't remember?"

"Jaysus, shut yer gob an' listen fer a second. That's what fiction's fer. Because stories can be interpreted lots of diff'rent ways, they get the truth across."

"So you think we've got to lie to tell the truth?"

"Lie to illuminate the truth, like all them stories I told ya about that have the truth hidden inside. Joseph and his coat a many colors, an' Sleepin' Beauty, an' all of 'em. All lies to get to the truth." She paused, thinking of a way to make her point. "Did yer man Jesus ever write a damn thing down?"

"Well, no, but the apostles—"

"All shite," she interrupted. "They didn't either. No, Jaysus spoke in parables that could be handed down, the truth hidden inside the stories. An' then what happened when them eejits Paul an' Augustine and the rest a those self-servin' fascists started to write? They distorted the whole damn thing. The word a God, my arse. Sure, some of it's still in there, but it's like any book, edited to appeal to the masses, distorted to suit the purpose of the writers. Liars, the lot of 'em," Anne said bitterly, and I had to smile. She was consistent, if nothing else.

"An' what have you got to smile about? Yer in hospital, half dead."

"You didn't even ask how I was feeling, you know that? You came in here already lecturing me, and it made me realize how much I've missed you these last few days while I was unconscious."

"Is that some sort of compliment? Because I may have missed it."

It was then that she took the paper from my hand and read the one word I'd written on it: *Kate.* I saw her eyes as she read it, and I knew it had hurt her. The light, the energy, seeped out of her. She said nothing. And that's how I knew how deeply that one word had cut.

"I'm not writing it for me. Not really," I said, trying to explain. "I mean, sure, they'll work as notes for the next time, to remind me, but—"

"Yer lookin' fer her," Anne said, cutting to the heart of the issue, as always.

"I wouldn't know where to start . . ." I admitted.

"Sure ya do. We tend to find each other, don' we? It's a rare occurrence fer someone ta come back among complete strangers, or too far from home. Look fer her where she'd want ta be, you'll find her." Anne looked lost and couldn't meet my eyes as she hesitated, then went on, "So, ya know where ta start, and the rest of it is done, inn't it?"

I knew exactly what she meant. *We* were done. Anne turned away. She didn't want me to see that her eyes were welling up, but truthfully, mine filled as well.

It's hard to explain what I was feeling, but I loved Anne. If I had to live a lifetime with her, I would do so gladly. But I knew that she wasn't the one. And I didn't know what to say to her.

"Don' say anythin'," Anne finally muttered, saving me one more time. "Ya don' need to. I knew it was comin'." Then she got up, squeezing my hand one last time. I held it tightly. I had to tell her . . .

"I love you, Anne."

"Don' ya think I know that, ya feckin' eejit? I've lived long enough to unnerstand that much. But I know what ya feel fer her, too." Her voice caught then, and I could see that she was getting angry at herself for being emotional. The anger helped her get control of her voice again, although it was softer than ever, and I had to strain to hear it. "I only wish I felt like that fer someone other than you. Or that anyone felt that way about me."

"Anne . . ."

"No. Shut yer bleedin' gob. I been through this kind of thing a thousand times, in hunnerds of lifetimes. It never hurts any less, but at least I know it passes. All things pass in their own good time. It's the one thing I know fer sure." She pulled her hand from mine and strode quickly to the door, stopping with her back to me for a moment. "Sean, sometime . . . When you're better . . . come back to me. I might even be able to help ya look. But right now, I need to be alone. The truth is, I envy the both a ya, and I just wish I could find what yer lookin' fer, too, someday."

"I'm sorry, Anne."

"Fer what? Ya done nothin' but follow yer heart, and most of us don't have the bollocks to do that much. Maybe that's why I loved ya at first sight. Long before ya ever knew Kate. An' we were good together until I lost ya. Somewhere in there, between lifetimes, you two found each other an' I been lost ever since." She stopped, and I thought she'd leave then, but as always, Anne needed to have her say.

"I still love ya, Sean. Always will. It's jus' . . . It's jus' sometimes it hurts too much ta stay. I hope ya find her. I really do. I love her, too, ya know. But I can' stand to see that kinda happiness aroun' me. Not when I've never had it. I'm jus' not that evolved yet. So go an' get her, but I don' know that I can help." She turned toward the door, then hesitated, turning back, pulling something out and striding back close enough to shove it at me. "Here."

"What's this?"

"The belladonna mixture. The full dose. Now that ya remember her, there's no point holdin' back all of it, is there? Ya might as well remember it all." Anne hesitated, then dropped it in my palm: "Declan ripped out pages of the journal to cover his arse and keep from goin' ta jail fer Black Friday an' the rest. My da, he took some because he was ashamed a what he done—but maybe I'm the worst. I ripped pages out bein' selfish. I dinn't want ta lose ya again. I was hopin' I'd have a chance to convince you I was the one you'd want ta spend this lifetime with. I burned them pages. I burned them out of jealousy, I guess, hoping the memory might be dim enough that you'd see me fresh . . . But I can't even compete with her dim memory, can I?"

Anne looked at me then, and I couldn't answer. I didn't need to. She saw it all on my face. She leaned over and kissed my cheek then and walked out without glancing back.

I looked down at what she'd left behind. A soft ball of belladonna and some other herbs. If I took it—if I remembered the rest—then maybe there would be some hint as to what happened to Kate.

There really wasn't much of a choice to make. I needed to see the end. I needed to go back to the Rock of Boho . . .

Michael

"Do you think he can forgive us?" I asked as I sat on top of the Rock of Boho, looking out over Ulster in all her majesty.

"I guess that depends on what ya think God is, don' it? If he's yer classic man with a white beard, a course God can fergive us, 'cause the bastard's perfect," Kate answered. She was lying on the warm stone, soaking up the sunlight that helped ward off an ever-chillier wind. "Or ya could ask the question a little diff'rently. Will we get forgiven so we can come back like good little children to learn our lessons all over agin'? An' the real question, boyo, if ya dare ta ask it, is can we fergive each other? Can we fergive *ourselves*? If we canna do that, we'll keep killin' and dyin' another thousand years, won' we?"

I'm not sure why I'm still surprised by the fact that almost every answer I get from an Irishwoman is a question or why their answers are so complete that they only raise more questions. I had been hoping for a simple yes, but I should have known better by now. It was late October, and Kate and I had been here for two and a half months, living off some of Coonan's cash and keeping a low profile. We rode the horses, Ciaran and the whole lot that her sister had brought up here, and we spent time playing with Kate's niece, Aliana.

I think Aliana was what had started us thinking of marriage and children and a real future. She was our flower girl when we married on September 16, and she'd been asking when she might be able to get a new cousin already. I kept telling her that we were trying all the time, but her mother didn't really appreciate the humor. To be honest, I didn't want children just yet. Not until we found a way to get out of Ulster, and Ireland. The States wasn't an option, but Australia or New Zealand might be possible.

That was the plan, anyway. At least for now. When things settled down a bit more, we were going to head south and get in touch with Patsy. Kate thought he might be able to help get us on a boat to France, where we were certain we could get help in getting to Australia. But right now it was still too hot for us to chance a move. On October 2, Declan had finally managed to infiltrate some of the operations of the British captain I knew so well. Five SAS men were killed that day. They had been posing as a laundry service, collecting information along with the laundry. Word got back to us through Kate's sister that the British had put out an alert for me, claiming I was behind the slaughter.

At least now I knew that I was still being used as a scapegoat, and that it was too soon to move. Instead, Kate and I spent our days walking the hills, usually ending up on the rock, talking about life, and the future.

"Maybe we wouldn' need ta be forgiven if we could remember how ta change things. We could pray an' have all our prayers come true," Kate mused, watching the clouds drift by.

"Wouldn't that be nice."

"It would. A long time ago, we knew how to pray," she said matter-of-factly, as if I should have already known that.

"And we don't anymore?"

"You tell me. Do ya feel it when ya pray, or is it all jus' words in yer head?" she asked.

I didn't have the energy for it. I was looking at the horizon, waiting for the British army or an IRA assassin, or even the FBI to come over it, on their way to get me. "Can't you ever just answer a question?" I asked, a bit more harshly than I'd intended.

"You'll never learn if I answer for ya," Kate reminded me, but then read my mood and backed off.

"Fine. This one time I'll tell ya. Prayer don' mean shite if ya don' use every particle of yer bein'. Ya can' just feel it in yer head. It's like tunin' a radio to receive the universe, an' our radios are full a static. We don' realize we're all made a the same stuff. We think we're all separate, so we can't talk to nature anymore. We can' talk ta God because we fergot that we're made directly from the same stuff he is."

"So, then, what do we do about it? We can't change the world."

"No? An' why not? Why can' we change the worl' the way people used to? Like Joan of Arc. She visualized and believed with her whole heart and defeated the damn English herself, dinn't she?" Kate sat up, irate, as if I were the one who was being irrational.

"If she could change the world, then why'd she end up burned at the stake?"

"One person can't counteract a black hole of negativity. Ya get a couple hunnerd thousand Englishmen hatin' ya, an' another few thousand Frenchmen jealous of ya', an' eventually their thoughts are gonna have an effect," Kate explained. "An' maybe she started doubting herself. In order for it to work, yer heart, yer soul, yer body, an' yer spirit all need to be in tune with each other. Prayer's an act of creation, an' the seed ya plant needs to be planted with absolute faith that it'll grow. Like a child." Her eyes were boring into me. I didn't need to look at her to feel it.

"Please, Kate. I want a child."

"Jus' not yet, is that it?" she asked. It wasn't an accusation, just a genuine attempt at understanding. That's one of the things I loved most about her. She rarely judged me—she just wanted to understand me.

"Maybe we need to change the world first," I said, delaying the inevitable.

"Then ya better get on it, boyo. I'm not gettin' any younger."

"Tell me how I change it and I will."

Kate sighed and put her arm around me, as much for warmth as to help soothe my tension. "Someday soon, Mickaleen, scientists will realize what we've known all along. The *only* thing that can change the world is a thought. Start by believin', then by doin', and soon you'll see all of creation believe in you, too. That's the way it works."

"And if there's a couple thousand Englishmen, a few Irishmen, and U.S. law enforcement working against me? Will I end up like poor Joan?"

Kate smiled, trying to make me feel better. "Weak-minded louts, the lot of 'em. I believe you can do it. That helps, don' it?"

I nodded, mostly to make her feel better, not because I believed in myself. She read my mood perfectly and stepped back, picking up the book she'd brought with her. From inside it she pulled out a faded yellow paper, folded in thirds. I could see spidery script on the other side as she held it out to me.

I stared at it and she put it in my hand. "Go ahead, read it. It was a letter yer uncle wrote to his fiancée, Erin, the night he took off with yer father for the States. A letter you wrote to me once, when I was the one havin' a hard time believin'. I think it's time you had it back."

"You've had it this long. Why give it to me now?"

"I was hopin' ya wouldn't need it. I was hopin' you'd find some faith in yerself without it. But read it an' remember the hopes ya once had."

Kate turned, heading down the hill, calling out to reassure me. "I'll be waitin' fer ya, Mick. I'll always be waitin'."

I looked at the letter, vaguely recognizing my own handwriting as I started to read:

Erin,

The mind has subdued the heart, the body imprisoned the soul. Our eyes have gone blind. We see no beauty, only form and function. Our ears are deaf, laughter and song just noise. When did magic die? When was it replaced by the machinery of science? When did life become biology and chemistry? When did miracles cease? The world is dead, and God with it, if we cannot remember our own divinity. One day I will return for you, and if my eyes are blind, if my ears are deaf, wake me from that terrible sleep and remind me of who I am. Remind me that we are one soul, part of a greater whole, and that I love you. I always have and always will.

Yours,

Sean

I let the wind rip through me, giving me chills, causing my eyes to tear. Kate had reminded me of who I was. The world didn't need to end here on this hilltop. It was all about to begin. I just needed to believe that it would.

MAYBE I DIDN'T have enough faith, or maybe I knew that my karma was too tarnished for me to deserve a quiet life with Kate just yet, but November had come and gone, and we were now in December, the darkest month of the year, coming up on all those ancient midwinter festivals of rebirth from Newgrange to Sol Invictus to the Son of God coming to earth for the first time. But all those victories of light over darkness came at a price. In spite of what Kate said, I still felt that forgiveness had to be earned.

The idea no longer scared me quite as much as it once had. Even if I forgot everything else, I knew I'd remember Kate sooner or later. But until I did, I'd be lost. I'd seen so many people lost in life searching for something, never knowing what it was. And now I knew what they were missing. They'd lost themselves and the ones they loved to the forgetting. I wasn't ready to let Kate go yet, so I stayed up there, by the Rock of Boho, waiting for a sign to show me the way out.

I got it that first week in December, when Kate's brother-in-law came back from Derry. He found me up on the rock and didn't say a word as he approached, just held out an envelope.

"What's this?"

"It's from a friend. An old friend." He turned and went back down the hill, leaving me alone with the single sentence on the page inside the envelope.

They know where you are.

—Declan

I guess that was a pretty clear sign it was time to move on. I walked slowly down the hill and found Kate inside the cottage, rereading *The Little Prince*. When she looked up and saw my face, she knew something was wrong, so I told it as honestly as I could.

"It's time."

"Fer what?" she asked, suspicious.

"To move on. Declan sent a note. They know we're here."

"Declan?" Kate was startled, unsure of his motives.

"He's still a friend, I guess. He's warning us. Maybe this one thing doesn't count for much after all we've been through." I shrugged. If Declan knew where we were and wanted us dead, we would be dead already. We both knew that. "We have to move. You should head south, get to your parents' house and find Patsy so we can get out of Ireland."

"What about you?"

"I'll meet you there, on Inchmore," I promised, looking her in the eye so she could see that I meant it.

"When?"

"I'll need to get across the border, and they'll be looking for me. I figure by December ninth, the latest. If I'm not there you should get out. Go without me, and I'll find you later."

I saw the doubt in her eyes. She didn't want to be away from me, and I didn't want to be away from her, but what else could I do? I had to keep her safe. "And if I say no?" she asked finally.

"Kate . . . The only way we can really be together, the only way we can have a family, is to get out of here. You know that. I want you to leave tonight. As soon as you can."

"And when will you go?"

"In the morning. I'll be gone in the morning," I told her, as truthfully as I could. Then I held her for the last time and made sure her sister and her family all left with her. I had a few things to prepare and was hoping the weather would cooperate.

I CALLED THE captain. I told him that I wanted to turn myself in, remembering what happened when they had come to arrest Coonan all those months ago. Then I called Declan, asking him for one last favor, telling him where I'd put my journal and camera. He promised he'd take care of it.

I climbed the Rock of Boho and settled in just as the night did, keeping the radio on until the batteries went dead. I really didn't need it to tell me what I already knew, that it was cold and getting colder and that the rain would stop soon. That was important. So was the shale. And so was the water.

Isn't the water always important? Lying just beneath the surface of the rocks, ready to break through, so everyone can take notice. Well, it was time for the water to surface again from where it had hidden underground. I knew that, even then.

The sound of limestone cracking is almost exactly like a gunshot in the cold crisp air. They say I came down off the Rock of Boho already firing. They say they all had to dive for cover. They lie. I was a marksman and would have stayed behind cover, picking them off one by one if I wanted to. No. I was there to pay a debt. I came out with my hands in the air, knowing that I owed a death.

Sean

I woke up hollow. I remembered it all. Kate. Kate at the Rock of Boho. Kate on our wedding day. Kate at the schoolhouse on Inchmore. And even more, before she was Kate, back so far I didn't know her name and it didn't matter. I remembered children, sons and daughters—Kate holding them at her breast. I could see her face in old age, lined with worry. Worry for me and for our family as she prepared to make her passage. I remembered, even then, promising I'd find her in the next life, and the next, and the next . . .

Actually, hollow doesn't begin to describe it. Nothing can when part of your soul is missing. Gradually my eyes focused, I remembered where and when I was, and I felt sick. I knew she wasn't here. I'd lost her somewhere as I made my own passage. The room was dim, but I heard someone shift in the one upholstered chair in the room.

"I spoke to Anne." It was Declan. I didn't turn to look at him. I didn't need to. I wasn't afraid of him anymore, and I knew why he was there. He'd broken a promise to me, and he felt guilty. "She tol' me what she gave ya, and I watched ya go through the rite these last few days . . . I guess that means ya remember it all now, don' ya?"

I closed my eyes, unsure. "Maybe. It's a dark glass I'm trying to see through."

"It'll get clearer, trust me. It keeps coming back in bits and pieces."

"Yeah, well, I remember enough to know that you broke your promise to me." I finally turned to look at him, and he was no longer intimidating. He was just Declan. I'd known him forever and loved him like a brother. Admittedly, a brother I sometimes wanted to kill but a brother nonetheless.

"Ahh, the journal. I sent it along now, dinn't I?"

"Not all of it. If you'd sent all of it, I wouldn't be here right now."

"It said too much, Mick. Hell, I had to kill the bloody prick who found it at the cottage just to get it back to ya. You'd have bollixed all of us up. I showed Patsy and Anne. I had to give them the chance to protect themselves from what ya wrote, and then I had to live with that fine bit of evidence all these years, waitin' fer ya to be old enough to deal with it. I had ta live knowin' it told all of our secrets. You'd written too much down, I'm tellin' ya . . ."

"No, it said just enough for me to know what I needed to know. You took it from me, and now I need to know the rest."

"You'll remember soon enough. It all comes back eventually. What's so important it can' wait?"

There was only one thing. "What else?"

He saw it then and nodded sadly. "I don' know where she is, Mick, I swear to ya . . ."

"What happened at the end?" I asked impatiently. "Not to me. I know that part. What happened to her?"

"Does it make a difference now?"

"I have to find her, and I have to start somewhere . . ."

"Still the investigator, are ya?"

"I need to know where she went."

"That's simple enough. She went looking fer you." Declan smiled sadly, as if that explained everything.

"No. That's not what I mean. How did she die?"

In the shadows, Declan shrugged, then paused, preparing to lay out the details of a story he'd told too many times. "Some said she took her own life, but I know that's not true."

"How do you know?" I asked, impatient for the answers.

"I saw it happen. She came back to Derry and found yer captain. Started tellin' people he murdered you and she had the proof. Next thing we knew she'd been arrested by 'im . . ." His voice trailed off. He expected me to assume the rest.

"And then?"

"The Brits say she stopped eatin'," he reluctantly continued. "But she went too quick fer it to be a hunger strike. Some say they beat her to death, but I saw the body, an there wann't a mark on her." He sighed deeply then, as if I were forcing him to say something painful. "You know how she died, don' ya?"

I shook my head, but I knew it before he said it. It was my fault. I'd done it to her.

"She died of a broken heart, boyo. She wanted ta leave this life. She jus' wanted ta find you. If ya go lookin', look to where she would go in search of you. Help her find you, and you'll find her."

Sean

I still remember it all. Not well, mind you. Not like it was yesterday. More like it was a vivid dream I once had. One of those dreams that makes you wake up sweating, heart pumping, feeling every emotion as if it were happening to you right then, and the stakes are real. I felt like a whole person for the first time in my life. I was no longer lost. I knew who I was, who I had been, and where I belonged. I felt like I'd woken up one morning to find that I'd been asleep and dreaming for my whole life, letting the real world pass me by, letting the one thing I needed slip away in the night.

And while I was asleep, I lost her. That's the only truth I know for sure. That I lost her, and that I'd miss her for the rest of my life unless I found her.

Kate.

God . . . I miss Kate. I don't know how else to say it, and words will never do it justice. I'm not that eloquent. The only thing that gave me hope was the searching. I tried for months, talking to everyone in her family, every woman that was related who was born after December 1972. But every time I looked at them, I knew my search would continue.

And I knew she was out there somewhere looking for me. Declan's the one who finally told me to go home. He thought maybe she somehow "crossed over the pond" and came to look for me in New York. Maybe she did. New York's a big place. But really, she could be anywhere.

My father, Aidan, picked me up at the airport. Actually, he picked me up at the curb and popped the trunk from his seat for me.

"Welcome back," was all he said as he pulled away and lit a cigarette.

"That's it? That's all you have to say?" I don't know what I was expecting, exactly, but after finding out he'd once been my brother, I expected *something* more.

"Sorry about the Mustang," he tried. "I know yer uncle left it to ya, but things happen."

"Did you even read Uncle Mike's journal?"

"Of course. I told you. Load a shite, right?" he said as he flipped off a cabbie he'd just cut off.

"Yeah. I guess." I shrugged, suddenly aware of why most people who could remember their past didn't share it.

I kept it to myself as I started to search for Kate, going back through the journal, beginning with the first letter I'd ever read. I finally understood why it was addressed to me, Sean. In the letter I'd sent to Aidan, I'd asked him to name his firstborn after me and my great-uncle, Sean Michael. Kate also knew that it was a family tradition to skip generations when naming children and took a chance when she addressed her letter.

Dearest Sean,

I know when you read this it may not make any sense to you, but you must come and find me. You must find out how, and when, it all ended.

Don't let them make me a martyr to their bloody cause. Martyrs are dead people, and I won't be dead, no matter what you think at first. And if ever I become a martyr, I'll be a martyr to my own cause, not theirs. I'll be a martyr for us. Only us. That's all that will ever matter to me and Mickaleen, right? Trust me, my eyes are wide open, I'm wide awake, and I know what comes next. It's not so hard once you've done it before. We both know we will find each other again. Just as I know you will try to find me. I believe in soul mates, in love. It's the hopeless romantic in me, but I know it's true and can say it because I've lived it. I'm the proof that it exists, and now I refuse to settle for anything less. I'll see you on the other side, and I vow to you, I will find you. If anything goes wrong, please, please, come looking for me . . .

Love,

Kate

For almost thirteen years I've searched, taking notes, keeping journals, finding old friends I haven't seen in lifetimes. Some of them wanted to kill me, some wanted to adopt me. I searched for clues and methods of contacting reborn souls from Tibetan monasteries to the Wicklow Mountains above Glendalough. I went back to Ireland to testify against Jimmy Coughlin, the man who was Coonan, for the Enniskillen bombing, and I used that time to reconnect with other people I'd known in Derry and Belfast, hoping they might know where Kate might be. When Coughlin escaped and disappeared to the Balkans where he ran guns for the Serbs, I followed him because he'd hinted he knew where Kate might be before he left. It was there that I saw him die again, before he could tell me what he knew.

After all my searching left me empty-handed, I started feeling a bit hopeless, until the night I saw you on the O'Connell Bridge. I went back to my hotel that night and found a picture of you, sitting in the cottage on Inchmore reading *The Little Prince*. Then I knew what I had to do. I remembered how much you love to read and what a hopeless romantic you always were. I knew in that moment that I needed to write this book, even if it was just for you and you alone. I can only hope that our story will strike a chord, and that what's essential to you, though written between the lines here and invisible to most, will bring you back home to Inchmore, where I should have been waiting for you on December 9.

Looking at you in that picture, I knew I'd made a mistake returning to the Rock of Boho. It wasn't our home. It never had been. If you ever remembered or even dreamed of what had once been, I knew you'd go home again . . . Home to Inchmore, so we could finish our right of passage.

That's why I'm sitting here in front of a low peat fire, inside the ruins of the old schoolhouse as I write this. It's almost midnight on December 9, 2008, and you're not here. If you were, I'd burn this book and not take the risk that someone might be able to dig up all the truths I tried to hide, but you're not. You're not . . .

I think that says it all, Kate. Tomorrow I'll send this book off, hoping that someone will publish it, hoping that however many copies it sells, one ends up in your hands. I *need* you to read this book. I have no idea where you are—or even *who* you are—but if you read this and it feels familiar to you, if you read this and it strikes a chord in you that makes you want to go to Glasson and see Lough Ree on a moonless night, or visit the Shale Ghosts of Mullingar Road, you *must* find me. If you're not sure, I ask only one thing.

Go to sleep now, and when you dream, dream of me. Remember me. I'll be waiting for you on Inchmore, by the ruins of the old schoolhouse on the ninth of every December from now until the next time.

For those of you who see the truth in this, I ask you only to believe that I will find Kate. Believe it like you believe planes can fly, that water is wet, and that the sky is blue. Believe it because you have eyes that see and ears that hear, and they tell you that hidden within this story is the truth.

The rest of you, who don't hear or see the truth hidden here, who read this story and don't believe in it, feel free to forget it. Write it off as just another story and let it slip away. It'll be for the best. Just call it fiction.

Sean Corrigan
Inchmore
December 9, 2008

ACKNOWLEDGMENTS

This book would never have come to pass if not for the help and support of so many people, so many that it seems to be more challenging to thank them all than it was to write the book. If I miss a few, send me a note for the next time. In the interim, I'd like to express my gratitude to the Irish culture and my extended family, for putting value on stories and embodying Kate's statement that "fiction is just the lie we make up to reveal greater truth"; my grandfather, Michael Nolan, for telling stories that no one in my family ever believed until they were verified after his death by strangers; my parents, for supporting my foolish dreams of making a living as a writer; my wife, Lynne, for gambling on me so many years ago and believing in me every day; my daughters, Kaileigh and Kiara, for inspiring me in every moment; Derek and Pearl Carrothers for their hospitality and stories of Ireland; the McGinley family; the island Nolans, especially Patsy, my tour guide; Mollie Glick, my agent, who made selling my first novel a dream; Mike Sword, my legal weapon; Chuck Adams, the most professional and respectful editor my imagination could conceive of; and last, but not least, all of the readers out there with "eyes that see and ears that hear."

I would like to thank the Millay Society for their permission to reprint Edna St. Vincent Millay's poem "To a Friend Estranged from Me," the full text of which is printed on the following page. It has been one of my favorite poems for longer than I can remember.

TO A FRIEND ESTRANGED FROM ME

Now goes under, and I watch it go under, the sun
That will not rise again.
Today has seen the setting, in your eyes cold and senseless as the sea,
Of friendship better than bread, and of bright charity
That lifts a man a little above the beasts that run.
That this could be!
That I should live to see
Most vulgar Pride, that stale obstreperous clown,
So fitted out with purple robe and crown
To stand among his betters! Face to face
With outraged me in this once holy place,
Where Wisdom was a favoured guest and hunted
Truth was harboured out of danger,
He bulks enthroned, a lewd, an insupportable stranger!
I would have sworn, indeed I swore it:
The hills may shift, the waters may decline,
Winter may twist the stem from the twig that bore it,
But never your love from me, your hand from mine.

Now goes under the sun, and I watch it go under.
Farewell, sweet light, great wonder!
You, too, farewell—but fare not well enough to dream
You have done wisely to invite the night before the darkness came.

Until the Next Time

A Homecoming: A Note from the Author

A Conversation with Kevin Fox

Questions for Discussion

A Homecoming

"Welcome home," said the customs agent at Shannon airport as he let me walk through without stopping. I thought his welcome strange. I'd never been to Ireland before, and it certainly wasn't home. Yet as I exited the airport into the misty air, I felt as if the customs agent knew something I didn't: that arriving in Ireland was a sort of homecoming.

I had traveled to Ireland to visit friends and to explore my family's past, most notably the past of my maternal grandfather, Michael Nolan. My grandfather had left the Irish Free State in 1921 after fighting the British in the Irish War of Independence and then his fellow Irishmen in the civil war that followed.

When I was five or six, my grandfather would take me to church and go through the motions of the Roman Catholic rites. On the way home, we'd stop at the store for rolls, pipe tobacco, and candy as he muttered under his breath about the priests and the hypocrisy of the Church. "Listen to 'em, Kevin. They say God loves you in one breath and that he'll let you burn in hell in the next. Ya gotta listen to what they're really sayin'. It's between the lines. It's what's between the lines of our lives that's honest. The words don' mean shite."

It was then that I began to pay attention to the inconsistencies in what people said and did, starting with my grandfather's purported Roman Catholic faith and his statements about what he would have done "in another lifetime," or how he thought that I was "an old soul, a wretched mean one, but an old soul nonetheless." When I pointed out his own hypocrisy, I got a lecture that was the beginning of an education that would benefit me even after my grandfather had passed on to the next life.

Since then, I've practiced what my grandfather taught me, reading between the lines of the written word, hearing the emotion and subtext of the spoken word, and constantly trying to see how culture and mythology affect people and their beliefs. It has served me well as a writer, but it didn't become part of my fiction until I went to Ireland.

When I arrived at the farmhouse outside of Enniskillen, I noticed that my host, Derek, had a love of storytelling similar to that of my grandfather. I got chills as his speech and intonations reminded me of the man who had told me so many stories as a child. One late afternoon when the valleys around Enniskillen were in deep shadows and the heights of the hills still glistened brightly, Derek led me up the hillside to see his horses and the sunset. I was momentarily distracted by the beauty of the landscape, but I focused once again on his words as I heard a familiar sentimental quality in them.

"For years the old man came right up this path with his donkey, exercisin' his right a passage," he said. I asked him to clarify what, exactly, a "right of passage" was.

"There are no roads to some places," Derek went on, "and the only way to get there is to cross another man's land. It's a man's right in Ireland. You can cross any man's land to get to your own, but you need to do it at least once a year to keep the path open. In another lifetime they tried to steal a man's land by preventin' 'is passin', but the law remains," he explained.

I couldn't help but remember my grandfather when I heard the phrase "in another lifetime." All the stories he had told seemed to come into focus at that moment, and I knew then that I would write about the country my grandfather loved and the stories he had never told but had left between the lines.

I would write about Lough Ree, and Inchmore, and about the men who died on the Mullingar Road fighting against the Black and Tans. I would write about the people who had been loved, lost, and then found again, and I would write about the old souls that he knew, fictionalizing his stories in *Until the Next Time*. The writing of these stories has, in some ways, been my own rite of passage, keeping a path open for me to the memory of the people I have known and loved, to my grandfather, and to an Ireland that once was and is no more.

A Conversation with Kevin Fox

Many members of your family are NYC policemen. Were they — and their stories — the inspiration for Michael's profession?

If you want to meet a great liar, talk to a policeman — especially one who has worked undercover. Darwinian laws are strictly enforced when your life may depend upon your lies, and your storytelling ability does more to protect your life than any gun. Since I come from a long line of police officers and Irishmen, I think evolution may have had some role in my family developing what my wife affectionately terms the Fox Factor — an inherent ability to embellish the facts. Whether it's nature or nuture, I can't say, but I remember dinners at my grandmother's house on Staten Island as my father and my uncles competed for attention with their stories, each using specific techniques to get reactions: horrific details, suspense, mystery, and most especially, humor.

Some of the stories involved complex characters, good men compromised by circumstance and history — criminals with good intent, if you will. The stories of the older generation that still had ties to Ireland involved similar characters dealing with the Troubles and the English occupation. In those stories the so-called criminals were the heroes, and I found the contrast between the Irish rebels and the American police interesting. The character of Michael was born from this tradition, as he is a man caught between his roles as a police officer and as a criminal, living in both of those worlds. He is forced to look at both civil rights movements, in the United States and Ireland, from opposite perspectives, coming to a fuller understanding through his divided role as criminal and cop.

You created a world with two parallel plots — Michael's experiences that the reader learns about through his journal, and Sean's journey twenty years later. How did you keep your characters and storylines straight while writing the novel?

Actually, the two plot lines were rather easy to keep straight, as they were thematically the same story and were designed to complement one another. In my mind, it was an easy way to compose a story dealing with the elements of karma and multiple lifetimes, as it was similar to a round in musical composition. The two voices were essentially singing the same melody at different times but still harmonizing, still operating in the same register. The plots and characters were on some basic level the same, operating in different eras, changed by time, and place, and circumstance, but with the same foundation.

The book is primarily set in Ireland. How much did you intend to use Ireland as a character?

While I believe the characters and ideas in the book to be universal and relevant to the present moment, the underlying philosophies and belief systems that inform the novel are ancient, and Ireland is a place that has a unique and continuous connection with its own past.

It is the one corner of Europe where the Celts were never truly conquered and assimilated, and because of this there is a deeply ingrained culture that bleeds through the overlying modern one. It also has a sense of magical realism, where all things are possible and where spirituality has never been completely replaced by modern cynicism. Even the government, as corrupt and rational as it can be, builds roads around raths for fear of disturbing the spirits of the place. The Irish culture also understands layered complexity, where nothing is as simple as it appears on the surface, where stories don't need to be factual to be considered emotionally true, and where "Celtic knots" are considered to be simple designs.

I couldn't imagine a better place to set a multilayered story full of love, loss, philosophy, and ancient beliefs that didn't let the facts get in the way of a good story.

Have you experienced or seen any of the ancient Irish rituals that you describe in the book?

The rituals in the book are based on bits and pieces of family tradition and phrases that are inherent to the culture, such as "in another lifetime" or "he's an old soul." It is not something that is on the surface or even admitted to in my own family but seeps out in unexpected moments. The eyes of an infant bring out the old beliefs as the baby's soul and "soul's age" is weighed by the depth of expression in his or her eyes.

In addition to family traditions, I've done a great deal of research into ancient Irish culture and its belief systems, as well as a variety of other traditions, including the mystery religions, Tibetan, Egyptian, Greek, and Norse belief systems. When examined in broader context, all of these have similar core beliefs and even similar rites of passage that share the essential elements of the one described in the book. After doing the research I have sought out and experienced several past-life regressions but have not, given that the awakening ceremony has as one element a near death experience, tried that ritual.

Reincarnation figures prominently in the plot of the novel. How important is this concept in Irish culture, and how do you feel most readers will respond to it?

I think most of the Irish would say that reincarnation has nothing to do with Irish culture — on the surface. But this is the interesting dichotomy in a culture that makes constant reference to "old souls" and "other lifetimes." The Celtic Church, including sects such as the Culdees, were different than the rest of the Roman Catholic Church, and until the tenth or eleventh century preached reincarnation among other Druidic traditions. Even after the Celtic Church was brought in line with the Roman rite, the culture outside of the church paid respect to ancient beliefs that would seem to be in contrast to the accepted religion, including an abiding belief in ghosts, little people, curses, and the power of cultural memory, which is a significant power in the book.

So while reincarnation is not part of mainstream Irish culture, I believe the once prevalent belief is still underground, like a hidden stream of water flowing beneath the surface. For this reason, I do think it will resonate with most people on some deeper level, and it's the reason I chose to tell the story from the point of view of two grounded cynics who do not have a belief in reincarnation. That, I believe, will be the point of view most readers will have as well. All in all, I'm not sure that readers need to believe in reincarnation in order to enjoy the story, but I do hope that at the very least the novel makes them consider how their world might be different if they did believe in it.

In addition to the mystery, suspense, and Irish history plot lines, Until the Next Time *is also a love story.*

I made a conscious decision when I decided to write a novel about multiple lifetimes that at its core there needed to be a love story. It wasn't that there needed to be one for storytelling purposes, but there did need to be one in order to be realistic, for I believe there is at least one love story in every lifetime, even if it is the story of a lost love, a doomed love, or vengeance for a love denied.

There is a definite cinematic feel to the novel. If your book is made into a movie, which actors could you see playing the main characters, Sean and Michael?

As a screenwriter and producer, I might answer that question very differently than I would as an audience member. I would also answer it differently from an authentic Irish perspective as opposed to a Hollywood financial perspective. Fortunately, Michael and Sean can be Irish-American, so Hollywood can have their stars in those roles without losing credibility. The best possible version I can think of at this moment that combines the ability of the actors, authenticity, and bankability would be: as Michael, either Johnny Depp or Leonardo DiCaprio, as both can pull off Irish looks and the inherent leading man/New York cop attitude; Sean, being the younger role, is a bit more difficult, but obviously Daniel Radcliffe can both act and draw a crowd, and Skander Keynes and William Mosley convey the right combination of naïve vulnerability and idealism.

What do you hope readers will take away from Until the Next Time?

I truly hope that anything I write, especially *Until the Next Time,* will make people think, question their underlying beliefs, and develop a perspective on the way they live that is not fundamentally rigid. I would hope to open their eyes to the inherent mystery and beauty that surrounds us every day but we often don't notice, focused as we are on this one moment in time. As this may be asking for a bit much from most readers, I'd be satisfied if they take away enough enjoyment to recommend it to others and to re-read the novel in order to find the other layers and themes that I tried to establish. If they can see the novel itself as a literary "Celtic knot" and unravel it strand by strand, following where they lead, to other works, ideas, and philosophies, I would be more than satisfied.

What are you reading right now?

As usual, I am reading several things at once, some simple guilty pleasures, some research for new ideas, and some to challenge myself. I enjoyed Dawn Tripp's *Game of Secrets,* Emma Donoghue's *Room,* Tana French's *Faithful Place,* and Michael Newton's *Destiny of Souls,* as well as Graham Hancock's older book *Fingerprints of the Gods.* But that's this week. Next week I may be back to some science fiction by Orson Scott Card or try to keep up with my daughter and read some good YA, like *The Absolutely True Diary of a Part-Time Indian* by Sherman Alexie.

Questions for Discussion

1. *Until the Next Time* begins with a dedication to "all those with eyes that see and ears that hear . . . You might not find the answers you look for in these pages, but perhaps they will help you to remember." Having finished the novel, what do you think that means?

2. Anne says to Sean, "The truth is always written in plain sight, even if it's between the lines an' not on 'em" (page 213). What message is she trying to send to Sean? What do you think the author is saying about the nature of truth?

3. Most of the novel's story is set in Ireland. How did the Irish backdrop and that country's turbulent history enhance the story for you?

4. Both of the phrases "right of passage" and "rite of passage" are used in the novel in different ways. How do they apply to the same events, and how are they applied with different levels of meaning at different times?

5. As a piece of historical fiction, *Until the Next Time* centers on events that actually occurred, including Black Friday, Bloody Sunday, the bombing of the Killyhevlin Hotel, the Battle of the Bogside, and so on. How does the factual basis give credibility to the narrative? Does the use of historical accuracy make you more or less interested in finding out how much of the rest of the story may or may not be factual?

6. At one point in the novel, Kate says, "Fiction is just the lie we make up to reveal a greater truth" (page 266), and at the end of the novel, Sean tells

those readers who may not believe his story, "Just call it fiction." What do you think Kate means by the first statement? If the first statement is true, does it really matter if the reader decides to call the story fiction?

7. *Until the Next Time* is told through the eyes of both Michael and Sean, in two different time periods. How does the time period influence the characters' actions and beliefs? How does Sean evolve throughout the story as he learns about his uncle's experiences in Ireland? How do his experiences parallel those of Michael?

8. Declan is present in both plots of the novel, past and present. Why do you think the author chose this character to bridge both stories? How does Declan's development over time parallel the political developments in Ireland?

9. Several times in the novel, different myths and stories are referenced as parables for reincarnation, including the biblical story of Joseph and his coat of many colors (pages 352 and 374) and the fairy tale *Sleeping Beauty* (pages 213 and 374). Do you believe that these stories have any meaning other than the literal one that usually comes to mind? Do you think that the author's interpretation of these stories is valid?

10. The novel presupposes that reincarnation is real and that some people are capable of remembering their past lives. If you could remember your past lives, would you want to? If so, would that awareness change the way you live your life? Do you think that if everyone remembered past lives, they would live their lives differently, and would that make the world a better place?

11. It is intimated but never specifically stated that Anne was Bridey in her previous life. How are those women alike? How are they different?

12. Throughout the book the author makes many religious references, including having Michael state that he has begun to see evidence of the old

religion everywhere, including within the Catholic Mass. Did that narrative line make you think about religion, or even mythology, in a different way?

13. At the end of the novel, Sean is alone, and the story's ending is clearly bittersweet. Would it have been more satisfying to have him find Kate? Why? Why not?

Kevin Fox is a producer and writer for the Fox TV series *Lie to Me,* and his professional screenwriter credits include the film *The Negotiator.* He splits his time between coasts, living in both Los Angeles and New Jersey. This is his first novel.

Join us at **AlgonquinBooksBlog.com** for the latest news on all of our stellar titles, including weekly giveaways, behind-the-scenes snapshots, book and author updates, original videos, media praise, detailed tour information, and other exclusive material.

You'll also find information about the **Algonquin Book Club**, a selection of the perfect books—from award winners to international bestsellers—to stimulate engaging and lively discussion. Helpful book group materials are available, including

Book excerpts
Downloadable discussion guides
Author interviews
Original author essays
Live author chats and live-streaming interviews
Book club tips and ideas
Wine and recipe pairings

twitter Follow us on twitter.com/AlgonquinBooks
facebook Become a fan on facebook.com/AlgonquinBooks

Other Algonquin Readers Round Table Novels

West of Here, a novel by Jonathan Evison

Spanning more than hundred years—from the ragged mudflats of a belching and bawdy Western frontier in the 1890s to the rusting remains of a strip-mall cornucopia in 2006—*West of Here* chronicles the life of one small town. It's a saga of destiny and greed, adventure and passion, hope and hilarity, that turns America's history into myth and myth into a nation's shared experience.

"[A] booming, bighearted epic." —*Vanity Fair*

"[A] voracious story . . . Brisk, often comic, always deeply sympathetic." —*The Washington Post*

AN ALGONQUIN READERS ROUND TABLE EDITION WITH READING GROUP GUIDE AND OTHER SPECIAL FEATURES • FICTION • ISBN-13: 978-1-61620-082-4

A Reliable Wife, a novel by Robert Goolrick

Rural Wisconsin, 1907. In the bitter cold, Ralph Truitt stands alone on a train platform anxiously awaiting the arrival of the woman who answered his newspaper ad for "a reliable wife." The woman who arrives is not the one he expects in this *New York Times* #1 bestseller about love and madness, longing and murder.

"[A] chillingly engrossing plot . . . Good to the riveting end." —*USA Today*

"Deliciously wicked and tense . . . Intoxicating." —*The Washington Post*

"A rousing historical potboiler." —*The Boston Globe*

AN ALGONQUIN READERS ROUND TABLE EDITION WITH READING GROUP GUIDE AND OTHER SPECIAL FEATURES • FICTION • ISBN-13: 978-1-56512-977-1

Water for Elephants, a novel by Sara Gruen

As a young man, Jacob Jankowski is tossed by fate onto a rickety train, home to the Benzini Brothers Most Spectacular Show on Earth. Amid a world of freaks, grifters, and misfits, Jacob becomes involved with Marlena, the beautiful young equestrian star; her husband, a charismatic but twisted animal trainer; and Rosie, an untrainable elephant who is the great gray hope for this third-rate show. Now in his nineties, Jacob at long last reveals the story of their unlikely yet powerful bonds, ones that nearly shatter them all.

"[An] arresting new novel . . . With a showman's expert timing, [Gruen] saves a terrific revelation for the final pages, transforming a glimpse of Americana into an enchanting escapist fairy tale."
—*The New York Times Book Review*

AN ALGONQUIN READERS ROUND TABLE EDITION WITH READING GROUP GUIDE AND OTHER SPECIAL FEATURES • FICTION • ISBN-13: 978-1-56512-560-5

Breakfast with Buddha, a novel by Roland Merullo

When his sister tricks him into taking her guru, a crimson-robed monk, on a trip to their childhood home, Otto Ringling, a confirmed skeptic, is not amused. Six days on the road with an enigmatic holy man who answers every question with a riddle is not what he'd planned. But along the way, Otto is given the remarkable opportunity to see his world—and more important, his life—through someone else's eyes.

"Enlightenment meets *On the Road* in this witty, insightful novel."
—*The Boston Sunday Globe*

"A laugh-out-loud novel that's both comical and wise . . . balancing irreverence with insight." —*The Louisville Courier-Journal*

AN ALGONQUIN READERS ROUND TABLE EDITION WITH READING GROUP GUIDE AND OTHER SPECIAL FEATURES • FICTION • ISBN-13: 978-1-56512-616-9